LORD *of* HONOR

DAVID

GRACE BURROWES

sourcebooks
casablanca

Published by Sourcebooks Casablanca, an imprint of Sourcebooks,
Inc.
P. O. Box 4410, Naperville, Illinois 60567-4410
(630) 961-3900
Fax: (630) 961-2168
www.sourcebooks.com

Printed and bound in the Canada.
MBP 10 9 8 7 6 5 4 3 2 1

To my ridin' buddy Donna, friend to me and to my ponies

One

OWNING A BROTHEL, PARTICULARLY AN ELEGANT, expensive, *exclusive* brothel, ought to loom as a single, healthy young man's most dearly treasured fantasy.

Perhaps as fantasies went, the notion had merit. The reality, inherited from a distant cousin, was enough to put David Worthington, fourth Viscount Fairly, into a permanent fit of the dismals.

"Jennings, good morning." David set his antique Sevres teacup down rather than hurl it against the breakfast parlor's hearthstones, so annoyed was he to see his man of business at such an hour—again. "I trust you slept well, and I also trust you are about to ruin my breakfast with some bit of bad news."

Or some barge load of bad news, for Thomas Jennings came around this early if, and only if, he had miserable tidings to share and wanted to gloat in person over their impact.

"My apologies for intruding." Jennings appropriated a serviette from an empty place setting and swaddled a pilfered pear in spotless linen. "I thought you'd want to know that Musette and Isabella got into a fight with Desdemona and are threatening to open their own business catering to women who enjoy other women."

Not a spat, a tiff, a disagreement, or an argument, but a *fight*.

Please, God, may the girls' aspirations bear fruit. "I fail to see how this involves me." David paused for a sip of his tea, a fine gunpowder a fellow ought to have the privacy to linger over of a cold and frosty morning. "If the women are enterprising enough to make a go of that dodgy venture, then they have my blessing."

Though *dodgy* wasn't quite fair. London sported several such establishments that David knew of, and each appeared to be thriving.

"Bella told Desdemona you had offered to finance their dodgy venture," Jennings informed him, taking an audible bite of pear and managing to do so tidily.

"Not likely." Was there a patron saint for people who owned brothels? A patron devil? "Felicity and Astrid are the best of sisters, but they wouldn't understand my involvement in that sort of undertaking, and, worse yet, their spouses would find it hilarious. I'll suggest the ladies apply to *you* for their financing."

He shot a toothy smile at Jennings, who'd taken a seat without being invited, a liberty earned through faithful service that dated back well before David's succession to the Fairly viscountcy.

"I could," Jennings mused, "but having seen the challenges facing my employer, I will decline that signal honor." He saluted with his pear.

"Such a fate would be no more than you deserve," David said, pouring Jennings a cup of hot tea and sliding the cream and sugar toward him. "Those women positively fawn over you."

Jennings lounged back, long legs crossed at the ankles as he devoured another bite of perfect pear. He managed to look more dangerous than attractive much of the time, but in his unguarded moments, his brown eyes and dark hair could be—and were—called handsome by the ladies. Then too, Thomas Jennings had a well-hidden protective streak roughly equal in breadth to the Pacific Ocean.

Jennings paused halfway around his pear. "Despite your strange eyes, the ladies are unendingly fond of you, too. No accounting for taste, I suppose."

"Their regard is a dubious blessing, at best. Will you at least accompany me to the scene?" Because the physician in David had to see for himself that matters had been resolved without injury to anything more delicate than feminine pride or the occasional crystal vase.

Jennings rose, pear in hand. "Wouldn't miss it. I have never been so well entertained as I have since you inherited that damned brothel."

While David had never been so beleaguered.

When he'd dispatched matters at The Pleasure House—a round of scoldings worthy of any headmaster, followed by teary apologies that would have done first formers proud—he departed from the premises with a sense of escape no adult male ought to feel when leaving an elegant bordello.

As cold as the day was, David still chose to wait with Jennings in the mews behind The Pleasure House for his mare to be brought around. Why David alone could address the myriad petty, consummately annoying conflicts that arose among his employees was a mystery of Delphic proportions.

"I've been meaning to mention something," Jennings said as David's gray was led into the yard. With a sense of being hounded by doom, David accepted the reins from the stableboy.

"Unburden yourself, then, Thomas. The day grows chilly." And a large house full of feuding women and valuable breakables sat not fifty feet on the other side of the garden wall.

"Do you recall a Mrs. Letitia Banks?"

"I do," David replied, slinging his reins over the horse's head as an image of dark hair, slim grace, and pretty, sad eyes assailed him. What had Letty Banks seen in David's late brother-in-law that she'd accepted such a buffoon as her protector?

"You sent me to advise her regarding investment of a certain sum upon the death of her last protector," Jennings went on as a single snowflake drifted onto the toe of David's left boot. "I did that, and she's had two quarterly payments of interest on her principle since then."

David swung up into the saddle, feeling the cold of the seat through his doeskin breeches. "All of which I am sure you handled with your customary discretion."

Jennings sighed. "I have."

Perishing saints. Thomas Jennings would scowl, smirk, swear, stomp away, or—on rare occasion— even smile, but he wasn't prone to sighing.

From his perch on the mare, David studied Thomas, a fellow who, on at least two occasions, had wrought mortal peril on those seeking to harm his employer. "This is a historic day. You are being coy, Thomas."

Jennings glanced around, making the day doubly historic, for Jennings displayed uncertainty no more frequently than he appeared coy. "She spends it."

Coy, uncertain, and indirect was an alarming combination coming from Jennings. "Of course she spends it. She is a female in a particular line of business, and she must maintain appearances. Whether she spends the interest or reinvests it with the principle is no business of mine."

"She's not spending it to maintain appearances," Jennings said. "I believe, despite this income, the lady is in difficulties."

David masked his astonishment by brushing his horse's mane to lie uniformly on the right side of her neck. He wasn't astonished that Letitia Banks was in difficulties—a courtesan's life was precarious and often drove even strong women to excesses of drink, opium, gambling, and other expensive vices. What astonished him was that Jennings would comment on the matter.

"Thomas, I would acquit you of anything resembling a soft heart"—at least to appearances—"but you are distressed by Mrs. Banks's circumstances. Whatever are you trying to tell me?"

"I don't know." Jennings's horse was led out, a great, dark brute of a beast, probably chosen to complement its great, dark brute of an owner. "Something about that situation isn't right, and you should take a look."

"Might you be less cryptic? If there is looking to be done"—and Mrs. Banks made for a pleasant look, indeed—"then are you not in a better position to do it than I? I've met the lady only once."

Months ago, and under difficult circumstances, and yet, she'd lingered at the back of David's mind, a pretty ghost he hadn't attempted to exorcise.

Jennings's features acquired his signature scowl, which might have explained why the stableboy remained a few paces off with the black gelding. "I haven't your ability to charm a reluctant female, and my efforts to date meet with a polite, pretty, lusciously scented stone wall."

Had Jennings noted that the luscious scent was mostly roses?

"You mustn't glower at the lady when you're trying to tease her secrets from her, Thomas. You aren't really as bad-looking as you want everyone to think."

Jennings took the reins from the groom, and gave the girth a snug pull. "Since coming into that money, she's let a footman and a groom go, sold a horse, and if I'm not mistaken, parted with some fripperies. She's reduced to taking a pony cart to market."

"Thomas," David said gently, "she is a *professional*. She would likely accept you as her next protector, and her financial worries would be solved. In her business, these periodic lapses in revenue happen. She'll manage."

Though the soft-spoken, demure ones usually managed the worst.

Thomas sighed again, a sigh intended to produce guilt in the one who heard it. "I am *asking* you to look into her situation."

Jennings never asked for anything. He collected his generous pay, occasionally disappeared on personal business, and comported himself as a perfect—if occasionally impertinent and moody—man of business. He was both more and less than a friend, and David was attached to him in some way neither man believed merited discussion.

And really, David could not muster a desire to argue with Jennings on this topic, not even for form's sake.

"I will look into it," David said, touching the brim of his hat before trotting off to his next destination.

◈

On this frigid, overcast day, the part of Town where the jewelers' shops clustered was in want of traffic. David perused the offerings at three different establishments, not seeing anything that appealed for his purpose. At the fourth shop, a less pretentious and ever so slightly musty incarnation of the previous three, he wandered between glass cases of yet more uninspired bracelets, rings, and necklaces, none of which were appropriate to a very young lady.

"She looks lonely to me," a male voice taunted.

"Lonely?" another man answered. "Or grieving. Does a mistress grieve? Mayhap we should offer her consolation."

"She grieves the loss of a man's money," a third added snidely. "Though look you, my friends, at a woman who is buying herself yet more jewelry when she has no one to give it to her."

Bullying. David knew the sound of it, from childhood on. While blond hair fit in well enough, and even some extra height might escape comment, a presumed bastard with one blue eye and one green eye was intimately familiar with bullying in all its forms.

And these three young sprigs were merely warming up.

A willowy brunette stood at the shop counter, her back to David, her reticule and gloves on the case before her. She was the object of this gratuitous meanness, though she knew better than to respond. She wasn't going to fight or flee; she was instead holding her ground.

David made a pretense of looking over the items in the display, hoping his simple presence would deter the young men from further mischief.

"Don't suppose this place has anything adequate for the likes of *her*," the boys started back in. "I heard Lord Amery never denied her anything."

Amery?

The title landed in David's awareness with a physical shock, for the rigid spine, plain brown cloak, and beaded reticule across the room belonged to none other than Letitia Banks. That shock smacked unmistakably of the hand of fate, shaking David's conscience by the scruff of its neck.

He swept up to the lady and possessed himself of her startlingly cold hand.

"Mrs. Banks, I am ever so pleased to see you again." He bowed correctly over that hand, and treated her to a decorous smile. When he straightened, surprise was receding from her dark eyes, though her gaze was guarded.

And still, to David, sad.

"Viscount Fairly." She curtsied. "A pleasure."

She'd withdrawn her hand, suggesting the sight of David would be a wary, cautious pleasure until she knew he wouldn't join in the taunting.

David aimed a look to his left, at the three lackwits who had gone quiet after a muttered "That's Fairly" had been hissed from one to his companions.

"Hello, Tavistock," David said with excruciating civility. "Bootley, and—forgive me if the name eludes me—Belchamp, I believe?" He turned away from them with such perfect unconcern that even simians such as they had to understand: their misbehavior had been noted, and any hopes they'd treasured of gaining admission to The Pleasure House had been blown to cinders.

Marking the first occasion in David's experience when owning a brothel had served a worthy purpose.

"Here you go, ma'am." A clerk scuttled forth from the faded blue velvet curtain partitioning off the back of the shop and put a small cloth bag into Mrs. Banks's hand. "A pleasure, as always."

"My thanks," she said, sliding the bag into her reticule.

David did not stay her with anything but his respectful manners, though the urge to restrain her with a hand on her arm was tempting. "Perhaps you wouldn't mind bearing me company for a moment or two longer, Mrs. Banks? I'd like to put a certain matter of fashion before a lady, if you'd tolerate my escort to your next destination?"

"Of course, my lord," she said in the same soft, controlled voice. "I've some gloves to pick up several doors down."

They walked out in silence, the street nearly deserted. The chill wind had picked up, and the sky had taken on a leaden quality. David signaled to his groom to walk the mare home, and hoped this difficult day wouldn't include a pair of ruined riding boots.

"Do you suppose it will snow?" David asked, offering his arm.

"My housekeeper says it will," Mrs. Banks replied, taking his elbow about as firmly as she might grasp, say, the tail of a hungry, sleeping dragon. "Her rheumatism hasn't been wrong yet."

David owned a brothel. He approved its expenses, signed contracts for its every pound of flour, head of cabbage, and lump of coal. He knew courtesans' clothes required laundering, the dishes from which they drank their tea had to be washed, and so forth, and yet, he hadn't pictured Letitia Banks with a housekeeper, much less one suffering sore joints.

"I really did have something I'd like to discuss with you."

She stiffened, as if she expected him to proposition her right there on the street, the sky about to dump more cold and misery on all and sundry. Her posture alone communicated that if David were to make such overtures, they'd be unwelcome.

Which was interesting, and not a little lowering.

"Do you truly have a pair of gloves to pick up, Mrs. Banks? Or may I take you somewhere we might have some shelter from the elements?" He had no particular matter to discuss with her, but the wind was bitter, and she'd been out shopping without even a maid to attend her on a day when most people would be snuggled up to a blazing hearth, a steaming pot of tea at hand.

And Thomas had been worried about her.

"The gloves can wait. We could return to my house, if you like." She ducked her eyes to the left at that offer, suggesting she'd forced herself to make it.

David did not want to return to the modest dwelling where, on the occasion of his brother-in-law's death, he'd paid a call on her months ago.

"I have a property only a few blocks distant that's not in use at present. If you'd allow it, I could look in on my staff and get a bite to eat. I'm realizing, as I stand here, that I've skipped my luncheon." For no discernible reason, or possibly to enhance his credibility with a bit of truth, he added, "I become irritable when peckish."

Particularly when he'd also foregone most of his breakfast for the entertainment of his man of business.

The lady treated him to a considering pause, the duration of three lazy snowflakes, before she let David escort her the several blocks to their destination.

"This is lovely," she said, looking around the entrance hall of a dwelling David had meant to rent out but hadn't got around to.

"I have a number of rentals throughout the city, this being one. Let me take your cloak, as it appears I'm short of staff."

When he raised his hands to undo the frogs at her throat, she flinched, a reaction any brothel owner— much less a fellow trained as a physician—recognized. David dropped his hands and stepped back.

Skittish. Of course she was skittish. They were

alone, David had a good five stone of weight on her, and half a foot of height, at least. "My apologies. I did not mean to presume."

"I'm just..." She fumbled the fastenings free, her hands shaking. "I was surprised, my lord, nothing more."

He deposited her cloak and his greatcoat on hooks in the hallway and offered her his arm. The notion that she might be anticipating a forcible sampling of her charms flitted through his mind like another of those cold, bone-penetrating gusts of wind.

"We'll summon reinforcements from below stairs," David suggested. "And I hope you will join me in some luncheon, though it's late for that. I won't last until tea if I don't eat something."

She dropped her hand from his arm when they gained the parlor. "You must accommodate yourself, my lord."

Mrs. Banks wasn't reassured by small talk—smart woman.

"I'm surprised you remember me," David said, lighting candles about the room with a taper from the fireplace. "If you give the bellpull a yank, we'll no doubt break up a rousing game of whist in the servants' parlor."

She tugged on the bellpull but did not take a seat. "You provided me funds upon your brother-in-law's death without asking anything in return. Why shouldn't I remember you?" She was too polite to mention his mismatched eyes, and she sounded unhappy with him for his generosity.

Or perhaps she was unhappy with herself for accepting it.

David had been unhappy too, because what sum, however great, could compensate a woman for what Amery had taken from her?

A knock on the door, followed by David's command to enter, admitted a smiling housekeeper.

"Lord Fairly. I thought I heard the front door." The little dumpling of a housekeeper, apron spotless, cap tidy, beamed at him as if his arrival were her every wish come true. "Staff's off today, but I am sure you and your guest could use a pot of tea and some victuals."

"Mrs. Moses." He smiled right back, a cheerful housekeeper qualifying as one of life's dearer blessings. "You would live in my dreams forever were you to provide some hot tea and cold food. We are famished."

Her smile grew brighter. "And will you be needing anything else?"

"I might be needing a room here for tonight, if you don't mind," he said, thinking of the pleasures of a London snowstorm and the perfect fit of his riding boots. "Don't go to any bother. As long as the sheets are clean, I'll manage."

"It won't be any trouble." Mrs. Moses curtsied and bustled off. She never moved at less than a full parade bustle, and David had never seen her discommoded. When he turned to face Mrs. Banks, he was surprised to see *her* expression had become discommoded indeed. "Have I given offense?"

"If you intend I share that room, you have." The weather outside was balmy compared to her tone.

"I do not." He might speculate, dream, ponder, or fantasize—he was an adult male of means without a current female attachment—but he was not *intending* anything.

"Then I apologize," she said, shoulders slumping. "But I am here with you, alone at a private residence, you know of my profession, I am in your debt, and you spoke of… biding here for the night."

"You don't know me well enough to understand I wouldn't presume so," David said. "Perhaps we might consider your misapprehension a reasonable mistake? Would you like to eat in here, or should we repair to the breakfast parlor?"

"Here. The fire's already lit."

And the room boasted two lovely bay windows, one facing the street, which would allow any passersby to note a woman in distress. A viscount—*even* a viscount—who owned a brothel eventually appreciated the brutal pragmatism any shopgirl acquired before her twelfth birthday.

"Shall we sit?" He gestured to a sofa upholstered in a blue brocade that went nicely with Mrs. Banks's coloring. His guest was turning out to be more than a little prickly, and he made the tactical decision not to seat himself beside her.

He fell silent while Mrs. Moses brought lunch and the tea tray on a cart, and then went smiling and beaming on her way, as if David entertained pretty, single women every day of the week—which he did *not*.

"You are looking at me most oddly, Mrs. Banks, as if you're surprised to see exactly the meal I'd requested of my housekeeper. Would you be so good as to pour?"

"Of course," she said, taking off her gloves and reaching for the pot. "How strong do you like your tea?"

"Just short of bitter. And most people stare at me, until they figure out that the problem with my countenance is that I have one blue eye and one green eye. Then they invariably don't know where to look."

"But your eyes are beautiful," Mrs. Banks remonstrated, sitting back without lifting the teapot. As soon as the words left her lips, she looked away, and now—*of all things*—a blush suffused her cheeks. "I do apologize, my lord, for making such a personal observation."

A blushing courtesan was not something even the owner of a brothel saw every day, and the sight was... charming, but also somehow discordant. Intriguing in ways that made a man, *a gentleman*, inconveniently curious.

"One doesn't apologize for a sincere compliment, Mrs. Banks." David's younger sister had paid him a similar compliment once, and Astrid Alexander was a stranger to flattery. "Our tea should be adequately steeped by now."

"As you wish." She poured and fixed his tea with cream and sugar, then passed him his cup, her hand still evidencing a minute tremor. The physician in David noted it, as did the man, and neither one was pleased.

"I've traveled a great deal," David said, "but I've found nothing anywhere to rival the simple pleasure and comfort of a cup of strong tea. When one is poor, such comforts are dear indeed."

"You consider yourself impoverished?" Mrs. Banks asked as she prepared her tea.

Before he answered, David paused to close his eyes and take his first sip of strong, sweet, nearly scalding tea, for bliss in any form was to be savored.

"As a child, I lived with my mother in a small town in Scotland. Our circumstances were humble, and the winters long and cold. My mother loved me, and I never understood how poor we were, because it was all I'd known."

"But your mother understood," Mrs. Banks guessed—accurately. "May I fix you a plate, my lord?" She might have been the hostess at some village at home, so correct were her manners.

"At least one." For David grew hungrier by the moment, also more desperate to provide the woman a decent meal.

As she arranged bread, cheddar, ham, and sliced apples on a plate, David discreetly studied his guest. Her dark hair and dark eyes were not pretty, not in the blond, blue-eyed Teutonic sense most Englishmen would be drawn to. She was not charmingly petite, not overtly flirtatious. She was, all in all, an unlikely choice as a courtesan—the best ones were—but even as he drew that conclusion, David had to admit the woman was... restful, like his sister Felicity was restful, even in the presence of her decidedly unrestful spouse.

Letty Banks moved with graceful, economical motions; she was comfortable with silence; she had good instincts.

And Thomas Jennings's hunch had been accurate: Letty Banks was in serious trouble, too.

～≪≫～

A man seeking to buy a woman's favors always bore a bit of calculation in his eyes. Sometimes the calculation was friendly. Sometimes the coin he offered was a promise, a ring, pretty words, soft caresses, or a bit of cash. More often, he didn't try to disguise his objective or his contempt for a woman who'd grant it.

Letty had become so cold, so hungry, she'd nearly stopped seeing the calculation and the contempt, and yet, in David Worthington's eyes she found… neither. Not for her, and *not for himself.*

"Thank you." He accepted the plate, letting his fingers brush hers, a fleeting warmth any woman of sense would disregard. "And you must join me, Mrs. Banks, else I shall feel like a glutton."

The tray bore a veritable feast by Letty's standards, and yet, she was already in his lordship's debt.

"I insist, Mrs. Banks," her host said gently. "You will hurt Mrs. Moses's feelings if you refuse her offering. She's quite sensitive."

Letty knew housekeepers, and had she gone 'round to Mrs. Moses's back door, she would have met with the domestic equivalent of a full-grown, well-fed bulldog, intent on guarding the master's last bucket of scraps.

"I am hungry." Famished, halfway to starving, if the fit of her dresses was any indication. One shouldn't lie, not to others and not to oneself.

Lord Fairly picked up a plate, and as she had for him, arranged a generous portion of ham, cheese, pale bread—crusts sliced off—and crisp apple slices on it. She accepted the food with a silent prayer of gratitude, making sure this time their fingers did not brush. By sheer discipline, Letty did not use both hands to cram the food in her mouth.

"I do not think Mrs. Moses's feelings could be so hurt she'd hold it against you for long, my lord. Given your charm, she'd sooner apologize for overloading the tray."

He looked pleased. "You accuse me of charm? My sisters say otherwise. They say I am entirely too dour and withdrawn, and because I don't go about in Society much, they might have a point."

Men did not mention their sisters to Letty Banks, though this man apparently did.

"Perhaps you are shy." She bit into an apple first, an apple that had been carefully stored in a cold cellar and still had most of its sweet crispness and only a hint of earth about its flavor.

"I'm not shy, exactly." Though his lordship's expression came close to bashful. "I enjoy people well enough, or some people, but I also need my solitude."

Letty made herself pause in her eating, a bite of cheese in hand. "Were you in my profession, you would have plenty of solitude." She ought not to have said that, but hunger was making her light-headed and more heavy-hearted than usual.

His lordship peered over at her, his sandwich two inches from a mouth that sported the even white teeth of the aristocrat who troubled about his hygiene. When he smiled, those teeth were in evidence, as was a warm benevolence that beamed from his gorgeous eyes and made Letty ache to be worthy of his regard.

His respect, rather.

"I'm sorry," Letty said, though she didn't put down

her bite of cheese. "That was a vulgar thing to say when you are being so... civil."

"Not vulgar, honest. I appreciate honesty, and I never considered solitude might be a large part of a courtesan's life. I have wondered, though, if the girls at The Pleasure House don't remain there in part because having other females..."

He trailed off, looking away toward the side window, though he hadn't drawn the drapes on either one. The flurries had thickened outside, whirling about on cold gusts and turning the day from gray to grayer.

"I believe," he said, topping up Letty's teacup, "I am the one who must now apologize. I should not have mentioned that establishment in your presence."

Steam curled up from her cup, putting her in mind of the incense that used to be part of the highest church services. "Whyever not? I send you business, you know. And I am a courtesan, of sorts, as you said. While I enjoy the company manners you show me, my lord, I understand that with women of my ilk, they are entirely discretionary."

She put the cheese on her tongue, savored the salt and tang of good, sharp cheddar, let it warm for a moment, then slowly, slowly chewed a bite of heaven.

Only to find her host's expression had become quite... severe.

"Mrs. Banks, every female is deserving of decent manners. I insist upon it in my establishment, and it pains me sorely that you would not feel entitled to the same treatment."

The cheese was so delicious, so devastatingly

nourishing to the body and spirit, Letty nearly missed the sense of his lordship's words.

She rolled up a slice of ham with her fingers, as he'd done. "Feeling entitled to manners and being shown them are two different things. You heard those young gentlemen at the jeweler's. I pay a price for who and what I am. I accept that."

One shouldn't resent a penance, though Letty did. She also ate the ham, which was perfectly seasoned, a bit smoky, a bit sweet. His lordship's quibbling over the civilities was all very impressive—perhaps his variety of calculation demanded manners—but a good meal was more impressive yet.

He sat back, making the chair creak and reminding Letty, that for all his golden good looks and exquisite tailoring, Lord Fairly was a large, fit man—as the late Lord Amery had been—and he had yet to state his true agenda.

"You shouldn't accept rudeness, Mrs. Banks. Boys in a pack like that want a whipper-in, lest they run riot. You have piqued my curiosity, however."

Hunting analogies found their way into all too many discussions of Letty's profession. She munched her ham and debated between the bread or the apple next.

"You mentioned you send me business," Fairly said. "In particular, you recently suggested Lord Valentine Windham might find someone suited to his needs at my establishment. He's a decent man, pleasant enough to look on, clean about his person, and so forth. If you are without a protector, Mrs. Banks, as those nasty boys implied, why not allow him your company?"

The question stunned her, both because it was more personal than if Fairly had propositioned her himself, and because it implied that a man she'd met on one other occasion months ago had intimate knowledge of her circumstances.

At what point did a woman become notorious?

"Young Windham was rather downcast to be rejected," he went on, "though I'm sure he was gracious about it. He likes you, you see, and probably would still be interested, were you amenable. And if Windham is unacceptable to you, perhaps my man, Thomas—"

He broke off when she stood quickly enough to provoke more light-headedness. Letty hadn't seen this coming, hadn't realized a brothel owner would know how to procure without even appearing to do so. Her disappointment was sufficiently profound that she had to move away from the food, lest she disgrace herself with the resulting upset.

"There's the problem, my lord, is it not?"

He rose as well, probably out of blasted good manners, and joined Letty at the bay window overlooking the dormant side garden.

"You have me at a loss," he said, standing at her shoulder, and heaven defend her, Fairly's scent was sublime, all spices and sweetness, sandalwood, flowers, and wealth.

"It doesn't do, your lordship," Letty said, the cold from the window almost welcome, "to like one's protector, at least not for me." And probably not for the women who worked for Lord Fairly, did he but know it.

"You have a novel approach to selecting a partner

for your intimate attentions, Mrs. Banks: you bed only men you don't like? I don't suppose the late Lord Amery was aware of your criterion."

His tone had become analytical, perhaps to hide his lordly dismay, for by his lights—his innocent lights, in some regard—whores were no doubt at all times to enjoy their work.

"Our conversation grows too personal." Though, somehow, not rude. Letty ducked around his lordship and returned to her seat on the couch and to the warmth thrown out by the fire. "I'm sure you meant no offense."

"Of course not," he said, resuming his seat as well.

He picked up a slice of apple from her plate—his plate was empty—and popped it into his mouth.

"You find this humorous?" she asked a touch sharply. She'd had plans for that apple slice.

"Eat," he said, his tone suggesting he liked a woman with some temper, the idiot. "If you had used such a severe tone on those puppies at the jeweler's, they would still be howling their indignation and surprise. Well done, Mrs. Banks."

He did not like her temper; he *approved* of it. Letty digested that, along with the rest of her cheese and ham, and a second cup of tea. The food settled, as good food would, and the tea…

The hot, strong, sweet tea made her want to cry. The pot sat swaddled in a thick white towel to keep the heat in, while Letty hadn't a thick white towel left to sell. Outside, the snow had picked up, and the distance to Letty's door stretched impossibly far.

The viscount struck Letty as the cuddling sort, and

he'd give off heat like a parlor stove. Would it really have been so awful to spend the night tucked up in his embrace, a hot breakfast brought to them tomorrow morning, and a sum of coins jingling in Letty's pockets when she parted from him?

The thought appalled her for its very wistfulness.

"The hardest thing…" She'd said the words aloud, though she hadn't meant to. She hoped he'd ignore her queer start, but he only regarded her from one blue eye and one green eye, both of which were beautiful, and… kind.

Those eyes had made him an outcast, had made him comfortable with being an outcast.

Letty broke a slice of bread in half, but couldn't get it to her mouth fast enough to stop more words from tripping forth. "The hardest thing was when he'd spend inside me. Lord Amery, that is."

She hared off back to the window, wrapping her arms around her middle against a cold beyond what the weather threatened. His lordship did not understand why a woman needed to hate her protector, and Letty would share that insight with him, even though he was a stranger and she expected him to remain so.

Fairly needed to understand that a woman raised to love her neighbor was slowly filling with hatred, even as her belly went empty, day after day.

"And that hurt you," he said, standing more closely than on their last trip away from the fire's warmth. "More than his indifference to your needs of a physical nature."

The only need she had left of a physical nature was the need to be left alone, or so she hoped.

Letty hadn't cried in months, not in years. Not when Herbert Allen had died, not when Olivia regularly failed to include even a word about Danny in her infrequent notes.

A hot trickle down her cheek informed her she was crying now.

"The worst hurt," Fairly went on, "was that he would risk getting a child with you, because that was disregard for the entire remainder of your life, and for the child's life too. A child you would have been solely responsible for, despite assurances to the contrary. And all so Amery might have a few moments, a few *instants*, of pleasure."

He had a beautiful voice to go with his beautiful eyes. He could have offered sermons on damnation and hellfire, and the congregation would have listened raptly, because that voice was kind and knowing. His touch, when he turned her by the shoulders and brought her into his embrace, was kind and knowing too.

Damnably, devastatingly, irresistibly kind.

He drew her against his body slowly, giving her the ongoing chance to flee, or offer him another scold for being too personal, but she stood in the circle of his arms without the strength even to return his embrace.

Two

LETTY BANKS WAS TOO SLENDER. THE PHYSICIAN IN David, an aspect of himself he'd often resented, took note of shoulder blades, nape, and wrist bones, all too much in evidence.

The man in him comforted her anyway, pressed her face to his shoulder, and stroked his hands over her back until she leaned against him.

She had apparently needed to cry, because minutes passed with him holding her thus. At no point did she slide her arms around him, but David didn't need her to. He could feel the heat rising from her body, and with it, a faint fragrance of roses. He'd caught the scent briefly before, when he'd bounced up to her full of flattery and ready to kill her detractors in the jeweler's shop.

The fragrance teased him now: subtle, feminine, sweet, and enticing.

She was skinny, and he also had the impression that she was exhausted in body and spirit. Something in the way her weight rested against him, something that sought shelter despite her dignity gave away her fatigue.

Her tears quieted, and still he held her.

"Don't apologize. A lady is entitled to her tears." He fished a handkerchief from a pocket without letting her go, and handed it to her, knowing she'd want to use it before allowing him to see her face.

Though Desdemona, Musette, or any other woman in David's employ would exploit a tearstained countenance to make him feel guilty—and do so quite successfully.

"I'm going to fix you another cup of tea," he said, walking her back to the couch with an arm around her shoulders. "You will drink it. You will also finish the food on your plate, if you please, lest I conclude my company has put you off your appetite."

A physician learned how to cajole like this—teasing and stern, both.

He took a seat beside her, their hips touching, and kept an arm around her back as he prepared her tea with one hand. He didn't look at her face all the while, though he wanted to. He wanted to see her eyes, wanted to know that the vacant, hopeless mask of the Covent Garden streetwalker would not gaze back at him.

"You must not be shy with me, Mrs. Banks. I have two sisters, both of whom are breeding—again—and I have many lovely employees of the female persuasion. Women cry, I assure you, and you have more to cry about than most."

She clutched the warm teacup with both hands, obediently sipping. When she put her tea down, he piled more food on his own plate and held it for her.

"Eat. Every bite, if you please."

"I am not that hungry," she said, a spark of dignity returning.

"You will hurt my feelings if you deny me the right to push sustenance at you after having provoked your tears." This was an understatement. She'd make him crazy if she refused his hospitality after he'd made her cry.

She regarded him dubiously then bit into a chocolate tea cake with raspberry icing, closing her eyes and making David's mouth abruptly go dry. She was not such a Puritan as she'd have him think—maybe not such a Puritan as she tried to believe herself.

"I really did need a woman's opinion on a certain personal matter. I wasn't making that up." *The hell he hadn't been.*

She paused in the consumption of her sweet, very much a lady interrupted at her pleasures. "I beg your pardon?"

"In the jewelry shop," David clarified. "I needed a woman's inspiration."

She eyed him warily as she slowly chewed on her second cake. "Regarding?"

Mrs. Banks was not long on charm—or guile—and what a pleasant change that was. "I must buy a present for a lady about whom I care greatly."

"A family member?"

"No. She isn't related to me, though I hold her in very great affection." Would cheerfully die for her, in fact.

Mrs. Banks brushed at her lap, as if crumbs might have had the temerity to fall there, but he could see she was also grateful for a change in topic.

As was David.

"I trust, my lord, you are not asking me to help you choose a present for your current amour?"

"I don't have a current amour, Mrs. Banks. I own a brothel, if you will recall." About which, he was *not* whining. "What would make a suitable gift for a little girl's birthday?"

Dark brows flew up, and she stopped fussing imaginary crumbs. He'd surprised his reluctant courtesan, which was more gratifying than it ought to be.

"Tell me about this little girl."

"Her name is Rose, and to her I am Cousin David, though the family connection is attenuated. She is earnest and shy, loyal, affectionate, and very busy. Her best friend is Mr. Bear, and she has recently become the owner of a stalwart steed named George. She has knighted him, however, so he goes by the sobriquet Sir George."

"You are serious. This matters to you." And that impressed her. David's wealth had not, his charm had not, his steady nerves in the face of female tears had not, his fine tailoring and mismatched eyes had not, but his effort to find a present for Rose had. Mrs. Banks chewed a short nail, eyeing him. "A puppy?"

Why hadn't he thought of that? "Too obvious, and the girl's parents might not appreciate the resulting mess."

"So a kitten is out too, or a caged songbird, though I've never approved of caging wild creatures. What does she like to do?"

"She thrives on movement," David said, and he, too, disapproved of taking wild creatures captive.

"Rose loves to be outside, and because she has neither siblings nor cousins her own age, she's usually in her mother's company. She has a terrific imagination, loves animals, and can draw with uncanny skill."

"Her first set of watercolors, in a wooden case engraved with her name and the date."

Far better than the set of grooming tools the girl's ducal grandpapa was rumored to have had made. David resisted the impulse to kiss Mrs. Banks on both cheeks. "Well done, Mrs. Banks. An excellent suggestion."

"Books," she went on, "inscribed by you, books of fairy tales about knights and princesses and dragons."

"Splendid. Even her step-papa will be impressed, and he is her knight in shining armor." The wretch.

"Gardening tools, because she likes to be out of doors, sized to her hand, inscribed. Some Holland bulbs, though it's not the proper time of year to plant them."

"Capital!"

"Her own stationery."

"You are a genius, Mrs. Banks. My troubles are solved."

She smiled at him, a true, open, winsome smile such as might send a man off on great quests and keep him warm on cold nights. "Which one will you get her?"

"All of the above, of course."

"You shouldn't."

"Whyever not? I am Cousin David, and I can do no wrong. Besides, she liked me best until she met her step-papa. He stole a march on me by wooing her mama. Sneak-thief tactics, if you ask me."

His indignation was intended to sustain her smile,

though that smile became... muted. Sad, even. "Do you know what your Rose would really like?"

He passed her two more tea cakes. "You must tell me."

"A friend. You mentioned she has neither cousins nor siblings her own age, and when she's out and about, it's with her mother."

Well, hell. "Her parents took her with them to Sussex not long ago, and there Rose had playmates for the first time in her life. When her mama told me that, I wanted to cry, to think of a five-year-old never having once had a playmate." Memories of his own childhood had risen up, though he felt no need to expound on that in present company.

"Then you be her friend," Mrs. Banks said, nibbling a lavender cake with lemon icing. "You take her on a picnic; you take her to Astley's; you read to her; you take her out on her pony. It isn't complicated."

She was more animated on this topic than she'd been about her miseries as a mistress.

"You are... right on the mark, Mrs. Banks. Have you raised children, then?"

He posed the question casually—too casually. The way she dispatched the second tea cake said she was not fooled.

"You might be surprised to know, my lord, once long ago, I myself was a little girl looking forward to her birthdays."

"Not so long ago," David corrected her. Her hand had no tremor now, suggesting she'd needed badly to eat.

Mrs. Banks dusted her palms, rose, and stood with

her back to the fire screen. "Such a day—it is pretty." Big, fat, lazy snowflakes drifted down through the late-afternoon gloom.

"Your housekeeper's rheumatism was correct," David said from her side. "And this weather looks like it could worsen into something inconvenient. Let me send for a coach and see you home."

"That won't be necessary, my lord," she said, turning and warming her hands over the fire screen. "I need to stretch my legs, and it's not that far."

At least a mile, in bitter cold with failing light. She didn't want to be seen emerging from his town coach, or she didn't want to tarry with him here while they waited for the vehicle to be brought from his residence.

A man who owned a profitable brothel—and property on three continents—could always order another pair of boots. "I'll walk you then, and no argument, please."

"If you insist."

"I do," David said, marveling that any female other than his horse on a good day should acquiesce so easily. "I spend much of my time dealing with my employees at The Pleasure House, and it's like herding cats. Nothing is more fractious than a determined woman, unless it's seventeen of them coming at you at once. If you'd oblige me, I'd appreciate it."

He *was* whining. Only a dozen women worked at his brothel, but the chefs counted for additional aggravation, as did the patrons.

David walked his guest to the front hallway and fetched her cloak from the brass hooks. He settled it about her shoulders then donned his greatcoat, gloves, and hat. He wanted to wrap his gray merino wool scarf around her neck but didn't dare.

Before he opened the door for Mrs. Banks, he recalled she'd been carrying a reticule, and retrieved it from the side table in the hallway. "Mustn't forget this."

"Thank you very much. Shall we be off before the light fades further?"

He offered his arm and matched his steps to hers with the automatic consideration of a gentleman. As they ambled along in the frigid air, his mind was occupied with a puzzle: the beaded reticule he'd handed to her contained the cloth bag from the jeweler's. The little sack should have held earbobs, a bracelet, a necklace, or perhaps a brooch with a clasp that had needed mending. What David had felt as he'd handled the reticule, however, had been the unmistakable clink of coins, and not all that many coins.

Why was Letitia Banks pawning her jewelry even as she turned down an offer of protection from a perfectly acceptable, attractive, pleasant young gentleman?

❦

Walking along beside Lord Fairly was a surprisingly painful business, for the handsome, blond viscount was everything Letty had given up.

No… He was everything she'd never had and would never have. Sophisticated, wealthy, good-humored, well-mannered, and with a bred-in-the-bone sense of consideration that made her want things she had once dreamed could be hers.

"Penny for them," he said when he'd escorted Letty halfway home.

"I have enjoyed this visit with you." Which ought to occasion pleasure rather than an inexplicable melancholy—her belly was full, after all, and she hadn't had to part with a single petticoat.

And for a few minutes, despite all her determination to the contrary, she'd cried on a man's shoulder and been… comforted.

With that thought, Letty slipped on the dusting of snow underfoot, the soles of her boots being worn smooth, though her escort righted her with no effort at all.

"I am almost sure I hear a but coming," he said, "perhaps of the same variety you inflicted on poor Windham."

Poor Windham, the handsome, wealthy, talented, musical prodigy of a duke's son. "I discouraged Lord Valentine out of motives other than spite, my lord."

"Befriend him," Fairly urged her. "He's recently lost a second brother, this one to consumption, the heir having died several years ago on the Peninsula. If your terms are clearly stated, he won't trespass."

"I will consider it." When the English put Napoleon on the throne.

"May I be honest?" Fairly asked, some of the pleasantness leaving his tone.

"Of course." Though she wished he wouldn't be. For two hours, his parlor hadn't been merely bearable, it had been *warm*. Fairly wasn't merely polite to her, he was gracious. The food had been plentiful and fresh, and the tea hot and strong. She'd put as much sugar in hers as she liked, not doled herself out a miserly serving and pretended it tasted just as good.

"I am quite frankly puzzled, Mrs. Banks. You appear to have no source of income, and yet you refused Windham. How do you sustain your household, if not by bartering your favors?"

She forced herself to continue walking, to keep to herself how mortifying his inquiry was. Perhaps by literally crying on his shoulder—in his arms, into his monogrammed silk handkerchief—she had granted him permission to presume this far.

"You needn't answer, of course." His tone was concerned rather than curious. "But your circumstances worry me."

"I appreciate the thought, though I am not your worry." She had lost the right to be anybody's worry years ago. Lost it in the vicarage rose arbor, within sight of the peacefully moonlit gravestones.

"You appear to be nobody's worry. Thus I am anxious, because you are a woman without protection, and my extended family had a hand in authoring difficulties for you."

"How do you reason that?"

"Your last protector was my brother-by-marriage. I have the sense Herbert did not comport himself well with respect to you, and sometimes it isn't finances needed to redress a wrong."

True chivalry, rather than pretty manners, empty flattery, or even the lure of coin, was a courtesan's worst, most beguiling enemy.

Letty increased her pace, despite the slick footing, and Fairly kept up—easily. "I had choices, my lord." How often had Olivia reminded her of that very truth?

"Somehow, Mrs. Banks, I doubt you had choices

in any meaningful sense. When the girls leave my employ, my most stern admonition to them is to always have their own money, somewhere, and to keep its existence and whereabouts a complete secret. Even so, I worry. A woman who has placed herself outside the protections of decent Society is always at risk for disrespect and worse."

For all his kindness, Fairly implied a fallen woman attained that precarious position all by herself, without aid from anybody else. The ire Letty felt at his judgment was pathetically welcome.

"You think I do not know the risk I've invited into my life?"

"No, you do not, not the way a streetwalker knows that risk when the pox gets so bad she can't ply her trade anymore. Not the way my employees know it when they end up with a baby in their belly. Not the way the actresses and opera dancers know it when their looks begin to fade."

How fierce he had become, and yet, Letty was not afraid of him. "Are you *scolding* me?"

"I am *worrying* about you," he replied, a thread of exasperation in his voice.

"Why?"

"You need someone to worry about you."

He could not know the pain his well-meant observation caused. "I most assuredly do not."

Fairly stopped and stared down at her as the snow swirled around them. For all they weren't the same color, his eyes were beautiful and… compelling. "You pawned your jewelry, you have no current patron, you turn away business, and you ate like you were starving.

You are pale and skinny. I apologize profusely, and for the last time, but I noticed these things."

"I wish you had not." She wished he had ignored her altogether, and was so glad he hadn't.

"What is so awful about a simple show of concern?"

"Is that what this is?" She dropped his arm, when what she wanted to do was cling to him. "Or, having ascertained my direction, will you come by Tuesday next and start ogling my bosom, dropping hints, and standing too close to me? Will you begin to pepper our conversation with double meanings and sly, lascivious innuendo as you serve me more and more wine? Will your exquisite manners desert you when your passions rise? And when I refuse your overtures, will you tell me I am a tease, a slut, and undeserving of your worry after all?"

Letty fell silent, trying to recall any other time when she'd lost her composure twice in the same day. A life of sin had not agreed with her, though a life of short rations didn't have much to recommend it either, for both caused her a sort of weary, hopeless shame.

Her tirade, so completely out of character with the rest of her interactions with Fairly, appeared to leave his lordship stunned, offended, and at a loss. He picked up her gloved hand by the wrist, put it back on his arm, and resumed walking through the thickening snow at a deliberate pace.

While Letty battled back another bout of tears.

"I have never," he said at length, "given anyone cause to doubt my honor, and I do not intend to start with you. Will you receive me, Tuesday next?"

She didn't answer, though he was observing the

courtesies, when in truth, he could barge into her home at any time and appropriate what she had given others more or less willingly.

"I am not propositioning you, Mrs. Banks. I am asking permission to call on you, nothing more."

His lovely voice was as cold as the snowflakes melting against Letty's cheeks.

He would call on her Tuesday next no matter what she said, so Letty remained silent until they'd reached her door. He led her up the steps of her house, onto a covered front porch. The housekeeper had lit a lantern for her, but in the increasingly dense snow, it cast little real light.

"Thank you, my lord," she managed, though that didn't seem adequate when her belly was full for the first time in days. "Thank you for bearing me company on my way home and for your conversation." She sensed he'd be offended if she thanked him for rescuing her in the jeweler's shop—more offended. "You will call on me next week?"

One way or another, she needed to know what his plans were.

"I will call. Whether you receive me is entirely for you to decide. Good night, Mrs. Banks." He bowed over her gloved hand, and waited politely while she opened the door and turned to leave him.

"Until next we meet, my lord," she said, her back mostly to him.

"I beg your pardon?"

"Until Tuesday." She stepped into the house and closed the door without further comment. Blast the man and his lovely eyes; she was already wondering how much he might pay a woman to tolerate his intimate attentions.

Though that woman would not be her. That woman would never be her again.

⊷

From behind the window of her front parlor, Letty watched Viscount Fairly walk away, his long-legged pace far more brisk than it had been at her side. He gave off a sense of energy and purpose rather than the exuberant high spirits of the young men newly down from university. David Worthington was not a boy, had probably never been a boy. He was in every sense a man, and that made him... tricky.

"Your tea, love." Fanny Newcomb put the tray on the low table before the settee, then straightened and regarded the falling snow dourly. "Won't be fit for man nor beast out there before too much longer."

She was a plump, gray woman, her face lined with the passing years and with concern for her employer. Fanny was also a connection with home, and for that reason alone, Letty would sell off the last bucket of household ashes before she'd let Fanny go.

"You are too good to me," Letty said, sinking down onto the sofa. Beside the tea lay two fresh, buttery pieces of shortbread—which they could not afford.

"Those boots have to be cold and wet. Best get them off if you're not to take a chill." Fanny's concern was served with a dash of scold, as usual.

"I did well at the jeweler's. Still, you need not have used new leaves for the tea." The scent of the tea was marvelous, and steam curled from the spout into the chilly parlor air.

"This is not a night for weak tea," Fanny said, tugging the curtains closed. "You were gone quite a while, and I was getting worried about you."

"I met someone," Letty admitted, glad for a chance to parse the encounter with a friendly ear.

Fanny gave up trying to drape the curtains so they entirely blocked the fading afternoon light. "Not a female someone," she concluded with some interest.

"I met him once before." Letty bent to unlace her boots, knowing the women at Fairly's establishment had ladies' maids for such a task—also coal for their parlor grates. "David Worthington, Viscount Fairly. He called on me when Herbert died."

"Is he related to Herbert?"

"No." Letty slipped her feet from her boots and tucked her legs under her on the sofa, because the parlor floor was positively frigid. "Not directly. There's some connection now through the in-laws to the surviving brother, but Fairly was not close to the deceased."

Thank heavens.

They fell silent as Fanny perched on the edge of an upholstered chair, fixed Letty a cup of tea, and passed it to her. Maybe some fallen women could observe strict propriety with their last and only employee; Letty was not among them.

"Just shy of bitter," Letty murmured, closing her eyes with the small bliss of it.

"Did this viscount fellow suggest he'd be interested in further dealings?"

Letty put down her teacup. "Must we discuss that, Fanny? I understand how strained my finances have become, but your wages are up-to-date, there's food in the larder for your meals, and the thought... I don't know if I can."

Worse, she was nearly certain she could not.

"Well, ducks, you have to do something, and sooner rather than later. Needs must. And certain burdens are a woman's lot whether she's married or not. There are fellows who can make the business bearable. Find one of 'em, or find another way to pay the bills, lest you spend next winter on a street corner or on your brother's charity."

On that mercifully brief summation of the relevant truths, Fanny withdrew.

Letty's reticule lay next to the tea tray, the beaded bag another small reminder of home, for it had been a gift from Daniel on Letty's sixteenth birthday.

She picked up the bag, hearing coins clink within— not enough coins, of course. Never enough.

In the cold, dark parlor, Letty ignored the coins, took out Viscount Fairly's silk handkerchief, and held it to her nose.

❧

When Tuesday came around, David nearly missed the time for his call on Mrs. Banks. Desdemona and Portia had gone at each other over Portia's decision to accept *carte blanche* from young Lord Ridgely. Desdemona had also entertained the man on occasion, and made comments disparaging his skills.

"Hell hath no ability to hurl the breakables," David

observed, "like a pair of women after a few glasses of wine. And all over some young twit's ability to keep it up."

Jennings put the bottom half of a porcelain angel on the mantel. "Or over Portia's ability to snag the twit's heart, while Des is left behind. That has to hurt."

David found the angel's wings under the piano and set them on the mantel among the collected shrapnel. "Yes, but Portia has to tolerate a steady diet of the twit, who doesn't strike me as any great bargain." Certainly not worth shattering hundred-year-old Meissen over.

"None of us are great bargains," Jennings said, surveying the wreckage in the main parlor. "At least not enough to merit this kind of display. Maybe they're angry as hell on general principles, and so they squabble with each other over the small things."

"Angry or scared. You'll have it cleaned up before this evening?"

"Of course, though Des has a black eye, and Portia's lip is split. We'll be a little shorthanded."

Such violence, and in a residence supposedly devoted to pleasure. "Then tell the ladies not to linger above stairs. Fortunately, the weather has turned cold as hell. Maybe that will keep things quieter tonight."

"Or make everybody want to snuggle up." Jennings glanced at the clock—mercifully unscathed—on the mantel. "You'd better toddle along if you're to pay a call on Mrs. Banks."

"Mrs…?" David was momentarily at a loss, though this appointment had loomed large in his awareness for days. "Mrs. Banks. Blessed saints, I'll be off then— dock the damages from the offenders' pay, and tell them I'll expect written apologies by week's end."

"You're cruel, Fairly. A nasty, heartless, cruel man."

In fact, the written apologies were not going to be easy, not when some of the women in David's employ were all but illiterate. He offered them the chance to learn to read, and without exception, they took advantage of it.

Mrs. Banks, he was sure, could read English, French, and Latin—fat lot of good it seemed to be doing her. When he knocked, her door was opened by an older woman in an apron and cap, who apparently couldn't be bothered to greet visitors with a smile.

David handed her his card, and she disappeared without offering to take his hat, coat, or gloves. He used the time to study what he could see of the house, and had to agree with Jennings that the place seemed subtly less well-appointed than it had months ago.

Cobwebs grew in the hallway corners, the rug running down the hallway was long overdue for a sound beating, and the air was so cold in the foyer David could see his breath. Perhaps leaving him in his greatcoat had been more consideration than rudeness.

"This way, if you please," the unsmiling woman said. She led David to a small informal parlor at the back of the house. The hearth sported a coal fire, though by no means would David have called it a cheery blaze.

"Mrs. Banks will be down shortly," David was informed. "Shall I be getting the tea, then?" The accent was Midlands rural, and the tone entirely put-upon.

"Why don't you wait until Mrs. Banks joins me, and she can decide whether libation is in order? I doubt I'll be staying long." Because even a tea tray was a luxury in this household.

David earned the barest indication of a curtsy for that remark, and was left alone in the little room to remove his coat, hat, and gloves unassisted. The last time he'd been here, Mrs. Banks had received company in the front parlor, a roomier, graciously appointed space at the front of the house.

Why was Mrs. Banks seeing him in this oversized broom closet now, and why was she making him wait?

"My lord." His hostess stepped into the room, carrying a tea service on a lacquered tray. "I would curtsy, but one of us might end up with a scalding, and I am looking forward to my tea." She smiled at him, a pleasant if not quite gracious greeting.

"Mrs. Banks." David bowed then took the tray from her. "A pleasure to see you again, particularly bearing the tea tray on a day such as this."

"The winters since I've come to London have been colder than any I can recall as a child. Shall we be seated?"

David was struck again by Letitia Banks's quiet loveliness. Here in her own home, she was more comfortable than she had been at his unrented town house. Her attire was simple—a brown velvet skirt, white shirtwaist, brown shawl, and wide red sash—but with her coloring, the shade and texture of the velvet were elegant rather than plain.

He sat at right angles to her perch on the couch, the better to enjoy simply beholding her.

"You must forgive me for using the family parlor," Mrs. Banks said, passing him a steaming cup of tea. "It is easier to heat, and gets more light. This room also has the advantage of being closer to the kitchen."

"I had wondered if you weren't making a comment on my station, though this is cozy, which given the weather, is a mercy." There. They had discussed the weather quite thoroughly, and avoided the notion that she had secreted him in the back parlor to hide the very fact that he was calling on her. "Have you considered the topics we discussed last week?"

He might have made more small talk, except he'd held this woman in his arms and brushed his thumb over the too-prominent bone in her wrist.

She paused in the middle of fixing her own cup of tea. "My lord?"

"Your finances merit some attention, Mrs. Banks." *Panic* might be a better word than attention, there being not a single tea cake on the tray, and the service being arranged to obscure, but not quite hide, chips in the lacquer.

She sat back, cradling the teacup in her palms, likely the better to treasure any source of warmth. "One should always mind one's finances."

She sounded as if she were quoting from Proverbs, though her teapot was wrapped in a thin, dingy towel that might once have sported some embroidery, and she looked paler than she had last week. David did not ask his hostess to pour him a second cup.

"I have need of a competent housekeeper for my estates in Kent," he said. "I own three, and I use only the one. You could have your pick of the other two." This was a stupid plan—a stupid *idea*, for David hadn't planned much of anything about this encounter, except that he'd see Letty Banks again. If she were in Kent, he'd find reasons to drop in on those other estates, reasons to stay there from time to time.

Perhaps remove there entirely, because this reluctant courtesan intrigued him inordinately.

"My thanks, but I cannot remove to Kent, my lord. I have obligations that require I bide in London."

He could not offer her a domestic post in London, for his family would drop in from time to time, and Letty Banks was likely known to at least his brothers-in-law.

As he considered a niggardly piece of shortbread that could not possibly be fresh, inspiration struck.

"You could instead be madam at The Pleasure House. The place is driving me to Bedlam, and if I don't do something with it soon, I'm likely to burn it down." And then, lest he appear desperate, "You could, in the alternative, ensconce yourself as chatelaine at my estate in County Galway, though it is remote as only rural Ireland can be."

"I cannot remove to Ireland, but why ensconce me anywhere at all?" she asked in a bewildered tone. "You hardly know me."

He knew her, despite short acquaintance. Knew she'd been saving those last few bites of shortbread, likely for days, in anticipation of his visit, knew were he not with her, she'd be wearing a second shawl for warmth, one that did not go at all with her ensemble. Yet more inspiration came to his rescue, the kind of honest inspiration she might appreciate.

"I have sisters. When our father died, he expected me to provide for them, but there were hostilities with Bonaparte, and I was prevented from returning to England. My sisters faced dire circumstances by the time I reached them, and they could easily have ended up living… as you do. My younger sister was barely out of the schoolroom."

Rather than comment on a recitation that surprised the man making it, she got up and poked at the fire, though she added no fuel to it, and her efforts sent a sulfurous cloud of coal smoke into the room. "What does a madam do? Specifically."

Mrs. Banks wasn't rejecting him out of hand, not yet, though clearly she wanted to.

"You do not entertain men." To her, that would be most important. "Not unless you choose to bestow your favors from time to time for your own pleasure. You are a combination hostess, mother hen, gunnery sergeant, and steward. The position is demanding. Mr. Jennings and I, between us, barely keep up with it. You wouldn't have to live on the premises, but there are private quarters for that purpose if you need them. The nights, particularly on weekends, can be quite late."

And the mornings early, when the girls were out of sorts and prone to squabbling, which was to say—always.

Mrs. Banks studied a small orange flame flickering above the coals, while the idea of depositing the burden of the damned brothel on her elegant shoulders gained appeal with each moment David considered it. She had the presence for it, the self-possession, the ability to manage unruly boys in perpetual rut and unhappy women.

"Please be more specific, my lord. Do I keep the books, decide who is to spend the evening with whom, choose menus, collect money? What exactly would I do, and for what kind of compensation?"

David badly wanted her to agree to this. He hated—yes, *hated*—seeing that smirk on Jennings's face almost every morning, and the headaches it presaged. He hated the way his in-laws teased him, and the way Douglas Allen, the present Viscount Amery, had simply admonished him weeks ago to find a madam, as if women willing and able to manage such a human circus could be found beneath any hedge.

So he schooled himself to apply his strongest negotiating tactics, and let the silence between them grow.

"The compensation, my lord?"

"Mrs. Banks, you have subdued that fire halfway to next spring. I beg you to resume your seat while we converse."

Get your opponent to give you something small.

She took her seat and unwrapped the teapot, revealing a predictably chipped article of imitation jasperware.

"Thank you," David said softly, the state of her tea service providing him needed encouragement. "Your duties can be somewhat flexible. If you detest bookkeeping, we can hire you a bookkeeper. If you are indifferent to wines, you may rely on the good offices of my sommelier. If you prefer not to interact directly with the domestics, we can hire you a house steward."

"Lord Fairly," she interrupted him through gritted teeth. "*What are my duties?*"

Something militant in her eye caught his attention, and abruptly, the discussion went from encouraging to… fascinating.

"Are you asking if one of your duties would be… *me?*"

Three

At David's question, Mrs. Banks nodded slowly, up and down once.

What answer did she want to hear?

What answer did he *want* to give?

Arousal, jolly and warm, coursed through him. Not the usual physical arousal that came from flirting and strutting, but something fresh, something optimistic, like a seasoned hound baying merrily on the scent of a fox new to the neighborhood.

He straightened the crease of his breeches and kept his legs crossed.

"You are a mature, worldly woman who has been without male companionship for some time. Is it so unreasonable to consider I might be worth your attention, should you be so inclined?"

How humbly he posited his intimate availability to her, how cautiously, when he hadn't made himself available to a woman since... He could not recall when, where, under what circumstances, or—this was not flattering—with whom.

His question left Mrs. Banks looking bewildered

rather than insulted or indignant. Too subtle, then? David shot his cuffs and tried again.

"When you yearn for a man's embrace, when your body aches for intimate gratification," he said, his voice dropping lower, "could you imagine availing yourself of my company?" For he could imagine providing her that gratification.

"Gratification?"

He might as well have been speaking Hottentot—or perhaps she simply did not fancy him in any degree, and this was how she conveyed her indifference. For that matter, she might not fancy any man—some of his employees were of a Sapphic persuasion, after all.

"As madam, you will manage the women," he said briskly. "Keep them well dressed, healthy, and in as good spirits as you can. They decide with whom they will pass an evening, or an hour, though you should be on hand to assist if the need arises."

"Assist? I thought you said I wouldn't…" She waved a hand in upward circles, as if that were the universal signal for coitus.

"Sometimes, two fellows get to scrapping about whose turn it is to go upstairs with a certain girl. You intervene before feelings are hurt."

"Intervene?"

The room had developed a puzzled echo to go with the stink of coal smoke. "They can figuratively draw straws. One goes tonight, the other tomorrow night. A second lady can be tactfully suggested, or they can all three go upstairs at the same time. It isn't complicated."

It *was* complicated and tedious and nerve-wracking,

and that was before Portia ˋand Desdemona began imbibing, or Musette's jealousy was aroused.

"I see." She gestured with the teapot; he shook his head. "And what if three men wanted to share her favors? Would she take all three upstairs at once?"

David shrugged, having run out of cuffs to shoot and creases to straighten. "I've seen it done. A woman can accommodate that many men, after all, but it's damned funny-looking. Rather like a rowing crew—the whole thing needs a coxswain calling the stroke."

The teapot hit the tray with a *clank*.

"My wages?" Mrs. Banks was changing the subject—also blushing furiously, though discussion of coin was difficult for some people. David tossed out a sum that reflected what it would be worth to him to get out from under the running of this particular business, and out from under Jennings's infernal smirks.

"I accept."

"Just like that?" The magnitude of his relief beggared description. "You aren't going to make me haggle, and toss in this and that additional consideration? You don't want Sundays off, your own gig, an account at Madame Baptiste's?"

She folded her arms, in one gesture turning herself into the embodiment of a female who'd made up her mind and would not be trifled with.

"Your establishment is not open for business on Sunday and Monday nights. I still have my own gig and pony, and I am adequately clothed for the present."

"Let's see about that," David said, rising.

Unease flitted through her eyes at this most prosaic request. "I beg your pardon, my lord?"

"I want to have a look at your wardrobe. What you might think is adequate may not be quite up to the mark. The Pleasure House maintains elegant standards, comparable to what you'd expect were you dining in the home of any peer. Your wardrobe must be worthy of your position."

And he sounded convincing when he delivered that lecture, because for her, he wanted it to be true: she would be well dressed in his employ. Elegantly well dressed, well fed, well compensated, *and well protected*.

She chewed a nail, flicking a glance at him that said he was daft, which perhaps he was around her—or brilliant.

"This way," she said, moving toward the door. "You might want your coat."

He ignored the advice, even as she added a thick red wool shawl to the brown paisley. She led him up to the second floor, the sway of her hips before him taking the worst of the chill from his blood.

"In here." She opened the door to a room at the back of the house, the one farthest from the noise, dirt, and stink of the street, closest to the heat coming up the stairwell from the kitchen.

There was a bed, of course, a pretty oak piece with a quilted spread of blues and browns, and a frame for bed hangings, though no hangings were in evidence, and the covers did not look nearly thick enough to keep a body warm of a night. The hangings had been sold, no doubt, or cut up for curtains.

The chamber itself was lovely if cold, boasting some light and a sense of comfort and repose. This was precisely the kind of room David would have envisioned for her: graceful, pretty, and unpretentious.

Wholesome, which was both a relief and, on an ungentlemanly level, an annoyance.

Mrs. Banks opened a large wardrobe in a corner of the room, sending the scents of sage and lavender wafting through the gloomy air. "I didn't entertain him here, if you're wondering."

"I beg your pardon?" David stood behind her, the scent of roses blending with the other fragrances drifting from the depths of the wardrobe.

"Herbert. The late Lord Amery." She kept her back to him as she fingered dresses, shawls, and chemises. "With him, I used the other bedroom, at the front of the house."

Well, of course. She'd kept part of herself private this way, by separating business and personal spheres. The girls at The Pleasure House did likewise, never bringing customers to their sleeping quarters, never sleeping in the rooms where they entertained. In some secret guideline for fallen women, this was apparently holy writ.

"This is a lovely room." What else was he to say? "Did you make the quilt?"

"A long time ago." She smiled faintly over her shoulder, a flirtatious smile, though she likely hadn't intended it as such. "What do you make of my frocks, my lord?"

He stood directly behind her for a long moment, ostensibly reviewing the contents of her closet, when in fact he was inhaling the subtle rosy fragrance of her, imagining his lips on her nape, and considering what she'd do if he pulled her derriere back against his thighs—all quite to his own surprise.

He spent the next half hour tossing her dresses onto the bed, suggesting minor refinements on this one, discarding that one, and frowning thoughtfully over another, all the while battling the distraction of inconvenient arousal.

From handling her clothing? From standing near her? Or was he attracted to Letty Banks because she was not even politely interested in him?

And he liked her for that, for not flirting, teasing, and trying to manipulate him through male appendages already quite vulnerable enough without a woman's grasp secured around them.

"You really do not dress to show yourself to best advantage," he said, handing her the dresses one by one to hang back up. "Why is that?"

"What would be the point? I looked well enough for Herbert's purposes, wearing only my shift."

"In the dark?" David asked, wishing the words back as soon as they left his stupid, thoughtless mouth.

"No." She ran her hand over the bodice of a green velvet carriage dress gone a bit shiny at the seams. "With candles blazing, my lord. Have you any other rude questions?"

Did you ever enjoy it? He knew better than to ask that, knew it was impertinent, personal, and irrelevant. If he asked that, he'd have to slap his own face.

"Some men," he observed as he passed her the last of the dresses, "enjoy having the candles out. Enjoy having to learn a woman's contours and preferences by feel and by the music of her sighs and whispers."

He was such a man, in fact, or he would be with her.

Mrs. Banks closed the wardrobe, turned, and leaned

back against it, her posture putting David in mind of a soldier facing a firing squad. "You have said I need not entertain men to earn my wages."

He wanted to kiss her, to mash her against the wardrobe and make her feel the rebellion against good sense going on behind his falls. At the same time, he resented her for inspiring his arousal, because he spoke of pleasure, and she quoted contract terms.

And he wanted to call Herbert Allen out post-humously, because the man had abused the lady's sensibilities unpardonably.

She turned her head, the only evasion their cramped quarters permitted. David told himself to step the hell back, but his feet did not listen.

But because he had been a physician, he noticed she was holding her breath, and that small suggestion that he'd become the bully allowed him to move away, closer to the weak light filtering in through the window.

"Your duties are as I've stated, Letty Banks, though nothing should preclude you from delighting in the pleasures a woman of the world might seek for her private enjoyment."

She let her breath out, perhaps because he'd retreated to the chillier space near the window, perhaps because he'd retreated into manners. "Steady income will be enjoyable, I assure you, my lord."

David held out a hand to her.

She blinked at his outstretched hand, uncomprehending.

"A bargain between business associates is often sealed with a handshake," he explained with what he hoped was a disarming smile—provided those business associates were male, and reasonably friendly.

Her smile was puzzled, her hand cold, and David trespassed the smallest degree on his good intentions by kissing her knuckles before letting her hand go.

"I'll have my solicitors write up our agreement and send it to yours," he said, holding the door for her. "Which firm do you use?"

"I don't," she said, following him down the stairs. "I don't have a solicitor."

"We'll remedy that." Truly, dear Herbert had not valued this woman properly. A mistress might be a commodity, but she ought to be a cherished commodity. "All of the girls who work for me have solicitors."

She stopped on the last stair, so their heights nearly matched. "They are not girls."

David wasn't about to call them whores. Not ever. "What are they, then? My employees?"

"They are *ladies*," she said, her hand on the newel post as if she were some monarch with her royal orb. "They are women, at least. They are not girls and haven't been for some time. And if you do employ girls, then our association is at an end, my lord."

"I do not employ any female under the age of twenty-one, nor have I ever." Though David hadn't realized it until this exchange with Her Majesty of the Non-Matching Shawls. "I assume you'll be able to start this week?"

She clutched those shawls more tightly. "This week? I can't begin this week."

Now, she intended to haggle? He remained one step below her, thinking she'd chosen her moment well.

"I need a madam, and you have accepted the position, at a very generous wage. You said nothing about needing time, Mrs. Banks."

"I'm asking for one week, and one week only, then I'll be your madam, and you will own my time, body, and soul—five days of the week. My days off will be my days off, or we have no bargain."

"One week," he said, not liking the idea *at all*. "Though you will join me at The Pleasure House this evening at six of the clock."

"Tonight?" She looked wary. She looked wary frequently, which would have put a lesser man—a less relieved man—out of charity with her. "Whatever for?"

"I want to show you the place, for one thing, and the clients don't wander in until eight, or seven at the very earliest. The ladies usually come downstairs about half eight. Tonight is the perfect time to look the premises over and acquaint you with the house itself. I'll fetch you in my coach, and we can dine when you've seen the place. Now, shall we retrieve my coat before I freeze to death standing on your stair?"

"Of course." She followed him back to the less frigid, more odoriferous parlor, though David had the sense she was profoundly preoccupied.

Well, so was he.

What manner of courtesan was indifferent to the thought of a new wardrobe, had no use for intimate pleasures, and blushed when discussing money? He left the premises uneasy with himself, because perhaps that kind of courtesan—the shy, proper, complicated kind—would really have done better as a housekeeper in County Galway.

Vicars did not allow whores around their children or their decent womenfolk.

Vicars did not bring fallen women into their family establishments.

Nonetheless, Letty braved the bitter cold; the stinking, crowded public coach; and the journey that took much longer than it should, and finally, finally found herself knocking on the door of the vicarage in Little Weldon.

"Letty!" Olivia greeted her with surprise rather than joy, but she opened the door nonetheless, as she'd promised she always would. "Come in, come in. We must not let in the cold."

"Aunt Letty!" Five-year-old Danny chorused from Olivia's side. "Aunt Letty has come to visit! Papa!" Danny tore off to deliver the news to his father rather than hug his aunt, while Olivia hustled Letty into the house.

"We weren't expecting you, Letty," Olivia remarked as she took Letty's cloak, bonnet, scarf, and gloves. "Is everything all right?"

The question held worry, as did Olivia's blue eyes, but it wasn't worry for Letty.

"Everything is fine. I have a new position, and for the present, at least, my situation is settled. I would have written, Olivia, but I left London on short notice, and I can stay only a few days."

Letty would not volunteer more than that about her changed circumstances, and Olivia would not ask. Their system was simple, and for years now, it had suited them both.

"You are always welcome." Olivia's expression

contradicted the plain meaning of the words, but further remarks were forestalled by the arrival of Letty's brother.

"Letty!" Daniel enveloped his sister in a tight embrace, and Letty's composure abruptly faltered. Nearly ten years her senior, Daniel Banks had always been her hero. He'd taken the brunt of their father's sour temper, tolerated Letty's ceaseless tagging along, and when she'd really, really needed it, he'd taken on her burdens without reproaching her. She clung to him for a long moment, then let him step back to inspect her.

Daniel was tall, brown-haired, brown-eyed, broad-shouldered, and too handsome to be a man of the cloth.

Also, too kind to be anything else.

"You are too thin," Daniel pronounced. "But a most, most welcome sight." Unlike his prim, blond wife, Daniel's sentiments were sincere. "How long can you stay?"

"The rest of the week, only. I've started a new position, and I demanded some time away before taking up my duties." The lies had been easy when offered to Olivia; they nearly choked Letty when given to her brother.

Daniel smiled at his wife. "Let's have some sustenance in the family parlor, if you please, Olivia. I must hear what my sister has been up to in old Londontowne, and I'm sure you will want to hear as well."

"Of course, Daniel." Olivia disappeared into the back of the house, obedient as always.

Daniel's expression lost its genial good cheer in Olivia's absence. "She doesn't mean to be so unwelcoming."

The irony of Daniel's pronouncement was profound, and yet he was oblivious to it—thank God.

"Olivia is perfectly civil, and I don't know when I'll be able to break free again, so I've come to spend what time I can with family."

"And Danny and I are pleased to see you, as always." He took her arm and led her into the parlor, seating himself beside her on the sofa. "You really do look too thin, Letty."

She was famished, and yet more aware that Olivia had shooed young Danny right back upstairs than she was of her hunger.

"I *am* too thin. I've been worried since losing my last post, but things are looking up now." She'd been raised in this house, raised to be truthful, no matter the cost.

"Tell me about the new position."

Letty fabricated a tale, of course, about being housekeeper to one of Viscount Fairly's less used town residences. She hated deceiving her brother, for he'd shown her nothing but kindness and understanding, but she couldn't disappoint him with the truth. He'd insist on her joining his household, which, for many, many reasons, would never do at all.

So she embroidered on the truth, avoided her brother's eyes, and listened for any sound indicating Danny might be rejoining them.

❧

"You are dithering, my lord."

With three words, Thomas Jennings could jeopardize his own existence, or at least his livelihood.

"I am choosing bed hangings," David shot back. "In case it has escaped your notice, it's bloody winter, and a woman needs proper bed hangings if she's not to fall prey to lung fever. How to choose bed hangings was not on the curriculum at St. Andrews."

Though *why* David was subjecting himself to this torment was simple: he wanted Letty Banks to sleep right here at The Pleasure House where he knew she'd be warm and well fed, not at that dusty, stinky, frigid little property she shared with her besom of a housekeeper.

Jennings wrinkled a not insubstantial nose and planted himself on a dressing stool upholstered with cabbage roses. "The burgundy, then."

David held up the swatch of burgundy velvet, which would make Letty Banks look pale, but then, so would the blue and the green. "Why?"

Jennings found something fascinating to study in the vicinity of his boots. "Won't show the dirt or the dust."

"Excellent notion." David tossed the burgundy velvet at him. "Have we had this flue cleaned recently?"

"Yes."

Thomas was pouting—or brooding. "When?"

"The first of the year, the same as we have all the chimneys cleaned on this property. There are other ways to keep a woman warm at night besides spending a fortune on velvet nobody will ever see."

David snatched the fabric from him and folded it into a tidy square. "You won't be keeping Mrs. Banks warm, Thomas."

Though he'd be keeping her safe, of course. Jennings was constitutionally incapable of allowing a

woman to put her safety at risk, and the employees of
The Pleasure House seemed to sense this about him.

"I own I am puzzled." Jennings rose from the dressing stool, the thing creaking as if in relief.

"You are not puzzled," David said, folding up the
blue velvet, which he'd nearly chosen because it was
a regal color, and he'd thought Letty—Mrs. Banks—
might prefer it. "You are baiting your employer, who
is not in the mood to be trifled with."

"I think you rather are," Jennings replied, running a
blunt finger over the mantel and inspecting it for dust.
"I think a good trifling might improve your disposi-
tion considerably."

David left off folding the length of green velvet.
The piece was clearly a castoff, asymmetric, the color
washed out across one corner. "What is that supposed
to mean?"

Jennings used the broom from the hearth set to
brush a stray bit of ash back into the fireplace. "A
week ago, you suggested I offer Mrs. Banks *carte
blanche*, now you're telling me to keep my hands off
of her."

David was not in the least fooled by Jennings's
impersonation of a chambermaid. A question was
being asked, one David could answer clearly.

"Thomas," he said gently, "I am, somewhat to
my own surprise, saying that very thing. You, the
patrons, that trio of expensive flirts in the kitchen, the
bootboy—you will all keep your hands off Mrs. Banks."

Jennings set the broom back where it belonged.
"Leaving only one matter undecided."

They'd spent much of the afternoon choosing bed

hangings, having the footmen replace the area rugs, the curtains, and the pillows, and having a chaise brought down from the attics. All in all, the formerly unused bedroom behind the kitchens of The Pleasure House was looking quite lovely.

Though it needed sachets hung on the bedposts and window sashes. Lavender was always pleasant, and rose could be very nice, too.

"And that undecided matter would be?" David asked, because Jennings was smirking again.

"Whether you'll be getting your hands on the lady."

David said nothing, for the answer to that question wasn't his to give.

❧

"Tell me," Letty said, a shade too brightly, "did the Doncaster sisters ever make good on their threat to move to Bristol to be with their niece?"

Daniel looked ready to launch gamely into that riveting topic, when Danny came hurtling into the room. "I want Aunt Letty to come see my pony!"

Letty smiled at the child's enthusiasm. "I didn't know you had a pony, Danny."

"It's not real. It's a rocking horse, so I can practice."

"Does your rocking horse have a name?" Letty asked, heart constricting at the earnestness in the child's expression.

"No, Aunt Letty. It isn't a real horse. It's a practice horse, like a toy."

"Don't be encouraging flights of imagination in the child," Olivia chided from her seat nearest the fire. "You would have him name the rocking horse as if it were a doll. And, Danny, you have interrupted your elders."

Letty stood and held out her hand to Danny. "Even if it has no name, I should like to see it. Danny?"

And Danny's parents let her go, which made every moment on the coach and all of Olivia's disapproving glances of no moment. Letty admired his horse, read stories to him, asked him endless patient questions about his studies, his friends, his hopes and dreams. Thrilled with the attention from his favorite—and only—aunt, Danny chattered on and on and on, until Daniel fetched Letty for dinner.

"Are there children in Fairly's household?" Daniel asked as he escorted her down the steps.

"He isn't married." Letty paused on a small landing to study a sketch she'd done of Danny as an infant, because this was not a discussion to be held within earshot of Olivia.

"How old is this Lord Fairly?"

"Probably about your age." Or five years Daniel's junior.

"I'm nearly two-and-thirty, Letty," Daniel reminded her, "and I would not, were I a bachelor, condone having an unmarried housekeeper eight years my junior, not even in residences I barely use. This is not what I would wish for you."

That disappointed tone was as close as Daniel would come to censuring her, and his words stung. How much more deeply would Letty be wounded were he to learn the truth?

"He's a very busy fellow, Daniel," Letty assured him. "I won't see much of him, and as soon as he does take a wife, she'll want to hire her own staff. This will do for now, and it will be a good character when I leave. Things in London are not so staid as they are out here."

They were more staid, in some regards, and so much less in others.

Daniel reached past her to straighten up the little sketch, which had hung slightly askew. "What you mean to say is, we are old-fashioned to a fault, which is the truth."

Letty allowed him to precede her down the steps, though she had a small scold of her own to fire off. "You don't fool me, Daniel," she said softly as they approached the dining parlor. "You aren't happy."

He had the grace not to contradict her directly, but his gaze slid away, and for a moment his handsome features looked... *bleak.*

Oh, Daniel, not you too. Please don't tell me you have made a bed you dread to lie in as well.

"I am not unhappy," Daniel said, his smile reappearing, though tinged with regret. "I am useful here, and the living is adequate. Olivia, though, is not—"

His words were cut off when the parlor door swung open and the maid of all work backed toward them, wheeling the kitchen trolley.

"Steady there, Nan." Daniel stopped the girl from bumping into him with a hand on her elbow.

Nan turned, smiling and blushing. "Your pardon, Vicar. Didn't know you was out there."

"No harm done." Daniel stepped back to allow the maid to pass, and Letty couldn't help but see the glance Nan shot her employer. The young woman admired her vicar, and just as clearly, Daniel ignored the situation.

Olivia was lighting candles on the sideboard in the dining parlor, the fireplace shedding additional light and making the room cozy.

"Shall we sit?" Olivia suggested. "This time of year, it's almost impossible to get food to the table hot, and cold soup has little appeal."

Daniel obliged by holding a chair first for his wife and then for his sister. He sat between them at the head of the small table and held out a hand to each of them.

"I'll keep the blessing short then, so as not to offend the dignity of the soup," he said with a smile.

He held each woman's hand while he said a few words. Had Danny been present and not consigned to a tray in the kitchen with Nan, the child would have completed a circle of hands held during the blessing. It was a lovely tradition, one of many Daniel had instituted in contravention of the rituals he and Letty had been raised with.

In his own quiet, smiling way, Daniel Banks was a fighter.

Letty gave her attention to her soup, finding it was in fact wonderfully hot and delicious. "Have you a recipe for this soup, Olivia? I can't remember when I've had better."

"No recipe. I use whatever is to hand, and we make do."

"It is good," Daniel added, patting his wife's arm. "You are a genius in the kitchen, Olivia. Your table makes me the envy of many men."

"Needs must," Olivia rejoined evenly.

Letty restrained herself from rolling her eyes, but

felt the barb just the same. *Needs must* when one couldn't afford a cook, when one couldn't afford but one maid, when one couldn't afford a real pony for one's only child…

Olivia would be like this until Letty got back on that vile, bouncing coach. Veiled hints that finances were inadequate, pious little asides suggesting Daniel wasn't a competent provider. Olivia would do no overt complaining, no blaming, no railing against an unjust God. She'd instead keep up ceaseless sniping and implying.

Daniel was either a saint, or so overcome by some misplaced guilt, that he'd put up with whatever snide innuendo Olivia served with each course.

Four days later, Letty was in some part relieved to find herself standing beside Daniel at the local crossroads, waiting for the horn blast to signal the approaching coach.

"Thank you for making this journey, Letty," Daniel said, peering down at her. "The weather is too cold by half, and the roads have to be awful. But seeing you has done me and Danny good."

"And I've loved seeing you, too."

He wrapped his arms around her and simply held her as they waited in the bitter breeze. She let her forehead drop to his chest, wishing for the thousandth time that she had the strength to confide in him. Her brother had never once judged her, never found fault with her, never offered her anything but loving kindness.

She couldn't risk telling him the truth, no matter how badly she feared what was to come, no matter how much she despised her choice of livelihood.

"Your chariot approaches," Daniel said, stepping back at a distant blast of the coaching horn. "I love you."

Those were the words of a brave man, because from Daniel Banks they were honest and true.

"And I love you," Letty said, stretching up to kiss his cold cheek. She felt tears threaten when Daniel caught her up again in a fierce hug and then handed her into the coach. The horses were thundering on their way back to London before she even had her handkerchief out.

❧

"You are back!" Lord Fairly spotted Letty as she came in the side entrance of The Pleasure House, his demeanor exactly that of a barn cat spying a limping mouse.

And wretched mouse that she was, Letty was glad to see him too. Glad he wasn't going to leave her to fend for herself on her first night as a madam, glad his smile was so genuine and pleased.

"According to your missive, I am to start my duties this evening," Letty said, noting not for the first time how quickly his lordship could move, like one of those hawks plummeting from a great height with unerring accuracy.

"That you are." He took her arm and paused in his forward progress long enough to kiss her cheek. "You have the most delightful scent," he observed as if to himself, and then he was off again, leading Letty toward the back of the house. "First, I must introduce you to the kitchen staff. I know they're busy, but it can't be helped, and this way, Etienne, Pietro, and Manuel will keep their flattery to a minimum."

She wore plain rosewater, and yet his lordship had noticed.

He spun her toward the kitchens, making Letty feel as if she were in the grip of a polite, charming human tornado—one scented with sandalwood and sporting a smile that ought to be banned by royal decree. The tornado brought her to a halt next to a swarthy, portly man shouting in Italian.

Fairly said something quietly in the same language.

Did Lord Fairly speak Italian in bed? French? Or was he silent, the better to hear a woman's sighs and whispers?

And where were these extraordinary, useless thoughts coming from?

As Pietro turned to her, his ferocious scowl melted into a smile. "Lord Fairly, and a charming lady, in my kitchen. This will only distract the help, but it cheers me, *bella donna*, to feast my eyes upon you."

"Mrs. Banks, may I make known to you Pietro Giancarlo Bertoldi Timotheus Verducci. Pietro, Mrs. Letitia Banks, who will be managing this house for me henceforth. You are to obey her in all things outside the kitchen, if you please."

Fairly smiled, though his words held a hint of steel. He'd introduced Letty to his fancy chef properly, too, indicating by sheer force of personality that Letty was to be treated respectfully.

Pietro lifted spaniel brown eyes to her and kissed her knuckles. "Though there is no universe outside the kitchen worth mentioning, I will obey you, Mrs. Banks, as directed."

"He lies," said a whimsical voice from the other

side of the long counter. "That one is not to be trusted. He skimps on the butter, you know."

"Mrs. Banks," Fairly began again, turning to a slim, handsome Gallic fellow sporting a hint of gray at his temples. "May I make known to you Etienne Charbourg de Vancourier; Etienne, the new mistress of this house, and your superior outside culinary matters."

"Madame." Etienne bowed over her hand and offered her a suave smile. "Do not trust the Italian, but do not even think of turning your back on the Spaniard. He flirts."

"At least," said the gentleman in question, "I flirt only with women. Madame, Manuel Cesar de Villanueva y Portemos, at your service. Enchanted." He bowed over her hand with utmost gallantry, but came up yelling in several languages when a resounding crash from the back of the room brought all activity to a hushed halt.

"Excuse us," Fairly murmured, pulling Letty by the hand from the kitchens. He tugged her down a short corridor into the office, closing the door firmly behind them as if they'd narrowly escaped capture by highwaymen.

"I avoid the kitchens at the start of the evening. The staff is quite busy, and I know next to nothing about what goes on, other than Etienne and Musette have undertaken a flirtation. How was your trip?"

Three Continental chefs at his beck and call, and his lordship looked beleaguered. Though how did Fairly know she'd left London? "My trip?"

He led her to a beautiful Louis Quinze escritoire

and sat her down behind it. "I assume you needed several days before starting this position, because you had matters to attend to outside of Town. Anything local you could have managed during the weekly hiatus in your employment."

Hiatus—a gap, a pause, a break to the common man. Lord Fairly spoke like a vicar. He wasn't being superior, merely using that all-too-quick brain of his to deduce things about Letty that were none of his business. He'd been the same way on their tour of the facility, showing her a supply of jade phalluses, a room sporting an entire wall of whips, riding crops, manacles, and blindfolds, and another room decorated to look like some sultan's tent—all with a sense of brisk, clinical disinterest.

Which had fascinated and appalled her as much as the premises themselves.

"So who are your people, Mrs. Banks?" he asked, taking the seat facing the desk.

"What business is that of yours?" And why had he seated her behind the desk and himself before it?

"Interesting word choice—business. I keep a record of next of kin for my employees. Most of them are recently moved to Town in search of employment. They hail from all over, and sometimes I can make an educated guess, based on accent, mannerisms, and so forth, but it's much easier simply to ask."

"Why would you want to know?" And when had he ordered the calling cards stacked neatly on one corner of the blotter? They bore Letty's name and the direction of the house in a tidy, flowing script, as if she were some baronet's daughter, not a newly minted madam.

That he'd have cards printed was both consider-ate and... wrong, for she'd have no opportunity to use them.

"When one is in strange surroundings," his lordship said with peculiar gentleness, "it can make a difference that someone else knows how to locate one's next of kin—in case of physical injury, death, difficulties, illness, that sort of thing. It's all too easy to die alone when one is far from home, Mrs. Banks."

He said this as if the opportunity had nearly befallen him, as if he knew what desperate thoughts a young woman alone and far from home might entertain in her worst moments.

"I should hope not to be doing any dying while here in London, sir, and if I do, I will hardly be con-cerned for my next of kin."

She'd be desperately concerned for them, of course. Would his lordship's family be similarly con-cerned for him?

"So you do have family. You might as well tell me who they are, Letty."

He could seduce with that teasing, confiding tone of voice alone. "Mrs. Banks, if you please."

"Sometimes I do please, sometimes I don't," he replied, rising. "Come, I'll introduce you around tonight and stay close to you. The dress will do, but tomorrow we are sending you to Madame Baptiste's. Spring is coming—one desperately hopes—and your wardrobe must be adequate to the challenge."

He held out a hand to her, and Letty found herself taking it.

"You like to hold hands," she observed as he once

again led her through the kitchens and up toward the front of the house. He'd pretty much dragged her by the wrist through the whole building on her last visit. She'd enjoyed the simple contact, enjoyed that at no time had Fairly intimated that he'd wanted to put the premises to their commercial use with Letty.

Heaven defend her, on some level she felt safe with this man.

"I like to hold hands with you," he replied, smiling over his shoulder. "In part, I like to see you get that puzzled, bothered look you're wearing now."

Letty couldn't help but smile at him, a smile that appreciated the impossibility of such a big, elegant man indulging in impishness. He stopped in the middle of a deserted hallway, his hand still in hers.

"She smiles," he said as if to himself. "She truly, truly smiles."

He smiled too, not the dazzling, exuberant smile, something far more personal and equally devastating.

"What's the other part, your lordship?"

"Beg pardon?"

"What's the other part? You said you hold hands with me in part to see me get that puzzled, bothered look. What's the other part?"

"The other part, Letty-love, is that I want you accustomed to my touch."

Years ago, she might have chided him for his impertinence—she was not his Letty-love— except he was her employer, and given the venue, endearments and hand-holding were more civilities than offenses.

Then too, nobody had ever called her Letty-love,

much less in such wistful tones, and she rather liked holding his hand too.

"Why should you want me accustomed to your touch?" she asked, glancing down at their laced fingers.

His smile faded, which was fortunate for a lady's composure. "Once we walk through that door, I want it understood by all that you are under my protection, and rather than hanging a sign around your neck, or calling out the first fellow to trespass, I will instead touch you. For the display to be convincing, you should look as if you're enjoying my attentions, hmm?"

He was logical. How did a logical man go about his seductions, and what was wrong with her, that she liked the notion he'd defend her honor if a patron of the establishment took uninvited liberties with her person?

"You want me to hang all over you?"

"Must you sound so appalled?" His smile was back: lovely, warm, and genuinely amused at her. "Nothing so vulgar as that, but let's practice a bit, shall we?"

She had no warning, not even a moment to prepare herself, before he stepped in closer and grazed his nose along her cheekbone. He stood, his head bent to her cheek, holding her hand and giving Letty a moment to wish they'd met under any other circumstances.

A courtesan, a whore, would pretend she enjoyed such attentions. How much worse was it that Letty enjoyed them in truth? Enjoyed his lordship's scent, his strength, his sense of energy and competence, and most of all, his sense of self-restraint.

"Relax," he murmured. "I'll behave, Letty-love, but you have to meet me halfway."

If she permitted him these liberties, she would be safe from the pawing and pinching of other men. And from him, affection would mean nothing, merely a courtesy extended her to allow her bodily privacy from other customers.

And yet, her heart sped up, and not with dread.

He'd introduced his staff to her with punctilious courtesy. He'd had cards printed for her that she'd never use. He'd given thought to how to safeguard Letty from uninvited advances, and he wanted to know she had people to worry for her, should illness strike.

Any woman would be attracted to Lord Fairly's charm, his good looks, his élan.

As Letty stood close enough to him that his breath fanned over her cheek, she forgave herself for the frisson of arousal his proximity caused. What alarmed her was that she respected this man, and—truly, she must master this lapse—she liked him, too.

"I'm about to kiss you, Letty," he whispered. "You will allow it?"

Her liking rose toward something more dangerous yet, because when—*when*—had any man ever asked for her permission before he kissed her?

She nodded but couldn't bring herself to turn her face up to his. She wasn't expecting it when his lips feathered against her brow, then her cheek, then the side of her neck. He nuzzled and sighed and took his time, following the contours of her face with his lips and his nose and his breath.

Just as the disappointing thought formed—*So, he isn't going to kiss my mouth.*—Fairly's lips settled gossamer light on hers, as if he rested his mouth on hers, waiting for her to take the initiative. When she didn't pull away or poker up—the two options she could have envisioned pursuing—the tip of Fairly's tongue teased along her lips. He'd used a soft, warm, flirting touch, playful and knowing. Letty opened her mouth to ask him what he was *doing*, but found to her shock his tongue insinuated itself *into* her mouth.

Heaven defend her. Her employer took lazy, decadent liberties with his tongue. He tasted; he explored; he seemed to grow taller as Letty clung to him. Her head was thrown back, their mouths fused, and her arms had somehow—she honestly knew not how—wound themselves around his neck, her fingers linked under the queue of blond hair gathered at his nape.

He eased away from the kiss, keeping his arms around her. Her wobbly knees appreciated that consideration, even as the rest of her wanted to step back, smooth down her skirts, and coolly precede his lordship into the front parlors—provided she could find them.

Who was she, that she'd thrust her tongue into a man's mouth? That she'd cling to him so shamelessly? That she'd *want* him to kiss her and kiss her and kiss her, endlessly?

And why had Herbert never kissed her thus? Why had he never held her hand?

"On second thought," Fairly said, his forehead resting against hers, "a sign hung 'round your neck might be the safer option all around. You practice very convincingly, Letty Banks."

A real courtesan, a woman who understood the

profession and accepted it for what it was, would have had something clever to say. Letty was not such a woman, and hoped she never would be. "I thought we were kissing."

"My mistake, for we surely were kissing after all." He bussed her nose, took half a pace back, and reached for her hand. Letty was glad he did, for she still needed some kind of support if she was to remain upright and yet move.

"Ready to face the lions?" he asked, opening the door and tucking her hand around his elbow.

"As ready as I'll ever be." Which was to say, not ready at all.

Four

"IF IT WARMS UP, WE'LL GET ANOTHER DAMNED SNOW-storm," David observed, poking at the logs in his madam's sitting-room fireplace. Logs were an extravagance he hoped she would not scold him for, though Jennings certainly had. "Do you prefer brandy, or perhaps a cordial?"

Because after hours of trying to remain close to Letty without hovering, of touching her hand, her hair, her *anything* with an appearance of casual affection, he needed a drink.

"May I please have a hot chocolate?"

So polite, in this most impolite of venues. "Of course you may." David opened the door and gave their request to the footman at the end of the corridor. "You may swill hot chocolate the whole night through if it's what you prefer. You mustn't spare the small indulgences, Letty. The nights are too long and the pleasures too few."

Sometime in the course of the evening, he'd gained the privilege of calling her Letty, though she did not call him David.

"What you require of me isn't that difficult," she replied, closing her eyes and resting her head against the back of the couch. "One smiles, greets, chats, and moves on to the next for more of same. One mustn't flirt too hard or give offense to any party, or be overly boisterous or overly withdrawn. One mustn't imbibe to excess or comment uncharitably on the social habits of others. Rather like a village assembly."

Not a comparison David would have ever thought to make. "You sound like you're reciting a catechism." And like she'd been to many, many village assemblies.

"I nearly am, the point being that superficial social interaction isn't that demanding when one has been trained to manage it. The gathering does take on a different air when couples are disappearing up the steps from time to time and grinning fellows are coming down."

"Noticed that, did you?" And she'd tried not to be obvious about her noticing too, while David had tried not to obviously watch her.

Perhaps he'd have two drinks. He took a place beside her, got his cravat off without swearing audibly, and began to wrench at a boot.

"You are disrobing."

"Partially," David said through gritted teeth. "You are welcome to do likewise."

"Would you like some help with that boot?" she asked, pushing to her feet.

He stuck his boot out, the same as he would have were she his valet or his... wife, while wondering whose boots she'd tugged off in the past.

"Do not," she warned, "think of putting your foot

on my person, sir. Or any other part of you on any other part of me."

"Duly warned." Did her defenses never waver? He rather hoped, for her sake, they did not.

Letty stepped over his shin and presented him with the fetching prospect of her derriere at eye level. With a strong tug, she had his boot off, dropped his foot, and stepped back to allow him to raise the other leg.

When the second boot was off, she held up both. "Where do you want these?"

"Outside the door. The bootboy will see to them while we have our nightcap."

A knock on the door heralded the arrival of their drinks, and David took the boots from her, putting them in the corridor before he took the tray proffered by the waiting footman.

"Your chocolate, madam." He bowed before Letty where she'd once again ensconced herself on the couch, then grabbed a pillow, slapped it down on the hearth, and lowered himself onto it.

Lest some part of him be tempted to touch some part of her.

He took a sip. "Chocolate is a good idea, but it needs something." He went to the sideboard, where he searched out a brown bottle with a label in Italian, and sloshed a goodly portion from the bottle into his hot chocolate.

"Try mine," he suggested. "If you like it, we'll doctor yours as well."

She reached for the bottle and sniffed. "Nuts?"

"Hazelnut liqueur. I came across it in Italy." He held out his drink, and she brought it to her lips.

Perhaps she thought he'd surrender it into her keeping, but instead—because he was a tired fool suffering an inconvenient attack of adolescence—kept his hand wrapped around the glass, so she had to wrap her fingers over his.

He was offering spirits to a lady in a bordello after midnight, and feeling both naughty and hopeful about the prospects.

Pathetic—or, perhaps, sweet. David held up the bottle. "Shall you?"

"A bit. I'm not used to spirits."

She attended rural assemblies, wasn't used to spirits, and kissed with all the wonderment and innocence of a new bride. David poured a sparing amount into her drink, though it was tempting to get her tipsy and himself drunk.

"So you're just going to sit there," David asked from his perch on the hearth, "all dressed?"

"Why would I remove clothing in your presence?" Letty replied, taking another sip of her drink.

She was baiting him—he was almost sure of it. "Because it's more comfortable and leaves less to do when one eventually succumbs to the arms of Morpheus? You are staying here tonight, I hope?"

"I could." Euridyce had taken lodgings in the underworld with more enthusiasm.

"Until the weather improves, I wish you would. The only people abroad at this hour of the night when it's this cold are up to no good. And we've an appointment with Madame Baptiste in the morning anyway. Would you like more hot chocolate?"

"I taste spices in this too—nutmeg, maybe, or

cinnamon. I'm probably going to fall asleep halfway through if I have another. The longer I sit here, the heavier my eyes get."

David gathered up their empty glasses a few moments later and used the bellpull, but didn't immediately sit back down on the hearth. Instead, he paused to shed his cuff links and turn up his cuffs. The room was cozy, and Letty ought not to have an apoplexy at the sight of his forearms.

"I'm taking your shoes off, Letty Banks, and you will permit this, seeing as you did, after all, wrest mine from me."

"I asked, your lordship, I didn't order," she said peevishly, but she made no protest as David eased her half boots off. Emboldened by her passivity, he slid his hands up her calf to untie the garter of each stocking.

"You are taking liberties." She sounded unsure, and not pleased.

"Your feet are safe with me, Letty. You can hiss and arch your back all you want, but you were on your feet for hours. Those boots of yours are an abomination against nature and fashion both, and I am going to ease your discomfort."

While increasing his own. He took her foot in his hands, and as the medical part of his brain noted a high arch and a second toe longer than her great toe—there was a name for this condition—the masculine part of him rejoiced to hold even this most humble part of her.

"Oh, my," she breathed, trying to sit up.

"None of that. You relax, and don't give me any trouble, or I'll peek at your ankles, or do something equally dreadful."

"Peek at my ankles, will you?" Letty eyed him dubiously then subsided on a sigh. "Where did you learn to do this, and what is it exactly you are doing?"

"I am simply rubbing your feet, as I like to have my feet rubbed at certain times."

Another tired, peevish glower. "Is this one of those times?"

"No. And don't you ask, Letty Banks, lest I shock you with the details. You did well tonight, by the way."

"You are changing the subject, but thank you. I was nervous, especially when I realized how many of those fellows scampering up your stairs are titled or in expectation of a title. You have an exclusive clientele."

She flinched as David dug his thumbs into a particularly stubborn knot of muscle in her arch.

"I don't think the titles matter much." He held her foot, using his thumbs to apply gentle, relentless pressure to the knot of muscle. How was it he'd never realized a woman's foot could be pretty? "What matters to me is that the patrons treat the girls—*ladies*— well, and certain standards of behavior are observed by all."

"What standards?" And then, as the knot in her foot relaxed, "Moses in the bulrushes…"

Moses in the bulrushes? An Old Testament oath, accompanied by the vision of Letty Banks sprawled on the couch, eyes closed, head back against the pillows, had David temporarily losing the thread of the conversation.

"I expect… I expect of the men simple decency," David said. "Manners, civility, discretion, the English virtues available to anyone who passes through the doors. I expect the men to hold their liquor and their tempers when they're under my roof, and those who don't aren't welcome back."

"And the women?" Letty asked, opening her eyes to regard him levelly.

"The women." *What women?* "They must act like ladies when they're downstairs, albeit particularly friendly ladies. Give me your other foot."

Another knock signaled the next round of hot chocolate. David added a dollop of liqueur to Letty's and a portion of the entire bottle to his.

"Now where was I?" He frowned at Letty, whose pink tongue was delicately swiping chocolate off her upper lip. "Ah, I was taking off your clothes."

"You most assuredly were not. You were going to tend to my other foot."

"That I was," David said, resuming his post so he could grasp her foot and ease the stocking off. "We are going to dress you from the inside out, you know. These sausage casings that you use for stockings are a thing of the past, Letty."

"You can say anything nasty you want. Just don't stop doing what you're doing to my foot."

Exhaustion and tipsiness were making inroads on her dignity when his charm and persistence had not. "Would you beat me if I were to stop?"

"Not if you'd enjoy it, and I think you would, particularly if I used one of my sausage casings to tie your hands first, and the other to gag you."

"Letty, you shock me." And would she please spout Bible verses while she beat him? "Such adventurous behaviors are foreign to my nature."

"I don't think it's possible to shock you, my lord." She'd adopted the contemplative tone of the overly observant—or the mildly inebriated, which shouldn't have been possible based on how minimally he'd dosed her drink. "For that I almost pity you."

His hands went still on her foot, and his simmering, unruly lust got doused in a cold bath of indignation. The shift must have registered on his face, because Letty laid a hand on his shoulder.

"I am sorry, David. I must be getting bosky, for I shouldn't have said such a thing."

No, she should not have, but she'd called him David. He resumed his attentions to her foot, one shaped exactly like its twin but for a small white scar near her little toe.

"You are correct," he said. "Little shocks me, particularly in matters between men and women. But your pity is unneeded. Finish your chocolate—I've kept you up past your bedtime."

His voice was admirably pleasant. When he glanced up to find Letty regarding him from dark, unhappy eyes, he revised that opinion. "I did not mean to sound peevish, my dear. Perhaps I'm the one up past his bedtime."

Letty withdrew her foot, leaving his hands empty.

"You perhaps cannot be shocked, David, but you can still be disappointed," she said quietly. "It is for me to apologize."

Her words, offered sincerely, soothed him, for she was right again: in his travels, he'd seen and done things most people went their whole lives without even imagining, but he could be disappointed still by his fellow creatures, and each disappointment carried with it a small, jarring element of sorrow, of outrage.

He rose and turned to sit on the couch beside Letty, looping an arm around her. She surprised him by allowing her head to rest against his shoulder.

She had called him David, not once, but twice.

"I should be shooing you out the door, sir. You're appallingly comfortable, though."

"I am not at all sure you've paid me a compliment."

"I have. If you'd told me two weeks ago I'd be cuddled up with you at midnight in a brothel, I would have slapped you soundly as soon as I stopped laughing."

Two weeks ago, she'd been too cold and hungry to laugh, and now, he would love to make her laugh. He was more likely to make her cry.

"Perhaps you would have slapped me." And perhaps she *should* have. That thought and the Old Testament oath and a recitation involving assemblies stirred David's snoring diagnostic abilities—and his conscience—to life.

She had been a good girl once, probably a better girl than many of his employees.

A good girl never saw the mischief headed her way until it was too late, and so David issued a warning. "You are cuddled up with me, as you put it, because you think I'm safe, and while I want the women upstairs to know they are safe from me, *you are not*."

There—cards on the table, every man, woman, or madam for themselves.

"You are not a rapist." She seemed sure of her point, a nominal consolation.

"True. I am, however, much to my surprise, a seducer."

"I've been seduced before, my lord, and it doesn't

have anything to do with hot chocolate and rubbing feet and cozy little chats at midnight."

"Then you've been seduced by an incompetent, Letty Banks." A damned, unworthy incompetent not fit to hold her... foot. "You want comforting, and I apparently want swiving. I'll offer you a world of comforts to get the swiving I want, and I've resources you can't even imagine when it comes to getting what I want. *You are not safe with me.*"

She raised her head to smile at him indulgently. "You are no good at this seducing business, my lord. Were you truly bent on seduction, you'd be fumbling at my clothes and making impossible promises, not issuing these warnings and assassinations of your own character."

"Do you want me kissing you?" And could kissing please be a euphemism for greater intimacies?

"You kiss..." She sighed and covered his hand with her own. She didn't hold his hand, didn't lace their fingers, she just rested her palm over his knuckles. "You kiss me to accustom me to your attentions, but..."

"But what? You're an experienced courtesan, Letty. You've been kissed at length by different men. I can't believe I have anything special to offer you in that regard."

Though if he were particularly foolish, he could hope—in the naughty, lonely part of him—he could hope he might be a little special to this woman.

"You are one of few men I've met who can withstand regular doses of honesty, so I will tell you you've made incorrect assumptions."

"Incorrect how?" he asked, turning slightly so Letty's head rested more against his chest. She didn't exactly snuggle up, but she remained relaxed against him.

"I am not so wickedly experienced as you might think," she said. "I came to London as a girl of eighteen, but found it very, very difficult to make my way. I was raised to be useless. I know my Bible, I can manage a small household, I can make small talk and turn a dress, but I lack employable skills. The agencies couldn't help much when I had no references, but I did manage to find work as a governess."

"And your employer seduced you," David guessed. "His wife found out, and you were turned off without a character."

"I quit without notice before his attempts at seduction got that far, and then, of course, employment was very hard to find indeed."

"Go on," David urged, taking her hand in his. Somewhere in London, a rutting cit deserved evisceration. More significantly, Letty deserved to have someone to confide in.

"I became destitute and took to sitting in the park just to be near people. I struck up a conversation with Lord Amery around the topic of duck hunting, and when he accidentally bumped into me for the third morning in a row, we had a very blunt and productive conversation. In his way, he was not unkind."

Not unkind. The bastard had ruined her, and he was not unkind. "Was it Herbert who took your virginity?" Because she needed to tell this story, David resisted the urge to nuzzle her temple.

"No," Letty said, a hint of regret in her voice. "I

was naive enough to permit someone in the village to take liberties, with the result that I felt uncomfortable back home. I chose to come to London, if that's what you're asking. Considering the many pitfalls awaiting the unwary here, I have been very lucky. I could have been picked up by an abbess, addicted to drugs, sold, or worse."

"You have been very lucky indeed."

He wrapped his arms around her, cradled her against his body, and tried not to recall that this house was full of women, good, formerly decent women, who could have told him similar tales and worse.

Perhaps sensing the shift of his thoughts, she did snuggle up then, letting him carefully untangle her coiffure and hold her while the fire burned down.

"Letty," David murmured against her hair, "when Herbert was with you, what did you feel?" This was a safer topic than what she might be feeling at the moment, and a far safer topic than the emotions rioting through David.

He thought she would not answer at first. Just because a woman decided to take off her clothes for money didn't mean she was equally comfortable revealing her feelings.

"At first I felt too much. I felt dirty, angry, hopeless, and betrayed—though by whom or by what, I know not. Then, I learned to not feel anything. When Herbert came around, I would simply stop feeling, shed my clothes, and leave my body in that bed. Life was bearable after that. I wasn't at all sorry when he died though, and for that I feel guilty and ashamed."

As a decent, God-fearing woman would feel guilty.

And now David wanted that decent, God-fearing, *fallen* woman with an intensity that made no sense. He had a house full of women available to him, in pairs and trios, if he so chose. Why did his errant lust have to settle on Letty Banks, recently of Rural Nowhere, and apparently, against all odds and anything approaching convenience, the next thing to an innocent?

❦

"How did it go last night?"

His lordship had joined Letty for breakfast in her office-sitting room, which suited his schedule better than hers. Letty was a heavy sleeper and did not awaken with the same boundless energy and mental acuity her employer appeared to enjoy. Still, in the two weeks she'd worked for him, he had yet to show her anything approaching rudeness.

He wasn't the same affectionate, attentive friend he'd been her first night on the job—nor did Letty permit herself any more reprises of tipsiness—but he was considerate, in his way. Letty was pleased to note, however, that he was dressed for riding, which implied he wouldn't be underfoot for long.

"Last night was quiet," Letty reported, pouring two cups of tea. She added a fat portion of cream and two sugars to his, and passed it to him before tending to her own.

Before she took a sip, she said a silent prayer of gratitude. For the tea, for the man who provided the tea, for the time he'd given her to find her balance in this new degree of fallenness.

"Custom is wanting because of this cold snap," he

observed. "If it doesn't break soon, we'll lose the early flowers altogether."

Which to him was probably as significant as any diminution in trade or revenue.

"It's February, my lord. February falls during winter. Now that we've discussed the weather, you will allow me some quiet in which to consume my tea."

He smiled at that, a bashful expression that preceded a respectful silence while Letty had her first cup. She was in a wonderfully warm chocolate-brown velvet dressing gown edged in red piping, and her hair was still in a thick, mussed braid. His lordship did not stand on ceremony with her, which, considering the early hour, was wise of him.

"Better now?" he asked when she'd set her cup down.

"There's hope," she allowed, reaching for the teapot. "But not if you want to harangue me at any length. I'm starting on the account books for the month this morning, and I expect I'll have questions for you."

"Good, because I have a few things I wanted to discuss with you too, the first being your penchant for repairing to your own domicile in the afternoons. It's inefficient and inconvenient."

Letty took her time fixing her second cup, rather than toss the contents in his lordship's handsome face. He had gradually ceased his escort of her during the evenings. Most nights, he still dropped in, making a casual display of kissing her cheek in greeting, and otherwise treating her as an intimate before others—a respected intimate. But he'd more or less left her alone otherwise, except for these random breakfast meetings.

The man provided her a job where she kept her clothes on—not a blessing she'd ever take for granted again—and so she marshaled her patience.

"I go home, your lordship, because it is home, because my clothing is there, my effects are there, and my privacy is there. I go home to give the ladies a break from me, and myself a respite from this house. I go home for Sunday, Monday, and Tuesday morning for the same reasons."

"Letty?" He'd called her Letty ever since kissing her, which made a sort of sense. "Are you enjoying adequate rest? You are crabby, and it isn't like you."

Letty wrapped the embroidered towel around the teapot. "You own this establishment, my lord, you do not own me. Where I spend my hours of leisure is none of your concern."

If anything, he looked more curious, or perhaps— confound the man—concerned. "What is so important about that cold, cramped, rented house, Letty, that you must return to it, day after day, when you don't even sleep there anymore? Have you such fond memories of the place?"

By the convoluted rules of honor to which he held himself with her, Letty supposed his lordship would consider the question fair. At that moment, she considered hating him a fair response. She hunched over her cup of tea and swallowed back miserable memories.

Fairly put a hand on her arm. "I am sorry, sweetheart, very sorry. I don't mean to be a beast. I must leave Town, and wanted to ask if you'd move here for the nonce. What was it you wanted to ask of me?"

Damn him and his charm, and why hadn't he offered to rub her feet after that first night?

"You insulted me," she said evenly, "with your reference to my memories at my present address. If their husbands said such cruel things to your sisters, you would be enraged on their behalves. I have no one to become enraged on my behalf, your lordship, but my feelings can still be hurt, though I am *just a whore*."

He probably thought the women in his employ survived on his coin. Letty knew better: most of them survived on their rage.

"As far as I know, Letitia Banks," he said carefully, "you take no coin for your favors, so whatever else you might be, you are not a prostitute. My words were thoughtless, and I do apologize."

She still had ammunition, and fired it because he apologized too easily. "When you taunt me about the time I spent… in that front bedroom, you disappoint me."

Saying that, and seeing the consternation crossing Fairly's handsome features, eased her hurt.

"I am sorry," he said again, picking up her hand and pressing a kiss to her knuckles, then keeping their hands joined. "Is this why you keep the house, Letty? Because I might disappoint once too often?" He freshened her tea, using his free hand to stir in cream and sugar. "You want an insurance policy in case matters here don't work out?"

Of course she did. "I am also responsible for Mrs. Newcomb, and this is hardly the type of establishment she'd fit into easily."

He visibly relaxed at the notion of a Problem He

Could Solve. "Would Mrs. Newcombe be willing to keep house here in Town for one of my relations?"

"She might." She would, if she were prudent. To the extent prudence was another name for practical self-interest, Fanny Newcombe was quite prudent.

"One doesn't get much more decent than Douglas Allen. He is the surviving brother of your former protector, but cut from entirely different cloth. He has a modest residence here in Town in a decent, quiet neighborhood. The wages won't be lavish, but neither will the duties be extensive."

Fanny wasn't earning her wages, with no one to do for and not much of a house to keep. Then too, Letty's fortunes could shift again on his lordship's whim.

He split a raisin scone and buttered both halves, holding one up for Letty to nibble. She bit off a morsel and chewed, because a fallen woman allowed a man to feed her, in every sense, and because his very lack of pretension appealed to her.

"You, my lord, are charming, considerate, and everything that is pleasant, while you are getting your way."

"And when I'm not?" He was rattled enough by her observation to take a bite of the scone from the same place she'd sampled.

"You have a mean streak, a ruthless streak, more accurately. Most of us do. Please, finish the scone."

Fairly looked down as if surprised to find one in his hand. "Etienne has a way with them, though I could do without the raisins."

"I'll have a word with him, and then perhaps I can have my breakfast and finish waking up. In peace."

For she would not have peace while Fairly was with her. She would feel safe, though, which was a puzzle.

"You will have a significant amount of peace, my dear. I am, as noted, off to spend some time with my sisters, then I'll hie myself to Kent, where I'm told the estates are going to ruin without my guiding hand. I expect I'll be gone for at least three weeks, probably longer, and I wanted to leave you my directions in case you have need of me."

Well, good. He drove her to distraction with his cheek kissing and scone sharing. "Won't Mr. Jennings be about to deal with emergencies?"

"No, he will not." He peeled raisins off the scone one by one and made even that undertaking look elegant. "Jennings has some leave coming, and then he'll join me in Kent. Watkins will be on hand, and I'll leave a messenger here for emergencies."

"We'll manage adequately without you." Pray God, they would.

"It is my fondest hope that you will. I'm overdue for a family visit."

Maybe it was the way he denuded his scone of raisins, like a small boy, or maybe it was because she was finally waking up, but Letty didn't want him to leave yet.

"Tell me about them. Your sisters, their children, where they live…"

She hadn't realized, when she'd asked the question, how his reply would torture her. He warmed to the topic easily, prosing on at length about sisters, in-laws, nieces, and nephews, until scones, raisins, and even the tea in his cup were apparently forgotten.

"You love these people," Letty said, "and you love

to be with them. Why haven't you set up your own nursery? Surely there's some competitive, male part of you that's tempted to jump into the race?"

He swept the discarded raisins into a pile on his plate and dusted his hands. "Felicity and Astrid regard my marriage as inevitable, and my brothers-in-law think duty to the title will also see me to the altar, but some of us were meant to be parents, and some of us were meant to be only uncles."

Thinking of Danny, Letty nodded.

"You just went far away, Letty-love. I did not mean to be grim."

"You don't sound grim; you sound resigned." As she was resigned.

His brows rose, though Letty was learning to read the warning signs. She stole three raisins off his plate lest he ask an inconvenient question.

"Was there something you wanted to ask me about other than my growing family?" he inquired.

"Yes, but it's… delicate."

He nudged the plate with its raisins a few inches toward her and crossed his arms, while somebody back in the kitchen started singing a naughty song in French. "If it's about money, Letty, be blunt."

"It isn't about money," Letty said, stealing three more raisins lest they go to waste. "It's about the ladies. They all… Their menses all occur… They're nearly synchronized, somehow, all of them."

"What?" He looked not appalled, but interested, the way a biologist would be fascinated with symptoms of a new lethal disease.

"Every woman in this house has started getting

her menses the very same week, most of them on the same day."

"Fascinating."

And the week before this *fascinating* phenomenon, the household was treated to felony assaults, hysterics, sulks, fights, and endless raids on the kitchen.

"Fascinating, if we're talking about a convent or a girls' school, but we're not."

"What do the women say?" He still looked intrigued, which tickled a fact from the back of Letty's mind: prior to assuming the title, his lordship had first apprenticed to a ship's surgeon and then trained as a physician. His employees hoarded up such details about him, which would probably make him uncomfortable if he knew.

"It's common, apparently," Letty said, arranging her cutlery so she'd be less tempted to sneak more raisins. "If a woman stays in one brothel for any period of time, eventually her cycle synchronizes with the prevailing schedule. Lord Valentine told Portia he'd heard of the same thing happening in harems."

"All of which is to say, you've presented me another reason to divest myself of this establishment at the soonest opportunity."

Letty stopped refolding her serviette. "*Divest yourself?*"

The song in the kitchen turned into a duet, Etienne and Musette, singing something about the cock crowing at dawn. His lordship eyed the remaining pile of raisins, his expression one of distaste.

"I'd sell this establishment in a trice, if I could be confident the next owner would take good care of the employees."

He was reluctant to call them ladies, and at that

moment, Letty was reluctant to refer to him as a gentleman. "I see."

"I've made no secret of wanting to be free of this place."

"You also failed to disclose that the business was for sale when you offered me employment here." And this made her want not simply to go back to bed, but to pull the covers up over her head and remain there until spring. She had liked David Worthington, and—more fool her—she had also trusted him.

When would she learn that her instincts regarding men had betrayed her most bitterly?

"The property is not for sale, Letty, but would you have come to work here if it were?"

Damn him. "I had no options, if you'll recall."

"You had options," he countered softly. He pushed his plate with the half scone and the pile of raisins on it directly before her. "Have you more to discuss with me, Letty? If not, then I'm off to spoil children, tease my sisters, and twit their husbands, but tell me something, Letty Banks."

Fairly's love for his family resonated with every cheerful, merry word, and Letty would have told him anything to get him on his horse.

"What do you wish to know?"

He picked up a single raisin and offered it to her on the end of an elegant index finger. "Are you happy with this position, Letty? Is there anything you would change, do differently?"

The dratted, confounded, *bothersome* man wanted her to enjoy the job he might sell out from under her, but somehow, she couldn't bring herself to lie to him.

Not about this too.

"I enjoy this position far more than its predecessor. I am grateful not to make my living on my back."

His expression was pained, but he could hardly chide her for plain speaking. "But?"

She was going to tell him this because he'd asked, and because she'd missed the man who'd been such a friend to her on her first night as a madam.

"In some ways, I am lonelier here than I was in my own household. There, I had much more privacy, whereas here, I am made familiar with the bodily cycles of a dozen women, who between them, might have one shred of modesty or tact. This is an adjustment."

"And?" His lordship's expression was hooded now, because he was hearing things he didn't expect to hear—didn't *want* to hear. Letty's feelings likely came under the heading of A Problem He Could Not Solve.

A problem nobody could solve. The lyrical duet in the kitchen was replaced by shouting—Musette was threatening to put Etienne's precious knives to a creative use. So much for the cock crowing at dawn.

"And I am a madam. I may not be any one man's plaything, but I am viewed as worse than simply fallen. I traffic in fallen women, or manage your traffic in fallen women, which makes me doubly outcast. Your patrons are polite to me, and the ladies are mostly delightful, but I am a pariah nonetheless. Your sisters could not acknowledge me, ever, and in all likelihood, they could not comprehend how I've ended up where I am."

Most nights, Letty could barely comprehend it herself.

"This is complicated for you. I am sorry for that."

Consumed with contrition, he was not. She hadn't

expected he would be, and yet, Letty still felt a touch of… disappointment.

"It is complicated, and it is simple," she said. "Whatever else is true, I must eat. The regular meals, those I quite simply adore."

"Not enough," his lordship remarked, rising. "You are still too thin, and when I return, I expect to see that you've gained flesh, my girl. People will think I'm working you too hard."

I am not a girl. More to the point, she was not *his* girl, his woman, *or* his lady.

Letty rose as Fairly did, simple manners suggesting she should see him off on his journey. Other than Musette, who'd apparently convinced Etienne to come back to bed, the other ladies weren't up yet, affording Letty some privacy as she walked with her employer through the kitchen.

"Safe journey, then," Letty said, lifting his greatcoat off a peg and holding it up for him. She waited as he buttoned up in preparation for travel through another cold, gray, blustery day. "You must want to see your sisters very badly."

"I should make it out to Willowdale before the weather does anything too miserable. You have my directions, feel free to use them."

His tone was brisk, as if his mind had already departed, anticipating the time spent with family and the matters to be seen to in Kent. Men of means were comfortable operating in different spheres, driving out with their mistress one day, their sisters the next, while Letty feared a lightning bolt would strike her every time she set foot in her brother's vicarage.

She was completely unprepared, then, when Fairly turned back to her and tugged the collar of her robe up around her throat.

"You'll be all right?" he asked, peering down at her.

"We'll be fine," Letty said, deliberately using the plural pronoun.

"So you're royalty now?"

"Be off with you. Safe journey home."

"Thank you," he said before dipping his head and taking her mouth in a kiss.

What on earth could he be thanking her for?

For him, he behaved, only tracing her lips with his tongue, tasting her mouth gently, nibbling at her lower lip, and pressing his mouth softly to hers. Letty slipped her arms around his neck and rose up on tiptoe to hug herself to him. When she eased her mouth from his, Fairly let her go, but his arms settled around her waist in a gentle form of contradiction.

"I will miss you, your lordship." She was not at her best this early in the morning, and kisses apparently magnified the muddling of her wits.

His hold shifted, became closer. "No, you will not. You will attract the notice of some fine fellow, lead him by his nose into a liaison that's both lucrative and enjoyable for you, and forget I ever inveigled you into working here."

She stepped back, let him go without any more words, and through the window watched him cross to the stables, where a gray mare stood patiently at the mounting block.

He hadn't sounded like he was teasing with that last little speech. He'd sounded in desperate earnest, like a man offering up a fervent prayer.

Five

THAT KISS HAD BEEN A LAPSE, A BREACH IN THE FORTI-fications David had been trying to erect between himself and his madam over the past two weeks.

And this royal progress from one relative's home to the next was an evasive maneuver, one David doubted would meet with much success. In two hours of trotting over bone-jarring ruts through toe-freezing cold, David could only wish he'd done much more than kiss his madam. The best he could hope for was that in his absence, some more worthy fellow would come along and win Letty Banks's affection.

When he reached Willowdale, home of his sister Felicity and her husband, Gareth, Marquess of Heathgate, David endured gentle interrogation from people whom he'd missed terribly—though not terribly enough to answer all of their questions honestly.

He marveled over the infant twins' new teeth, tossed his older nephews aloft enough times to alarm any mother, rode out in the bitter weather with Heathgate, and made himself available for quiet chats with Felicity. The visit with his sister Astrid and her husband, Andrew, Earl of Greymoor, followed the same pattern, with the exception that Greymoor, lighter of heart and more laissez-faire than his older brother, did not attempt any inquisitional discussions.

Either that, or Heathgate had—in the fashion of siblings who are also friends—already communicated the substance of his interviews with David to Greymoor.

David's final stop before changing course for Kent was the home of Guinevere and Douglas Allen. Gwen was a cousin to Heathgate and Greymoor, while Douglas was the surviving brother of Astrid's late husband, Herbert. On the last day of his short visit in their household, David made it a point to sequester himself in the library with Douglas.

While David liked his brothers-in-law, his affection for Douglas Allen was based more on the man himself and less on family associations. Douglas was tall, blond, handsome, well-mannered, and reserved to the point that his demeanor could be mistaken for aloof.

"So you're off to Kent on the morrow?" Douglas asked as David examined a woodcut of a fluffy, academic-looking hare reclining in the snow.

"I am. My steward claims he forgets what I look like, and that we will never succeed at spring planting unless I subject myself to his attentions for the next few weeks." His steward grumbled something to that effect, at any rate. Or in that general direction. More or less.

Douglas remained where any sensible man ought to, right by the study's cozy fire. "In this beastly cold, one can hardly believe spring will ever arrive. I know the hour is early, but Heathgate sent over a case of his best as a housewarming gift. I've been waiting for someone to share it with, and you will soon be departing."

"A tot in anticipation of my travels would suit. Gwen seems to be having an easy time of it," David remarked. While both Heathgate and Greymoor had prevailed upon him for a medical opinion of their wives' interesting conditions, Douglas had not.

Yet. The other family description for Heathgate's finest was "Heathgate's bribing stock." Douglas passed David a glass of excellent whiskey, and poured a smaller portion for himself.

"If Guinevere weren't having an easy time with this pregnancy," Douglas mused, "you would probably be the only one she'd even think of asking about it. I believe she wants you to attend her, but won't ask for fear you'll turn her down."

"I *will* turn her down." And why hadn't David seen this coming?

"Why?" Douglas hunkered by the fire, a poker in his hand. "Guinevere doesn't trust men in general, particularly not when it comes to personal matters, but she trusts you as both a physician and a friend—as do I."

A weight pressed down on David's heart, of bad memories, poor judgment, responsibility, and friendship.

"Do you recall, Douglas, when Felicity had such difficulty with the twins?"

"I do," Douglas replied, the fire blazing up as he added a log. "And I recall that the medical knowledge you were able to impart to Greymoor was integral to saving your sister's life, as well as the lives of both children."

A merciful God had saved the lives of all concerned, possibly abetted by the Earl of Greymoor and his stubborn little countess.

David took a steadying sip of his drink. "Any pregnancy, no matter how many times the mother has safely delivered, can reach that same point, where a decision must be made as to which life to sacrifice. I do not want that responsibility, so I don't practice medicine. It's as simple as that."

To be truthful, he didn't want to even *discuss* the practice of medicine.

"I doubt it's at all simple," Douglas said, straightening and setting the poker back on its stand. "I respect your decision, nonetheless. If you would suggest some alternatives to Guinevere, I'm sure she'd appreciate it."

And thus, Douglas's innate consideration eased them past a difficult moment.

Though another had yet to be faced. "I appreciate your understanding, Douglas, and I shall prevail on it further before I resume my travels."

Enduring more miles of bitter wind, frozen mud, and a dull ache that wasn't entirely sexual.

Douglas lounged back against the mantel, the very picture of a country squire at home amid his books, though his aim with a pistol was not to be trifled with, and his eye for details even more accurate. "So be about your prevailing, then."

"I need to apprise you of a certain matter." David resumed his study of the professorial hare and half turned his back on his host, the better to afford himself and his host a modicum of privacy. "The topic I raise may have no significance to you at all, or it may give offense, but I want your word you'll give me an honest reaction."

"My wife claims I am incapable of dissembling. She says it's a shortcoming when a man becomes a parent."

Must he sound so pleased to have his wife's opinions?

"I've hired Letitia Banks as my madam at The Pleasure House, and because she had intimate knowledge of your late brother, I thought you should be aware of it."

Douglas remained where he was, his expression bemused. David waited, not knowing whether to expect laughter, disapproval, or indifference.

"I liked her," Douglas said, which prosaic pronouncement David could never have anticipated. "We met on only one occasion, but she wasn't at all what I anticipated—not that I've your experience with fast women."

For which the man should be grateful. "You *liked* her?" And when had Douglas met her?

"I liked her," Douglas repeated. "So much so that prior to making my wife's acquaintance, I fleetingly considered establishing an arrangement with Mrs. Banks."

Douglas was not stodgy or pretentious, though people often mistook him for both. He was careful and shy, and enjoyed a sense of moral self-assurance David envied. No topic was too delicate if Douglas believed it needed discussion, and in this, he was well matched with his Guinevere.

"You considered a liaison with Mrs. Banks, but discarded the notion. May I ask why?" Why would any man?

"Several reasons," Douglas said, still exuding an air of

contentment and relaxation. "First, I concluded that Mrs. Banks, while as fair-minded as the next woman, might not view an association with the surviving Allen brother favorably, regardless of the monetary compensation."

"You were afraid she'd turn you down," David paraphrased, still stunned that Douglas had considered taking a mistress—any mistress—much less his late brother's paramour.

Douglas looked down at his drink, but he didn't partake of Dutch courage. "The situation was more complicated than that."

"You're tormenting me on purpose."

"You may not practice medicine, but I still hold you to standards of confidentiality regarding personal matters."

"Did you just insult me?"

"No." Douglas held up his glass to the light, the way a jeweler would examine a high-quality stone. "I'm stalling, but here's the rest of it: at the time, I was not sure I could have done justice to any woman. I did not want Letitia Banks to think ill of another Allen brother."

David silently dubbed himself the world's biggest, most obtuse fool. "I am sorry to have raised an awkward topic. I knew you had a difficult year, but I hadn't realized…"

He did not miss the intimate confidences inflicted on a physician. Did not miss them at all. David downed his drink and set the glass on the nearest level surface, which happened to sport a copy of Smellie's old treatise on childbearing.

Douglas's eyes lit with humor. "The matter has

resolved itself, as my wife's condition will attest. You have been a friend to me, and I would be one to you now."

David mentally braced himself for a gentle, well reasoned, spectacularly awkward sermon, which reaction Douglas apparently perceived.

"You're prepared to repel boarders. I'll fire a broadside instead: in my opinion, you and Mrs. Banks would suit."

Several beats of silence went by, while David tried to comprehend that Douglas Allen, Viscount Stick in the Mud himself, was encouraging a liaison between David and Letty Banks.

Douglas hoisted his drink a few inches in David's direction. "I have silenced the glib and sometimes charming Lord Fairly. How marvelously gratifying. I should call my dear wife to stand as witness."

"You think Letty Banks and I would *suit*?" It was one thing for David to desire a woman and flirt with her, quite another for his friends to encourage such mischief.

"You are an odd duck, Fairly. I say this, knowing full well the label is applied to myself frequently. You don't go about in Society unless you are tomcatting— and you've apparently foresworn that activity in recent months altogether. You don't dabble in trade; you shamelessly and profitably wallow in it. You happily saw your father's estate pass nearly into escheat rather than risk scandal to your sisters, and you own a brothel but do not sample the charms of your employees. You are a saint by some standards, a lunatic by others."

Could one be both? "Douglas, I had no idea you've made such a thorough study of me, but whatever is your point, assuming you have one?"

"Letty Banks can handle you," Douglas said, and his tone suggested this was high praise. "She is kind, perceptive, and intelligent, also honorable within the limits of her station. You respect her, and you have no other current attachments, at least not that your sisters or their husbands know of."

Because Douglas, too, would be kept apprised of the family gossip.

"How did you and Mrs. Banks meet, if I may ask?" David refreshed his drink, but wasn't surprised when Douglas declined.

"She contacted me when she was pawning her jewelry. She'd learned that some of the pieces Herbert had given her belonged to the estate, and returned them to me."

"She sold them back to you?"

"She *gave* them back to me, reasoning that Herbert could not give her what did not belong to him. To her, the transaction was simple. Mrs. Banks regarded the right to wear those jewels as Astrid's, at least until I married."

"Letty has said nothing about any of this." Though she'd been hoarding coal and rationing her tea leaves, and the sum Thomas had invested for her was all but gone.

"She wouldn't say anything," Douglas replied. "The situation reflects poorly on my brother's memory, who for all his faults, provided well for her during their association."

Douglas understood this sort of moral clarity, while David understood hunger and cold.

"And on the strength of your one meeting with her, you think Mrs. Banks and I would enjoy each other's company?"

Douglas resumed his place by the cozy hearth, to all appearances a gentleman happy to prose on about his acres and his broodmares, rather than his friend's next choice of inamorata.

"I don't know Mrs. Banks that well," he said. "All I am trying to say is that Mrs. Banks is lovely, honorable in her way, and available. You are similarly situated, and in need of… recreation."

Outside, scattered snowflakes began a sidewise dance toward the cold, hard earth. "You are presuming to comment on my personal life?"

"I presume," Douglas said, "because I owe you, and I can plainly see that you are lonely as hell. I know from experience that lonely men do stupid things. Becoming intimate with Mrs. Banks would not be stupid."

"Lonely and lecherous are not the same," David retorted, purposely using crude language with a friend who was himself never vulgar, because this snow would likely keep up the entire distance to Kent.

Douglas did not so much as twitch an eyebrow. "Indeed, they are not. Loneliness can kill a man; lechery is easily managed by any fellow over the age of twenty-five."

The scold was all the more effective for being delicate. "You think I should simply bed Letty Banks?"

"No, again." Douglas's calm should have been a warning. "Bed her if the two of you are so inclined, but my opinion is that you should marry her."

Long moments of silence ticked by, while David stared incredulously at a man he considered a friend, someone he respected as eminently rational, shrewd, and observant to a fault.

But also *kind*. Douglas was reserved and much concerned with propriety, but he was also painfully kindhearted.

"Damn you, Douglas Allen. I'll bite: Why should I marry Letty Banks?"

"I'm not going to tell you that your title means you have to marry someone," Douglas began as patiently as if he were teaching a catechism. "You will pressure yourself to marry and produce an heir and a spare—you're an English peer, after all—so one could say that you *should* marry, not that you must."

"One could." Though Douglas, in his orderly, rational, goddamned reasonable way, was apparently not.

"Mrs. Banks would be a scandalous choice, of course. But your sisters both married amid scandal, and they've been happy for it nonetheless."

"My sisters' husbands would not appreciate my choice, were I to take Mrs. Banks to wife." Because a rake reformed was a hypocritical bastard, and a pair of rakes reformed was a heavenly chorus of how-could-you's and I-told-you-so's.

Douglas waved a hand. "The only true reason for you to avoid scandal is to ensure your marital options remain flexible. Heathgate and Greymoor were a couple of scapegraces before they married; they can hardly point fingers at you. And as far as that goes, my impression was that Herbert was the first man to offer Mrs. Banks his protection. Other than whatever missteps she took out in the shires, she is not known intimately to any living man."

"You are saying she is only slightly used goods, and if I want her, I should have her."

Douglas leveled a stare at David, as if willing insight into the brain of a lout. "My wife," he said softly, "thought herself slightly used goods. She hid with the shame of it, because her family's wealth allowed her to do so."

David had the grace to look away, to acknowledge the punch in the gut Douglas had just delivered to his conscience. Douglas—proper, stodgy, reserved Douglas—had schemed and planned and moved heaven and earth to marry his slightly—badly—used Guinevere.

"Letty isn't Gwen." Though even a moment's reflection pointed out similarities between them.

"And you are not me," Douglas agreed, oh, so very pleasantly. "You are wealthy, you have the devotion of your sisters, you have properties from here to Halifax to which you can repair, and you have wit, charm, and influence in abundance. No." Douglas took David's half-empty glass from him. "You are certainly not me."

"I'll consider your counsel." The very next time he became too drunk to ignore it.

Or all the way to damned, freezing Kent.

"See that you do. Now, you are due to spoil my daughter, who is at this moment stuffing treats into that market hog thrust upon us by her ducal grand-father, though it's hard to fault Sir George, when he takes such good care of Rose while hacking out."

"She hasn't come a cropper yet?"

"No, thank the gods." Douglas's expression was the epitome of a papa who regarded his daughter's pony as his first rival. "I'm not sure my heart could take that, and Moreland would be on the premises, demanding explanations of the pony at gunpoint. With Guinevere in an interesting condition, such mayhem and riot must be avoided."

"Are you worried for Gwen?" Douglas seemed so composed—at all times, under all circumstances.

"Not worried, terrified. She delivered Rose without complications, but that was years ago."

In the dead of winter, Surrey was producing an excellent crop of anxious prospective fathers.

"No matter how concerned you are, your job is to be the soul of patient good cheer, to shower your wife with affection, and to exude confidence and optimism. Consult Heathgate and Greymoor if you need further pointers. They've both become proficient at dealing with gravid wives."

Douglas raised a thoughtful eyebrow, which from him qualified as an indication of burning curiosity. "Shower her with *affection*?"

Oh, for God's sake. "In abundance. She's not concerned about getting pregnant, so you might as well enjoy the resulting lack of inhibition."

Douglas straightened up the already tidy set of glasses remaining on the sideboard. "My wife has assured me of the same, but one feels hesitant nonetheless."

"Listen to your wife," David admonished. "Once the baby arrives, Gwen will need weeks to recover from the birthing. Then it will be weeks more, if not months, before the child sleeps for more than a few hours at a time. You're newly wed, Douglas, don't deprive yourself *or Gwen* of the pleasures to be had now."

"Pity," Douglas said, shifting the decanter half an inch to the left.

"What's a pity?"

"Pity you don't practice medicine any longer," Douglas murmured, absolutely straight-faced. "One could certainly use your sage and comforting counsel if you did."

❧

"David?" Guinevere, Lady Amery, found him packing his belongings after a noisy midday meal en famille with young Rose. "There's a fellow in the kitchen who's been sent for you from Town. He says his news is urgent, and asked that you attend him at once."

David slung his saddlebags over his shoulder, his first thought that Letty might have found other employment. "Let's see what he's about."

The man in the kitchen was Watkins, not the messenger David had left with Letty, but the head footman and a trusted retainer.

Watkins bobbed a bow. "It's sorry I am to be botherin' ye, yer lordship, but Mrs. Banks said it were urgent."

Which meant—thank ye gods—Letty was still at her post and capable of giving orders. "What's urgent, Watkins? You can speak freely here."

Watkins darted an anxious glance at Gwen, who rolled her eyes at David and withdrew from the kitchen without further comment.

"It's young Portia, my lord," Watkins said. "She's in a bad way, and the quack won't come, even when Mrs. Banks went to fetch him personally."

"Is it flu?"

Watkins colored to his ears. "I don't think so, your lordship. I think it be a female complaint. Mrs.

Banks didn't want to bother you, but it's been since Thursday, and Portia's faring very poorly."

"So I'm to come to Town, is that it?" David asked, mentally rearranging his travels to detour through London, because Letty would not have sent for him unless the matter were serious.

"If'n you please. Mrs. Banks is worn fair to a nubbin worryin' for Portia, and Desdemona is fit to be tied. Portia's at Mrs. Banks's house, where she'll at least have peace and quiet."

Only the very ill needed peace and quiet that badly. Watkins was worried too, as was David.

"Let your horse rest, Watkins, and I'm sure there's a toddy to be had and some victuals in the meanwhile. I'll see you back in Town."

"Best bundle up, my lord. It looks to start snowing again, if you ask me."

❦

"Letty? It's David, and my hands are full with the tea tray, so open the damned door."

He'd come. All Letty could think as she opened the door was that he'd come, and his presence would mean a lot to the woman dying in the bed.

"What in the hell is wrong?" His lordship put the tea tray down on a bureau and took a step toward her, but Letty nodded toward the bed, lest she collapse into her employer's arms.

"Portia's bleeding to death." Letty kept her voice down, though the stench in the room likely proclaimed the truth loudly enough. "She went to Old Meg, at least that's what the women told me. Portia wouldn't say a thing to me, and apparently timed her visit such that most everyone was getting their courses—her bleeding wouldn't have been unusual, then."

"Old Meg?" Fairly added a short, filthy oath as he sat on the bed. "You know who she is?"

"I gather from your expression she's not a midwife."

"She's a damned butcher," Fairly shot back. "She's an abortionist, a whore whose protector slashed her face rather than let her leave him. She took to her trade when her looks were ruined, but she's as jealous of the young women who come to her as she is likely to help them. Many do not survive her assistance."

Something else to hate about this new occupation Letty had taken on. "I sent word to Ridgely that Portia's health was gravely endangered, and he didn't bother to send a reply."

"Ridgely is probably the reason Portia went to Meg in the first place. We'll need hot water, towels, lye soap, and some laudanum if you have it."

Letty returned with the hot water—thank heavens Fanny was at least keeping the well full in the oven—and found her employer in his shirtsleeves with his cuffs turned back to the elbow.

"Have you ever assisted at a birth?" he asked as he used the soap on his hands, wrists, and forearms.

"I've been present. What are you going to do to her?"

"I will try to save her life. You are going to have to fold back the covers, Letty, and clean Portia up as best you can before I touch her. Can you do that?"

She passed him a clean towel, one of the last ones in the house. "I can, but I've changed the linens enough to know she's literally a bloody mess."

"Then we'll change them again, and sooner is better than later."

Portia was not only a bloody mess, she was a bloody, stinking mess, and yet, his lordship was undaunted.

"Change the towels and ease her legs up so her knees are bent."

Letty complied, though how one woman could lose so much blood and yet draw breath she didn't know. "I ought to send for a parson, but I doubt one would come."

As Letty swapped clean towels out for the soiled ones, fresh blood seeped from between Portia's thighs.

"Bend her knees, and if I send for a damned priest, the man will come posthaste."

Letty turned her head rather than watch what came next. Portia remained inert on the bed, but Fairly was soon swearing softly.

"That damned old bitch. I need bandages. Linen if you have it, and fast, and we're going to bank the pillows under her hips to help slow the bleeding."

He tossed a length of bloody, curved wire onto the brick before the hearth, and Letty wanted to be sick as she passed David a wad of cloth.

"Infection is almost a foregone conclusion," he said, "but Portia's young and otherwise healthy. She might pull through and surprise us all." He worked in silence for a few minutes, then stepped back, his hands bloody, and motioned for Letty to replace the covers.

"How do you know all this?" she asked, for not every physician concerned himself with matters of midwifery.

He recommended scrubbing his hands, turning the remaining water pink and soiling the last clean cloth.

"Once, long ago, in a land far away, I thought I might have had it in me to become a healer. I was wrong."

And yet, Portia might live. "So what do we do now?"

"We keep her comfortable and watch for infection. She should eat as much organ meat or beef as we can get into her, and drink beef tea to help her replace the fluids she's lost. White willow-bark tea and feverfew if she spikes a fever, and various other infusions for pain and inflammation."

His gaze as he regarded the still figure in the bed was far more that of an aggrieved friend than a treating physician. "In any case, she will be a long time getting back on her feet, and her previous profession may no longer be available to her."

Because she'd be too damaged, which meant she'd also never have children. Any woman would feel that as a loss, and not a small loss.

Letty smoothed a hand over Portia's brow, which was not—yet—fevered. "I could shoot Ridgely." Shoot him in an unmentionable location.

"My poor Letty. You've been dealing with this for four days, and you are exhausted. Portia won't be stirring for a while. How long has it been since you've had something to eat?"

Portia might not *ever* stir. "Mrs. Newcombe tried to get me to eat something yesterday, I think—maybe the day before." Tried. Probably mentioned in passing that food might be a good idea.

"Mrs. Newcombe needs to be taken firmly in hand," Fairly said, draping the damp, streaked towel over the back of a chair. "She should have kept up with the wash, at least."

Letty moved around the room, collecting soiled towels and sheets. "Don't fuss. It's too late for that, and I'm too tired to defend anybody."

Also, too heartsick.

❧

"I'll watch over her," Desdemona said, "and plan a bad end for Lord Ridgely while I do."

David might have smiled, but the woman was not joking. He pushed to his feet, every joint and muscle protesting movement away from the chair by the hearth. "If Portia stirs, get some willow-bark tea into her. It's bitter, nasty stuff, but it can help with fever and inflammation."

Des took a seat near Portia's head and smoothed her friend's hair back. "We should cut her hair."

Portia was vain about her long, dark hair, and with good reason. "Cutting her hair won't help, despite what the herb woman told you growing up. Your prayers just might. Call me if she worsens." David never importuned or took liberties with the women who worked for him, but before he left Desdemona to take up the sickroom vigil, he kissed her forehead. "We'll all be praying for her."

"God does not listen to the prayers of such as I, your lordship, else I would not have ended up where I did."

David was too tired to debate theological conclusions, particularly when they were supported by both logic and grief. He closed the door to the sickroom, realizing the hour had grown late while he had tended his patient, but at least Letty's house was no longer frigid.

Thinking that Letty would want to know how Portia fared, David tapped on her door. He pushed the door ajar and slipped into her room when he heard no response.

"Merciful saints." He hadn't meant to say the words aloud, but he'd caught Letty at her evening ablutions.

"My lord."

By the rosy light of the fire, she did not blush. She reached for her dressing gown and slipped into it, but not hurriedly—perhaps she was too exhausted to hurry, for David did not think she was capable of coyness.

"I'm sorry. I did knock."

He was *not* sorry. He was a man, also a former physician. He appreciated the wonder that was the human body, and he appreciated the specific wonder that was Letty Banks too. In the few instants it took Letty to gather her wits and cover her nudity, he studied feminine proportions designed to hold a man's interest—she was slender through her pale belly, but curved through the hips. Her breasts were generous, the breasts of a woman, not a girl, full and slightly heavy.

David noted details—a dark thatch of curls, an asymmetry of the knees, ribs still a bit too much in evidence—and he absorbed the whole of her. As a younger man, he would have treasured the womanliness of her unclothed frame, but in those few instants, he lingered on the imperfections, the details that made her different from what he'd expected, and different from—and more precious than—any other woman.

She tied the belt snugly around her waist, but the gesture was too little too late. David had seen the lovely abundance of her breasts, seen how the pale column of her neck turned to join her shoulders, noted the flare of her hips and the flat plane of her belly. By the light of a generous and well-stoked fire, he'd seen *her*.

Her unexpected nudity hit him low and hard, a blow to his self-restraint all the more stunning for being unforeseen.

"I did not hear you. I was preoccupied," Letty said. "How is Portia?"

Letty's feet were bare. David wanted to slip out of his boots and give her his wool stockings, or scoop her up and tuck her into the bed.

"Portia is faring better than she should. Desdemona kicked me out of the sickroom and told me get some rest. If you don't put on some slippers soon, you will come down with lung fever yourself, Letty Banks."

She sat on the bed, his words having no more impact than the wind moaning outside the windows. "I cannot recall being this tired ever, but if you think I'll allow you to navigate the streets alone at this hour, sir, you are sadly in want of sense. You might as well sleep here."

Her hair hung over one shoulder in a thick, glossy braid. David had seen Letty's hair done up in a braid before, but he was seized with a desire to see it freed of all constraints.

And she was nattering on about… "*Sleep here?*"

"The bed is large enough. The fire in the front parlor is not lit, and the sofa is the only other possible place to put you. I trust you've shared a bed at some point in the past?"

Not for years, if passing afternoon recreation was discounted. "Of course I have. May I make use of the wash water?" Because, apparently, he was going to subject himself to the sublime torture of sharing a bed with Letty Banks. He was tired enough, and the

weather more than nasty enough, that the alternatives bore not even a moment's consideration.

Dispirited enough, too.

"The ewer on the hearth holds clean water, and tooth powder is behind the privacy screen. I can't offer you a dressing gown, because I gave Herbert's few effects to charity."

She moved behind the screen, and David heard her stirring about. "You didn't sell them?"

"That did not"—she paused... to yawn?—"seem right."

He suspected her retreat behind the screen was to afford him privacy to use the wash water. Such consideration was oddly... touching, and if he did not take immediate advantage of it, he'd fall asleep where he stood.

"Where shall I put my clothes?" He wanted her to know his clothes were coming off. He'd been in them the livelong day, and Letty was no stranger to the unclad male body.

Letty emerged from the screen, a nightgown evident beneath her robe. "The back of the door has hooks."

He'd known that, of course. "Letty, if I'm to wash—"

Was there any prospect more ridiculous than a grown man explaining to a madam that he was about to disrobe? Letty apparently did not think so, though her smile was sweet rather than mocking. When she ought to have climbed into the bed, she instead crossed the room to slip her arms around David's waist and rest her forehead against his chest.

"I was so glad to see you today. I nearly cried with relief."

His family was glad to see him. He was almost sure of it, even if they never came close to crying in relief at the sight of him. Before he could wrap his arms about her, she shuffled off to climb into the bed.

She'd turned the sheets down, but that bed would be cold.

David unbuttoned his waistcoat. "The warmer is in Portia's room?"

In the shadows, the covers rustled. "Mmf."

He pulled his shirt over his head, his arms protesting the movement. The rustling paused, then resumed, then stopped.

Was this how a woman felt when a man had paid her to disrobe for him? Uncertain, shy, a bit aroused, and silly?

No answering movement came from the bed. David put aside awkward questions, tugged off his boots and stockings, then undid his falls.

He'd never been particularly self-conscious about his body, never given a thought to taking off his clothes when sharing a bed with a woman, and yet, he wanted Letty's permission before he burdened her with his nudity.

"Letty-love?"

Nothing, not even a sigh.

He shucked out of his breeches, used the wash water, and climbed into the bed next to the woman already fast asleep under the covers.

❧

Letty was cheating.

Instead of saying her prayers, kneeling by the

bed—the only posture from which evening prayer could be heard by the Almighty—she was saying her prayers snuggled under the warmth of her quilts.

She was cheating not only by praying under the covers, but also in the content of her prayers. Good King George did not receive mention, or his queen, or his progeny, or the Archbishop of Canterbury. Letty's own family was relegated to a passing reference, though Portia received mention.

What Letty prayed for most was fortitude, for the prospect of David Worthington, unclad and washing off at the end of a long day, made her throat ache and her insides restless. He was beautiful, the weary grace of his bathing impossible to ignore. Firelight gilded lean flanks, muscular limbs, and a torso worthy of any hero from antiquity.

And then her prayers turned to thanksgiving, because finally, years after parting with her innocence, Letty Banks experienced what it was to want a man.

She allowed herself the space of two deep, even breaths to appreciate the object of her desire from behind nearly closed eyes, to memorize the magnificent bodily proportions and severe male angles of his face, then closed her eyes.

A cheat she might be, but not a hypocrite. Letty did not pray for forgiveness for her prurient longings; nor did she pray that she'd be delivered from them. She prayed instead that the images she'd seen of David Worthington as God made him stayed with her into her dreams.

And into her old age.

Six

DAVID AWOKE TO WARMTH AND THE CERTAINTY THAT he was not at any of his various domiciles. The scent of roses came to him next, and a vague worry—

Portia. Though if she'd worsened in the night, Desdemona would have fetched him.

As the relief of that realization warred with the temptation to let sleep reclaim him, David's gaze fell on a copy of *Grose's Dictionary of the Vulgar Tongue* on the night table, and the rest of the puzzle snapped into place.

He was sharing a bed with Letty, her knee casually pressed against his thigh. And just as he knew he'd at various times cuddled her close during the night, he also knew he ought to get out of that bed, find his clothes, and check on his patient.

"Don't go." Letty hadn't moved, hadn't given herself away by so much as a change in her breathing, but she regarded him from her pillows, her gaze solemn and alert in the gloom. "The sun's not even up yet."

Staying in bed with her while she slept was stupid; staying in bed with her when she was awake was…

stupider. What came out of David's mouth next was stupidest of all.

"I should tend the fire." Because if the coals went out, somebody would have to start the thing all over, and David did not trust the lazy housekeeper to do it. Then too, cold air could dampen arousal more effectively than could stern lectures about common sense.

Letty reached past him for a glass of water, took a sip, then offered it to him. When he'd accepted her offering, she pushed his hair off his brow and settled back against the pillows, their exchange having all the familiarity of a couple long married.

"You banked the coals thoroughly before you came to bed."

She'd been peeking the previous night, then. The knowledge cheered him. "Letty, if I stay in this bed—"

They'd make love. Share a little pleasure, scratch the itch adults of both genders enjoyed scratching. His cock could think of no better way to start the day. So why was he hesitating?

"You could have any fellow at The Pleasure House, you know. All of them. A different title for every night of the week. Why me?"

When he feared she might laugh at his question or mock the insecurity trying to mask itself as curiosity, Letty instead shifted closer, draping a leg over his hips. "You will think me ridiculous."

He scooted to the middle of the bed, near enough to tuck her crown under his chin. "Never. Not about this."

Letty's nose was cold. David knew this because she buried her face against his throat, and used the leg she'd hitched around his hips to draw herself closer.

"I have never understood desire. As a girl, I understood that to leave my father's house, I'd have to engage in certain acts with my husband, and I was curious. I understand curiosity. When I got to London, I was no longer curious, though I became resigned. I thought perhaps loneliness had something to do with it, and then too, one must eat—"

David kissed her, lest her confessions become more heartbreaking. "You deserve desire, Letty Banks. You've parted with your innocence and nearly starved as a result. The goddamned least you deserve is desire, pleasure, and satisfaction."

And she trusted him—*him*—to give them to her.

"I am a madam," she said, in the same tones she might have said, *I have given my kingdom for a mess of pottage.* "I would learn something of desire."

"Right now, you are the woman sharing a bed with me. The woman who will share pleasure with me."

David trailed his palm over her nipple, letting that movement be the only caress he offered. He would accustom her to his touch and to the pleasures it could yield rather than distract her with more kisses—for now.

Letty's fingers came up to encircle David's wrist where his hand poised over her breast, her touch was neither restraining nor encouraging.

"You will enjoy this, Letty-love." A mandate, instead of a prediction. *David* enjoyed it, liked the ease and warmth of being snuggled up with her, the sense of wonder and intimacy.

"I might."

"You might enjoy this too, then," he murmured,

closing his fingers gently over her nipple and offering her the slightest pressure. She closed her eyes in response, while David detected the barest arching up against his hand, the smallest token of encouragement.

This should have felt like work. To move so slowly, one caress, one sigh, one touch at a time—it should have been frustrating, and even tedious, but encouraging Letty's passion was no more work than unwrapping a long-anticipated gift. Even a casual partner deserved the courtesy of arousal, but David was also learning Letty, learning her responses even as she was learning them herself.

The realization was humbling and exhilarating, and even greater than the gift of Letty's responses was the gift of her trust.

"Kiss me?" she whispered.

Satisfaction rose up, fueling greater arousal. She had asked him for something, a small something, by arching her back slightly. A not-so-small something by asking for his kisses.

To his utter pleasure, she followed up her request by taking a small kiss for herself.

And we're off.

But it was the most languid start to an erotic race David had ever known. Letty's lips trailed over his, her tongue shyly inviting his into the kiss. She did arch her back then, pressing the fullness of her breast against his hand with unmistakable entreaty. He obliged, letting his caress become a gloriously sensual exploration of the weight, contours, and responsiveness of her breasts. And even as he provoked more arching and sighing from her, he deepened the kisses, using lips, breath, and tongue to orally mimic the act of copulation.

"I wasn't going to allow this," she whispered.

He had to focus on her admission, another gift that surpassed the mere, predictable endearments the situation might have merited. "You weren't going to allow me to touch you?"

"I wasn't going to allow myself to want."

Maybe a woman who'd lost her innocence had to learn the art of not wanting, because much, *much*, was no longer hers to even wish for. That conclusion brought with it anger and sadness, which had no place in the same bed with a man who sought to bring his lady pleasure.

David trailed his mouth down her neck, then along her sternum. He pillowed his cheek on the swell of one exposed breast and paused deliberately.

He wanted Letty to anticipate his next touch, and wanted time to gather his wits. The last thing he could afford was to rush her, to give her any excuse to marshal her defenses or to direct her practical, thinking mind to what happened when intimacies became meaningful.

She wanted to know about desire, about intimate and pleasurable bodily sensations.

Lest his own mind hare off in the direction of desires of the heart, David raised himself over her, and slowly—giving her time to anticipate—lowered his mouth to her nipple. Her hands came around the back of his head, again neither pulling him to her nor thrusting him away, as if her fingers and palms could eavesdrop on the pleasure he was visiting on her breast.

And pleasure it was. When he drew on her nipple, he surrendered to bliss shot through with bright streaks of something hotter and more intense. A sigh that edged toward a groan escaped Letty, and David paused, treasuring even that sound, before resuming his pleasuring. Her fingers moved on his nape, massaging, and eventually, holding him to her.

But so lightly, only a hint of an embrace, the merest suggestion of an invitation. The pace of their caresses, like the deliberate steps of an old pavane, forced David's own arousal to unbearable intensity, but still he held back. Letty was becoming interested, but she was not yet in pursuit of a goal. She was letting David lead her, because a need for her own gratification hadn't yet begun to drive her.

David moved his mouth to the second breast, which allowed him to lean more of his weight onto his lover. In response to his cock's insistent demands, he flexed against the crest of Letty's hip. Moving felt good, not good enough, but better than completely ignoring his own wants, so he set up a slow, lazy rhythm, pressing himself to her hip, then easing back, only to press in again.

Letty's hands went on a quest, slipping down his back, around his hips, then back up, into his hair, over his face, and off again. She had the most provocative touch: light, curious, and increasingly bold. When her fingers feathered over David's throat, chest, and face, pausing to explore his lips, it was his turn to sigh and moan.

"Easy, love," he murmured, "or we'll finish too soon."

Her hand stilled over his heart. He covered it with his own and dropped his forehead to her collarbone. Their position was a variation on the embrace of the waltz, with her arm around his back and their hands joined. Letty waited unmoving, and again, David had the sense she was trusting him, willing to follow his lead for yet a few more steps.

Because he'd managed to find the most innocent madam ever to preside over immoral commerce in the history of London.

He glossed his palm down her breastbone, taking his time, exploring the contours of her ribs, then the smooth, flat plane of her belly and her hip bones. She remained still as his hand trailed lower, holding her breath physically and perhaps emotionally as well.

"Let me pleasure you," he whispered, kissing her neck below her ear, where her rosy scent was sweet and strong. "Let me ease the ache for you."

He entreated, because what she wanted was an experience of pleasure, and what David wanted was to give that to her, and in a way her previous paramours had sadly neglected to do. For reasons novel and unexamined, he needed to be different from his predecessors, and was curiously grateful for their ineptitude.

He shifted up, enough to kiss Letty properly, and found to his horror that tears had gathered in her eyes. The sight pierced him with a profound sadness, and worse, a tenderness for Letty, who should have been beyond the reach of tears when sharing intimacies.

"I want only to pleasure *you*, Letty," he said, sifting his fingers through the curls shielding her sex. "We needn't do more."

As it turned out, he hardly needed to do anything. His fingers learned the soft, damp contours of her intimate flesh, and explored the responses he could inspire by attention to the seat of her pleasure.

"I'll go softly," he whispered, kissing the corner of her mouth when she wrapped her grip around his wrist. "Close your eyes and trust me."

She would never entirely trust him, but she might tolerate him as a lover. That thought made him patient, determined, and attentive, such that her every little sigh and hitched breath informed his fingers, his mouth—and his self-restraint.

Pleasure took her silently and beautifully. She turned her face into David's throat while her body convulsed, the contractions of sufficient strength he could feel them as he palmed her sex.

She remained against him when it was over, burrowed into his embrace, her restraint and misgivings nowhere in evidence.

Something peculiar turned over in David's chest. She'd trusted him, just as he'd asked. Maybe not quite as much as he'd wished— and when had he ever courted a woman's trust?—but she had. He would not betray that trust with selfishness now.

They remained thus for several minutes, Letty's breathing gradually returning to normal. When David levered his body over hers, she allowed it, her hands finding their way to his hair, and then in slow strokes, to the long muscles of his back. He settled his weight on her, hoping it brought comfort, at least.

"May I ease myself on you, Letty?" He punctuated the question with a slide of his hips that had his cock gliding along Letty's damp flesh. In reply, she brushed her lips across his, then wrapped her arms tightly around his waist.

Acceptance, then, of a request, if not of him.

David repeated the movement, a slow hitch of his hips that moved his cock tightly against her.

For long moments, he was content with that pleasure. He toyed with the knowledge that he could change the angle ever so slightly and be inside her. She was a madam and assuredly not a virgin, so she knew well the risks she ran with what she allowed.

If he'd asked for more, she might have granted it, but as arousal rose in David's blood, he also knew that permission was not going to be enough. When—not *if*—when Letty took him as her lover, it would be because she wanted him for herself, not because she *permitted* him liberties.

So he rocked against her slowly, savoring the heat and feel of her beneath him. She held him closely, not the embrace of a woman tolerating an obligation, but the embrace of one who could become his lover.

He lifted his hips to trap his cock against her belly, and thrust a few more slow, powerful strokes. As he came in hard, hot spasms, Letty kissed him on the mouth.

The relief David tasted in that kiss eradicated any lingering sense of frustration. It vindicated his judgment that Letty hadn't been ready to take him as a lover in the fullest sense of the word, though that mattered little compared to how much intimacy she was willing to grant him.

David's satisfaction was more than sexual as he returned Letty's kiss. He was content, for now, to have given her as much pleasure as he could, to have shared pleasure with her. The contentment surprised him, but there it was.

He straightened his arms, fished on the night table for his handkerchief, and used it to swipe gently at Letty's stomach and then at himself. He tossed the handkerchief aside and rolled onto his back, wrestling Letty into lying against him.

He should probably offer her some conversation, but he was too content for words, the sexual lassitude blending with a sweetness words might disturb.

He was thus inordinately pleased when Letty's hand stole over his chest to cover his heart. She rustled around in the covers until her head rested on his shoulder and her leg lay across his thighs. David wrapped her hand in his, and his arm around her shoulders, a feeling of such peace and rightness enveloping him that he almost told her about it.

Sleep, fortunately, came to the aid of his common sense, and he and Letty both drifted off, warm, content, and for the present, not lonely at all.

∽

Letty woke alone, the covers tucked in around her and a pot of tea under a towel on a tray beside her bed. Her body was rested, contented, and pleased with its new knowledge of satisfaction and desire, but her mind was groggy and overwhelmed. David, no doubt the bearer of the tea tray, was likely downstairs, ordering Mrs. Newcomb about, and making himself at home in yet another household of women.

How could Letty face him? She'd invited him

to share intimate pleasure with her, invited him to remain in her bed. Fatigue and pragmatism might account for ending up in the same bed with him, but loneliness, foolishness, and even wickedness had been involved in the passion that had followed.

Tea before further self-castigation seemed a good idea.

Letty sat up to pour herself a strong, aromatic cup. She was pleased to find the room uncharacteristically warm because David had also built up the fire. Oh, to be taken care of... David's thoughtfulness was as seductive as his kisses, as his arms, warm and strong around her, as his voice, rumbling beneath her ear in the darkness.

Her musings were interrupted by a hard rap on the door, followed by David's smiling presence in her bedchamber. He bore another tray, and wore a towel over his shoulder.

"I've brought you sustenance." He set the tray on the night table, went to the window and pushed back the drapes to let in a gray, wintery light. "The weather is still foul, but the snow has slowed down. I expect you are hungry?"

"I am." For food, too.

He sat on the bed at her side and shifted the tray to her lap. "I made you some pancakes, and there's jam and butter, as well as a coddled egg. I couldn't find the pepper, but salt should do. You have no fruit in your pantry, Letty. That will not serve."

He was nervous. He had the peculiar competence to whip up pancakes and coddled eggs, he exuded his usual casual charm even unshaven and sporting a towel over one shoulder, and yet, Letty was certain he was nervous. "Thank you for breakfast, for the tea, and for building up the fire and for…"

Heaven defend her. She was nervous, too. More nervous than she was hungry.

"Hush," David said, putting two fingers over her lips. "Eat your breakfast and drink your tea."

No awkward discussions, then, which was fine with her. Letty began by slathering butter on her pancakes. "Where did you learn to cook? I didn't think culinary skills were a prerequisite for becoming a viscount."

"They aren't." David settled himself cross-legged at the foot of the bed, a posture Letty had not seen another grown male adopt. "But for the first quarter century of my existence, the viscountcy was the last thing on my mind. I traveled extensively and often had only myself or Thomas Jennings to rely on. One learns to make do, or to do without under those circumstances. And badly prepared food can kill as effectively as a bullet, and much more slowly."

"Is that why you have three professional chefs at The Pleasure House?" Letty asked, adding strawberry jam—her favorite—to her pancakes.

"In part, also because I am self-indulgent with my wealth, and unlike most of my station, my palate craves variety. Then too, had I only one chef, that one would think he ruled the kitchen, and by extension, a part of me."

Letty shied away from the ramifications of having one woman in his bed.

"You wouldn't tolerate that very well," she said. Nor would Letty, though chatting her up over pancakes didn't bear much relation to controlling her—did it? She set aside philosophy long enough to take a bite of hot, scrumptious, buttery pancake. "I would say, based on my breakfast, that you could let all three chefs go and still make shift quite nicely. This has to be the best breakfast I can remember having."

He glowered, like an enormous cat not pleased with his bedmate. "Does the kitchen really take such poor care of you when my back is turned, Letty? You could use more flesh, you know, not that I'm complaining."

No discussion, but some innuendo at least. She misaimed the knife and got a smear of preserves on her wrist.

David uncoiled himself to prowl up the bed on all fours and kissed her cheek. "Letty, you mustn't be self-conscious. Not with me. We've moved beyond that, haven't we? I want us to move beyond that."

His action and his tone suggested that in his mind, they'd arrived to some new arrangement, one that allowed him to prepare her breakfast and to give her orders.

"I *am* self-conscious." She lifted her wrist to lick the jam away, then thought better of it and used the serviette. "A madam I can be, David, but this business of moving beyond... You've given me much to consider. I do not think I am suited to what you have in mind."

"I beg to differ."

Letty smoothed her hand over the blankets, and sought words both honest and placatory, because his lordship was likely already picking out the house where he'd keep her, and the coach he'd make available for her use—all without meaning her the smallest insult.

The very opposite, in fact.

So she tried to meet his version of respect with her version of truth.

"You are too much of a gentleman to say it, but we can both admit I don't know what I'm doing. Having spent time with you in this bed, I must admit I am more confused regarding... copulation than ever."

David's expression became unreadable, and Letty hated that every bit as much she hated the blush creeping up her neck.

"Yet copulation is your stock in trade."

She was apparently going to offend, nonetheless. "Not by my choice. I want to eat, to have a roof over my head, to put a bit by. That is a different agenda entirely from wanting men to desire me, and knowing what to do with that desire."

Which competence, she doubted she would ever acquire.

David scooped up a half-eaten pancake with his bare fingers, took a bite, then put the remainder on Letty's plate and sat back.

"But I do desire you, Letty-love. At the risk of sounding arrogant, I believe you desire me as well."

"I won't argue that." More than ever, she could not argue that.

"Is it, Letty," David said slowly, "that you think I will cast you aside? I always part friends from my liaisons, I can assure you, and I am generous, both in bed and out."

The issue was now overtly under discussion, and David's expression was perplexed. Very likely nobody, nobody *ever*, had declined an invitation to share erotic pleasure with David Worthington.

And for such good reason.

"You will cast me aside, or I will cast you aside," Letty said, swallowing past a lump of pancake. "And I believe you are being honest when you attribute amicability and generosity to your partings, but I am not prepared to... to..."

And yet she nearly *had*, with no forethought at all. If he'd wanted to visit the risk of conception on her, she would have permitted it. Eagerly.

"I am trying to understand your reservations, Letty, and so far all I can come up with is that you are shy. I rather like that about you, but it hardly signifies as a reason to deny yourself the pleasure you deserve."

"I don't want to whore for you." A pathetic, honest sentiment.

"Letty," David said gently, "as young as you are, you would have to hold the post of madam at The Pleasure House for years before you have enough put by, as you say, and if someone else should own the business, you haven't even that prospect to rely on. Would you not rather earn a comfortable life, sharing pleasure with a man who holds you in affection and a certain respect?"

A certain respect—a certain private, socially irrelevant respect. His argument boiled down to a miserable truth: she could whore for him, or whore for somebody else, but if she wanted to keep body and soul together, she'd whore for somebody.

Maybe many somebodies.

They'd attempted this conversation once before, in this very house, and had made little progress with it. But now, thanks to David's single visit to Letty's bed—at her not-very-well-advised-in-hindsight invitation—she had a glimpse of what he was truly offering her. Her reputation was gone, and her future precarious, as David had delicately reminded her.

But when she was in his arms, held, cherished, desired… the chill of that future receded. Letty sent up a short, heartfelt prayer for wisdom, and failing that, self-restraint.

"The issue, my lord, is perhaps that I hold you in a certain affection and respect, and that I would like to continue to do so. What if there's a child? Have you children, that you can answer that question from experience, or will you simply make me more promises?"

He helped himself to a sip of her tea this time, which Letty took to be a prevarication rather than a presumption.

"You were subjected to Herbert Allen's attentions on a regular basis for a long period, and you did not conceive. Perhaps children need not concern you greatly."

"That is an ignorant answer." Also mean, though he wouldn't have intended it as such. "Particularly from a man with medical training. The problem could well have lain with Herbert, and you know it."

The unassailability of her riposte, or perhaps the vehemence of it, had him rising from the bed.

"So we'd have children. I love children, and even had a child." He crouched before a fire that was already blazing merrily. With his back to her, he poked at the coals, making sparks dance up the chimney. When he'd bludgeoned the fire thoroughly, he replaced the fireplace screen but kept his back to her.

"What became of the child?" She did not need to ask, because any extant child of his would have had his loving devotion, but he apparently needed to tell somebody.

"The child lived but a few hours. I will admit that I cared little for the mother, at least by that point, but for the child... In the few short hours of that child's life, Letty, I found out what real heartbreak means. This business, as you refer to it, between men and women, it has never affected me the way that one tiny, wretched baby did. I don't often speak of it."

"But you tell me this now." Inflicted it on her, more like. "Why?"

David turned to face her, the poker grasped in his fist like an old-fashioned claymore. "Were you to give me a child, I would treasure that child. Your baby would know no want, no deprivation, no hurt that a wealthy, titled father's love and care could prevent."

He had merely stated the obvious, for a man of his means would be expected to provide well for a love child.

"And would your love for that baby entail ensuring that his or her wicked mama have no contact with her own child?" Letty asked gently.

The intensity in David's eyes cooled, and disappointment sank like a stone in Letty's gut. Generosity he could well afford; nonetheless, he hadn't thought through the consequences of his lust to any save himself, no different from any other man driven by the dictates of his cock.

David set the poker aside and leaned a shoulder

against the bedpost. "Your question is valid. I will consider it."

A more honest response than many other men would have given, and much less than Letty's heart demanded.

"Well, don't stand there glaring at me as you do," Letty muttered, turning back to her breakfast. "You cooked enough for an army, and I can't possibly finish these pancakes. I will take on the egg, if you'll attempt to clean up the pancakes."

He stayed leaning against the bedpost for a moment, while Letty hoped he wouldn't refuse the only olive branch she'd been able to find.

"You are a good sport, Letty." He accepted the plate from her and resumed a place at the foot of her bed.

"And you are a good cook. We must still work together, regardless of what else goes on between us— unless, of course, you fire the women who eschew your attentions?"

Her question was far from casual, though it merited her a smile.

"I wouldn't know. None have ever refused me, except present company." He put a forkful of pancake into his mouth, chewing thoughtfully. "I really am a competent cook, aren't I?"

"You are frightfully competent at any number of endeavors," Letty muttered.

"Am I, now?" he said softly before taking another bite of pancake.

He kept his attention on his pancakes, though Letty had the sense her comment had pleased him. As they concluded breakfast in companionable silence, it occurred to her that even a man as competent as David Worthington could still have insecurities.

The thought was equal parts intriguing and confusing.

❧

David took himself home that afternoon, dealt with some correspondence, slept fitfully, achieved no clarity of thought *whatsoever* regarding his madam and her place in his life, and then—after a detour to Lord Ridgely's rooms—came back to Letty's to check on his patient. And if he happened to run into the lady of the house, and happened to blame her for his night of poor rest, that was pure coincidence.

"Is Portia going to be all right?" Desdemona asked when she'd closed the sickroom door.

The concern on Desdemona's face had been absent on young Ridgely's, though David had made sure his handsome lordship had worries aplenty before parting company with him.

"She's holding her own," David said, "but infection could yet take her. Every hour she doesn't run a fever, doesn't start bleeding more heavily, or otherwise get worse, is an hour closer to restored health. You can stay with her, Des, but don't agitate her."

Desdemona slipped back into the sickroom without another word.

David saw no evidence of Letty's excuse for a housekeeper, so he took himself to Letty's private parlor and found Letty ensconced on the sofa, a tea tray before her.

"May I have a cup?" he asked, dropping down beside her. May he have her intimate attentions for an hour, a day, or a lifetime? Because that question now haunted his every waking hour, driven by equal needs to safeguard her welfare and secure her interest.

"Of course." She fixed his tea, while he kept to himself an uncomfortable truth: he'd slept better when he'd shared a bed with her.

Well, damn and drat the luck.

"Am I a managing, overbearing, interfering lord-ship?" David asked when he'd taken a bracing sip of strong tea.

"Very." Letty tucked a brown-and-red knit afghan more closely around her. "But well motivated and charming about it. I doubt most people even know you're manipulating them."

Manipulation was worse than managing—more honest. "Portia said the way I go about looking after people is as bad as a fat customer who can't finish… As smothering and annoying."

She didn't laugh, which suggested Portia had expressed herself delicately. David hadn't laughed either, because if he was not to manipul—*manage* Letty into accepting his protection, then how was he to overcome her reservations?

For he assuredly wanted to. A man needed his rest.

"I don't see your tendencies as a bad thing, neces-sarily," Letty said. "You are frightfully intelligent, generous to those under your protection, generally practical, and reasonable. Why shouldn't your world be ordered to your preferences?"

"Because I apparently don't limit myself to ordering my world," David replied, and why did tea have to taste better when consumed in her company? "You may scold me for further interfering in Portia's affairs. I've had a chat with Ridgely, and he'll be sending along some funds to assist Portia in opening her dress shop."

"Recovered his sense of Christian charity and decided to support free enterprise, did he?"

Letty approved of David's actions, which was a relief. "Either that or he wasn't keen to meet me at twenty paces. I award the boy a few points for prudence, for I would have felt no compunction whatsoever about blowing his feeble brains out."

Yes, *over a whore*. David had taken particular pleasure in emphasizing that point, for Ridgely had given Portia the funds to go to Old Meg, and her direction—after making plain that Portia's offer of carte blanche depended on making use of Ridgely's funds in the manner prescribed.

"If he ever sets foot at your establishment again," Letty said, "our dear little Musette will gut him like a fish. You, however, would have blown a hole through his hat, David Worthington, or at worst winged him, and you know it. More tea?"

"Thank you, no," David said, rising. "I will take my leave of you, and return on the morrow to endure more verbal beatings from my patient."

And frustration regarding his madam, whom he wanted to bed, protect, and scold in equal measure.

"Before you go," Letty said, her expression becoming guarded.

He did *not* want to argue with her, and he *did* want to sleep with her. Also to swive her silly. The sooner he was on his horse, the better. "Just tell me, whatever it is."

"It's about money." Letty remained seated, and rearranged the tea service on its tray. "I am having trouble with your books. I cannot be sure, but I think some expenditures are overstated for the quantities purchased."

He had hired her to manage his establishment. That she'd take this aspect of her position seriously should not have surprised him. "Are you certain?"

"No. I have totted things up for this month only. I want to go back through January and create a budget for March. We keep a file for receipts, you see, but everything is crammed in there, no order, no method. I'll have to sort through all of that before I can say if the problem is simply a matter of misfiling or mislabeling an expense."

"Then sort away. Neither Jennings nor I have had time to properly look over the books for the last quarter at least. I wouldn't put it past any of the three chefs to skim, though I would expect them to be clever about it. Look into it, but don't spend too much time searching for lost pennies. Sometimes the effort to recover what's gone missing exceeds the pleasure of having it restored."

His words left innuendo hanging in the air, and not the sort of innuendo that would land a man in bed with his madam. Before he could misstep further, David kissed Letty's cheek and took himself back out into the frigid, windy day.

Becoming intimate with Letty had not been a mistake, but rather, a revelation. She was the least qualified mistress he could have chosen, and for that reason, the woman he was most determined to have under his protection. On that befuddling thought, he turned his steps in the direction of his solicitors' office, and dared the sullen sky to dump more snow on him.

Seven

"YOU NEEDN'T SKULK AROUND TO THE BACK."

As Letty stood at his back door, David shot a glower over her shoulder in the direction of the mews, clearly unhappy with her for using a servants' entrance.

Which was just too perishing bad.

"It's Sunday, your lordship," Letty chided as she brushed past him into the spacious empty kitchen of his town house. "People are about and at their most pious. I should not be seen merrily thumping on your front door."

Letty removed her bonnet, taking in spotless counters, gleaming copper-bottomed pots, and a tea kettle steaming on the hob. Also a copy of *The Wealth of Nations* facedown on the table, suggesting her employer had been lurking here in his kitchen, waiting for her.

"That reminds me." David went to the hallway and bellowed for a footman. "Take the knocker down, would you, Merck? I am not at home, save to family in a dire emergency." He picked up the ledger Letty had brought and offered her his free arm. "Let's away to the library, and we'll study your figures, unless you'd like a tour of the house first?"

Of course she would, so she might torment herself with visions of her employer in his private rooms, or preparing for bed of a night. Perhaps he'd planned as much when he'd made the unusual suggestion that they meet here.

"This is not a social call, your lordship." It wasn't a call of any sort; it was a meeting between employer and employee to discuss matters that ought not to be overheard at the business location. Portia and Desdemona were yet at Letty's house, or she might have invited his lordship there instead.

David's expression became cajoling, though his gaze was wounded. "It's just a house, Letty."

He honestly wanted to show her his house.

Of all the sins he might entice her into, touring the house was not so very wicked. On the strength of that dubious logic, Letty allowed David to show her first the understory, where the kitchens, butler's pantry, servants' parlor, laundry, stillroom, and storage were located. All was spotless, tidy, and pleasant, much like The Pleasure House.

The ground floor was a testament to good taste and quiet elegance. The scent of beeswax and lemon wafted from gleaming wood surfaces—the floors, furniture, even the wainscoting shone with good care and excellent craftsmanship. The house bore small touches of pleasure for the eye—a hothouse rose in a vase in the hallway, a small painting at eye level of a quiet domestic scene.

"Is that a Vermeer?" Letty asked, stepping closer.

"It is. Greymoor gave it to me. Said it was going to waste on his estate in Sussex—no one ever saw it there."

Letty closed her eyes and let a wave of something— wonder, sadness, longing—pass through her. What kind of world did David Worthington live in, that family would casually gift one another with the work of an old master?

The exotic was subtly in evidence as well, small stone carvings of chubby, smiling fellows, that to Letty's eye looked Eastern in origin. A little elephant in a dark wood sat on an end table, the shine of the piece so lustrous it begged to be touched.

"I rub him for luck," David said, following Letty's gaze. "I was shipwrecked off of India, and this little piece of the cargo floated by, followed by a sizable spar. I snatched onto the spar and later found him washed up on the beach beside me."

"You have had such adventures."

"Traveling," he said dryly, "is often more adventurous than one would wish. Let's go upstairs."

More torment, more pretty, exquisitely tasteful rooms that underscored how different Letty's station was from her employer's. They started with a formal drawing room and a family parlor, then three guest bedrooms, and David's suite of rooms—a sitting room, dressing room, and bedroom. Each chamber was both elegant and comfortable, the colors lighter than Letty would have guessed, given that she was visiting a bachelor household. David's bedroom and sitting room held more delicate, aromatic roses, and a cat—a large, long-haired gray cat—sat in the middle of David's huge four-poster.

"What a magnificent specimen he is." In two quick strides, Letty was leaning onto the bed, scratching the cat, for every self-respecting vicarage sported at least one cat, and she'd missed their company. "And you have such a wonderful rumble," she told the cat, stroking plush fur. "He's exactly what I would have imagined you would have for a pet. Elegant, self-possessed, and lord of all he sleeps on."

David lounged against the bedpost, his expression similar to the cat's. "Was that a risqué comment?"

"Not about a cat," she replied, straightening from the bed. "You have a lovely house, my lord. Shall we go downstairs?"

His rooms bore his scent, spicy, vaguely Eastern, and beguiling, and the sooner Letty had her nose in the blighted ledger, the better.

"Soon."

Abruptly, Letty recalled they were in his *bedroom*, with no one to chaperone except a cat, whose morals were only slightly less suspect than his owner's.

Or, of course, her own.

David prowled over to her and brushed a lock of hair off her neck. The gesture was casual, not even erotic, and yet when he walked around behind her, Letty's heart began to beat hard against her ribs.

She had one instant—between when his breath warmed her neck and when his lips brushed softly across her nape—to pull away. He repeated the caress, and the effect was… aggravating. Letty had told herself she'd exaggerated his skill and his appeal. Told herself she was merely lonely, he was attractive, and his attentions were flattering.

She had not exaggerated his skill, damn him, and damn his deft, delicate kisses to unlikely places, too.

"I want to take you to bed, Letty," he murmured. "That bed, right there. I want to make passionate love to you, not carefully appease our lusts." His arms crossed at her waist, which meant he could settle a hand over each of her breasts.

A single white rosebud in a blue porcelain vase graced the night table, reminding Letty of a summer night when she'd lost her future in a rose arbor.

"Nothing has changed, my lord. You can still get a bastard on me, and I will not be your mistress." She made her declaration in tones more forlorn than resolute, and let her head fall back against his shoulder.

"Come with me to the library," he said, stepping away. "I've put the solicitors to work, and they've drafted a document you must see. I was hoping," he said as he led her through the house, "that you might simply melt into my arms, swear undying lust for me, and avoid the mundane considerations. But you won't, for which I adore you, of course. And though I don't want to offend you, I do want you, Letty."

He said this with the air of a man who'd argued himself to that conclusion, and as he towed her through the house, he was a man on a mission other than seduction.

When they reached a paneled library—more perfectly placed roses, a cozy fire, and the scent of well-cared-for old books—he went to a desk and extracted a document tied with a red ribbon.

"Read this, please." He slapped the document into her hand, like a gauntlet cast down before an opponent, then went back to the desk and perched upon its writing surface.

The paper was expensive and watermarked with a crest Letty presumed was his. She sat before the fire and read the words tidily set forth, or translated them, for the document was legal.

"Well?" he asked when she looked up.

"This isn't very well drafted."

Clearly, not the reaction he'd anticipated. "You want more money? That can certainly—"

For pity's sake. She took up a perch beside him on the desk, feeling self-conscious that she should have to instruct him on a matter of business, though bless him a thousand times, he'd grasped the basic idea.

She would not whore for him.

"This document provides that I be paid a generous sum certain, upon proof that I have conceived a child, David, that's all. The child need not be yours, the child need not survive birth, nor does the child even have to be born out of wedlock. The document doesn't serve your interests at all."

He regarded her for a moment with what Letty thought was consternation. "Portia's circumstances are an example of mere conception ruining a woman's prospects. I don't want to see that happen to you, Letty."

"I would not do as Portia did." Letty needed for him to know that. "There is no requirement—"

"A difficult delivery," he retorted, "even a difficult miscarriage, can mean your circumstances forever change. Portia may be taking her life in her hands should she *ever* bed down with another man. Barring a miracle, she'll find no tolerant yeoman to be her husband. If her dress shop fails, then what is left to her?"

Portia wasn't stupid. She'd be back on David's doorstep with another well-rehearsed plea for support, and Letty would not blame her.

"I take your point," Letty allowed, "but all this document requires is that I disclose my condition to you. You do not require that the child even be conceived while you are extant, or—"

"Enough quibbling." David rolled up the document and retied the ribbon with a tidy bow. "My sister Astrid bore Herbert Allen a child nine months after the man's death. Herbert could not have attested to the paternity of the child, Letty, and when I am not around to look after my child is precisely when I want you to have this money."

"You are not being very prudent." Somebody had to impress this upon him, for it appeared his lordship had nobody to look after his interests. "The likelihood I would bear you a posthumous child is small, David. And your solicitors would not willingly part with this sum after your death anyway. How am I to even prove conception, if it comes to that?"

David helped her off the desk and extracted a pen, inkpot, and blotting paper from a drawer. "The funds will be in Douglas Allen's hands. He thinks well of you, and he will be sympathetic to any woman faced with the prospect of raising an illegitimate child."

As Portia had slowly recovered, Letty had told herself David was avoiding her, rethinking his options, or coming to his senses. He'd been tightening his hold all the while, even to the point of recruiting *minions*.

Letty pretended to examine a cutwork snowflake framed behind the desk. The paper was so exactingly rendered, she expected if she touched it, it would be cold. "I've met the present Lord Amery only once, but he struck me as both proper and decent."

"That's a good description of Douglas. Before she married him, his wife spent five years raising a child on her own. Douglas loves them both, and is a truly good man. He will dispense the funds, should it come to that."

Which meant David had at least one true friend. Letty dipped the pen and affixed her signature to the page, then dusted it with sand—all without taking a seat at his desk. "Lady Amery's child would be little Rose?"

"Yes." David crossed to the sideboard and poured two drinks. "She loved every one of the birthday presents, by the way."

Plural. He had not heeded Letty's suggestion that he show restraint in his material generosity. "She loves *you*," Letty rejoined. "How do I establish that I've conceived, if the obvious evidence isn't yet available?"

David passed her a drink, and she didn't bother asking what it was. Anything he served to a guest would be delectable. "Carrying a child leaves medical indicators, subtle changes to your body any skilled physician or midwife will be able to note."

And had he made different choices, David might have been one of those physicians, just as Letty might have been a curate's wife. "Is this a toast we're making?"

She'd caught him off guard—a moment to savor. He set his drink aside, and when another man would have come closer—presumptuously closer—David instead turned his gaze to the cheery fire. "Does that imply," he said over his shoulder, "that you will sleep with me, Letty? That you will let me make love to you, copulate, have sex?"

"You need not be so blunt. I take your meaning."

And yet, she also understood, because he kept his back to her, because he was a man of delicate sensibilities, that her answer mattered to him.

"I will never again," Letty said slowly, "be respectable. I don't like that, but there it is. You make it possible for me to have some security, regardless of my fall from grace, and you are right: I deserve consolation for my loss of reputation. So I will make love with you, David, and I will enjoy it for as long as I can, but you must not expect me to…"

He came no nearer, but he turned and watched her closely with his beautiful, mismatched eyes. "Yes?"

"You mustn't expect me to be your fancy piece, to flounce around the theatre with you, to parade in the park at the fashionable hour. I need privacy in our dealings. I am not sleeping with you for money."

And she was not sleeping with him out of any wide-eyed notions that their relationship was a romance, which left… *what* as her motivation? Loneliness? Foolishness, perhaps? Selfishness?

Still, he did not touch her. "I understand that. You will be paid to raise a child, Letty, if a child should be conceived. You receive nothing simply for taking me as your lover."

That somewhat annoyed summary assuaged Letty's beleaguered sense of decency, though his words weren't entirely accurate either.

"To be your lover is not *nothing*. It is the furthest thing from nothing, at least for me, though I'm not exactly sure how we go about this."

He leaned an elbow against the mantel, smiling slightly. "I fall upon you and tear your clothes off right here and now, then chase you naked through the house, for starters. With the exception of Merck, who will not come above stairs unless I ring, the staff is off at services or visiting family, after all."

He was teasing her, a kindness that imbued Letty with exactly half an iota of confidence. "You have it backward, my lord," she said, strolling toward him. "I shall fall upon you and do the chasing."

"My mistake," he said, wrapping his arms around her.

Letty leaned into him, resting her forehead against his chest, for her knees had gone abruptly unreliable.

"We go about this, Letty, however you would like. I can come to you at your house or at The Pleasure House, or you can simply stay with me here from time to time."

His sandalwood scent was soothing, while his willingness to accommodate her was unnerving, underscoring that at her insistence, theirs was not a professional relationship. Had she taken his coin, he might have set terms—times, places, even days and hours and articles of clothing. Herbert certainly had.

But now, they must talk, must negotiate and discuss, which was a measure of intimacy Letty had not anticipated.

"My preference," he went on, "would be for you to remain with me tonight and perhaps tomorrow night, and we will see how we go on from there."

Letty nodded and stayed right where she was, burrowed against his chest, his exotic scent enveloping her as did the heat from his very body. The notion of entertaining him at her own house was insupportable, and besides, Mrs. Holcombe was soon to take another post in one of Douglas Allen's lesser-used residences. Letty was considering allowing the lease to lapse.

"Are you unsure, Letty-love?"

"Not unsure." He'd met her terms, given her what she'd said she wanted. "Anxious." And sad, because in accepting him as a lover, a pleasurable, intimate, and temporary companion, she'd forged a compromise between her conscience and a heart grown perilously weary.

"I will not deal with you cavalierly, Letty. I keep my promises."

"We will try very hard not to hurt each other." And they would fail. In fact, he already had.

"Would you like to go upstairs now?" He grazed his lips across Letty's brow, so he spoke his words against her skin.

What she wanted was to be good again, to be innocent and whole in ways a sixteen-year-old girl could not even comprehend were precious.

"You would like to *go upstairs* now," Letty said, though *going upstairs* was a homespun euphemism for deeds that with him would be more breathtaking than words could convey.

"I want to cherish you, Letty, in the broad light of day. I want to worship you with my body." His word choice was unfortunate, echoing phrases of the wedding ceremony—unfortunate or humorous.

"Let's go upstairs, then," she said, leaning up to kiss his cheek.

He kept an arm around her shoulders as he led her from the room. When they got to the bottom of the stairs, he startled her by slipping another arm behind her knees and lifting her against his chest. She curled into his strength, knowing the romantic gesture was for her, and appreciating its sweetness.

In her mind, they would be as if married by this act he contemplated. She would not offer herself to another after she had taken David as her lover. And she knew better than to reveal that bit of foolishness to him.

Not today, not ever.

❧

David paused outside his bedroom door and dipped so Letty could lift the latch. She made no protest when he walked right through the sitting room and carried her to his bedroom.

Something in him rebelled against his own head-long desire, though, so rather than deposit her directly onto the bed, he instead settled her on the sofa turned toward the hearth.

"Are you hungry?" he asked, kneeling before her. He'd touched her feet before, and it seemed a safe—and biblically humble—place to start. "Or would you perhaps like a bath?"

She put a hand on his nape, a curiously chivalric touch. "I want only you."

He said nothing, lest he babble a response. This entire endeavor—an intimate association with virtually no financial protection for her—left him at sea, and yet, it was what Letty wanted. He finished with her shoes then untied her garters, rolled down her stockings, and sat back. "You can manage from here?"

"If you'll unhook my dress and undo my laces."

What he knew of Letty's history suggested he'd had many more intimate partners than she—at least three continents' worth—and yet, no happy, sophisticated detachment descended as he contemplated the next hour. She rose and presented him with her nape.

This was fortunate, for it meant she could not see his hands shaking as he undid the myriad fastenings down the back of her dress. "I'll leave the privacy screen to you."

She sent him a curious look then disappeared into the corner of the room behind a japanned screen. David's first priority was to banish the damned cat, his second to get himself naked.

"Letty?"

"Just a moment."

"My dressing—"

She emerged from behind the screen wearing David's favorite dressing gown, a lovely green velvet lined in blue silk. "I did not bring any extra clothes with me," she said, smoothing a hand over the fabric. "I did not anticipate, that is—I hope you don't mind."

Did not mind that she'd been too innocent to foresee why he'd lured her to his house on a quiet Sunday morning?

David had everything off but his breeches, and he'd managed all but a few buttons of both falls, his thoughts as undone as his clothing.

Could he please her?

Could he *pleasure* her?

Was she truly attracted to him, or simply tolerating his advances the way women could with men they could not afford to offend?

She smoothed her palm over his dressing gown again, her fingers betraying a slight tremor.

"Letty, come here." Wariness flashed through her eyes at his blunder. "Please, would you come here and allow me to hold you?"

She crossed the room to stand before him, the hem of his favorite dressing gown dragging on the carpet. "I had not planned on the day taking this turn."

He slipped his arms around her, he, who had been planning on taking this turn with her for weeks. If he'd shown an ounce of interest in any other woman at The Pleasure House, that woman would have been plotting and scheming toward this moment as well, as would any other lady in Polite Society with whom he waltzed more than once.

"Shall I call for the carriage, Letty?" The question cost him.

Against his chest, she shook her head. "Don't expect much. I gather from listening to the women at The Pleasure House that Herbert's demands of me showed a lack of imagination all around."

She blamed herself for not knowing more of debauchery. "No toys?"

Another shake of her head.

"No games? No bindings? No drugs or potions?"

She shot him a puzzled look. "Is there a list somewhere, of what constitutes a proper romp in bed?"

Every culture kept such lists somewhere. David kissed her nose. "Will you play a game with me?"

The wariness was back, more forcefully, and though she didn't leave his embrace, she withdrew emotionally. "What sort of game?"

David found it necessary to tuck her more closely against him, so he might address his request to her left temple. "Just for today, might you indulge me in the fiction that you are simply Miss Letty Banks, and I am merely Mister David Worthington. We are attracted to each other, and fate has intervened to allow us to act on that attraction. We are not employer and employee. I am not a viscount, and you are not a madam. You are merely Letty, and I am David."

Rather than allow her to scoff at such foolery, he kissed her mouth. Today marked a shift in their dealings, and he would seal this new bargain with a sweet, slow kiss.

"Thank you," Letty said, drawing back a half inch. "And in that spirit, that fictional spirit, you must decide how we go on. For you see, I have never had a lover before."

When he closed his arms around her this time, the feeling was different, more tender and yet more desperate, because despite all of his experience—swiving, rogering, fucking, shagging, ad nauseam in ten different languages—he had never *been* a lover before.

When he kissed her again, she met him. Leaned into him, sank her fingers into his hair, and plundered his mouth and his wits both. They half stumbled onto the bed, and she laughed when he sent his breeches sailing in the general direction of the privacy screen.

"Laugh at me, will you? Naughty wench." He rose up over her on all fours, wishing he had more clothing to pitch across the room if it would make her laugh.

"I've always wanted somebody to call me that," Letty said, drawing her thumb over his chin.

"Wench?" He treasured her odd admission, because the wistfulness in her eyes said this was truly a wish.

"Yes. I was raised in a pious household, though the local tavern was a friendly place. When I had occasion to go to The Tired Rooster, the serving girls always seemed so merry and full of fun."

David slipped down to hug her, lest she see what this sort of nakedness did to him. "Then I shall call you wench, and you will feel merry and full of fun. Kiss me, wench, and let me love you."

Nothing came between them. Not coin, not unequal status, not social expectations, and certainly not the bedclothes. David kissed Letty until she was shifting restlessly beneath him, then probed at her sex with his cock enough to know she was damp and ready for him.

"Stop being polite," Letty muttered against his throat. "Stop asking."

He left off tracing her eyebrow with his nose. "I'm not to give orders, and I'm not to ask. What does that leave?"

She kissed his mouth and undulated in such a way that her curls kissed his cock. Had she practiced that exact maneuver, she could not have made it more arousing. "Take what you need. I need you too."

Need. The word she'd chosen was startling, courageous, and accurate. He drove forward, seeking her heat. She gloved him with her sex, her sigh breezing past his ear like a benediction. In the last reaches of his rational mind, it registered that Letty had kept on not one shred of clothing, not a bracelet, ring, or silk stocking when she'd come to his bed. And her very lack of artifice was a more powerful aphrodisiac than all the tricks, games, toys, or stratagems could ever be.

In David's long history of seductions, encounters, and trysts, and even a few orgies, his initial coupling with Letty was embarrassingly unsophisticated. They kissed, he mounted her, slid home, and started thrusting.

But the sensations… Ah, God, the sensations.

For the first time, David Worthington, Viscount Fairly, accomplished swain on four continents, wasn't in control of a sexual joining. Letty was making love *with him*, arousing him, driving his passions into a spiraling coil of want and pleasure rather than providing him a performance or a mutual accommodation.

"Slow down, love, or I'll spend."

"Spend," she whispered. "Hold nothing back."

She held nothing back, but instead locked her ankles at the small of his back and urged him closer. The slight shift in the angle of her hips gave David better purchase, and as he thrust more strongly, she began to shudder around him.

She had no artifice in this either, made no attempt to delay her pleasure, to duel with him for greater displays of self-restraint or control. A soft groan slipped from her, full of desire and longing as she bucked hard against him.

Her pleasure was too much for him. He pounded into her endlessly, the mindless violence of his release coming from a place in him as primitive as it was honest, as it was foreign to his usual habits.

When the storm abated, David lay full length on Letty's limp form. His mind would not work, his body could barely move.

"Merciful suffering saints," he breathed, chest heaving as he raised his torso up by slowly straightening his arms. He stared down blankly at the woman in his bed. "God in heaven, Letty…"

"Thou shalt not take the Lord's name in vain." She kissed his mouth and used her hands to urge him back down to her. "Though there was certainly something of heaven in that."

He let her hold him, needing her arms around him, not understanding what had been so *different*. The sexual pleasure had been unprecedented, though he'd barely offered Letty a moment's teasing beforehand.

Some lover, he.

"I'm too heavy," he murmured against her shoulder, trying to retrieve his manners.

"Hush," Letty admonished, her hand stroking the back of his head. "Just hush. You feel lovely."

Yes, he rather did, feel lovely. He gave up trying to puzzle it out, gave up his attempts at manners, gave up fretting generally, and dozed in contentment on Letty's sweet body.

When he awoke, he was still right there, lying heavily over her, his cock slipping from her sex while she continued stroking the back of his head. Her hand stilled on his nape when he gazed down at her. She wore such an expression of affection that David felt… shy.

Also profoundly pleased.

"Cloth," he muttered. He levered off of her, retrieved a basin and towel from on top of his bureau, and brought them to the bed. His own ablutions were brisk and efficient, but when he wrung out the towel and gazed down at Letty, he was momentarily at a loss.

"You are going to be so sore." He held the cool cloth to her sex. Multiple continents of erotic experience, and he'd fallen on her like a beast. Even in her inexperience, she had to know she'd been ill-used.

"Stop mumbling. Get under these covers, lest you take a chill." Letty held up the covers for him as he climbed back into bed. If he touched her again, he might become aroused, or possibly weep, so he curled up on his side, facing her.

"Letty Banks, I have never before had to apologize for my conduct in bed, and yet—"

She put her fingers over his lips. "You don't have to now. I don't want to know that polite, careful, controlled man who can find his pleasure without engaging his passions. I want to be in bed with *you*."

"You make me sound like a courtesan." Or like a viscount who managed his way through life.

Letty's thumb brushed over his nipple, and she studied the effect of her touch. "You aren't a courtesan, but you are as careful as one."

"Not with you." David rolled to his back, turning his head to regard her. "Would you like me to take you home now?" Lest he abuse her generosity yet more.

She left off playing with him, her expression suggesting he'd blundered again. "What I would like, is to be held."

And she'd wanted somebody to call her wench. He

threaded an arm under her neck. "Then come here, Letty Banks. Come here and let me hold you."

She wrapped her arm around his waist, hiked a knee over his thighs, and let him hold her.

⤷

"By the time I was thirteen, I hated the entire New Testament by heart."

David's hand on Letty's neck paused, while across the room, a shower of sparks shot up the fireplace flue. "That is a lot of hate for one very young lady, Elizabeth Temperance Banks."

He'd apparently read her signature, and even murmured her name twice in the throes of passion. Letty carefully did not remark on the pleasure of being called by her Christian name.

"When your papa's the vicar, there's a lot of New Testament," Letty said, and such was David's ability to encourage confidences that she didn't roll over and draw the covers over her head. "I hated soup grown cold because grace took so long. I hated kneeling, my left knee in particular hates kneeling to this day. I hated Sundays, because the weather is always fine on Sundays until services are over, and then it's miserable. I hated and hated and hated."

While her brother Daniel had learned to love.

David's hand resumed its slow, soothing caress of her nape. "Most adolescents are rebellious. My aunts were determined I should go to university, but I pouted and sulked and raged until they let me go to sea for several years as a surgeon's apprentice."

Letty was at sea, though with David spooned around

her in his big bed, she was also firmly anchored. "I haven't discussed my childhood in years." Hadn't had anybody to discuss it with.

"You've been preoccupied with survival. Given your upbringing, I'm surprised any of the local boys were brave enough to sin with you. Was your foray into romance another rebellion?"

Of course it was, though Letty hadn't taken the time to realize that. "He wasn't a boy. I sinned with the curate, of course. Isn't that how the farce is usually cast?"

She must have surprised her worldly, sophisticated lover, because he gathered her against him, bringing the scent of country-washed sheets and freshly bathed man closer. "Letty, I am so sorry."

Because her back was to David's chest, the tears that rose up didn't need to be dashed away. "Not as sorry as I was."

Sorry, humiliated, bewildered, and hurt. Very hurt. When David rearranged her so she lay along his side, Letty hadn't the strength to thwart him.

"You loved him." David used the sheet to dab at her cheeks. "Must I find this wretch and call him out for you?"

What a hearteningly violent offer. "You need not. Hell should await such a one as him, or so I hope. I did not love him. I flirted with him, and he made promises, and all I could think was I would be out from under my father's roof if those promises were real. The curate was handsome—there's a rule somewhere that all penniless curates must be handsome—and when I told him I wasn't interested in further dealings with him, he went to my father and confessed our misdeeds. I was so stupid, so painfully, wretchedly stupid."

David kissed her stupid, damp cheek. "You were not stupid. You were young, and he was wicked. The curate told your father that your charms had tempted him beyond his strength, that he repented sincerely of his lapse, and that he'd offered you holy matrimony, but in your wantonness, you'd refused him. He saw no recourse but to seek the forgiveness and guidance of his spiritual superior, who happened to be your father. And there you were, caged between a lying, self-serving bastard, and your father's judgment. If the man's not dead, I can make him wish he were."

Maybe this was what had allowed Letty to join David Worthington in his bed. All that exquisite tailoring and all those fine manners hid a savagery Letty found attractive—an honorable savagery.

"He eventually became a vicar." Daniel, who'd made it a point to keep up with church gossip, had worried that the news might *upset* her. He hadn't been as reluctant to tell her of the man's eventual death from natural causes.

David's caresses trailed over her hair, and beneath Letty's cheek, his heart beat in a steady tattoo.

"As a physician, I became familiar with a number of poisons. I've always thought a slow poison would be a good revenge. One could watch the victim fading. You might bear that in mind for future consideration. In any case, I'm glad you didn't marry him."

The fire in David's room was no paltry bed of embers, but it did not cast enough light that Letty could fathom his expression. "You're glad because I'm available for romping with you now?"

And was this romping, exchanging memories and regrets naked under the covers as the fire burned down?

"A mere romp would never trust me with her cold soup and sore knees, Letty Banks. I'm glad, because if you had married that curate, then night after night, you would have been required to offer your body to a man you did not respect, a man who did not respect you. The law would not have protected you should he have become violent or diseased. On the path you chose instead, you were intimate with a man you at least felt a passing fondness for."

She had not loathed Herbert. He'd been bluff, self-indulgent, and generous for show rather than out of good-heartedness, but not mean. "You aren't... wrong," she said.

"I'm right," David rejoined, kissing the center of her chest. "If a protector's attentions become distasteful, you can send him on his way. There's nothing he can say to it. The life you've chosen is hard, but you've kept a control over your fate and a dignity the curate's wife would never have had."

Everything in Letty came to a still point, as if she could strain to hear a far-off, faint angel chorus over the braying of the parson in his pulpit. "You think I made the right choice?"

Because if even one person agreed with Letty's choice, even one, then she might hold on to that dignity in truth.

"I know you did. Also the more difficult choice. Imagine the pity you would have been showered with when your husband strayed again. Imagine the piety ascribed to you, the martyrdom, when some other sweet, sheltered young lady tempted him to sin yet again. And again. And again. Like a physician, a man of the cloth has private access to women at their most vulnerable. Your curate knew that."

Letty sat up, the better to reenvision her entire adult life. "I would have hated that. I would have been filled with hate, every day. For my own husband—for *myself*." And raising children in such a household would have made the whole awful, sordid business worse.

David sat up beside her, hiking his knees and wrapping his arms around them. "I came to hate the woman I married."

Letty's thoughts stopped midflight, knocked out of the sky as if by a raptor. "You're *married*?"

Eight

So GREAT WAS DAVID'S FOCUS ON THE ADMISSION Letty's honesty had provoked, that her dismay took a moment to penetrate.

"And if I *am* married?"

"Then we are not lovers." Letty started to scramble off the bed, as if David were that deceitful, treacherous cleric from her youth, or something worse.

"My wife is dead."

She stopped, one leg over the side of the bed. "Dead?"

And because he was desperate for Letty to get back under the covers, he added, "Neither she nor the child survived childbirth by more than a few hours." The words no longer hurt the way they should, which was an entirely new sort of pain.

"They died nearly a decade ago and an ocean away. I'd finished my medical studies as a proper physician, and thought to practice in the New World. I was smitten, not with the lady herself so much, though she was a comely young widow, but with the idea that somebody might stand with me through all of life's vicissitudes."

That *anybody* might stand with him. Fortunately, he'd given up on that bit of foolishness.

Letty resumed her place beside him on the bed. "Lifelong loyalty and fidelity are quaint notions. Others have found them appealing." She rubbed his bare back, the way a fellow rider might have after a bad fall in the hunt field, to help him regain his wind.

"Though her family hid it from me when I courted her, the lady had a fondness for the bottle, and all my efforts to limit her consumption only provoked her into drinking more. She'd already conceived by the time I'd admitted the magnitude of the problem."

He managed to sound as if he recited a case history, but this small tragedy still didn't feel like a case history. With Letty sitting on the bed beside him, he admitted he never wanted it to.

She mashed her nose against his arm. "You were not stupid. You were young, and she was wicked."

Her misappropriation of his words gave him a reluctant smile. "Wench."

The hand on his back slowed. "I'm sorry. I'm not sorry you're free to be in this bed with me now, but I'm sorry you were hurt."

"My pride was devastated. I was a physician, a healer, and my own child——" A tiny, beautiful scrap of life, who had fought hard for a few hours and then fought no longer.

Letty gently but firmly pushed him onto his back, then straddled him and settled herself over him. The fire burned down, the shadows grew deeper, and David fell asleep in the sweet, silent comfort of Letty's loving.

❦

"Marry me," David coaxed. His hand was wrapped around Letty's breast, the warmth of his grasp more comforting than erotic.

"Good morning," Letty managed, "and not fair, that you have already used the tooth powder."

"Of course I have. I have company in my bed. One observes the civilities under such circumstances."

A proposal of marriage was a civility? "Well, let me up, your lordship, so I can observe the civilities and perhaps have a bit of privacy."

"No privacy for you," David replied, but he lifted off of her, and when she cast around for his dressing gown, he reached behind him and handed her her own brown velvet instead.

"I sent for some of your things."

Letty bit back the castigating lecture that welled up, because David looked so... guilty. So vulnerable.

"You have every right to be angry," he said, tugging the dressing gown closed over her chest. "I should have asked you first, but I gave the order, and didn't think better of it until the footman had gone. I'm sorry, Letty. I know you asked for my discretion."

She tied the sash on her own garment, though his was the more luxurious and bore his scent. "Once you ordered me a bath in your chambers, your staff knew we weren't exactly discussing business up here."

Though they needed to discuss business, because to all appearances, someone was stealing from him.

"I meant what I said, Letty."

"About?" She left the bed to find her very own toothbrush by the wash basin.

"I want you to marry me."

She glanced at him in the mirror over his dressing table, then slipped behind the privacy screen and set about brushing her teeth. Not "Will you please marry me?" but "I want you to marry me."

Though bended knee and pretty phrasing would have made no difference to her answer.

"I'll fetch breakfast," David said, perhaps knowing Letty wouldn't be pushed into the discussion he apparently meant to have. When he'd left, Letty tended to her more personal needs and set about rebraiding her hair.

What on earth had got into David now, that he was talking about marriage? For God's sake, it would never do, never do at all, and Letty saw with brutal clarity that she was going to have to hurt him even more than was inevitable. And worse yet, as much as she was going to hurt him, she was going to hurt herself more.

If Letty married David Worthington, Olivia would make good on every one of her threats, Daniel's prospects with the church would be in ruins, and little Danny would suffer for the rest of his life—to say nothing of the mischief Olivia might wreak even on a viscount's good name.

By the time David reappeared with breakfast, Letty had decided on an air of amused curiosity.

"Is there a reason you're proposing now?" Letty asked, helping herself to a slice of buttered toast when David had seated her at a table near the window.

"Because I want to marry you," he replied, his own breakfast apparently of no moment to him. "You are a vicar's daughter, after all, Letty. It isn't as if you were whelped in Seven Dials."

And girls who were born in the slums didn't deserve pretty proposals on that basis alone?

"I am a whore, David, and you are a wealthy viscount. We would never be received, and we will not suit." Despite how convincing his little game had been, they would never suit.

He sat back, no longer the lover, but once again the shrewd, aristocratic negotiator. "We spent all night in that bed, suiting marvelously. I rather hope we suit some more in the near future. I don't care two farthings for being received at Court, and you do care for me, so what is the problem?"

Letty set down her toast and busied herself with the tea service—antique Sevres of course, the colors exactly matching his eyes. Amused curiosity was insupportable. "That was sex, and you know it."

"It was more than sex, and *you* know it."

She did. Even in her relative inexperience, she knew what had passed between them had been different. *Special*, God help them both.

"Please, can we not argue about this? I have reasons, David…" What plausible lie could she manufacture? What version of the truth wouldn't have him galloping off to tilt her windmills into submission?

He eyed her teacup, which shook minutely in her hand. "What reasons, Letty?"

"There are things you don't know about me," she said, a safe enough truth. "And if you did, you would not be making this very generous, rash, unthinkable proposal."

She managed a sip of tea, realized she'd forgotten to add sugar, and set it aside.

He looked, if anything, more determined. "Are you married then, Letty?"

"I am not now, nor have I ever been married," she said, adding a silent *thank God*. Oh, there had been pressure on her to marry—very, very considerable pressure.

"Is it that you fear you could not bear me an heir?" he asked, a hint of the physician creeping into his eyes. "My opinion is knowledgeable, Letty, and I can assure you I've found no signs of problems with your reproductive health."

This from the very fellow who'd suggested she might be barren? "Were you *examining* me?"

"Of course not." He added cream and sugar to her tea, then poured himself a cup as well, and his hands shook not at all. "But I notice things, Letty, like the fact that all your parts are working, in the right location, and of the proper dimensions—and I observe with all modesty mine are as well. There is every likelihood we would have children—scads of them, in fact."

Letty rose abruptly, lest she smash her teacup. She could not, could *not* allow her imagination to stray off into thoughts of what it would be like to marry David, to have his child. A single child, much less scads of children.

The sitting-room window overlooked a snowy back garden. All was bright and clean under new-fallen snow and sparkling morning sun, while inside Letty's heart, all was gray, bleak, and dirty.

David's arms slipped around her from behind.

"I do not want to hurt you, but you must see that I am not a suitable wife for you. For the sake of your children, David, you shall put this notion from your head."

She sensed the shock that coursed through him at her words. He would understand, having been raised as a bastard, what scandal could do to a child's world.

"I am disgraced, David," she reminded him. "I have been seen at your establishment by many, many titled gentlemen. I may not have spread my legs for them, but that detail will not resurrect my good name."

Nothing would resurrect her good name, but *his* good name was still hers to protect.

"Are you running away, Letty Banks? Are you saying my attentions were distasteful to you, and that I must let you go now?" She could feel anger boiling through him, but something else, too, something she was loath to hear in his voice—bewilderment.

"I'm not asking you to end our association. I am asking that you drop this notion of marrying me. In fact, I insist on it." She had the power to insist because he'd handed it to her willingly, though now she wished he had not.

"You insist because you have been seen at The Pleasure House, or because of these things I do not know?"

Damn him, his tactical mind, and his gentle, unbreakable embrace. "Both."

He stroked a hand over her hair. "I know more than you think I do, trust me."

David Worthington knew entirely too much about too many things, but not everything.

"Perhaps you do. That doesn't change the fact that sooner or later, you, or our children, would resent me and resent my past. When you marry, your wife must be above reproach in every way."

"My sister, the marchioness, is a bastard," he said, his hand on her hair heartbreakingly gentle. "Heathgate married her, not knowing if it was possible to whitewash that. The truth of Astrid's birth was known to Greymoor when he insisted on making her his countess. Douglas had to face down the formidable Duke of Moreland to win Gwen's hand. We are not saints, Letty."

"And all of those secrets," Letty replied, "are buried beneath the lives of their children. They could explode at any point, and the children would be among those who suffer. *You know this, David.* You've lived with the consequences of parental missteps, allowed them to separate you from your sisters, watched your mother suffer for them. You of all men understand my concern."

Apparently the vicar's daughter could deliver a convincing sermon. David turned her in his arms and held her while an eddy of cold air trickled across her bare feet.

"Stay here today," he said. "I have matters to see to, but they won't take me all day, and I would like it were you to remain here."

His quiet suggestion was a strategic move, as if he knew she would not refuse him this request when she had just refused something of much greater moment. A ruthless streak, indeed…

"And what am I supposed to be doing," she asked, looping her arms around his waist, "while you are off on the King's business?"

"I have a well-stocked library, and you brought your ledgers with you. You can read, you can work on the ledgers, you can keep me company, or you can soak in your bath all morning. Or perhaps you'd like to visit the shops and indulge in a few feminine fripperies. Have you seen the Menagerie?"

"I have not." Nor would she, with him, for seeing the sights was as public as attending the theatre together. "When one's livelihood is in question, touring the sights doesn't rate very high." Then too, she'd no desire to gawk at caged animals, regardless of their species or gender.

And she really should spend time with the ledgers, because something was off about The Pleasure House's accounting.

He kissed her cheek, bringing Letty a whiff of tooth powder and sandalwood. "And when your livelihood wasn't in question?"

"If I ever reached a point where I felt all the work to be done was taken care of, I might like to see Richmond Gardens, but until that day..."

"Your education," David said, kissing her forehead, "has been neglected. Recreation is important, Letty, as is appeasing one's curiosity, and getting out of ruts from time to time. You'll find some of your clothing hanging in the wardrobe in the dressing room. When you're dressed, meet me in the library."

He stepped away and disappeared into the dressing room himself, and Letty had the sense of a fairy tale coming to its necessary, if not ideal, conclusion. With the quickness characteristic of him—when not in bed—David was moving into his day, their interlude in his bedroom taking its place under the heading "recreation," no doubt.

Exactly where it should be.

When she arrived to the library, David was sitting at his big desk, impeccably attired in a gentleman's informal day wear.

"Do you use a valet?"

"On occasion, but seldom in the mornings," David said without looking up from his reading. Letty stood a few feet from him, feeling more than a little out of place.

David held out an arm, still without looking up from his reading. "Come here."

Reluctantly, Letty stepped to his side, much of her joy in the past twenty-four hours draining from her. *Marry me. Come here. Meet me in the library.*

Their interlude hadn't been recreation. *She* was the recreation.

David looked up from his reading and wrapped his arm around Letty's waist.

"This morning, I will be busy. First, Thomas will come and harangue me about various business matters, ordering me to do this and that, and see to the other. He is quite the martinet, is Mr. Jennings. Then I will see to my correspondence until luncheon, which is usually served at one of the clock. I have two social calls to make this afternoon, between which I will ride in the park, but I should be back here by four of the clock to take tea with you."

His recitation of the day's schedule was rapid-fire, his diction precise. He had an empire to run, and run it he did. If he moved at this pace every day, and often stayed late at The Pleasure House, when did he sleep? When did he see his many nieces and nephews? When did he make use of this impressive library?

And why did Letty abruptly feel as if some of the tears aching in her throat should be for him?

"So what, Letty Banks, would you like to do this day?" he asked, pulling her onto his lap.

She'd like to marry him, of course.

"I would like to spend the morning at my house, and do some shopping this afternoon. I also have mending—Monday is for mending—though I can meet you for tea, if you like."

The mending would keep, or Fanny could see to it—the woman had done little enough since making plans to leave Letty's household—though stitching together what had torn was an oddly soothing undertaking.

"You don't want to laze about naked in my chambers all day, on the off chance that I might enjoy your favors rather than the occasional cup of tea?" David nuzzled her breast, but when Letty made no reply, he stopped.

"Letty, I was teasing."

"Were you?"

"Mostly." He rested his brow against the fullness of her breast. "I am new to this… situation, just as you are. Be patient with me, Letty, please?"

Had any man, ever, *asked* for her patience?

"You would have me set up in a tidy little house in a quiet neighborhood. All my bills sent to you, and my schedule always open for your pleasure?"

And what was wrong with her, that she hadn't allowed it?

"If asked a year ago," he replied, sitting back, "I might have said that is exactly what I wanted from a mistress. I wanted a pleasant convenience and value for my coin. But you are not my mistress, are you?"

"No. I am not."

And she could not be his wife, which left a vast, cold desert of unfulfilled wishes and frustrated longing between them.

"I want as much as you are willing to give me, on your terms and at your convenience. This is an affair, Letty, not an arrangement. By your order, it cannot yet be more."

"Yet?"

"You have refused my suit," David said, dropping his arms from around her. "I do not give up easily on my objectives."

"I am not an objective." Not a convenience, not a wife. What on earth was he *doing* with her?

He stroked a hand along her cheek. "You are so serious. We are involved for the sake of mutual pleasure. If you want to spend the day at your house, then we'll have the carriage brought 'round, and I'll see you at four. It needn't be complicated."

"A plain coach." A sop to her dignity. "And I will see you at five." She'd see to her mending, knowing it was a kind of penance imposed by the vicar's daughter on the woman who would never be anybody's wife.

"I'll wait tea for you. And know that you will be distracting me as mightily with your absence as you do with your presence."

He smiled at her, a smile Letty had rarely seen from him: sweet, warm, quietly radiant. It filled her with a sense of well-being, of connection to him, and contentment. This smile wasn't for show, but was instead a genuine reflection of his private joy.

"I'll be thinking of you as well."

And she did think of him as she went about the mundane tasks of keeping her rented house in usable condition, as she took a solitary luncheon in her own kitchen, and as she patrolled the shops, making very few purchases but satisfied with what she'd bought. By the time she returned to her house and took up her mending, she was tired—she and David had kept each other up late the previous night, and he'd been awake early, eager to get to his library and the work that awaited him there.

As David's unmarked coach rumbled through the streets back toward his town house, Letty came to the realization that her emotions—uncertainty of his regard, a sense of being neglected simply because he had other matters to deal with, resentment of his other responsibilities, and unwillingness to surrender her day to him—they were old feelings, familiar to her from her childhood.

At the vicarage, her father and mother had always been available to members of the congregation, regardless of the day or the hour. The vicar's children understood that service to God could not wait for a child's nightmares to be comforted or her artwork to be admired.

How odd, that a viscount's unpaid mistress and a vicar's daughter should have that much in common.

❧

When Letty joined David in the library, he took foolish satisfaction from the fact that she was twelve minutes early.

"I've missed you, Letty-love." And those were foolish words, also true. He drew her against him, wondering if she'd notice he'd doubled the number of roses placed about his house.

"You've had a busy day, I'm sure."

Not the words he'd wanted to hear, though she seemed in no hurry to leave his embrace; but then, "I've decided to accept your proposal" wasn't a likely greeting.

"I had good news today." And because he'd had no one, not even Jennings to share his news with, David kept his arms around Letty, lest she see the glee in his eyes. "A ship I'd thought lost came into port today, six weeks late. The captain was blown off course in a storm, and laid over in some obscure little bay to make repairs."

"That is good news indeed," Letty said, hugging him gently. "You must be especially grateful, having weathered storms at sea, and knowing how dangerous they can be."

"I am." Though ebullience figured into his emotions, too, as did exultation and profound relief. She'd put her finger on a truth: all of his commercial endeavors earned his attention, but the seagoing vessels held a place in his heart that harked back to the terror and wonder of his adolescence. "Are you falling asleep, my dear?"

"I'm enjoying a nice, cozy hug. They come my way with lamentable infrequency."

"I'll speak to your employer about remedying that oversight."

She pulled back and frowned up at him. "You're jesting. I'm never certain with you."

"And you're tired. I kept you up last night." Though he himself did not feel tired, he felt… pleased to see her. "Shall we sit? I don't like the idea that you're uncertain with me."

And yet, he liked that she'd admit as much.

Letty allowed him to walk her over to the sofa, but when they sat, she took a place a good two feet away from him. "My uncertainty isn't something you can address."

"How can you say such a thing when—" A knock interrupted his rejoinder, which was a good thing. Faint heart might not win the fair maid, but lecturing her was likely to send the lady pelting for the door.

David waved off the footman who'd wheeled in the tea cart, and set the tray down on the low table before the hearth. "You'll pour out?"

"Of course. Your staff takes excellent care of you."

The tray sported more than tea fixings and a few pieces of shortbread, David's usual late-afternoon fare. Small sandwiches—no crust—crisp apple slices, and pretty little frosted tea cakes graced the platter—silver, rather than the everyday Sevres.

Downstairs was rallying to the lady's cause—or perhaps to David's.

"They're paid to take good care of me," David said, taking a seat closer to her. "Two sandwiches, please, but I'll hold off on the cakes." The sight of her fixing him tea soothed something in him, not an anxiety so much as a tension.

She passed him a plate, and poured herself a cup, holding it under her nose for a moment before sipping. "Even your tea is difficult to decipher."

"It's a blend. I went on a gunpowder spree for a while, but this suits me better in cold weather. Am I difficult to decipher, Letty?"

"In some things."

She took a sip of her tea, and because her expression suggested she was truly savoring it, David savored the pleasure of watching her.

"When you greeted me, for example," she said, "I was somewhat at a loss."

He'd hugged her, plain and simple, though the pleasure of it had been neither plain nor simple. "*That* was complicated?"

She set her teacup down and picked up a sandwich, but didn't eat it. "You held me, and I could not tell…"

"I was glad to see you." Surely that had been obvious?

The sandwich went back on her plate. "But were you in a state of inchoate arousal? I felt… *you*, but I haven't the experience to know what contours are consistent with—that is, whether even in an unaroused condition, a man might be…"

David had never had occasion to study a woman's blush so minutely. Color rose up Letty's neck and washed over her features and even her ears.

"Letty, would you oblige me for a moment?"

"Of course."

He drew her to her feet and wrapped his arms around her, bringing her flush against his body. "I'm not now aroused. This is what I feel like when I'm merely glad to see you and not anticipating erotic pleasure. Any more questions?"

She ducked her heated face against his neck. "A madam would have known. Any woman of experience would have known."

A wife would have known, at least by the end of the first week of marriage.

"Not unless she and I were regular partners." He didn't turn loose of her, but rather, nuzzled her ear. "For the past year, I have found myself possessed of significant self-restraint where the ladies are concerned, a nearly alarming amount of self-restraint. If you need to sleep tonight, then sleep you shall."

He allowed her to resume her place on the sofa, though the source of her upset was... endearing. Touching, even, and a bit silly. Men could not tell if women were aroused under any but the most intimate circumstances, and yet, the species survived.

She passed him his plate, which still sported a sandwich and, now, a single tea cake. "You've been self-restrained with women or indifferent?"

A bite of sandwich allowed him a moment to ponder the distinction. "At some point, excesses of self-restraint can feel like indifference." Or boredom?

Letty's blush faded, though she still didn't pick up her plate. "Caution, then. After your sister nearly died delivering twins, you became cautious. Would you like more tea?"

He held out his cup, and yet, Letty had served him another insight: Felicity's harrowing delivery of the twins *had* affected him, and not in any positive sense.

"Eat, Letty-love. I didn't tell you about the emeralds."

She took a nibble of her sandwich, and even that— the plainest food David's kitchen could muster— seemed to please her tremendously. This cozy tea tray was different from the first one they'd shared, and yet, not different enough.

"What emeralds?"

"If my ships are traversing the tropics, I send them out with extra stores of netting."

She paused between bites. "And you will tell me why?"

"Infants, in particular, seem to do better if their beds are under netting. They get fewer fevers, and that is a profound advantage—it also keep the mosquitoes away."

The library had never struck him as a cozy room, but rather, as the place he worked. Books were found here, and a sizable desk, upon which sat the largest wax jack in the house. The walls held art—art was supposed to go on walls—but the space had had no sense of… haven to it, until Letty had served him tea here.

"What has the netting to do with… emeralds, did you say?"

She was more concerned with the tea tray than with jewels, and more concerned with his day than the tea tray.

What man wouldn't love—

David jammed the tea cake into his mouth, knowing it was chocolate and raspberry, not tasting either flavor.

Something about some gems…

"Emeralds, a bag of emeralds, and they appear to be excellent quality. My captain left some netting behind at this obscure little bay, as a token of his thanks for the hospitality. Apparently, it's the custom in that region to repay a token with a token."

"And your token was a bag of emeralds?"

"Enough to make every tar on that ship comfortable into a ripe old age."

She dusted crumbs from her fingers, poured herself a second cup of tea, and studied him. "You enjoyed the practice of medicine, didn't you?"

The human body, man might eventually understand; the mind of woman, never. "How do you reach that conclusion?"

Letty passed him a second tea cake and kissed his cheek. "Your secret is safe with me, David. I saw you with Portia, and I can promise you, there isn't another ship owner in all the realm who's sending his ships out with extra stores of netting for purposes of goodwill with the locals. Emeralds are worth more than rubies, aren't they?"

"More, even, than diamonds." He munched his second tea cake, sweetness and a hint of lemon gracing his tongue. Her question brought to mind a line from Proverbs: *She is more precious than rubies: and all the things thou canst desire are not to be compared unto her.*

"Would you like another sandwich?"

"No, thank you." He wanted simply to sit with her as the day slid into darkness, to bask in her company, and that would not do. "If you don't object, I have reading to do. You're welcome to grab a nap while I finish up down here."

"And then I won't be able to sleep tonight," she

said, pushing the tea tray to the side. "Do your reading. I've brought work."

Because he employed a number of fallen women, David could conclude with some confidence that not another such lady in all of London would turn to work and tell him to get back to his reading. Letty's counterparts at The Pleasure House would have pouted, flounced, fumed, tantrumed, and otherwise extracted vengeance for a man's neglect.

Letty produced a cloth bag—she'd brought it in with her apparently, and he had been too busy greeting her to notice.

Too busy hugging her.

He ran his hand over a patchwork of blue and brown velvet. "Pretty bag."

"You see here the mortal remains of the curtains in my father's study," she said, drawing out an embroidery hoop. "Sun is hard on velvet, but few fabrics will check a draft or a sunbeam as effectively."

Velvet blocked air and light, in other words, and she'd kept a version of those curtains as a memento. Her stitchery, by contrast, was full of colors.

"My mother used to embroider flowers on everything," David said, though he'd forgotten this about her. "Handkerchiefs, pillowcases, my shirts. Her flowers were not as delicate as yours." He touched a rose that shimmered as if illuminated by real sunbeams. "Will you embroider a handkerchief for me?"

She poked the needle up in the middle of a pale pink bud, gilding its edges with golden thread. "Of course. Is your mother's love of flowers the reason you keep flowers here in your house?"

Letty had bent her head near her hoop, and she drew the needle up and down, up and down, in a rhythm so fundamentally feminine David might have been watching a Renaissance tapestry come to life. When he didn't answer her question, she paused and studied her initial efforts.

"I thought you had reading to do?"

"I do."

And yet even when David moved to his desk and picked up his pamphlet, he merely held it and watched her making tiny stitches with golden thread.

Letty Banks kept handing him pieces of himself, little insights, small appreciations, connections that he, in his headlong, self-important sprint through life had missed. Of course the flowers were a tribute to his mother; of course he had enjoyed the practice of medicine; of course Felicity's difficult delivery had affected him deeply...

"I want to make love to you," he said quietly. "Now."

Letty looked up at him again, and then, without a word, put down her embroidery hoop and rose. She didn't wait for his escort; instead, she preceded him up the stairs, walked into his bedroom, and took off her shoes and stockings. David followed her a moment later, and taking his cue from her, also started disrobing.

He wasn't particularly aroused, though he was aroused enough. He knew only that he wanted closeness with Letty, significant closeness, and he hadn't any means other than his body to bring this about.

This joining was also erotically unremarkable. Again, they kissed, he mounted her, and then eased into her body. She was ready for him, her body welcoming, her hands roaming his skin with eager curiosity. She moved with him, let him set up a slow, lazy rhythm, and didn't seem to need anything more than him, moving inside her.

He held back, determined to savor the lovemaking, the sound of Letty's sighs, the feel of her mouth on his skin. And he sensed that she comprehended his mood, his need to join with her, for her caresses were easy, her touch light.

She comforted him in a way he hadn't realized he needed comforting.

He'd thought himself beyond infatuations, though surely, this upwelling of tenderness toward her could be only that?

Her caresses became lavishly caring, imbued with tactile lyricism as she stroked him everywhere, as if she were unwilling to lift her hands from his flesh. Her body hummed with the silent pleasure of loving him, of being loved by him, and David's awareness of where he stopped and she started, blurred.

He moved languidly in her, sending a sweet, relaxed pleasure through his body, one slow, deep thrust at time. His hands brushed at her forehead and then into her hair; his mouth brushed over her features. Every caress, every undulation of his hips, every kiss they shared surrendered into her keeping some burden he'd felt but never named.

She cared for him. She said it in her sighs and caresses as clearly as if she'd printed it in *The Times*, but she said it as a woman would. Such tenderness could come only from the heart, from the soul. From the good places…

"Elizabeth," he whispered, moving yet more deeply inside her. "My sweet Elizabeth…"

He uttered her name, the name she'd trusted to him alone, and felt her desire take flight. The pleasure shimmered through her, through him, and back again, in endless cycles of satisfaction and sentiment. He took her with him into a place of light, oneness, and communion, and held her there, as she held him.

Resting on his forearms above her, David gradually returned to awareness of his surroundings. Something numinous had happened to him in Letty's arms. Something indescribable, transcendent, and unprecedented.

Something he was wise enough to accept without attempting to analyze, label, or take apart. But this loving left him feeling as if all of his considerable sexual experience put together was so much folly, compared to what he could share with Elizabeth Temperance Banks.

❧

Letty dragged her hands through the silky abundance of David's hair, his undone queue a metaphor for her emotions.

"You have the sweetest touch," he said, resting his cheek against her shoulder.

"And you are the sweetest man." She turned her face to kiss his cheek. "I never want to leave your bed." Or his embrace, or the ambit of his soft, private smile.

How had she landed in such trouble so quickly?

He inflicted that particular smile on her, the one that made her insides hop about like robins at a puddle on the first spring day. "The sentiment is mutual, my love, but I forgot to set dinner back, so we will shortly be dining on cold victuals if somebody doesn't bestir himself."

My love. That was part of her trouble right there. "Lucky me, I do not qualify as a himself."

"Letty?" He brushed her hair back, and studied her with beautiful, serious eyes. "You are... special to me." He held her gaze for only a moment before leaving the bed and moving to the other room.

"And you are special to me, too," Letty murmured to the empty room.

Special was likely a sophisticated man's way of warning her that he might care for her, but he was not smitten. Prudent people did not become smitten, and for all her mistakes—because of her mistakes—Letty had thought of herself as prudent.

She sat up and found her dressing gown at the foot of the bed. As she crossed the room, she caught a glimpse of herself in David's dressing mirror and was astounded at what she saw.

Her eyes were luminous, her hair falling around her in soft waves. Her skin glowed, and her smile was secret, knowing, and altogether feminine. Her father would have said she looked wicked, and her father would have been wrong.

This is how David sees me? Does he ever see himself as I see him?

For long moments, she regarded the woman in the mirror, amazed at the beauty, grace, and mystery she saw in her reflection.

And observing her folly was David, propped

against the doorjamb and smiling faintly. "Her name is Elizabeth Banks. She is a woman more precious than rubies."

How easily he flirted. "More precious than netting?"

"More precious than a good meal after a fantastic loving," David replied. "But only just, so get in here and let me feed you."

To Letty's amazement, the mood didn't dissipate when they left the bed. It lightened, but the tenderness and regard still hummed between them as they dined in his sitting room. Between one bite of trifle and the next, Letty had the thought: *this is the kind of harmony and closeness in which children should be conceived.*

She choked on her sweet, which provoked David into whacking at her back, then pressing a glass of wine into her hand.

"Stop fussing, Dr. Worthington."

Her form of address startled him into retreating to his side of the table. "My apologies. Perhaps you'd like more wine."

She'd like him beside her throughout the meal, throughout the day, throughout…

"So what," Letty asked between more bites of trifle, "did your treatise have to say about childbed fever?"

He watched her chew the way a new mother watched her firstborn fall asleep on a winter night. "The topic isn't appetizing, Letty."

"I asked because I am curious, but if it will put you off your feed, then I can ask later. Will you finish this for me, please?"

He accepted the remains of her dessert. "The author's suspicion is that the illness is preventable, if proper precautions are taken." Before her dessert was gone, he was summarizing theory and giving examples of practice, complete with proper Latin terms and medical phrases.

"You should hear yourself," Letty said, recalling the bumbling attentions she'd endured from Little Weldon's medical practitioners. "One would think you were rooting for your team at a cricket match, you're so convinced of your position."

David used a tiny spoon to stir the salt in the cellar, as if stirring tea leaves. "I know I get carried away, but people die over this—women die—and when the mother is gone, the newborn stands little chance of surviving without her. Most families don't have the luxury of wet nurses and nannies, and endless supplies of clean nappies. This topic matters."

"It does, and it matters to you."

"I have endless respect," he informed the salt, "for women, you know."

Letty regarded him patiently, rather than mention that owning a brothel might contradict his words, because in some sense, he was speaking the truth.

"When Felicity had such difficulty with the twins, I was tempted to take Heathgate to task," David went on. "A woman doesn't get herself pregnant—not once in recorded history has a woman impregnated herself—and so I blamed him. He and Greymoor have both indicated clearly, though, that while they are capable of restraint, their wives are not keen on it. My sisters are cursed with bravery and faith in life, beyond what I could muster in their circumstances."

How that must bewilder him. "And," Letty said,

taking the salt spoon from him and setting it aside, "they are both carrying again. You are very worried about them." Worse yet, he did not know how to share his worries in any way that would lessen them. Merciful heavens, Letty knew how that felt.

David looked away, toward the fire blazing merrily in the hearth. "Felicity especially, though Astrid, being the more diminutive, could also have difficulties."

"So who is attending them?"

He turned a thoughtful gaze on her. "I don't know."

"I'd find out, if I were you." Letty helped herself to a spoonful of the remaining trifle. "If you aren't satisfied, then suggest someone you have faith in. This is too important, David, and your family looks to you for guidance in this area. So guide them."

"As simple as that?"

He'd lost a wife and child; he probably hadn't shared that with his family either. "It is simple," she admonished him as she passed him a spoonful of dessert. "You know what you suffered when your sister had difficulties. Imagine what her husband and children would suffer were she to die. They will listen to you, David, and you are in a position to choose more wisely than they can."

"And when"—he took the bite from the spoon Letty held—"did you become an expert on me and my abilities?"

Letty put the empty spoon down. "You chose to read a medical treatise rather than *nap* with me."

"I'll talk to Heathgate," David said, "and Greymoor, and Amery."

Nine

FOUR WEEKS INTO HIS AFFAIR WITH LETTY BANKS, David had come to dread Tuesday mornings. On Mondays, Letty would do her accounts—muttering all the while that something was off—or read in the library while David tended to correspondence. If she had errands to run, he'd take her about in the coach, bringing his letters with him so he might read while she shopped. And while desire was ever present for David, the first firestorm of lust had burned down to pleasures that could be paced, savored, and enjoyed.

As always, on Tuesday mornings, David made slow, sweet love with Letty in that dark, quiet hour before they rose.

"Do you fence today?" Letty asked, her fingers drifting through David's hair.

"At ten, and I'm to meet Greymoor, Heathgate, and Amery for luncheon."

"You should enjoy that." She caressed his ears, a touch he particularly enjoyed. "You haven't seen them for some time."

She would never accuse him, never ask a difficult

question directly, and yet David knew exactly where the conversation was heading.

He lifted himself away from her, disentangling their bodies. "I have neglected my family." And because he could not face her as he made that admission, David rose from the bed and busied himself with the sheath he'd used, only to find the damn thing had a small tear near the tip.

"Then you must make time for them," Letty replied as he washed off with cold water. "Though as to that, David, they don't seem to find much time to check in on you."

She chided in hints and innuendo, and he hated it. "They are avoiding me."

"I see."

"What do you see, Letty-love?" He tossed the sheath onto the hearth, where it crackled, then smoked, then burned.

"David, you need not reserve your weekends for me. You love your family, and I'm sure they miss you."

But I love you too.

The sheath turned to ash, and David returned to the bed, arranging himself over his Puritan mistress who wasn't his mistress or his Puritan. "Why won't you marry me?"

Beneath him, she shrank away. Not a physical withdrawal, for in fact she lay still, but every other part of her went away from him.

"David, not now."

"Did you honestly think I wouldn't ask again? I want to marry you, to sleep with you every night, not merely twice a week. I want our children to be legitimate. I want to raise them with you, not visit on birthdays or Yuletide, assuming I can sneak away from my other obligations. I want to take you out on my arm. I want my family to love you as much as I do. I do not think"—he dropped his forehead to hers—"that I am asking too much, to have the woman I love for my wife, and devote the remaining years of my life to her happiness."

The woman I love... Oh, he was in for it now.

Letty jerked silently under him, an odd hitching of her body, as if he'd slapped her. He gathered her in his arms and rolled them so she was sprawled on his chest, an embodiment of the weight his heart carried everywhere of late. "I am so sorry. Don't cry, Letty, please don't cry…"

She did cry. As he rocked her and soothed and crooned and comforted, Letty cried as if she'd lost her best friend, which was both disturbing and frustrating, because David could not fathom her stubbornness.

He hurt for her, and he hurt for himself, for the future he wanted to share with her that she rejected, again, and for no reason. When she lay quiet in his arms, he put the question to her.

"Can you at least tell me why, Letty?" Had he ever held a woman this closely and felt her struggling this hard to keep him at a distance?

"You know how much you love your nieces and nephews? How you dote on them all, remember their birthdays, miss them?"

"Yes." Even Jennings had their birthdays memorized.

"I love children that much too."

This was apparently all the reason she would give

him, and when they parted that morning, David tried to tell himself that all couples went through rough patches and spats, that not every weekend could be sunshine and roses, that time could heal many problems.

But his renewed proposal had opened a breach between them, and he knew it.

※

"Good evening, sir." Letty smiled and curtsied at the gentleman who'd just swept in the front door. "Welcome to The Pleasure House." Though he looked vaguely familiar, Letty was certain she hadn't seen him before. He was tall, with damp reddish-brown hair, green eyes, and features that would be handsome were they not scowling so fiercely.

"It is decidedly not a good evening," he bit out, diction more crisp than the night air. "I am looking for Mrs. Letitia Banks."

"You have found her," Letty said, keeping her smile in place. "And what may I do for you?"

"You will please fetch Lord Valentine Windham to me," the man said, slapping his gloves against a muscular thigh. "I can hear him playing the piano, so don't attempt to dissemble and tell me he's not on the premises."

The fellow was big, agitated, and rude.

"If you will follow me to my office, we can summon Lord Valentine to attend you there."

He looked like he wanted to argue, so Letty marched off in the direction of the servants' passage that would spare her grouchy guest a trip through the parlors. She left him pacing her sitting room while she ordered tea, brandy, and sustenance.

"Mrs. Banks," her visitor growled, "I do not have time to observe the niceties. If you will please fetch Lord Valentine?"

"And your business with him would be?"

"Personal."

The food and drink arrived, and rather than allow her footman to gawk, Letty took the tray at the door and sent him off in search of reinforcements.

"Lord Valentine will join us when he has completed the sonata he is playing. He's on the slow movement, so it shouldn't be that much longer."

"Oh, for God's sake, if it's that damned Schubert, it could go on another half hour or more."

"Then you have time to eat something and enjoy a hot cup of tea." Though Letty's visitor looked like he'd rather be smashing the parlor furniture over Lord Valentine's head.

"Mrs. Banks, when my father may be dying, I do not have time for tea and crumpets." He ran his hand through damp chestnut hair in a gesture reminiscent of Lord Valentine.

The puzzle pieces snapped together.

"Lord Westhaven," she said gently, "particularly if your father is dying, you need to be mindful of your own care. Eat, please, and your brother will be here soon enough."

He eyed the door, and looked for one moment as if he might go storming through the house, grab his errant brother by the scruff of the neck, and haul him bodily into the night.

And wouldn't the gossips have a holiday then?

"No one saw you come in," Letty said, for Lord Valentine had never described this brother as anything less than hopelessly proper. "Nobody except Watkins, and he is very, very discreet."

"Watkins?"

"My head footman. How do you like your tea?"

"Strong, plenty of cream and sugar," Westhaven said, managing to sound peevish about even this admission.

Letty held out a hand. "Give me your cape. There's a fire going in the next room as well, and we can at least start on drying you out."

When he'd surrendered his sodden cape—a sumptuous black garment woven of lambs' wool—Letty handed him a mug, not a delicate little cup, but a mug, of hot tea.

"You might as well eat," she said when she'd dealt with his cape. "Your brother will be here shortly, and the food is good."

He gave her a curious look, and picked up the bowl and spoon. "You aren't joining me?" he asked, taking a seat before her hearth.

"It's a little late for manners, your lordship. I'm sorry your father is ill."

"God, so am I," he said, sounding not at all imperious. "This is good." In the ensuing minutes, the soup disappeared, as did bread, butter, cheese, and slices of pear.

"Shall I ring for more?"

"No, thank you." He sat back, having left not one scrap of food on the plate. He was a ducal heir—a largish, restless ducal heir, for pity's sake—but he ate as if nobody fed him regularly.

"Has he been unwell for long?" Letty asked, refilling Westhaven's mug of tea.

"No." Westhaven watched her hands, something in his appraisal male without being disrespectful. "Moreland is hunt mad, and because winter was late this year, he thought to get in one more week with the hounds before the ground softened. A chest cold became lung fever, and he isn't rallying. The physicians have been bleeding him regularly, but I see no improvement."

And clearly, Westhaven wanted desperately for his father to rally. "If he dies, you are left with the dukedom."

"And may God help me," Westhaven muttered, scrubbing a hand over his face.

"Letty?" David's voice cut in softly from the door. "Have you a visitor?"

She hadn't seen David in days, and the mere sound of his voice set her insides fluttering. He'd spent the previous weekend with his sisters, and had left Letty to her own devices since. They'd kept in touch by writing notes, though Letty was trying hard to let something unspeakably precious die.

David came to stand beside her, which was telling, when a duke's son lounged by the hearth.

"Lord Westhaven awaits his brother," Letty explained. "There is illness in the family, and Lord Valentine is needed."

"Not the duchess, I hope?" David said.

"His Grace," Westhaven replied. "Lung fever, and as stubborn as Moreland is, he isn't getting any better."

"Who attends him?" David's hand had slipped into Letty's, while she stood beside him, relishing the small contact and wishing ducal heirs to perdition.

"Perry, assisted by Stephens," Westhaven replied wearily. "They are underfoot constantly."

"And utterly useless," David shot back. "They will bleed him to death, Westhaven. Get rid of them, or at least forbid any more bloodletting."

"They are his personal physicians. I couldn't get rid of them if I tried." Which must have been brutally frustrating for a man so taken with his own consequence.

"Then try harder, unless you crave the dukedom that badly."

"That's the last thing I want."

David left Letty's side to rifle her escritoire. He scrawled something on a piece of paper and shoved it at Westhaven. "These men are competent. They won't talk to your mother like she's three years old, they won't let your father bully them, and they will offer effective treatment. Other than bleeding him, what are Perry and Stephens doing?"

"Drinking vast amounts of brandy, cluttering up the sickroom." Westhaven helped himself to a third cup of tea, then offered Letty a look that was probably the ducal version of sheepish. "They mutter about humors and vapors and such, but I haven't really seen them *do* anything."

"The congestion should be treated with steam and poultices," David said, making more notes. "The inflammation and pain with willow bark tea. Use laudanum sparingly, and only if he isn't getting any rest, and for God's sake, keep offering him food and drink."

"Westhaven?" Lord Valentine Windham stood in the doorway, looking handsome and bewildered. "What on earth could bring you to a brothel?"

"His Grace," Westhaven said, draining his mug of tea. "Moreland has taken a turn for the worse. I thought you would want to know."

"Of course I want to know, and might I say, you look like hell yourself."

"Valentine," Westhaven growled, one fist going to a hip. "I did not jeopardize my own health and that of my horse for the privilege of trading insults—"

"Now, children," David interjected, "you have more important things to do than scrap in front of the neighbors. My coach and team are waiting in the mews, and you, Westhaven, may borrow my cloak." He swept it from his shoulders and settled it around Westhaven's shoulders in an oddly fraternal gesture. "It's pouring out there, and cold as Hades. Watkins!"

The footman came on the run, then left to fetch Lord Valentine's cloak as well.

"Letty." David turned a smile on her that featured a number of perfect teeth. "Have we any of the medicinal stuff on hand?"

"Of course." She left the room, knowing full well David was being more than hospitable to a pair of ducal offspring. He'd conjured this errand to give him privacy with the Windham brothers, though Letty was at a loss to fathom why.

❦

David turned back to his guests in time to see Westhaven's gaze following Letty's retreating figure, and the poor sod wasn't even subtle about it.

"That," Westhaven said pensively, "is one particularly fine woman. She has…"

"Grace," Lord Valentine said wistfully.

"Not only grace," his brother mused. "It's more—"

"It's more," David said, "that she's spoken for, and you can't have her." Westhaven would never stoop to the company of a woman who wasn't at least nominally associated with the peerage, in any case—would he?

"At least for now," Westhaven concluded.

They were very civilly glaring at each other when Letty returned moments later with two silver flasks and Windham's coat. Oblivious to the undercurrents, she handed the brandy to David and held up the cloak for Lord Val, who slipped into it, buttoned up, and tucked a brandy flask in the inside pocket.

David handed Westhaven the second flask. "You will heed my advice regarding your father?"

"I will talk to Her Grace first, but I will be blunt. And as for the other topic..." He paused and studied the silver flask before slipping it into a pocket of David's borrowed cape. "The word I was searching for was *gentility*, gentility deserving of far more than this."

Westhaven might be overly impressed with himself, a dull stick, and duty bound to the exclusion of anything resembling fun, but the blasted man wasn't wrong.

"No argument there," David said. "Watkins, see their lordships to the porte cochere."

Lest one of them come sneaking back to make calf eyes at David's... madam.

David closed the door and turned to the lady. "Mrs. Banks, I am stranded here for the nonce. Have you dined?"

And have you missed me as much as I've missed you?

"I have not had supper," Letty said, smiling at him *pleasantly*. And how David hated that smile, for she used it on every patron to cross the threshold. "It is good to see you again."

"And you." Good and awful. "You look tired, Letty. Have things here been that busy?"

And so they dined together, talking about the business, about ledgers that didn't balance, about how the suspicious expenditures came from the kitchen, which made the matter complicated. David spoke of his visit with his sisters and their families, about the never-ending rain that had replaced the never-ending snow, and finally about nothing at all.

"The coach should be returning shortly." David crossed his utensils over his plate. "I'll see how things go in the parlors, then be on my way."

Letty folded her serviette in tidy quarters by her plate. "You are welcome to stay here tonight."

He'd never slept at this establishment, hadn't felt he had the right. "Is that what you want, Letty?"

Now her wineglass had to be lined up two inches from her plate and serviette, both. "It is who I want."

"And you're who I want, but this is not how I want you."

She clutched the serviette in a tight ball. "David…"

"Pax, Letty." He smoothed his fingers over her knuckles, needing any touch he could have from her. "I apologize. I will stay with you and be glad of your company."

Before David permitted himself what Letty offered, he made the rounds in the front rooms, pausing to chat with almost every patron and flirt with most of the ladies. He found his way back to Letty's office after midnight, coming upon her curled on the fainting couch, fast asleep. Silently, he removed his coat, cravat, and cuff links, regarding Letty critically as he did.

She had lost flesh, and she had been too slender to begin with. Faint bruises shadowed her eyes, and when he'd joined her earlier, she'd held his hand almost desperately. While visiting his sisters, David had tried to reason through his situation with Letty, to no avail. Quite simply, he could not force her to marry him.

And yet their brief separation had been hard on her, if her appearance was any indication. He'd sent her several notes, to which she'd replied, though the contents had been business related. The only personal aspect to them had been that Letty signed hers with an *E*, something only David would have understood.

"Sweetheart?" He sat at Letty's hip and kissed her forehead, but she didn't stir. "Letty?"

Still no response.

David crossed into the bedroom, turned down the covers, stoked and screened the fire, ran the warmer over every corner of the sheets and pillows, then returned to his sleeping beauty.

"Up you go, love," he whispered as he lifted her in his arms and carried her to the bed. She stirred, but didn't even open her eyes until David sat her on the bed and bent her forward so he could unhook her dress.

"You stayed," she murmured. "I thought you'd left."

Had she wanted him to go?

"Hush. Let's get you into bed." It was scant effort

to pull off her dress and stays and untie her chemise. When she was naked and curled under the covers, David took off his clothes, locked the door, and climbed in beside her.

He wrapped himself around her, which provoked a soft sigh as Letty linked her fingers through his. Otherwise, she didn't move.

As Letty slipped back into slumber, David felt… bereft rather than sexually frustrated. He'd gone about his evening anticipating intimacies with Letty, and now…

Aroused as he was, it didn't seem right to impose on her. He'd tried to stay away from her, to get his thoughts in order, to see if he even *could* stay away from her, and ten days later, his thoughts were not in order, and he'd proven nothing.

As he was drifting off, Letty shifted, and then he was gently pushed onto his back. She settled herself on top of him, her breasts pressed to his chest, her sex caressing his cock with a slow, rocking glide of her hips. She brought him patiently back to full arousal, and then slipped her body over him, shallowly at first, then to a deeper penetration.

"I have missed you so," Letty murmured against his throat.

For David, almost lost to sleep, the loving was dream-like, a languid, sweet joining in the warm, silent darkness. On and on, Letty loved him, stroked him with her body, kissed him, and let her hands wander over his chest, neck, face, and arms. Pleasure stole upon him in delicate, shimmering increments, and then a trickle turned into a quiet, relentless torrent of erotic satisfaction.

As the pleasure ebbed, David held Letty close, his hands tracing patterns on her back.

She was crying again, her tears wetting his chest. He had been cruel to create a separation without discussing it with her, and she was obviously close to exhaustion.

"It it's any comfort," he murmured, "I haven't been sleeping either, and I've started at least a dozen letters to you each day. I make art of your name on my blotter, and wonder what you're doing at each moment of the day and night. I long for you when we're apart, and when we're together, Letty…"

She kissed him to silence.

"When we're together," she said, "I am so full of feelings that I don't know where to start should I try to express them, and I want to touch you and touch you and touch you…"

"And touch you," David concluded. "Letty, it can't go on like this."

"I know. David, I know."

He let her drift back to sleep, their limbs entwined, still no closer to a solution than they had been weeks ago, but more heartsore than he could ever recall being.

And yet he suspected his suffering was nothing compared to Letty's.

❧

"I've become pathetic," David said, offering the short version of events.

"You?" Douglas Allen, Viscount Amery, countered. "My role model for all matters involving savoir faire and grace under fire?"

"I've asked Letty Banks to marry me, Douglas. If

you tell my sisters or their spouses, I will denounce you in public." They were in the stables at Douglas's new property, saddling up for a ride about the grounds, so Douglas might show off his land.

"And how does proposing make you pathetic?" Douglas asked, patting the shoulder of a sturdy bay gelding.

"She turned me down." David rested an arm across his mare's broad rump, though it would mean a crop of gray horse hairs adorned his fine wool riding jacket. "More than once."

The sturdy bay investigated his master's left breeches pocket. "It's a lady's prerogative." Douglas produced a bit of carrot for his horse. "We ask, they decide. If they say yes, they legally become our property. It behooves a woman to be choosy, I should think."

A lady. Douglas knew Letty was a lady; no one had had to tell him. "Spoken like the father of a six-year-old daughter." Also like an honest friend.

"Which daughter, thank God, is not in love with anybody other than Sir George," Douglas said, referring to the pony Rose's ducal grandfather had given her. "But you, I think, are in love with Mrs. Banks— need I say, I told you so?—which means we must ask if she is in love with you."

Yes, we must, at least a hundred times a day, and more often at night.

"She doesn't say," David replied, hefting a saddle onto his horse. "But Douglas—"

"Sometimes," Douglas interrupted, which was fortunate for David's tattered dignity, "a woman expresses herself without using words."

"Letty can be very articulate without saying a thing. She cares for me, and I almost think if she didn't, she'd have married me."

"You are not going to accept that she simply doesn't love you," Douglas concluded, feeding his horse a second treat. "Your instincts, which are legendarily canny, tell you otherwise. While my own are nowhere near so reliable, I note that you seem to be in much the same position I was with Guinevere."

"How so?" David asked as he fastened the girth.

A third bite of carrot was crunched out of existence. "I proposed to her, knowing we cared for each other, and she turned me down. Her refusal did not comport with her expressed sentiments regarding me; ergo, it wasn't that she wouldn't marry me, it was that she *could* not."

Ergo? A syllogism of some sort. David's heart was breaking, and Douglas was spouting logic. "Mrs. Banks, despite her title, is not married."

"Do you know that for a certainty?" Douglas snugged up the girth on his gelding and ran the stirrup irons down the leathers.

"I have only Letty's word regarding her unwed state."

"How much do you know about her?" Douglas asked as he slipped a bit into his horse's mouth.

I know I love her, which ought to be all that matters. "Not nearly enough. I know her real name is Elizabeth Temperance Banks, she was raised as the daughter of a dogmatic, humorless vicar, and her mother died before she came of age. She came to London after a curate dishonored her. When she refused him further favors, he confessed their sins to her father, making her situation at home intolerable."

"Came to London from where?" Douglas asked, fastening the bridle straps. "Raised the daughter of whom, whose living was provided how, and to what extent was she truly dishonored, or was she guilty of breach of promise? Or promiscuity? And where is the evil curate now? Wasn't it you who told me good decisions are based on good information? How can you decide your next steps when you have so few facts to predicate your future upon?"

David petted his mare when he wanted to launch himself fists first at his best friend. "How does Gwen tolerate being married to a man who has an abacus where his heart should be?"

"She loves me," Douglas said without a hint of arrogance, "and that abacus is part of what will make this property prosperous, eventually. Guinevere claims I'm also quite the passionate fellow under appropriate circumstances, though the woman is given to occasional flights on certain topics."

"Of course you are, and Gwen is a very appropriate circumstance, which is why a blessed event is in the offing, less than nine months after the wedding."

Douglas didn't exactly smile, but the humor in his eyes was smug as he swung up onto his horse.

As they rode out through the muddy, greening fields, Douglas's words stuck with David. What did he *know* of Letty? Douglas prattled on about the land, about Gwen's plans to run it jointly with the adjacent property, Enfield, which was owned by Greymoor.

"What do we hear about Rose's grandpapa?" David asked as they turned back toward the stables.

"That His Grace was damned lucky," Douglas replied.

"Moreland is tough, but from what Lord Valentine told Guinevere, the duke had been bled nearly dry by those quacks attending him. He's still recovering, albeit slowly. The duchess is insistent that he give up riding to hounds, and he's adamant that he won't."

Oh, to be able to insist on anything with Letty. "If Westhaven sells the hunting box, then the question is all but moot."

"The duke has any number of cronies owing him favors, in Parliament and otherwise. He can cadge a mount for a week in the shires," Douglas replied. "And I almost wish he would. Guinevere purely hates him for trying to keep us apart. I can't say I blame her."

"How did you manage it, Douglas? When you thought there was no hope at all—what sustained you?"

Douglas leaned low over his horse's neck to duck beneath a branch of oak just leafing out. "What sustained me when I feared losing the love of my life? I struggle to answer you. I suppose on one level it's a kind of religious conviction, a sense that a just God would not permit any other outcome than the one I felt myself born for. Guinevere was meant for me, and I for her. I could not accept any other reality, and would not even try."

"So it was stubbornness?"

"In part," Douglas allowed, pausing while David ducked the same sturdy branch. "A stubborn belief that we were meant to be together, not so much because that was the easy option, but because I would not survive any other. I suppose one might term it sheer animal desperation."

And how typical of Douglas, that he could discuss such a notion calmly.

"That concept has the ring of authenticity. When Letty turns me down, citing the need for my viscountess to have a spotless reputation, then what I feel is sheer animal desperation to convince her otherwise."

Douglas halted his horse outside the stable and remained in the saddle rather than dismount.

"You have finally fallen, my friend," he said gently, "and as Guinevere has predicted, you have fallen very hard indeed. So it might interest you to know that the housekeeper we hired from Mrs. Banks's household has received at least three letters while in our employ, and every one has been posted from a place called Little Weldon, Oxfordshire."

Had they not been mounted, David would have hugged his friend. "Douglas, you are a prince among abacuses. Now, shall we go up to the house so that I might flirt with Rose, annoy Gwen, and admire her great, gravid dimensions?"

Douglas swung off his horse. "My wife is a sylph, Fairly. A wraith, a delicate creature whose husband will blacken your eyes if you so much as mention words like *gravid* in her presence."

David slung an arm across Douglas's shoulders. "Getting cranky, is she? Can't stand to lie on her back for even five minutes? Ducking out to use the chamber pot every time you turn around?"

"And sending me murderous glares all the while," Douglas said. "Heathgate claims it will all settle down in the last month, but we have a way to go yet before I can test his theory."

Douglas was not one to worry needlessly, and yet, he was worried. "Honestly, Douglas, how is

Gwen? Are her feet or ankles swollen? Can she eat and drink normally? Is she inordinately vertiginous, has she fainted?"

Douglas's steps slowed, as if what awaited him at the house was not entirely a cheering prospect. "Physically, Guinevere seems hale, but she is frightened, and while the fellows you recommended are reassuring and competent, they are two hours away, and they are not you."

"I deserved that," David said as they gained the back terrace. Pots of daffodils lent a note of cheer, though they thrived only because the location was sheltered.

Douglas snapped off a single bloom, then a second, very likely one for Rose and one for Gwen. "Guinevere trusts me, you, Greymoor, and Heathgate, but the idea of having some strange fellow attend her has no appeal. She dreads the thought of giving birth." Douglas stopped outside the back door. "I would do it for her if I could."

This was Douglas's version of love, of being in love, and to David, who'd brought children into the world—and seen some of them leave shortly thereafter—it was true love, indeed. "Wait to make that offer until you see what the ordeal consists of."

"I remember my mother," Douglas said, looking haunted, "screaming for hours when Henry was born. My father went to his club, and Herbert and I were left in the nursery to manage as best we could."

"I'll talk to Gwen," David said slowly. "I'm not promising anything, but I will talk to her. You and Gwen and Rose are…"

And abruptly, he couldn't form words as a lump rose in his throat and the wind got in his eyes.

"I know," Douglas said, opening the door and leading the way through. "To us, you are too, and if we have Letty Banks to thank for your willingness to consider using your medical knowledge again, then she is too."

❧

Letty spotted Fanny Newcomb wending her way up the walk toward their favorite tea shop off The Strand. If a new walking dress and a cheery smile were any indication, Fanny was enjoying her position as housekeeper for Viscount Amery's little-used town residence.

"Oh, my dear." Fanny took both of Letty's hands in hers. "How I have missed you this age. You are entirely too thin, Letty, and you have no color at all."

"I'm a bit tired, but it's good to see you. I can't stay long, though. A war was brewing among the chefs in the kitchen when I left."

"Men," Fanny scoffed as they were led to a table. "They must make everything a battle. What a body was thinking to hire not one but three men for the same kitchen is beyond me. You be careful, my dear, lest you be caught up in the affray."

"I am careful. I have no authority regarding the business of the kitchen. I am merely a diplomatic presence." And that was thanks only to a vicarage upbringing, oddly enough.

Fanny tugged off a pair of crocheted gloves—also new—the same shade as her green walking dress. "Your viscount should be the one knocking heads and enforcing order, though he doesn't seem the kind to get his hands dirty."

Letty saw an image of David's hand, covered with Portia's blood.

"He isn't my viscount, Fanny, but you're right: he enforces order by lifting an eyebrow or making a joke."

Fanny peered at her over the menu. "Do I detect a note of admiration in your voice?"

And was that a new bonnet to go with the new dress and new gloves? Amery must believe in paying his help well, which notion pleased Letty. "I admire whoever is paying my salary, Fanny, particularly when I'm allowed to keep my clothes on into the bargain."

"Hush, my dear. You may be beyond shame, but I am not."

"My apologies," Letty replied in a sheepish whisper. As they placed and then received their orders, the topic shifted to pleasantries, the weather, and the magnificence of London's parks in the spring. Not for the first time, Letty wondered why she continued to keep these weekly appointments with somebody whom she no longer had anything in common with.

What would the Viscountess Amery say about her housekeeper taking tea with a madam? Did Fanny care so little for the goodwill of her employer?

"How much longer do you think you will hold your current position?" Fanny asked, swishing the dregs about in her cup.

And just like that, Letty was grateful for a sympathetic ear. "I don't know. I enjoy much about the position—including the generous wages—but it is not decent employment, and I can't get my mind past that fact." Then too, his lordship was looking to sell the place, and like livestock conveyed with a rural property, the ladies—and Letty—would likely be considered part of that transaction.

"You should get the viscount into your bed," Fanny suggested quietly. "He has the coin, and he's clean. He fancies you, Letty."

Letty stared at her empty cup and wished she'd stayed home. Fanny might be beyond shame, but she wasn't above handing out shameful advice.

"He's a good man, Fanny. A better man than I deserve."

"So don't deserve him," Fanny rejoined, patting Letty's knuckles. "Take his money and lead him a dance or two."

"I'm doing well enough for now, better than I was last year at this time, and without leading anybody any dances. I must be getting back, so I'll leave you until next week."

Fanny slipped on her new gloves and bonnet, said nothing while Letty paid the bill, and parted from her at the corner.

Fanny had been housekeeper at the vicarage for a few years as Letty had grown up. She was a link with home and a familiar face, but Letty couldn't help but feel ashamed when Fanny alluded to leading the viscount in a dance or two. And those remarks, encouraging Letty to find a new protector, to prostitute herself again, always made their way into the conversation, even as Fanny chided Letty on small lapses in propriety.

Next Wednesday, I am going to develop a megrim, and this time I mean it.

Ten

LETTY RETURNED TO HER OFFICE THROUGH THE SIDE entrance off the kitchens, and indeed, pandemonium reigned. Etienne accused Pietro of using his knives, and Manuel insisted that Etienne was poaching on his recipes—as best Letty could tell from the polyglot shouting match that included sufficient quantities of English cursing. Musette's name popped up a time or two—Etienne's "angry little Frenchwoman"—as did the names of several other ladies.

Letty wasted the better part of an hour sorting through the details, smoothing ruffled feathers, and ensuring preparations for the evening were under way. Dealing with kitchen politics in a brothel bore a startling resemblance to parish politics in Oxfordshire.

The evening passed easily enough, the moderating weather ensuring that the parlors were more often full and the ladies kept busy. Letty had become so used to mingling with the patrons that she did so by second nature—also like a parish assembly—even as she kept her eye on the ashtrays in the smoking parlor, the clutter of dirty glasses to be cleared, and the dishes on the buffet to be replenished.

"That," Lord Valentine Windham said, taking a place beside her in the main parlor, "is not an expression of pleasure. My dear, you look positively woebegone."

His green eyes missed little. Letty tried for a smile anyway. "Hello, your lordship. I am lost in thought, and because the hour grows late, a bit tired."

Lost in thoughts of David. Again.

Windham fussed the lace at his cuffs. "The hour is not late for you, Letty Banks. And you've been looking peaked for the past two weeks, if you ask me. Of course, I am not a physician, am I?" The last question was offered in such bland, conversational tones, that Letty abruptly felt very tired, indeed.

"Was there some significance to that remark?"

"You're missing your Lord Fairly," Windham said. "I don't suppose you'd consider finding solace in my arms, would you?"

His grin said he was teasing, though Letty had the uncomfortable sense that perhaps he wasn't *merely* teasing.

"Things run more smoothly when he's here." *She* ran more smoothly. "I spent much of my afternoon listening to three grown men argue—in several languages—over recipes for hollandaise and the sharpness of their knives. They need to know someone takes them seriously, and they would rather that someone be Lord Fairly."

"As would you, I gather?"

Valentine Windham was the Duke of Moreland's son, which might explain why Letty didn't tell him to take his too insightful questions and go make music with them.

"I manage the patrons well enough, and the ladies are comfortable with me. The account books are gradually getting straightened out, and the various merchants accept me adequately."

"But?"

"But we all know I'm not Fairly. And he is the owner." Though David was no more suited to owning a brothel than Letty was to running one.

"Have you considered buying him out?" Lord Valentine asked, casually sipping his drink. "He's grumbled about this place endlessly, and because he must eventually take a wife, he'll someday need to get rid of it."

The observation wasn't unkind, though it was bracingly, painfully honest. "How could I afford to buy him out? I am paid well, but I have obligations. I can put some by, though nowhere near enough to purchase a business as profitable as this."

Windham raised a dark eyebrow, looking very much a duke's son and more like Westhaven's sibling.

"What obligations could you possibly have? Aging parents living in a cave by Hampstead Heath? A crippled, blind sister begging with a tin cup in Greater Mud Puddle? A brother who gambled away the family farm near Cow Crossing Wells?"

Letty gave up on smiling altogether, resenting the mockery a titled man could make of what was reality for too many people. "It's Little Weldon, Oxfordshire, and nothing so dramatic as that. I need my gowns to wear, don't I?"

He leaned two inches closer. "Do you really want me to answer that?"

Sometimes, Letty missed the vicarage. Perhaps that was why she'd ended up in a brothel, because she'd been ungrateful for her upbringing. "I wish you wouldn't do that."

"Do what? Flirt with you? I should think it simply another meaningless exchange in an evening that is filled with them, for you at least."

Letty closed her eyes, fatigue and a howlingly inconvenient case of the weeps dragging at her. A real madam would have known what to say to such comments—or she might have slapped his lordship soundly.

A real madam might, in the alternative, have taken his handsome young lordship to bed and swived the smirk right off his face.

"In the first place," she began, "while the flirtation may be meaningless, *you* are not meaningless. In the second, I am not comfortable flirting in a venue where it is expected that flirting with me could lead to something... more."

"You see my flirting as a renewed attempt to gain your favors?"

"I fear that's what you're about." Or did she hope he was, because then the puzzle of what to do when David lost interest in her would be solved.

"Put your fears to rest," Lord Valentine said, offering her a genuine, if wistful, smile. "I merely want you to know, Letty Banks, that even though Fairly can't seem to pay you sufficient attention, I do enjoy your company."

He laced their fingers, making the gesture more than a drawing-room gallantry. "You have been a friend to me, my dear, and there are few others about whom I could say the same. Please remember that you have a friend, too. Short of calling Fairly out, there's little I wouldn't do, should you ask it. And that includes making you a loan sufficient to buy this place, if that's what you decide you want."

What on earth should she say to that? Fanny Newcomb, who'd known her since birth, encouraged her to further vice, while this lordling offered her a casual fortune out of simple… decency.

"Try not to look surprised." Windham kissed her knuckles. "Much to my father's consternation, I own companies that specialize in the importation of fine musical instruments from the Continent, and manufactories that build pianofortes here in England. Though my social life is sadly impoverished, my personal coffers are not."

"Your offer is generous, also surprising, my lord."

"Think about it," he said, patting her hand and returning it to her. "And now I will take my leave of you, to put yonder fine instrument through its paces once again. Would you like to hear anything particular?"

She would like to hear again that she had a well-placed, wealthy friend—except all of Lord Valentine's wealth and charm might simply be a patient version of pursuit.

"What I like most is when you play without written music, your own compositions that you make up as you go. Such a talent leaves me in awe, your lordship. The beauty you create with your hands is almost too much to bear."

Windham bowed as properly as if he'd met her at a village assembly. "For flattery such as that, I will play for hours."

He would play until he'd exorcised whatever demons were tormenting him, and sometimes he did play for hours. Lord Valentine had an uncanny knack for making the music that suited the hour and the mood of the evening, too. Tonight, he spun a slow, lyrical melody, one that drifted from the treble, to the tenor, accompaniment flowing under, over, and around it as he crossed hands to follow his muse.

Perfect music for putting her in the mood for bed.

A bed she'd rather be sharing, but only with David Worthington.

～

"I didn't know you'd come in." Letty stood by the door, her smile friendly without being *personal*. "Have you had supper?"

"I have," David said, rising from the fainting couch in her office and wrapping his arms around her. Letty hadn't flown across the room to embrace him; she'd hovered by the door, a pleasant, noncommittal greeting in place of the leap of enthusiasm she might have shown him.

He had done this to her, put her on her guard, wary and mistrustful.

"I'm glad you're here," she said, leaning into him and resting her forehead on his shoulder. "So glad."

Something inside David eased. "How was the evening? I confess I'm hiding back here, and I have no intention of leaving the private quarters, Letty."

"You've been hiding a lot lately," Letty said, straightening the folds of his cravat. The gesture was wifely; the observation was pure Letty. "I mean, you haven't been much in evidence here, and your staff is remarking your absence."

His *staff* was indeed remarking something. He dropped his arms, the better to see her eyes when she flayed him with guilt. "Who is giving you trouble?"

Besides her employer.

"Etienne, Manuel, and Pietro went at it in high dudgeon this afternoon and Musette chimed in with various threats of violence." Letty knelt to poke at a perfectly cheery blaze. "There's jealousy afoot, both personal and professional. The ladies could hear them on the third floor, and the footmen were placing bets regarding the likelihood of bloodshed. Somebody in that kitchen is stealing from you, possibly several someones. It grows... tiresome."

"I can believe that," David said, wondering if—should he crouch down beside her—she'd let him tumble her on the hearthrug, and then disapproving of himself heartily for the notion. "You've spared me and Thomas Jennings both the pleasure of attempting to intercede, though I understand it's hardly a chore you enjoy."

"They're fretful, David," Letty said, shifting to sit on the fainting couch, the poker across her knees. "They need to know you appreciate their efforts. And the ladies miss you as well."

He sat beside her, hip to hip, set the poker on the hearth stand, and brought a hand up to gently massage the nape of her neck.

Not because she enjoyed it—though she clearly did—but because the pad of his thumb ached to stroke that soft flesh and to tease the downy hair that escaped her tidy coiffure.

"And what about you, Letty Banks? Do you miss me, too? Or do you more often wish me to perdition these days?"

"I wish you with me," Letty said softly, "and I wish this house full of flirting, drinking, swiving fellows somewhere else."

The good news, and the bad. She wished *herself* elsewhere.

"They are paying your salary, those flirting, drinking, and particularly those swiving fellows." *He* was paying her salary, but the swiving fellows allowed him pretenses to the contrary.

She curled over to lean against his shoulder. "Do you ever think of closing this place?"

No, he did not. Not any longer, because this place of immoral commerce meant he had some connection to her beyond what she allowed him in bed.

"And doing what with the property?" he asked, taking pins from her hair. "The building is almost too big to be a town house, unless, like Devonshire, you have various children, a wife, a mistress, and the ability to manage them all under one roof."

"You could do anything you pleased with the property: sell it, turn it into gentlemen's rooms to let, use it to house some of your businesses. The house is pleasant and pretty enough."

And gentlemen's rooms in a former brothel would have a wonderful cachet. Jennings had made the very same point, damn him. David undid the single thick braid Letty had wound into a coronet, then spread her hair in long, loose skeins down her back.

"I've thought about closing the business, Letty," he

said, trailing his fingers down the silky length of her mahogany tresses. "And then where would the ladies be? I've considered selling the place as well, and the same concern makes me hesitate."

Lately, it made him hesitate. Three months ago, he'd been ready to give the place away.

"You would have to sell it to someone you trusted. Do you suppose Valentine Windham might buy it?"

She had an answer for everything, also beautiful hair, and the most beguiling rosy scent.

"I doubt he has the means, and neither Westhaven nor His Grace would approve." And for the first time, David honestly appreciated old Moreland's propensity for meddling in his children's lives.

"Lord Valentine has the means. Tonight, he offered to lend me the money to buy it from you."

Utter glee at the prospect of shedding the property warred with… terror at the idea that Letty might buy him out. "Are you considering it?"

"I am not."

Relief burned through him at her words, though for the life of him, he ought to sell her the place. Selling the brothel to Letty would accomplish three dearly sought outcomes: First, it would relieve David of the enterprise entirely. Second, it would ensure Letty had financial security for the rest of her life. Third, it would ensure the ladies were well taken care of.

"So you don't want to own this establishment?" Something they had in common. "Why not?"

Letty kissed his jaw. "I never aspired to be a madam."

Oh, *that*.

David shifted so he could undo the hooks on the

back of her dress. "You aspired to eat, to have a roof over your head, to put a little bit by." He swept her hair aside in a slow caress and kissed her nape, and even there, she bore the scent of roses. "I can't say the prospect of years of squabbling chefs, violent altercations among the employees, lecherous young lords, and the rest has great appeal as a steady diet."

He fell silent for a few moments, content to kiss the juncture of her shoulder and neck, and the soft, soft skin between her shoulder blades. Next, he peeled back her dress and rested his forehead on her nape, a man condemned to protect her best interests, such as those might survive in her present situation.

"Letty, you could make enough in five years here to retire outright, if you lived frugally off in the shires. You could be the one selling this business at an enormous profit, and spending the rest of your life in relative peace."

Without him. He wanted to bite her, to hold her in place the way a stallion pinned a mare in season with his teeth.

"Do you want me to buy it?"

She sounded breathless, and that was wonderful, because it meant this awful conversation would soon be over. David pushed her gown from her shoulders and went to work on her chemise and stays.

"What I want," he said, "is not under discussion. If you want this business, I am sure we could come to terms. Why do you wear so many clothes, my love? The hour grows late, and I am on fire for you."

"I wear so many clothes because my employer insists that I be properly attired from the skin out."

She was taunting him with reason, which was most unfair. David pulled her to him, her back to his chest. "I could bend you over this chaise, hoist your skirts, and pleasure you witless with you half undressed. Nobody need shed a single additional piece of clothing."

Though they would, at least temporarily, let this vexing topic drop.

"You could, or you could let me relieve you of every stitch of your fine evening attire, lie naked with me on the big, soft bed in the next room, and spend hours castaway with pleasure."

David swept her hair aside again, let his hand drift up to cup her breast, and brought his lips close to her ear.

"Let's do both."

⤜⤛

"Are you haunting your own establishment?"

Windham posed the question from the piano bench, where he was still quietly plying the keyboard, though the hour neared three in the morning. David paused by the decanter, poured them each a healthy tot of brandy, and brought one glass over to the pianoforte, where he set it on an ornate silver coaster.

"I might be. What of you?"

"Thinking," Windham murmured. "I always do my best thinking when I'm playing through the night."

"You won't be playing through the night here, old man." David sipped his drink and dropped onto the bench beside Windham, so they were shoulder to shoulder, facing opposite directions. "The ladies have all gone to their beds, the staff is nearly done cleaning up, and it's long since time you were toddling off to your own quarters."

"You're kicking me out then?" Windham asked, bringing his music to a gentle cadence. "Letty usually trusts me to see myself out."

"My dear Letty," David said *quite* pleasantly, "is adrift in the arms of Morpheus, so I'll be the one seeing you out."

Rather than get up and take himself off, Windham reached for his drink and took a slow, savoring—taunting?—sip.

"Between the quality of this instrument and the caliber of the liquor served, you make it damned difficult to recall exactly where home is and why one would want to frequent the place."

"Clean linens," David said, wondering where Windham was biding these days. "Solitude. The chair that has conformed itself exquisitely to one's anatomy. One's cat, exactly where one's cat should be. The ability to navigate the premises in complete darkness without bruising one's shins. A comfortable place to become inebriated without having to face the elements at the end of the evening. Need I go on?"

"Gracious God. Is that all home is to you?"

Windham was intent on mischief tonight. Perhaps his father had been bedeviling him—or his mother. Moreland's duchess was not to be underestimated.

David shifted so they were both facing the keyboard. "My home is also the location of my personal business records and various artifacts and curios that have sentimental value. My country seat is entailed with the viscountcy, but a comfortable enough place to visit."

"You are impoverished," Windham said, closing the cover over the keys and caressing the wood with an index finger. "Though your wealth is the envy of your peers."

"I try not to let my peers know the extent of my wealth, but what is home to you, then, if you're so disdainful of my definition?"

He knew better than to ask that question, but somewhere, Letty had had a home, and it hadn't been where she'd kept her personal business records or become cozily drunk of a frigid evening.

Windham's version of thinking meant he opened the cover and ran his left hand over an F-major scale, descending two octaves, then ascending.

"Home is where my late brother Bart taught me how to make a flatulent noise with my armpit," he began. "We laughed so hard we were soon… Well, never mind. Home is where Westhaven will always make time for our sisters' concerns and needs, no matter how tired, distracted, or upset he is with my father's latest misbehavior. Home is where my brother Victor finally succumbed to the peace of death. Home is where those I love most dearly in all the world will always be safe and warm and welcomed."

This recitation required that David finish his drink. "So you are a poet as well as a musician?"

"Letty Banks would be home to you," Windham said quietly. "Night after night, she makes this business of yours what it says it is: a pleasure house, a place where a man can indulge his petty vices, safe from the judging eyes of the world. All the while, she watches for you, hour after hour, and she waits for you. I honestly don't know what makes her more upset: when you join us here, or when you don't."

"Your concern, Lord Valentine, is touching. Are you offering to succeed me in her affections?"

Windham closed the cover and shoved off the piano bench. "Nobody will succeed you in her affections. She will grow old and lonely, and what you've offered her will be all she knows of love, pleasure, or human companionship. The woman loves you, and you are taking more from her than if you'd robbed her blind and left her bleeding in a ditch."

"And would your tirade," David asked, rising as well, "be directed otherwise if you knew I'd repeatedly offered our Letty marriage?"

Even in the flickering candlelight, David could see his companion was astonished.

"I am shocked, not that you would make the offer, but that she would refuse you," Windham said. "I have five sisters and a brace of female cousins. Letty Banks lives for the sight of you."

"I wouldn't go that far," David said, settling into a comfortable chair near the hearth. "She enjoys my company, as I do hers."

As understatements went, that one would round out the evening nicely.

Windham remained standing over him, like some angel of judgment. "She hasn't your ability to mask her feelings. For anyone who knows her, her eyes give away her emotions. You, by contrast, are not much more familiar with her than you are with the other women here, and you've been coming around this place less and less."

"I would do Letty no good whatsoever were I to fawn over her more than is needed to ensure she doesn't suffer unwanted advances."

Silence stretched while David felt a tidal pull from the private apartment at the back of the house, where he'd left Letty in an exhausted, well-loved slumber.

"I wonder," Windham said musingly, "if she has a husband stashed away back in Little Weldon."

Husband? The very word dashed across David's fatigue like cold water.

"Where?" Douglas had said the housekeeper—Mrs. Newcomb—had received letters from Little Weldon, and Letty had said she'd come to London with Mrs. Newcomb.

"Little Weldon, Oxfordshire," Windham said. "I offered to undertake a business arrangement with Mrs. Banks earlier this evening, when she said she had obligations back in Little Weldon that tied up her capital."

"A business arrangement?"

"For God's sake, Fairly, I'm not offering her carte blanche. She'd make a terrible mistress."

"She would?" David asked, bristling for reasons he didn't want to consider. Windham had proved entirely insightful enough for one evening.

"Of course she would," Windham scoffed. "I see that now. She loves too deeply. A little affection, some friendship between a man and his mistress is fine, but Letty Banks is made for loving, not swiving."

The same conclusion David had been hammering his conscience with for weeks.

"For a man who hasn't gone up the front stairs once in all the time you've been bivouacking here," David observed, "you've made a thorough study of matters between men and women."

"I most certainly have not," Windham said, his gaze going to the damned piano the way some men might watch the love of their lives walk away. "At the risk of burdening you with confidences, I understand Letty's demeanor because in certain regards it reflects my own."

"You have obligations back in Little Weldon too?" And would another drink truly be a bad idea?

"Of course not, but I am more comfortable making love than swiving. It's hardly well done of me, and more inconvenient than you can imagine— particularly for a man who is trying to elude parson's mousetrap. But there it is, probably part of my artistic temperament."

Whatever that meant. "Did Letty happen to mention the nature of her obligations in Little Weldon?"

"My love life doesn't fascinate you," Windham said, picking up an empty pink Sevres vase from a spot on the mantel formerly occupied by a porcelain angel. "I am devastated. The only thing I could surmise about Letty's obligations is that they affect her finances. Should you wish to learn more, I suggest you ask her." He set the vase down and aimed an equally curious look at his host.

Who was not half so worth examining as antique porcelain.

"She keeps secrets, Windham, and those secrets are part of why she won't consider my suit."

"Part of why?"

In for a penny... "Neither she nor I care that we would not be welcomed at Court, and I doubt Letty gives a fig for being accepted among the beau monde. A quiet life would, in fact, suit us both. I suspect she is unwilling to marry me mostly because she knows our children may not be received by the best families."

"You will have to convince her then, that being loved is more important than being received," Windham replied. "And unearth her secrets if convincing doesn't work."

Convincing had already failed repeatedly. "Bring the decanter over here, Windham, and have a seat. There's a small task you might be willing to undertake for me. A small task requiring significant discretion."

❧

Cold, wet seaweed wrapped itself around Letty's waist. She'd been to the seacoast only once, and had no idea what seaweed wrapped about one's middle felt like, but this was her dream, so reality was of no moment.

The seaweed gradually warmed and became David's hands, stroking themselves over her breasts, her arms, her back. On and on his hands drifted, caressed, teased, and brought her to arousal. When he slid into her gently from behind, Letty felt her body contracting around him—not a dramatic, earth-shaking cataclysm, but rather a pleasurable greeting between lovers.

David thrust into her, prolonging her pleasure generously, but not attempting to force it to any greater intensity—which he could do and often did. Letty laced her fingers through his where they kneaded the fullness of her breast.

"Missed you."

"Missed you too," David whispered back. "Relax, Letty, and dream on."

She almost could, so undemanding was he. Lately, each night he joined her in bed, his approach was different, as if he'd show her all the pleasures she would miss when they parted. One night, Letty had awakened to find that he was penetrating her body with a jade phallus, and to her shock, she had been on the verge of satisfaction before she'd become aware enough to sense her pleasure came from an *object*. When she had scooted away in indignation, David had seemed bewildered, even hurt.

"I want to make love with *you*," she'd tried to explain.

"There's nobody here except me."

"But you are not inside my body. That *thing* is."

"And what of this thing," David argued, sliding a finger inside her. "Is *this* thing unacceptable to you, Letty? I fail to see the difference between my hand and what is wielded by my hand."

"It isn't a difference you see," Letty said, feeling tears threaten for no definable reason. "It's a difference you feel"—she tapped her chest—"here."

He'd desisted, of course, and given her a very traditional, pleasurable loving, but it had reminded Letty how ill-suited she was to the role of mistress, and how much broader David's experience was than hers. The ever present anxieties—that she bored him, that he would grow tired of her, that she was too difficult, that they simply did not belong together—had undergone considerable growth since that night.

Another time she'd awakened to find her wrists tied to the bedposts. Again, she'd been less than pleased, but she had kept her complaints to herself, and found, in David's hands, restraints could heighten pleasure.

Still another night, David had suggested she might take him in her mouth, and that, she had to admit, had been fascinating, pleasurable, and the fulfillment of some very private daydreams, probably for both of them.

Tonight, it seemed, would be less adventurous. David stroked into her from behind, Letty's head resting on his arm. He took his time and built Letty's arousal slowly. She'd already found pleasure once, however, so her fuse was short.

"Will you come again for me?" The dratted man had somehow divined that Letty liked his naughty talk. "I want to feel you come, Letty. You caught me by surprise the first time."

And because he was never content to torment her with only words, he gently rolled first one nipple then the other between his fingers.

Desire coiled beneath Letty's womb, as well as the same sense of desperation that likely fueled David's sexual devotions.

"Letty, will you answer me?" He slowed his thrusting, as if listening for her response. "Do you want to come again?"

"I do." If she tried to wiggle against him, he'd only tease her more.

"You want me to make you come now?" David asked again, nudging at her with his cock.

"I want you to make me come now," she confirmed, sighing on the penetration. "And hard. So hard I scream for you." *Because I will surely cry for you.*

"I can do that." His tone held approval—he liked it when Letty was demanding, and he liked it better when she was beyond even pleading. He didn't move any more quickly or deeply. He lazed along, all languid patience and slow, soft caresses.

Letty was on the verge of offering him some very clear direction, when he withdrew on a gentle retreat, rolled her to her back, and without warning thrust into her hard, and kept on thrusting. After a startled moment, Letty locked her legs around his waist, got her teeth into his shoulder, and braced herself for an explosion of pleasure.

"Oh, God, *David*... Merciful heavens, *David... David...*"

He was getting worse, in some sense. Letty was nearly certain he hadn't spent—he never did anymore unless he wore a sheath, but what he visited upon her had become much more intense in recent weeks. Unbearably intense, and unbearably precious.

"You kill me," Letty said against his chest when she could talk again. "The pleasure approaches violence, David, and to be honest—"

"Yes, Letty-love?" He was all tenderness again, a placid, golden lion, content to caress her with indulgent gentleness. "The pleasure approaches violence... For me too, you know."

"I am almost afraid of you sometimes. What are you trying to prove in this bed, David?"

He was silent for a long moment, and Letty was

concerned that she might, again, have offended him intimately. His touch didn't change, however, it remained… sweet.

"Maybe I am trying to prove that I am still myself. That I haven't changed for loving you."

Loving her. Letty weathered that blow as best she could, cradled in his arms, his body sheltering hers, even as her heart went howling into an internal wilderness.

"And why would it be such a bad thing to change a bit, to adjust, or grow?"

He kissed her nose, probably to make sure she wasn't crying. "You hoist me on my own petard, Letty, for I see now that when one changes, even for the better, one loses something of one's old self, doesn't one? You tried to make this point with me some time ago, I think."

Letty snuggled the covers up around them, even as David slipped away in some sense that had nothing to do with the physical. "What part of yourself do you think you will lose?"

David extricated himself from her embrace and from her bed, firelight gilding him as he tossed away the sheath and tended to his ablutions. The dimensions he sported confirmed that he had not spent inside her, which Letty took for a consideration toward her, and a form of self-torment for him.

"You do trust me," David said, climbing back into the bed and wrapping his arms around her.

Which in no way answered her question. "I do. In this bed, at least. I trust you more than I trust any other person, you may depend on that."

He lay back, hands laced behind his head, not

touching her because, Letty knew, he had his own issues with trust. "You don't trust me enough."

She thought he'd leave the conversation there, on that sad, if honest, note, but David wasn't finished.

"The part of me I am afraid to lose," he said quietly, "is the part that believes affection between paramours is quite sufficient, and any further degree of entanglement purely a bother. That part of me is a sensible fellow, and he's spared me much heartache."

And that part of him was still trying to make him think he could happily own a brothel.

Letty tucked herself against his side and rested her knee on his hairy, muscular thigh. She remained cuddled next to him, listening to his heart beat, until sleep tugged at her.

"I love you, you know," she murmured long, quiet minutes later. He made no response, assuring her, as his steady heartbeat had, that her words would be held safely in the darkness while her lover slept.

Eleven

"LITTLE WELDON IS A BUCOLIC LITTLE BACKWATER," Valentine Windham reported as Fairly handed him a healthy tot of whiskey. "And the handsome vicar appears to be a saint among men. He was, however, the previous curate, so I'm thinking he's your man— or Letty's man."

"Describe him."

Val lounged back in a comfortable chair near the hearth, thinking the viscount looked decidedly short of sleep.

"Vicar Daniel is about our height, perhaps three-and-thirty years of age," Val said, trying to recall details. "He is well favored, dark-haired, and obviously a gentleman, but his study is that of a scholar as well. He rides a horse Greymoor would enjoy—a big, handsome, athletic beast with a wide streak of mischief— and he has the most extraordinary brown eyes."

Fairly looked up from his desk and stopped trying to fit together some pieces of shattered porcelain. "Extraordinary *how*?"

Valentine searched for more words, frustrated by

an inability to choose accurate terms when describing another man. A gentle lilting tune in A minor came to mind instead, one with a sturdy baritone accompaniment.

"The vicar's eyes are kind," Val said, "or more accurately, compassionate. Kind and understanding together. He's not a fool, but he doesn't judge, either. I gather his predecessor was an old dragon, and Daniel's more humane approach to scripture is much appreciated. The ladies would be cramming into the pews for the pleasure of observing him; the men would like him because he's unpretentious and without airs."

"*You* liked him," Fairly accused, frowning at a small pair of snowy porcelain wings.

"Very much," Val admitted. "I was prepared not to. I wanted not to, in fact."

Fairly hadn't touched his drink, and peered around the confines of a roomy library the way a cit peered around in an art gallery—as if he'd never seen his own books before, never seen a hothouse rose gracing an end table. "What changed your mind about the vicar?"

"That's hard to put a finger on. He apologized for his own untidy study; he suggested that being a vicar's wife is hard on a woman. He rode that damned horse as if it was *fun*, and when I wanted to accuse him of flirting with a lovely widow, all I could observe on his part was simple concern for the woman. I could not find one iota of evidence upon which to suspect he's a seducer of innocents."

Fairly set the wings down on a handkerchief amid what looked like the remains of a shepherdess or an angel, and crossed to the fireplace, brandishing the iron poker like some household halberd. "Seducers are invariably charming and disarming. Did anybody mention Letty?"

"No one. I made a few comments that should have provoked mention, at least of the old vicar's family, when I had my dinner in the common of the local watering hole. I might have caught a few raised eyebrows, an odd glance between the neighbors, nothing of substance. No one had anything to say along those lines but what a good fellow the current man is. Nauseating, really."

"You took three days to determine essentially nothing?"

Determining that Oxfordshire had more than its fair share of pretty widows was not *nothing*.

"The widow suggested the vicar and his missus are disappointed not to have more children, and that their union is not blissful. What union is?"

"Damned if I know," Fairly muttered, surrendering his poker to the hearth stand. "Certainly not my parents', and from what I can gather, not Letty's parents' either."

While Valentine's parents still flirted after thirty years of marriage. On that baffling thought, Val rose. "If you've no further questions for me, I'm off to seek my bed, a hot bath, and some victuals."

"Stay here tonight," Fairly suggested. "It's pouring out there, dark as pitch, and your horse has gone far enough. I keep the first bedroom on the right prepared for guests, because my brothers-in-law will occasionally avail themselves of my hospitality when they're in Town unaccompanied."

"Obliged," Val said, sitting back down and tugging

at his right boot. "And this potation, if I do say so myself, is superior even to what you serve at The Pleasure House."

"It's superior to what Prinny serves himself." And Fairly would know exactly what the regent served his guests. "This is from Heathgate's distillery, his personal reserve. God knows how old it is. He sends over enough to keep on my good side."

"How fare the marchioness and the countess?" Val asked as he wrestled with his second boot.

"My sisters enjoy good, if gravid, health. I'm more concerned about Amery's viscountess."

Val looked up, surprised. He'd met the present Lady Amery when Moreland had taken a notion to meddle in the woman's affairs. "Guinevere strikes me as an Amazon, one of those frighteningly competent women who could hurl thunderbolts with deadly accuracy and so forth."

"She can," Fairly said, and his expression suggested he heartily approved of her ladyship as a result. "But consider the prospect of, say, passing something the size of a melon from your body, and see how sanguine you become."

"I've considered how much Her Grace must love His Grace," Val replied, staring at his muddy boots. "She bore him eight melons, and none of us are petite, save little Eve, who arrived several weeks early."

Fatigue was making him daft. Or perhaps the memory of a pretty widow had something to do with a sudden, baffling sense of envy regarding the Duke and Duchess of Moreland's marriage.

"Did you happen to visit the cemetery?" Fairly

asked, resuming his seat and recommencing his fiddling with the shards of porcelain.

"You are like a dog with a bone." Or like a man besotted for the first time in his life. "The late Vicar Banks and his wife, Elizabeth, are interred, side by side. No other Banks there, and I read every legible headstone."

And he hadn't seen any sign of the widow's late spouse gracing the churchyard either.

"So we really don't know much more than we did," Fairly said. "My thanks anyway. Sometimes the failed experiment tells you more than the one that simply confirms your hunches."

Failed? Three days in the saddle, three days without a decent piano, and one stolen kiss in an overgrown wood to compensate for that lack?

The experiment, as Fairly called it, was not a failure, not for Lord Valentine. He'd be going back to Little Weldon, perhaps as a local landowner, or simply to see the lovely widow again, and sit sipping lemonade on her back porch. He took that pleasant thought up to bed with him, and dreamed in the happy, pastoral key of F major.

❧

With rain drenching the morning in gray torrents, Letty went back to her private quarters, a cup of chocolate in hand.

"I love you, you know," she told the cup.

She'd said those words a week ago to David, who had been scarce in the intervening days—and nights—suggesting Letty's declaration had not fallen on sleeping ears. Whether he'd heard her words waking or sleeping made no difference, because in making the admission to herself, Letty had allowed some emotional safeguard, some self-discipline, to lapse.

As a result, the prospect of seeing him again had acquired another level of anxiety and another level of desperation.

Voices raised in anger, coming from the kitchen, interrupted her introspection—Etienne and Musette, having another one of their rousing Gallic differences of opinion. Half the time, the matter at issue was no more important than whether lavender was an herb or a flower, so Letty tried not to get involved. They had never escalated into violence—though some pots had been hurled in anger—and if Musette wanted to offer her favors on her own time, that was her business.

A soft knock had Letty rising from the bed, her chocolate unconsumed.

"Good morning, Letty." Not "Letty-love," not "my dear." David looked as tired and worried as Letty had ever seen him.

"Come in," she said, stepping back. "I hope you brought the coach, David Worthington. You do not need to be out in weather such as this."

He'd shed his greatcoat in the office-sitting room, though his hair and cravat were damp. Before she could scold further, David wrapped her in his arms and held her fast. He'd always exercised a kind of restraint with her, never using his full strength to hold her. He used that strength now, embracing her so desperately it seemed he was trying to seal her body to his.

"What is it? David. Tell me."

"Gwen's baby. The child is coming a few weeks

early, and her fancy London physician, whom I personally recommended, won't attend her. It's two hours on horseback out to Surrey, and I've every suspicion he simply doesn't want to come out in this rain and mud, though his note pleads another urgent case."

"You have to go." Letty kissed his cold cheek. "Lord Amery is your dearest friend, and from everything you've said, his wife is his world. He's lost too much already to lose his wife and child to a damned rainstorm."

Particularly when David would hold himself responsible for any harm befalling Lady Amery or her baby.

"I've made the vicar's daughter curse, for which I apologize. Will you come with me?" He put his question to Letty's temple, which she suspected was a way to hide his face from her view. "My sisters are both quite pregnant, and I can't ask it of them. Gwen has nobody else, nobody she's close to. It's a messy business, Letty, but not something to leave to servants, and there's no midwife in the area worth the name."

When had David asked her for something substantial? When had he truly needed her for anything?

"I'll come. Of course, I'll come." How many lyings-ins had she attended with her mother? Usually, she'd remained in the parlor or the kitchen, making sure the family functioned despite what transpired in the birthing room. Occasionally, with the poorer families, only Letty and her mother had attended, and once—

"Bring a change of clothes," David said. "The birth could take that long."

Letty took a precious twenty minutes getting dressed, packing a bag, gathering up some supplies, and giving orders to Watkins. At the last minute, she suggested David send a note around to Lord Valentine, asking him to discreetly oversee the parlors for the next few evenings.

Then they were in a well-sprung, luxuriously appointed traveling coach, speeding through the muddy streets.

"Why did you come?" David asked when they'd left the worst of the London streets behind them.

Because you asked me to. "Growing up at the vicarage, I learned that some things transcend our petty vanities. Death will bring together family members who've been squabbling for years, and sometimes, they finally do apologize and find some peace. When a baby is on the way, all that matters is that the baby and mother come safely through the travail. Once that has been accomplished, I can be a fallen woman again, you can be a nabob, brothel-owning viscount, and Amery can be a prosperous member of titled society. Until that happens, however, we will be focused on a shared objective, to the exclusion of all else."

David took her hand in his, his grip blessedly warm. They'd been in such a hurry, neither was sporting gloves, and Letty was glad for it.

"On board ship, when a storm hits, it's the same. Nobody argues, grumbles, or complains about the cold coffee. The entire ship, officers, crew, and even passengers labor to the limit of their strength to bring the ship through safely. I've seen it with serious illness too. Have you done this before?"

This? Violated every principle of propriety because David had been the one to ask? "I have attended some

lying-ins, though I would hardly call myself experienced." Mama had been experienced though, and
she'd discussed childbirth very frankly with a daughter
who could also well have ended up as a vicar's wife.

"Medically, it's rarely complicated." David's grip
on her hand grew painfully tight. "But, Letty?"

"Yes, my love?" Endearments were not going to
help, but that one had slipped out, and David looked
more pleased than surprised.

"I want you… I want you to look after Gwen, of
course, and Douglas might need some tending as well,
but most especially, I want you to promise me—"

The coach hit a rut, pitching David's heavy frame
into hers. He smelled of soap, wet wool, and worry.
He righted himself slowly, as if mashing his body into
Letty's were a fine idea, one he parted with reluctantly.

"Look after *me*," he said. "I haven't done this
since… for quite a while, and I care for these people.
I would not be doing this, but the local midwife is a
horror, and there is no one else to help."

And thus, the nature of the real problem began to
reveal itself.

"Why shouldn't you be doing this?" Letty asked.
"I've heard you rattling off nostrums and prescriptions.
I've seen the number of medical manuscripts littering
your desk, David. You are, whether you admit it or
not, a trained physician with a thorough knowledge
of surgery. What kind of looking after are you asking
me to do?"

"Don't let me kill anybody. Please God, don't let
me kill anybody."

This was not a request so much as it was a prayer,

and Letty was no angel to grant such a boon. She brought his knuckles to her lips and kissed his hand.

As if he *could* take a life. "I will not let you kill anybody, David. I will not.

"Thank you."

Her calm, her confidence in him, seemed to buoy him somewhat, at least to the extent that when Douglas, the present Lord Amery, ushered them into his home, David could muster a semblance of good cheer.

"Thank God you've come," Douglas said. "This has been going on since last night, and Guinevere is quite uncomfortable." Given what Letty knew of his lordship's personality, dear Guinevere had likely been shouting down the rafters in her "uncomfortableness."

David shook Douglas's hand then held it between both of his. "You know Mrs. Banks. She has relevant experience, and Gwen will be glad of another woman."

"Mrs. Banks." His lordship bowed and turned for the stairs, his manner suggesting Letty could have been a dancing bear and she would have received the same perfunctory courtesy. "Guinevere is in the guestchamber. She claims this is a spectacularly untidy business."

David shot Letty an amused look, while a bewildered footman stood by. His lordship had forgotten to afford his guests time to remove their capes and hats, so they extricated themselves from their outer clothing as they climbed the steps.

"Exactly what time last night did Gwen start having contractions?" David asked.

"Approximately eleven minutes after midnight," Douglas replied, as if failing to note the seconds involved a gross oversight on his part. "We'd just gone to sleep. She woke, and her belly was mounding up, but she wasn't doing anything to make it mound up, and she couldn't stop it from mounding up. She said this was the way Rose had started as well. I'm babbling." He stopped outside a heavy oak door and closed worried blue eyes. "I don't mind telling you, I am terrified."

When David seemed not to have any rejoinder to this heartfelt confidence, Letty patted his lordship's arm. "Her ladyship is too, while the child is merely impatient to be born. Trust Lord Fairly and your wife. These things happen literally every day, and you did go through it once before."

Douglas peered at her, as if noticing her for the first time. "I did?"

"When you were born," David supplied. "As did we all. Now, chin up, old man. You have a wife to reassure, and a birth to endure."

The viscount knocked on the door, waited a moment, took a deep breath, then sauntered into the room, all appearances of fatigue and worry apparently left outside the door in anticipation of a trip to the rubbish heap.

"Guinevere?" he inquired pleasantly. "Haven't you had this baby yet?"

&cᴏ

Two miles beyond the Wellbourne driveway, Letty was still ominously silent, having withdrawn in some way David loathed. She'd been all calm good cheer in the birthing room, her competence soothing David,

Gwen, Douglas, and probably—once the lad had made his appearance—the baby.

A healthy, robust boy, thank the Deity.

"Are you relieved to be away from the happy family?" David asked, staring out the window on his side rather than study Letty's impassive expression. They sat side by side, not touching.

"Relieved, though not because Lord and Lady Amery were in any way ungracious. I simply didn't belong there, under normal circumstances. I am pleased, however."

"Pleased?" Letty *did* belong with David's friends, who had treated her with more warmth and appreciation than even the sentiment of the moment had required. She did not belong at his brothel.

"They love you so, David. They have worried over you, and not known how to be family for you. I am pleased to see you are not alone."

Letty had come to his rescue, risked horrendous awkwardness, and subjected herself to a front-row seat at the most intimate, loving moment a family might share, and yet she was pleased for the man who had dragged her there.

"You don't want me to be alone, as you are alone? No one to love you, to be family for you, to worry over you?" Seeing Letty with the new baby had done this to him, made him fierce and angry and determined—more determined.

"I am not alone," Letty said wearily, "and please do not let us fight merely because we were together these past two days in a new way. I won't trespass on that. You needn't toss me off the property in anticipation."

He wanted to marry her, not send her packing. "What are you talking about?"

She reached for the grab strap while the coach rounded a corner and David took her free hand in his.

"I saw you practicing medicine, sir. You were brilliant, with Guinevere and Douglas both. You managed to bring a child into the world without…"

"Yes…?" He'd managed to assist Gwen and Letty to bring a child into the world, which was miraculous enough.

"You never… *saw* Gwen," Letty said, dropping her voice. "Intimately. You didn't see her. You didn't put your hands on her privy parts."

"She and Douglas are modest." Most mothers were modest when attended by a male physician, and Letty had been stunningly competent in the birthing room. "It was nothing of significance."

"To her ladyship, it was very significant." The coach was steady, but Letty kept hold of the grab strap. "When you're expecting, the experienced mothers tell you not to worry about the indignities of birth. They want you to think that having strangers see you naked, in pain, afraid, and unable to control your body will mean nothing when you hold the child in your arms. Those women mean it kindly, but they lie."

David didn't interrupt her, because Letty bitterly resented this kindly lie, as, David suspected, many first-time mothers did.

"You don't forget, David. You don't forget a minute of it, not the smells, the sounds, the mess, the loss of privacy. Yes, the arrival of the child is special, but it's too easy to tell a mother that she shouldn't mind a bit of what happens to her just because there's going to be a child. She does mind. She minds very much."

For long silent minutes, David watched the damp, green countryside passing by; then, without looking at Letty, wrapped an arm around her shoulders. When Letty let go of the strap and snuggled up to his side, he rested his cheek against her hair, her rosy fragrance steadying him for the next words to be shared.

"I was so scared, Letty. So hopelessly, mindlessly scared."

She cuddled closer.

"The last child I delivered," he said very softly, "was my daughter. She came early, and neither mother nor child survived long. I'd arranged for the midwife, because my wife did not hold me or my training in great esteem—and I would not have chosen to attend her in any case—but the child arrived in the middle of a storm, another damned storm, and my wife's buggy had overturned. I had no time to fetch help."

Hadn't had time even to sober up the mother before the poor little mite had come into a cold, difficult world. He'd had time to pray and curse and hold his daughter as she breathed her last.

"I am so sorry, David. So very, very sorry. I am sure, no matter who had attended your wife, no matter how skilled, the outcome would not have changed. Nobody could have done better for your wife and child, and your willingness to attend them made a difference to them both. I know it did. You did the best you could, and that is all anybody can ask of us."

Those were the words he'd needed to hear for almost a decade: *Nobody could have done better for your wife and child, and your willingness to attend them made a difference to them both*. To hear the words from Letty eased a knot in David's chest and created a lightness where rage had been.

The lightness, he realized, was sorrow—simple, common, everyday sorrow that, while painful, was somehow an improvement over years of silent rage.

❦

Letty had lost her virginity in the vicarage garden on a summer night when the full moon had provided illumination nearly as brilliant as day. The better to enjoy the moonlight, she'd chosen a bench under a leafy rose arbor, a spot out of sight of the vicarage windows.

In hindsight, she could admit that a young man with whom she'd flirted on occasion, and kissed twice previously, might have convinced himself she'd been waiting for him; except she hadn't been.

She'd been waiting for years, for *life*, for something beyond a bucolic congregation that gathered in a stifling church in summer and a frigid church in winter, each season bringing a particular sort of stench to the service.

Wet wool and coal smoke for winter, sweat in summer, and mud and manure for the in-between seasons, when rain and hard work were present in equal abundance.

Her handsome curate had kissed her that night, too, and at first the kisses had been sweet, if flavored with summer ale. And then the kissing had become different, accompanied by a serpent-like tongue invading Letty's mouth, and fumbling hands insinuated under her skirt.

She'd thought she'd been committing the sin of fornication; in truth, her sin had been stupidity.

These thoughts were on her mind as she and David returned to The Pleasure House, the name of the establishment feeling ironic. No pleasure dwelled in that house. Unhappiness, rather, lived at that address, with its housemates despair, weariness, and deceit.

David handed her down from his traveling coach and did not immediately climb back inside. He was going to escort her to the door, at least, which was kind of him.

"Musette and Etienne are out of charity with each other." His tone suggested the children were squabbling again, though Musette's shrieks struck Letty as particularly desperate.

"Etienne flirts with all the ladies, but Musette cannot abide that he also flirts with the footmen." Because even the chefs must serve up misery to somebody at The Pleasure House.

David offered his arm as they walked under the porte cochere. The day was warm and still in the way brought on by the season's first few blasts of real heat, heat that caught even the bugs and birds by surprise.

"Shall I have a word with him?"

"It can't hurt." If David intervened in this altercation, it would mean he came inside, which on this day, Letty needed him to do.

"You're sad, Letty-love. Is it the baby?"

Yes, it was the baby, and that David would

understand that and bring it up was a comfort. "The child will suffer in this life. His parents will love him, but he'll suffer much."

David ushered her into the back entrance of the house and kissed her cheek, which meant they could hear Etienne's rapid French counterpoint to Musette's screeching. Etienne claimed Musette was impossible, an irrational, stubborn little creature, and he washed his hands of her.

Letty's father had called *her* stubborn, so had the curate. "This is not one of their usual spats."

The rest of the house was quiet, the way children knew to be silent when Papa had come home stinking of gin and spoiling for violence.

"Musette Martinique Duvallier!" David called, leading Letty into the kitchen. "What can this riot and mayhem be about?"

He'd spoken French, which had the effect of silencing the combatants for a few instants. They both began to speak at once, with the guttural and percussive diction of the French when in a temper.

Musette claimed to have gone with Etienne to market, not to enjoy his skinny, leek-scented company, but so she could steal from the kitchen accounts, because raising a child took coin. Etienne claimed the child could not possibly be his.

Which was either a lie or a Continental exaggeration.

David tossed his hat on a hook and began speaking in the soft, conciliatory tones he'd likely learned as apprentice to a ship's surgeon, where violence was common and medical supplies limited. Nobody need fret over a few pilfered coins. Musette was to understand Etienne was upset, and Etienne was to comport himself like a gentleman, if either expected to enjoy a continued livelihood.

Letty's sense of despair and weariness crested higher. She'd heard these same tones before, though it had been Daniel trying to "speak peace unto the heathen," as Letty's father had thundered without ceasing. Because she was not following the words, but rather, the tone and subject of the exchange, Letty saw what David did not.

Musette was not attired in the elaborate lace and flounces in which she plied her trade, but rather, in a white dressing gown cut in simple, elegant lines. Despite the quality of the garment, it hung on the small woman, as if she were a child parading about in her mama's finery. Her dark hair was caught back in an off-center bun, and her brown eyes glittered with hopeless desperation.

For Musette had a knife. She held it in her right hand, so it glinted from among the folds of her dressing gown, a flash of steel amid drapes of white silk— Musette's entire wardrobe favored virginal hues.

Fear pierced Letty's soul, cutting through sadness, fatigue, and even despair in a keen, sharp slice. Musette would not be comforted. David's arrival had distracted her, but clearly the woman had been upset for a long time, and with good reason.

For raising a child did, indeed, take substantial coin.

"You know nothing of this man, this overpaid, rutting *cook*," Musette hissed, her gaze fixed on David. "You are the so-lovely owner of this sty of vice, and you have more than enough coin for ten lifetimes, while we women have nothing. I hate you."

Letty knew that sentiment, knew that Musette did hate David, at least in that moment, as well as Etienne and every man who'd ever leered at her.

Mostly, though, she hated herself.

"Musette, my dear, you are upset, and understandably so," David said. "Etienne has not behaved well, and you are concerned for your child. The child will be provided for, I promise you."

My dear. Those were the wrong words, for they had Musette's knife hand twitching. David should not have used passive voice on a woman spoiling for action—her child would be provided for, though David had not said by *whom.*

"David." Letty spoke softly, but if David heard her, he ignored her.

"Listen to the viscount," Etienne added, and Letty winced, because two men patronizing Musette at once would hardly placate the woman. "He is wealthy, and he keeps his word. The child shall not want. Shame on you for stealing from his lordship, Musette."

Shame on you. The most unjust, inflammatory, *stupid* words to fling at a furious, heartbroken woman whose future had veered from grim to doomed.

Musette's hand twitched again, so the length of a wicked blade flashed before Letty's eyes. From where they stood to Musette's left, the men would not see the weapon. In their male hubris, in their smug confidence that the angry little whore could be placated, they would not suspect their peril.

"The viscount is wealthy," Musette spat. "Like a king, too wealthy to enjoy his own women, but he offers us to any who walk through the door. The viscount runs a livery stable, rides for hire." She raised her arm. "I hate you worst of all, Viscount."

As the words left Musette's lips, Letty made a dive for David. Musette would hurt someone, anyone, because the suffering inside her—for herself, for her unborn child—had parted her from hope and reason.

As the knife flew, Letty managed to shove David hard enough to knock him from its path, and then a cool, mean dart of agony hit her high on the back of her shoulder.

"Sacre bleu!" Etienne snatched Musette into his arms as pain spread from Letty's shoulder, down her back and arm, into her mind.

She had been pierced, again, without intending that such a fate should befall her, and again, the pain and bewilderment of it rendered her immobile and speechless. Dimly, she perceived a commotion at the back door, caught sight of Valentine Windham's worried face, and heard David's voice over Musette's screaming.

"Letty's taken a knife. Etienne, get Musette the hell out of here, Valentine get my goddamned medical kit from the coach, and, Letty, don't you dare die on me."

❧

David walked out into the long evening twilight and turned his steps from The Pleasure House toward his home. Home, where Letty lay in uncomfortable slumber, perhaps even now suffering with the fever that could take her from him.

She, who had given him back so many wandering parts of himself... His ability to use his medical knowledge, his love of flowers, his ability to love a woman, and to be in love with her.

His willingness to become a father.

He walked along Mayfair's shady, dusty streets, guided by instinct, mentally adding to the list. He tried to summarize the gifts she'd given him, the things she'd found in him that he hadn't known he'd misplaced, and the word that kept cropping up was *heart*. Letty had put the heart back in him, the courage to love, regardless of consequences, because that was what love compelled one to do.

He considered his own needs and Letty's needs, as far as he understood them, and he knew a reckoning was not far off. Along with the courage to love came the daunting requirement to sometimes—often—let go. David had loved his mother, and let her go when his aunt had relocated him to England. He'd loved his grandfather, to lose him to death. He'd loved the practice of medicine, he'd loved his wife for a time, and with his whole heart, he'd loved his daughter.

And once again, because he loved, the time had come to let go.

❧

Two days into Letty's convalescence, the mundane variety of infection arrived to plague her. The wound itched, throbbed, hurt, and hurt some more. David poulticed the injury with some concoction of minty herbs Letty had never encountered before.

That night the pain became a nasty, nagging beast sitting on her shoulder. David stayed with her, despite her repeated admonitions that he should not neglect his work. He played endless round of cards with her, held her hand, read to her, and wrote a letter for her to Mrs. Newcomb. At one point, he left to dash off a note, and then returned. Forty-five minutes later, Letty heard a piano lullaby drifting through the house.

"I sent for Windham," David said. "I hope you don't mind, but he's been asking after you, as has his brother."

"Westhaven?" Letty replied, incredulous. "That man…"

"Yes?" David poked up the fire, though the room was cozy.

"He has hidden depths." For the earl, who'd dropped Lord Valentine off for an assignation with the Broadwood, had been swift to come to Letty's aid, regardless of her station. "He'll make an excellent duke one day."

"He's not in an easy position," David said, jabbing at the logs on the hearth. "And he about fretted himself silly over you when I was stitching you up."

"I was hoping I'd imagined him there."

"He was more than helpful, Letty. He thanked me for giving him the names of competent physicians to treat his father, but now I am the one in his debt."

The music drifted around them, bringing a sense of peace that Letty had been missing. All of those hours she'd smiled, chatted, and discreetly orchestrated evenings at The Pleasure House, Windham's music had been a subtle, comforting reminder of grace, beauty, and joy. The music comforted her now too, as did the thought that Lord Valentine and his brother had assisted David in her rescue.

David wandered around the room—David who'd

thought to bring Lord Valentine and his music here for her—while Letty withstood a surge of love for him, a wish that he be happy and have all his heart desired.

Tears sprang up, a common nuisance of late. David had only ever asked one thing of her—that she give him her hand—and she would not oblige him.

"Letty?" David looked up with that uncanny instinct he had where she was concerned. "Love, are you crying?"

He took a place beside her on the sofa, drew her carefully against him, and wordlessly stroked her hair. She recalled then that Westhaven had done much the same thing while she'd lain in a fog of pain and medication under David's needle. There were good people in David's life, people who would love him when Letty moved on.

Even as the words formed in her mind, she knew them for a lie. When a heart broke, there was no help, there was no comfort; there was only pain and time and more pain.

Twelve

THE STRAINS OF VALENTINE WINDHAM'S PIANO DRIFT-ing through the house told David he still had company, and so he rose from Letty's bed, covered her carefully, and left her door open that the music might comfort her even in sleep.

The infection could worsen, but in the past twenty-four hours, it had been content to aggravate without truly threatening. Letty was young, healthy, and she'd had good care. Moreover, she was an obedient patient, and David hoped her recovery would be uneventful.

Hoped?

He'd prayed without ceasing for nothing else. The last time he'd prayed with the same undignified, begging desperation, he'd been pleading for the life of his unborn daughter, and his prayers had been answered—for all of five hours.

Silently, he made his way to the music room at the back of the house. Windham sat at the keyboard, his only illumination a single carrying candle on a table inside the door. David suspected the composition wasn't from memory, it was from Windham's apparently limitless imagination, a sweet, lyrical adagio that filled the house with peace and beauty.

Music to heal by. In the dim light, David poured two brandies from the decanter on the sideboard, and left one sitting on the piano's music rack. The other, he kept with him as he stood at the French doors overlooking the back gardens. Windham played on, giving David time to enjoy the music for himself. The moonlit garden, the pleasant heat of the brandy, and the tender lyricism of Windham's playing washed over him, leaving him aching so miserably for Letty that had he been alone, he might have wept.

He was alone. Whenever he was away from Letty, he was alone.

Gradually, like the moon sinking to the horizon, Windham brought his playing to a close. The music faded into the sounds of the evening—the soft breeze, the song of a night bird, the singing of the crickets.

"How's Letty?"

With the piano gone silent, the growl of a tomcat preparing to trounce a rival or argue a lady into submission came from the mews.

"She's sleeping," David said, his gaze on the garden shadows. "Thanks to you. She's growing restless, which is good, but she still has a long way to go before we can pronounce her truly mended."

"And her spirits?"

The first tomcat was joined by a second feline— perhaps a rival, perhaps a lover—and from the sound of their caterwauling, pitched battle was imminent.

"She is cheerful enough, to appearances, but she could have died, and that will take a toll." A proper physician would have inquired about Letty's spirits. David had not dared.

Windham tidied a stack of music nobody had played in ages. "And your spirits? The knife was meant for your heart."

"Not in the sense you mean. Musette is angry at life, and I was a convenient target. Or perhaps she was homesick—she and Etienne will depart for France by week's end and never set foot on English soil again."

"Musette was angry at you, and one wonders if Letty might be as well."

Letty had collected some self-appointed guardians, Windham and his brother among them, which was a fine thing. Out in the alley, the combatants—or lovers—joined battle, the hissing and yowling prodigious, until a sudden silence ensued.

"I hope," David said softly, "Letty will always think of me as a friend."

"But?"

"But I am *undoing* The Pleasure House. Owning a brothel no longer suits my interests." Never had, and never would. Why had it taken him this long to admit that simple truth?

"You're not selling it?" Windham asked, rising and coming to stand beside David at the doors.

Somewhere beyond the garden wall, a batch of kittens was being enthusiastically conceived, which ought not to be an occasion for sadness—or envy— though it was.

"Selling that establishment won't serve," David said. "I might have sold it to Letty, but neither she nor I aspire to make our coin in the flesh trade. Anyone else would be too likely to take advantage of the women—even more than I do—and cut corners, and so forth."

"Why this sudden change of heart?" Windham settled in for a comfortable lean against the doorjamb. "It's a perfectly profitable, well-run business, and if you don't supply the need, many others—with a lot fewer scruples—will. One hears even the Church of England owns a few discreet establishments, so why shouldn't you?"

David tried to be grateful for Windham's willingness to play devil's advocate. This decision wasn't something he'd had a chance to talk over with anybody—and who would he discuss it with? Jennings would shrug and march out smartly, David's in-laws were arse over teakettle agog over their latest progeny, Letty was trying to recover from a knife wound...

"The decision has been under consideration for some time, though it cannot be implemented of a sudden. Portia, Desdemona, Etienne, and Musette are already moving on in one sense or another. I simply won't replace them. Bridget and her entire clan can be installed on one of two estates in western Ireland, if they're willing. It will go like that, one footman, one chef, one... woman at a time, until they're all taken care of, unless one of the women wants to buy me out."

Windham scratched one broad shoulder on the doorjamb, the way a cat might. A very large cat. "So if I offered to buy it from you, you'd turn me down?"

David flicked an assessing glance at his guest, but could tell little in the moonlight. This might be more devil's advocacy, or it might be the beginning of a business overture from the duke's son who chafed mightily against his father's meddling.

"You would certainly be welcome to buy the property itself, but the practice of prostitution is not something I want to personally facilitate anymore."

"Unless, of course"—Windham's voice was sardonic—"you're procuring the services for your own enjoyment."

"Your sisters are showing, Lord Valentine," David said mildly. "I cannot speak for the rest of my life, and you probably shouldn't speak for yours, but it is time I take a wife and have done with the things of my boyhood. I may find a suitable mistress, between now and when I wed, but only if the arrangement is entirely satisfactory to her."

Though finding a mistress generally entailed looking for same, and David could not imagine such an undertaking.

"And you think Letty will be that mistress?" Something about Windham's tone bore a hint of the growling and hissing in the alley.

"She will not." On this point, Letty had been clear from the start. "She will not accept coin, in any sense, in exchange for her affections. I respect her preferences in this regard." In all regards, because when a man was in love, what else could he do?

"You will cast her aside because you *respect her*?"

"My dear man," David said evenly, "I am not casting Letty aside. She, by contrast, has waited patiently for me to realize that I am the one being cast away. And lest you feel the need for further inquiries, I will not allow Mrs. Banks to suffer poverty or want, regardless of the dictates of her pride. She put her life at risk on my behalf, and that entitles me to see to her welfare in at least a financial sense."

Which was some relief, but little satisfaction.

"You've informed Letty of your decision?" Windham asked, his tone now more curious than indignant.

"I have not." And he dreaded the task heartily, for all it was the right thing to do. "I suspect she senses my thoughts on the matter."

"Westhaven might have her."

David would have bristled at this observation, except Windham's words bore more warning than lewd speculation.

"Valentine, if she thinks herself unworthy of me, a mere viscount-come-lately, whom she loves, what could possibly make your brother think she'd have him, heir to a dukedom?"

Windham pushed away from the door with his back and crossed to the piano, likely a sign that he found the next words difficult.

"Westhaven isn't as… perceptive as you are. He would have her for his mistress, I'm thinking. And Mrs. Banks might consider it, on the grounds that she doesn't particularly like him."

This again?

"At times, neither do most people, but that will be up to Letty. I will ensure she has adequate finances to render consideration of such propositions purely a matter of her own whim. I can't see Westhaven being comfortable with a mistress who can afford to leave him, but that will be none of my business—or yours."

A silence stretched, while a breeze lifted the scent of honeysuckle into the room and Windham closed the cover over the piano keys. He touched the instrument the way David touched Letty, a blend of torment and reverence in his caress.

"How can you do this?" Windham asked finally. "You love that woman, and you know she loves you. How can you neatly cut your lives apart, as if this kind of feeling can be found any day of the week? As if you're removing stitches that have served their purpose? She was willing to *die* for you, Fairly, and you think this is the appropriate response?"

Bless the man for his tenacity, and damn him for his late-night sermons.

"I know this is the appropriate response, for she cannot marry me. And if I were to force her to remain at my side, I would be killing her, by slow, well-intentioned degrees, over months and years. We'd have children, and for the children, she would try to be happy, try to make me happy, but she deserves more, and she's right—any child of hers does too."

David had reached this conclusion on the coach ride back from Wellbourne, when thoughts of his daughter had refused to fade. He'd held that baby for a few hours, and those few hours were never far from his heart. How much more entangled would a mother become in the happiness of a child she'd carried beneath her heart and nurtured at her breast?

Windham finished his drink in a single toss, and set his glass down a bit too hard on the music stand. "So you'll marry another?"

Perhaps the hardest question of all, and Windham

was not David's conscience, that an entirely honest answer was required. "I will try to find a woman with whom I can be content, because again, Letty would feel responsible were I to remain unwed. I will encourage her to find happiness without me as well."

"This"—Windham waved his hand toward the piano—"this melodrama is more than I can grasp, Fairly. People who love each other should be together, and you believe this as well. Your sisters married for love. Gwen Hollister married for love, despite all my dear father's machinations to the contrary. You can tell yourself that your contented marriage will be for love as well, but it won't be for the love of your wife, you idiot, and that simply isn't right."

David said nothing, wishing Letty believed as Windham did: people who loved each other ought to be together. Maybe Letty did believe that, but she wasn't willing to accept that *people who love each other should also trust each other*, and on that detail, the entire balance shifted.

"I hope," Windham said slowly, "you reconsider this scheme, Fairly. I don't like many people, but I like you, and I more than like Letty Banks. I would see you both happy. More to the point, I would see Letty happy, and your prescription sounds to me like a nostrum guaranteeing a damned lot of foolish, unproductive suffering. I'll see myself out."

He took the sting from his words by laying a hand on David's arm before departing, but Windham had hit a nerve: David's decision to close The Pleasure House and settle a sum on Letty would allow him to part from her before his frustration and hurt feelings could fester and poison their relationship further. This choice would allow Letty to take up a life of obscure virtue, where no strangers could take intimate liberties in exchange for coin. It would allow David to get a legitimate heir.

It would meet so many practical, desirable ends— while absolutely, unequivocally causing a damned lot of foolish, unproductive suffering into the bargain.

⤙⤚

As the pain in Letty's shoulder subsided, the pain in her heart grew.

She and David ate every meal together, and if he had appointments that took him away from the house, he managed those while Letty napped in the after-noons. When he walked with her in the back gardens, he put an arm around her waist or took her hand in his. The evenings they spent side by side on the sofa in the library, David pretending to read medical treatises, Letty staring at poetry.

He washed and braided her hair, managing it so that her injury stayed dry. He read to her, he hung a ham-mock in the shade that they might lie in one another's arms and simply rest together, he curled up with her each night until she fell asleep, and shared breakfast with her in the morning.

But he did not sleep with her, did not kiss her on the mouth, did not offer her the touches of a lover. The wound in her shoulder was healing, but other wounds were tender, their healing not yet begun, their worst suffering yet to be endured.

Letty did not want to speak of their parting, any

more than she'd wanted to lose every shred of respect-
ability she'd been raised with, and David, perhaps
sensing her dread, would subtly turn the discussion
whenever Letty tried to bring up the future.

They shared the sofa in the library, a cozy fire
taking the chill from the rainy evening, a tea service on
the low table before them. She could lift a full teapot
with her left hand now, though David scolded her
when he caught her at it.

"How will I regain my strength if I don't use my
arm?" Though she didn't particularly want another
cup of tea.

"Strength comes back slowly," David said, taking the
pot from her grasp. "In small steps, and all your patience
will be for naught if you overdo. Let me pour."

The moment was upon them, with no warning,
no preparation, even though it had been approaching
since the day Letty had agreed to become his madam.

"David, you cannot protect me indefinitely from
the risks and effort involved in making my own way.
I will manage. I always have."

He returned the pot to the tea tray and enshrouded
it in white linen. "You will manage without me." He
might have diagnosed her with a wasting disease in the
same bleak tones.

Yes, she would manage without him. He needed
a wife whose past would not obliterate his place in
Polite Society, and she needed… to be welcome to
visit occasionally in Little Weldon, and pretend her life
in London had not become every cautionary tale her
papa had ever preached against.

She kissed his cheek, the movement pulling her

shoulder. "If we've only a little time left to share, let's not waste it—particularly not by pretending this doesn't pain us both."

David slid his spectacles down his nose, folded them, and placed them on the tea tray next to the pot. His movements were unseeing and gingerly, like those of an old man.

"A little time?" he said softly. "Pain us?" He threaded an arm around her waist, drawing her closer. How much easier and less honest would it have been if he'd pretended to misunderstand her.

"Letty, I do not want to lose you. To lose you will devastate me."

She heard in his voice that the process of accepting that loss had already started, and she replied accordingly. "To care for someone should not be devastating, David. Not if it's truly caring for them. You were working up to this topic, too, so don't pretend otherwise."

He drew her onto his lap, so her injured shoulder bore no weight and her uninjured side rested against his chest. "How did you guess I was considering this?"

"Your eyes. You have the most beautiful eyes." They were sad eyes, though. She understood that now.

He was quiet, his cheek resting against her hair. Letty felt his heartbeat, felt him searching for kindness when pain lurked on every hand. She should never have become his madam, he should never have taken on ownership of a brothel, and they should, neither of them, have permitted an attachment to form.

Much less a love to flourish.

"You will stay with me until you are healed. I can

remove the stitches then, rather than inflict weeks of itching and bother on you while the sutures dissolve. Then we'll see what's to be done."

"I will stay that long, but no longer." Letty neither knew nor cared what was to be done, other than the fact that their inevitable separation would soon be effected. The thought should bring relief—she tried to force herself to feel relief—but relief was not the emotion that lodged like a bone in her throat.

She had become his madam, he had taken on ownership of a brothel, but those decisions could be reversed. Letty very much feared that the attachment she'd formed for David never could be, and that she'd never want it to be in any case.

❦

"Your stitches come out tomorrow, Letty," David said after seating her at breakfast one bright and pleasant morning.

She used her good right hand to lift the teapot. "And then?"

This was a courtesy, that she would ask him how he preferred to lose her. David knew Letty could climb into a hackney and disappear, and in some ways that might be kindest.

"I will have the staff pack most of your belongings today, and transport them back to your house. I've taken the liberty of having some minor repairs made to the premises in your absence, and of installing a maid of all work, along with a man of all work. You will also find, Letty Banks, that your wardrobe and effects from The Pleasure House have been moved to your dwelling."

David had packed them himself, unwilling to allow a violation of even her sartorial privacy.

He spoke briskly, not knowing how else to push the words out. Letty couldn't possibly think he'd expect her to continue her employment at The Pleasure House, and yet he'd not broached this aspect of their situation.

Hadn't been able to.

"Whatever you think is best." She brought her tea to her mouth, having added neither cream nor sugar, when he knew she enjoyed both.

"Are you turning up meek on me, Letty? Showing a biddable streak at this late date?" He guided her hand back to the table and doctored her tea.

"This is difficult, David. I appreciate that you are giving thought to how we should go about it."

Her appreciation was a wretched, rank stench in his soul. He stirred her tea and set the cup and saucer before her. *People who love each other should be together.* But that was selfishness on his part.

"Tell me, Letty, that this is what you want." He did not ask her if leaving him would make her happy, because he had the small satisfaction of knowing it would not.

"This is what must be."

Glorious morning sunshine poured in the windows, a bouquet of roses graced the table, some bloody bird chirped its idiot head off in the garden, and David had never felt closer to violence under his own roof.

"Here's what I propose." Where were the damned tomcats when a songbird needed murdering? "We will spend today together—I have documents for you to read, and I suspect you will want to argue over them with me—and then tomorrow, after breakfast, I will escort you to your house. I will not expect you to resume your duties at The Pleasure House"—he would not permit her to—"and you will be free to pursue whatever path beckons you."

"What kind of documents?"

David suspected she did not care; she was humoring him.

"We're not going to eat breakfast, are we?" He certainly wasn't. "Very well." He held out his right hand. "Let's to the library, and we can commence a rousing donnybrook, perhaps to give us an appetite, perhaps to ease what lies ahead."

Letty hadn't even commented on the fact that she wasn't to return to The Pleasure House, further proof that she'd realized she didn't belong there.

He sat her down at one of the chairs across from his desk and took the other one himself. "These"—he handed her a sheaf of papers—"are what you need to read and eventually sign."

If he had to forge her signature, he'd see the documents executed.

"What are they?" Letty asked, paging through them.

They were the only means David could devise of placating his conscience.

"First, you'll find the deed to your house and its grounds, in fee simple absolute, and all its furniture and furnishings. If anybody asks, you're a widow, lest your title to the property be questioned legally, but they won't ask."

He'd made sure of that, and should anything

happen to him, say, for example, a ten-year-long spate of inebriation, Jennings would make sure of it, and Douglas would make sure of it as well.

"Second," he went on, "I've drawn up a trust document that puts a sum certain at your disposal, interest income in perpetuity, etc. Third, there is what amounts to a custodial quitclaim deed on any right, title, or interest I might have in children born of your body, though obligating me to support same, provided they appear within one year of the date of signing. Am I going too quickly?"

Letty stared at the papers while holding herself very erect in her chair. David covered one of her hands with his and went silent, thinking that in some ways, lawyers dealt with more suffering than did physicians. When Letty remained in her chair, still, tense, and barely breathing, David nearly snatched the papers from her, wanting to tear them to bits.

Lest he do just that, he rose. "Say something, *do something*. Tell me I have offended you, hurt your feelings, misread the situation, been too miserly—anything, but don't sit there *suffering* this recitation."

She grabbed his hand and pressed her lips to his knuckles. "David, you needn't have done this. My love, you need not."

My love. Were he not her love, she wouldn't have allowed him to do this, but she would have eventually left him, nonetheless. This was a miniscule but real consolation.

He sat down again and drew his chair closer, but made no effort to retrieve his hand. Letty curled over it, and David hunched in, his shoulder to hers, stroking her hair with his free hand.

"The documents make it real," he said. "These details, arrangements, logistics... they make the ending reality."

Letty nodded, her grip on his hand desperate.

He spoke, because words were also something she'd allow him to give to her. "When my mother died, matters remained to deal with—in what clothes to bury her, what to put on her headstone, what flowers to put on the casket, who the pall bearers should be... I resented my aunt's unwillingness to tend to these details. She'd known her sister much longer than I'd known my mother, after all. But Aunt would not act, and it was largely left to me. I understand now, the wisdom that drove her."

"Wisdom?" Letty asked, raising bewildered eyes. "This torment of documents, funds, and deeds is wisdom?"

"These arrangements give me something tangible to focus on, Letty. Something to do that helps me acknowledge what you mean to me, what you will always mean to me."

She started crying in earnest, and David slipped an arm around her waist, brought her head to his shoulder, and simply held her as she wept out her heartbreak and despair.

He crooned meaningless comforts to her, stroked her hair, her face, her hands. He imprinted on his memory—for the thousandth time—the rosy scent of her, the feel of her lithe warmth against his body, the way she yielded in his embrace without question. And still, he feared, it wouldn't be enough.

They spent the day talking little, touching constantly. By consent, dinner was a glorified tea tray.

Through a long, mild evening, they lay in the hammock and held each other, Letty's head on David's shoulder, David's arms wrapped around her.

"What will you do?" he asked as the last of the light faded.

"I don't know. Go home, perhaps. Find a cottage somewhere to live out my life in peace. Think of you every day and night."

"And I of you."

"Will you hire a replacement for me at The Pleasure House?"

"I think not." Nor a successor.

For a time, they feigned sleep for each other, but in the garden, in their hearts, night was falling, and soon, they were forced back to the house.

❧

For years, Letty had prayed with a sense that her communication with heaven was not earned.

After David had escorted her up from the garden, she'd climbed into bed and lay unmoving, trying to pray prayers of gratitude—for David's generosity, his caring, his bone-deep decency and honor—and failing miserably. Then she tried praying for strength and for guidance and for strength again, which also brought no comfort. She fared a bit better when she prayed for David's happiness—surely the Almighty would not begrudge a good man some happiness?—and then she prayed simply for sleep and the oblivion it would bring.

But even that prayer was destined for frustration, when deep in the night a beloved warmth enveloped her, a beloved scent wafted into her awareness, and a beloved hand stroked her cheek. David settled his weight over her, letting her know he did not intend a platonic sharing of warmth and affection.

Thank *God*. Letty's hands coursed over David's back, seeking, caressing, memorizing.

"We must be careful," David whispered. "Your wound—"

Her *wound*, indeed. "Love me. Please, David, please just love me." She leaned up to kiss him, his mouth, his eyes, his jaw… She was frantic, desperate to touch him everywhere, to possess him and be possessed by him.

"Hush. Easy, Letty-love, easy. We have all night. Be easy, and let me pleasure you."

They had all night, but only all night.

His kisses were slow, lazy, savoring, not the kisses of a man who would never hold his love again. David was playing a final game, for his kisses were those of a lover secure in the affections of his beloved, confident of a future with her full of such pleasures. He eased the clothes from her body without Letty even being aware of it; he caressed her arms, her chest, her shoulders, her face. His hands moved slowly, in soothing, knowing strokes that comforted even as they aroused.

"Give me your weight, David. I need to feel your weight when we join."

"You shall have whatever pleasure you desire, my love. Whatever is within my power to give you." He settled into her body, taking some of his weight on his forearms, but resting on Letty as well. He clearly understood what she sought, a sensation of joining over as much of their naked skin as possible. A *definiteness* about his presence in her bed.

For surely, his absence tomorrow would feel very definite, indeed.

He began to move inside her, to advance, retreat, and advance again. His thrusting was slow, powerful, and so familiar and dear to Letty that tears threatened. Even as the tears closed her throat, her body sought pleasure from his, craved it, demanded it.

"Please," she whispered. "David, *now*."

He laced his fingers through Letty's where her hands lay on her pillow. "Come with me. My love, my Elizabeth, come with me now."

Letty's fingers closed tightly around David's as heartbreak, desire, and love coalesced, mingling pleasure and sorrow in such torrents that she could only hold on to him, tighter and tighter as the loving went on and on.

When David was silent and sated above her, Letty still held his hands. "I will miss you and miss you and miss you, my love." For he was her love, and always would be.

"And then," David murmured against her throat, "I will miss you some more."

They made love again, slowly, sweetly, murmuring endearments and orders and pleas and wishes into the darkness. They brought each other pleasure, tenderness, sorrow, joy, strength, and in some odd, irrational way, hope.

But when Letty awoke the next morning, she was alone. She rolled over to where David's scent lingered on her pillows, breathed in the memory of their last night together, and then forced herself to face the day.

Which was absolutely, without exception, the hardest thing she'd ever done.

❦

One of the many wonders of the human body was that when physical pain reached a certain point, the mind granted oblivion. Pain could inebriate the senses every bit as effectively as strong spirits, yet the heart's capacity for suffering was without limit.

David marveled at the intensity of the ache suffusing his every muscle, bone, and breath, even as he and Letty ate a subdued breakfast, each stealing glances at the other—searching, remembering, longing glances. Their hands brushed frequently; they poured tea for each other; they made meaningless small talk simply to hear each other's voices.

David had lost loved ones before, too many, but those losses were not ones he chose, then orchestrated and executed. Like performing a surgery on oneself, an excision of the heart perhaps, without anesthetic.

When they'd lingered over the meal as long as possible while eating as little as possible, David offered Letty his hand. "Your stitches?"

Letty clasped his fingers. "Where?"

"Your bedroom," he said, rising and holding her chair for her. "I'll get my kit and meet you up there."

He left her at the stairs and watched her retreating figure, the sway and twitch of her skirts, the absolute dignity in her spine.

She belongs here. She should be my viscountess, she and no other.

He wasn't young enough or foolish enough to vow never to marry another, but he did wonder how on God's great green earth he would bring himself to contemplate such a thing, even for Letty.

Spend time with the children, she'd told him as they lay in the hammock the previous evening. Clever, merciless woman. He fetched his medical bag and found Letty wandering her sitting room, touching this and that, probably to avoid looking at the clock—as he was.

David gestured toward the sofa. "Have a seat, and prepare to be surprised at how simple this part of it is. The stitches come out much more painlessly than they go in."

Letty sat and loosened the sash of the dressing gown she'd worn down to breakfast. David took the place behind her and gently peeled the garment back from her shoulders, exposing bare skin.

"You were naked beneath this at breakfast?" he asked, unwillingly amused.

"I was not. I took my nightgown off when I came back up here."

"Of course you did." A good physician had the knack of distracting patients with idle banter, with questions and chatter. "The wound, if I do say so myself, is a work of art. You'll have barely any scarring, Letty."

Though who would ever admire that art?

"And I will have the ability to predict storms," she replied, because such conversation was part of the walk to the gallows they would share with each other.

"What will you do this afternoon?" David asked, using small, sharp scissors to snick at the stitches.

"Probably nap and go through a quantity of handkerchiefs. I have a letter or two to write. What about you?"

"In place of handkerchiefs," David said, tugging the threads, "I will likely go through a quantity of brandy. I've warned Jennings to leave me in peace for the balance of the week, and I've told my sisters I will be quite busy in Town for the next little while."

As wounds went, this one had healed beautifully.

"You must not brood, David. You must go out and tend to your business and see your family. They will fret over you—continue to fret over you, I should say. And you must let your staff coddle you. Do not neglect your rest or eschew the company of your mare when the weather is fair enough for hacking out."

She knew which platitudes a physician offered most often.

"And you," David said, taking the last of the stitches from her flesh. "You should rest, stroll in the park, and laze about eating tea cakes. I never did fatten you up to my satisfaction, though you've at least gained some flesh in these past weeks."

"I won't overdo, lest you find out and inflict your wrath upon me, but I must see to my future."

The stitches were gone, and abruptly, it was time Letty dressed. David wrapped his arms around her waist, when he should have been on his feet and making plans to meet her downstairs in half an hour.

"I hate this." He rested his cheek against her bare shoulder. Just that, a small lapse in his efforts to return to the fiction that he was her physician, her friend, her companion, and not her lover.

"I know," she said, placing her hands over his. "And I think, maybe in another day, or another week, maybe I will be stronger then, more at peace with this never-ending ache, but I won't be. Far kinder, I think, to simply abide by the plan we've laid out."

"Kinder but by no means easier." He sat back, kissed her nape, and eased her dressing gown up over her shoulders. "There you go," he said, forcing a lightness into his voice. "You are still not to lift anything heavy with that arm, still to rest, drink extra fluids, and eat as much red meat as you can. You lost a lot of blood, and while you are not at risk of infection, you are not fully recovered either."

"No," she said, "I am by no means fully recovered."

Thirteen

DAVID APPARENTLY HAD ENOUGH EXPERIENCE IN sickrooms—rooms rife with suffering—that he could be brisk, efficient, and even cheerful, when any sane person would run howling from the scene. His deft hands made short work of Letty's braid and coronet, and no lady's maid ever provided more competent assistance.

Maybe this was how soldiers felt going into battle against tight odds. Did they don a false bravado, put on more for one's comrades than oneself? Did they suddenly become so achingly dear to one another that tears threatened moment by moment? Did they become unable to contemplate anything beyond the looming hours of terror and loss?

David finished with the hooks of Letty's dress in silence, dropped a kiss on the side of her neck, and withdrew. She felt his absence like the loss of a talisman, a cherished symbol of luck and safety, as when someone had stolen her father's Book of Common Prayer from his study. She took a last look at herself in the mirror, seeing a lady in better finances and even worse spirits than she'd sported before meeting David.

"You're simply afraid," she told her reflection. "Afraid you won't endure the pain of losing him. Also afraid you will."

Letty tied a bright red sash about her waist, her ensemble the same one she'd worn one of the first times David had come calling upon her. To know he'd recalled such a detail comforted her, to know she was parting from a man who *could* recall such a detail devastated.

David was waiting for her at the bottom of the stairs, smiling slightly, though the expression in his eyes was anything but cheerful.

"You're going out for a hack," Letty said, and why must he look particularly fetching in his riding attire? "Fine idea. Your mare will take good care of you." Though leaving him to the good offices of a mere horse felt wretchedly like abandonment.

"I'll ride later, perhaps after the heat of the day. I thought we'd take the coach to your house."

Taking the coach would allow them to sit, touching and holding hands, in relative and quite improper privacy—and it would allow her to cry.

Thoughtful of him, as always.

He led her down the steps and turned to hand her up into the coach, when Letty paused to look back at his house.

"We have been happy here," David said.

"As happy as two people could be." And as miserable.

Though the horses were kept to a smooth walk, all too soon the journey ended.

"We are here," Letty said, needlessly, of course. "Will you come in? I do not want to make my farewells to you in this coach."

He should not set foot in her house, not ever again. They both knew it. She should not have asked.

"I will come in," David said, opening the coach door, for the groom apparently knew better than to intrude. "Only for a moment, and no farther than the front parlor."

Letty allowed him to precede her from the coach and then escort her up her front steps and into the house. He didn't knock, he simply opened the door and ushered her through, as if they lived there together and had merely been out shopping or making calls.

In the front hallway, David undid the frogs at Letty's throat, then stepped back as she removed her bonnet and gloves. He took off only his gloves.

"Whatever you're trying to find the words for," Letty said, "just say it."

She expected a swift good-bye, a peck on the cheek, something painful but soon over, like a competent surgery.

"You will note a few changes," he said, slapping his gloves against his thigh. "When you napped, I needed something to occupy myself, so I replaced the curios and knick-knacks you'd sold, took care of the minor repairs, had the gutters and chimneys cleaned and the windows reglazed. I also took the liberty of adding some books to your parlor shelves, and the larder has been provisioned with what staples and foodstuffs I thought you might need."

He fell silent, while Letty wondered if he'd ever made such a thorough confession as a boy. A bouquet of roses sat on the table in the front hallway, and the Vermeer hung in discreet pride of place above it. A small silver angel that looked very like a porcelain angel she'd particularly admired at The Pleasure House stood, wings outstretched, beneath the Vermeer.

"It's lovely of you," Letty said, though she could not bear to study the angel. "It's *loving*." She looped her hands behind his neck and leaned into him. "Thank you."

"I hoped you'd understand." His arms settled around her waist; his cheek rested against her hair. They stood like that, silent, not clinging, but unable to part.

I will miss you so.

"Letty?"

She stepped back at the question in his voice.

"If there's anything," David said, "anything at all, that you need or want, or even think you might enjoy, you must send word to me through Jennings, and I will see to it. I am still your friend, and hope you will be mine as well."

He might manage this friendship-through-Jennings, while Letty dreaded the day Jennings would brusquely let slip that his lordship was negotiating an engagement with some earl's daughter.

"I will not trespass," he said, pulling on his gloves. "I fully expect you to sell this house and repair to some rustic cottage, perhaps without even letting me know your direction. But not yet. I still need—"

She put two fingers against his mouth.

"We both need to know, at least for a little while longer, that the other is in familiar surrounds, safe, and not too far away, adequately cared for. I expect I will sell this house, eventually."

"Not just yet," David concluded, relief in his eyes.

"Not just yet," Letty agreed, and maybe, if the ache in her heart grew any worse, never.

A painful silence went by, while Letty tried and failed to find one more scrap of business to transact that might put off David's leave-taking.

He took her in his arms. "Good-bye, my Elizabeth, my love, my friend."

She would not cry. For the love of God, she would not cry. This parting was her doing, her last best gift to him and his future, and she would not make it any more miserable for him than it already was. "Good-bye, my David. I love you so," Letty whispered, clinging just as tightly.

"Don't watch me leave, Letty." He brushed a kiss to her cheek and kept his forehead to her temple. "I won't be able to walk away if I know you are watching me, tears in your eyes, your heart suffering the same agony as my own."

"Go then. I won't watch." But she held him still, for long, long minutes of pain and sorrow and gratitude and love.

"Elizabeth. Farewell, my love."

When she released him, he turned abruptly, and without pausing to meet her eyes or speak another word, passed through Letty's door and out of her life. She collapsed against the door, thinking she might just die there, so great was the weight of misery pushing up from her chest, into her throat, and down through her body.

And yet, she had insisted on this separation, not only for herself, but also for David.

That thought had her dashing to the parlor, there to stand behind a lace-curtained window. David had dismissed the coach and walked past the house in the direction of his own dwelling. He didn't turn to see if he could discern her figure behind the curtains, didn't stop, as Letty had, to give the place a final glance.

He had the strength to walk away from her, from them. She could not have done it, could not have borne it had she been the one responsible for taking those steps.

Oh, she loved him terribly. She loved him, and she must not fly from the house to beg him to turn around, and love her—have her—on any terms, any terms at all, for just a small while longer.

For she loved others, too, others with no wealth, no consequence, no titled relations to smooth the path, and their well-being was in her hands every bit as much as David's was.

And then he did turn, pause, and lift a hand to his lips. He blew her a kiss and waved a small, courtly salute before resuming his progress down the street. The gesture brought such a shaft of joy to Letty that laughter welled up through her tears.

He'd known, *he'd known*, she would disobey and peek, and need that final offering of goodwill and intimate understanding. How it pleased and comforted, to be understood and cared for that way, even in parting.

She flopped down on the sofa and let the tears run their course.

They'd done it, she and David. They had parted, and managed it with love and kindness and even some dignity.

Though she took peculiar pride in that accomplishment, she also wished they hadn't been quite so determined and successful. Now that the process of separating was under way, she knew she could never ask it of David again. She could not endure a relapse of intimacy, not even a relapse of contact. It would hurt both of them far, far too much.

❧

A wise old bishop, over several tots of sherry, had once delicately pointed out to the newly reverend Daniel Banks that his relationship with his own father would likely be the most fertile ground he encountered for learning the true meanings of the scriptures. Daniel, only beginning his theological journey, had been railing against his father's judgmental, harsh, and intolerant approach to his calling.

The bishop had smiled and settled his considerable fundament into a comfortable chair by a cozy fire. "But young Daniel, do you not now sound as judgmental, harsh, and intolerant?"

And thus, thoroughly chagrined by the bishop's gentle reproof, Daniel's real education in his chosen profession had begun.

That education had gone on, day by day, week by week, with insight and wisdom coming from odd places. Daniel gained particular comfort from time spent with the elderly and the ill, for they often demonstrated a courage and peace, even an optimism, that humbled him. His spiritual education was more about his own shortcomings and humanity than about verses of scripture or brilliant sermons.

He had learned that very day, for example, that he was capable of adultery. The realization was disquieting, but not as devastating as it should have been. Oh, he hadn't *committed* adultery, but the actual committing of the sin was a technicality compared to the willingness to commit it.

Olivia had been called away to her mother's bedside. A bout of influenza the winter past had weakened his mama-in-law's lungs, and she had been failing since.

So Daniel had handed Olivia up into the northbound stagecoach, knowing it would be several weeks until her return, and he'd turned his steps back toward the vicarage with a curious, surprisingly *unguilty* lightness. The best weeks of summer had stretched before him and Danny, free of strict mealtimes, free of strict bedtimes, free… of so many needless parental rules and consequences. Danny was a bright, well-mannered child, one any father would be proud of.

Olivia, by contrast, was becoming more like Daniel's father and less like a woman who was grateful she had a child to love and care for in the first place.

Just that afternoon, Danny had gone off to play with the local squire's sons, and Daniel had used the free time to take Beelzebub for a gallop, one that had them cantering up the track to the widow Ellen FitzEngle's property. She'd greeted him graciously as always, and strolled her fairy tale flower gardens on his arm with the same friendliness she invariably showed him.

Then, in the shade of her porch, the warm summer air redolent of honeysuckle and petunias, Daniel had kissed her.

And what a soul-gratifying, joyous, heartrendingly

lovely thing it had been, to kiss a woman once again with passion. Ellen had responded generously, allowing him every liberty a kiss could encompass, when she should have slapped his face and gone haring off to the bishop.

When Daniel had found the resolve to lift his mouth from hers, she'd remained in his arms for a long moment. He'd held her, his emotions rioting from shock at his own impropriety, to relief that he still could feel passion for a woman, to an absurd urge to laugh and kiss her again.

Ellen had smiled up at him. "So Olivia has gone to Mama's, and you want to know if you can be naughty with your friend the widow?"

Put like that, Daniel's urge to laugh, to kiss her again, faded. Ellen must have seen the change in his eyes, for she tucked her face against his chest, sighed, and then turned to take his arm and continue their stroll.

"You don't want to *be* naughty," she concluded as if to herself. "You want to know if you *could* be. As if you'd found the decanter your papa hid on the top shelf of the pantry, and you want to know you could tipple, though don't actually take a sip."

"I never found a hidden decanter," Daniel said—inanely. Nor had he hidden one himself.

Ellen's smile broadened. "The decanter was hidden somewhere, Daniel. Maybe it was an inordinate interest in butterflies, or a taste for gothic novels, but your papa had his guilty pleasures. We all do, and you are entitled to yours."

She was so calm. That kiss had rocked him physically, emotionally, *theologically*. Until ten minutes ago, he'd been a virtuous husband, whatever that meant. Now he knew the freckles dusting Ellen's cheeks were the same cinnamon hue as her hair, and she tasted of peppermint tea.

He found a bench under a huge willow and sat beside her. A stream burbled by a few feet from the willow, and the scent of roses sweetened the air.

"I must apologize, of course. I am not entitled to guilty pleasures at the expense of a lady's virtue, and you have never led me to believe I would be. I simply…"

She took his hand, the contact reassuring rather than flirtatious.

"One becomes lonely," she said, "and when the loneliness goes on and on and becomes part of one, it grows roots and can begin to destroy one's very foundation, like this tree whose shade we enjoy now. You are a lovely, lovely man, Daniel, and I would have to be blind not to see that Olivia neglects you terribly. That you have an occasional lapse of sainthood does not make you wicked." She laced her fingers through his and squeezed his hand. "It makes you human."

"You are more than understanding." Perhaps he'd known she would be.

"Understanding," she snorted. "Is that the word for it, when you've slept alone for five years, and yet you can recall your husband's intimate affections each and every night as you dream? At least I do sleep alone. I cannot imagine what a torment it must be to share a bed with a spouse who isn't… receptive to conjugal relations."

Daniel resigned himself to having a very personal discussion with someone against whom he'd intimately sinned.

"Olivia would humor me, were I to impose on her." She'd humored him every time he *had* imposed, beginning with their very wedding night. He'd considered it a mercy the urge to impose had stopped plaguing him years ago—mostly stopped plaguing him.

"Straying would be the easier option, Daniel, and Olivia would be relieved if you did."

Many men extolled the companionship of widows, and Daniel began to see why. "You are undoubtedly right. She wants me to stray." And what did it say about the state of a man's marriage—a vicar's marriage—that his wife hoped he'd sin?

Ellen leaned forward to pinch off a blue pansy gone droopy in a crockery pot beside their bench. "Mean women enjoy knowing every option before a man is a painful compromise. When you are faithful, she can feel virtuously martyred, because the animal passions are beneath her. If you cheat, to use a vulgar term, then she is righteous, and you are guilty. A better bargain for her."

Something had changed in the pretty, reserved Widow FitzEngle's world, or in her view of the world, and Daniel suspected it had to do with making the acquaintance of a certain Mr. Windham who'd come nosing about the shire ostensibly in search of property several weeks past.

"I love my wife. I do."

"Keep telling yourself that, and you will likely end up even lonelier."

"Whatever do you mean?" He gazed at her in surprise, not because her words made no sense—they made too much sense—but because of the acerbic tone in which she'd uttered them. Ellen was not an acerbic woman.

While Olivia, in all her quiet and piety, was.

"I do not know the woman you call your wife, Daniel, whom you believe worthy of your love, but Olivia Banks is a narrow-minded, hypocritical, mean-spirited, petty little twit, and I cannot like her or name one person in Little Weldon who does."

"She is pious," Daniel reported, bewildered, "and sober, but not without charity or affection or friendly associations."

"She lords her piety over every other lady of her acquaintance, and her charity is dispensed with such condescension that most people would rather refuse it, though that would hurt your feelings, so they don't." Ellen pulled her hand from his and swiped at stray locks that had escaped from her braid. "Her Lady's Charitable Guild is a pit of vipers, all of the members currying favor with the vicar's wife, and at one another's expense."

Ellen was confident of her words, and her tone left no doubt whatsoever regarding her sentiments.

"I cannot absorb what you are telling me. Olivia is my helpmeet. She visits the sick and those lying in. She has taken the burden of the parish books entirely from my shoulders, and has done so for years without complaining. She tends the household accounts so I might have more time for my parishioners."

Bad enough for Daniel to harbor regrets about his marriage, but for the entire parish to regret it…?

"You are a good, godly man, Daniel, and I am sorry

to offend, but your wife is the cruelest bitch. I would give anything to make that not so."

"Bitch." He repeated the word softly, wishing it didn't resonate with some honest, miserable, long-silent part of him. "Bitch," he muttered again, more softly. He hadn't used the word about a human female since going up to university, and before then only when not in his father's hearing.

While the bees buzzed over the glory of Ellen's garden in spring, she recited to him a litany of meanness: Olivia belittled her husband, criticizing him for spending his "pittance" of a salary to feed his fancy horse, for his inability to condemn the myriad sinners and slackers about Little Weldon (and the one true, habitual drunk, for that matter), for not providing young Danny with sufficiently firm guidance.

"You are a good man, and Olivia would have her coven believe she married a selfish, spineless, puerile cipher, whose only chance of maintaining the appearance of competence at his calling rests with her selfless devotion."

Daniel suspected Ellen was being diplomatic. She presented him a picture of a woman who was not merely petty, venal, and frustrated, but *hateful*.

"I believe you," he said at length. "I believe, at any rate, that Olivia comports herself when out of my company in a manner that forces you to draw this conclusion about her."

Bitch. He knew full well the implications of the word, and it struck him with the force of unacknowledged intuition as an accurate epithet for Olivia. She criticized him, subtly, particularly when Letty came to visit, and Olivia had to constantly imply that he was not a competent provider, while insisting that managing the finances was no burden for her. She criticized Danny for not mastering skills that he was too young to even attempt. She criticized the parishioners for their parsimony, their sloth.

But she was a clever bitch, for her criticisms were carefully couched.

"Now, Danny, you mustn't feel bad if you are slow at these simple sums. That would be arrogant, to assume that because other boys can master them, you can as well…"

"Living at the vicarage," she'd said to Letty in Daniel's hearing, "gives one endless opportunities to practice economies and the virtue of self-denial."

"Isn't it a shame," she'd observed the day before her departure, "that George Dalton's wife must bear him yet another child when he's too intemperate to provide for the ones she's presented him already? The poor woman…"

To Daniel, the Daltons were happy enough, and the *poor woman* seemed quite proud of and contented with her smiling George. But Olivia was full of "Isn't it a shame…?" and "We must remember to pray that Lorna Hamilton finds some self-discipline…" and "How blessed we are, that unlike Cheevers Miller…"

Beside him, Ellen played with the end of her thick, coppery braid. "Are you very upset?"

"I am disappointed in myself, but reassured, too, for having been… naughty with you, as you put it. And as for Olivia… I have known her lack of warmth was a disappointment to my flock for some time. I didn't want to admit how much of a disappointment. That, I find, is the more disconcerting lapse."

Ellen went after more fading pansies. "And you still don't want to admit what a disappointment she is to you."

Daniel watched her hands, saw competence in them, and the dirt worked into the creases. Again, he had the thought that this was a different Ellen FitzEngle. One who had always been here; he'd only had to offer her a naughty kiss to waken her.

The idea amused him, which wasn't polite—or pious—at all.

"Perhaps I can barely begin to comprehend what a disappointment she is to me—and to Danny." What a difficult pill that was to swallow—little Danny did not choose to be born, and he did not choose his circumstances on this earth.

"You will pray about this," Ellen observed with some amusement. "Do me one favor."

"Anything," Daniel replied, meaning it. The woman could see him defrocked, and instead, she was defending him to his own conscience.

"Do not pray for absolution because you asked a friend for one kiss, a kiss that you could ask for from no other. It was just a kiss, Daniel, a lovely, sweet kiss. I thank you for it, in fact. You meant me no dishonor, probably just the opposite."

"Not probably. I esteem you greatly."

"And yourself not enough," she retorted. "Come." She rose. "As it appears I will be unable to further corrupt you with my florid charms, let us repair to the cider jug and what comforts simple friendship might avail us. We wouldn't want Olivia to have any pretext for additional righteousness, and we are, after all, merely lonely."

Ellen was unconcerned about the kiss itself, and perhaps she was right. Walking along beside her, Daniel realized that while Ellen was dear, lovely, and undoubtedly a woman, she was also convenient and discreet enough that he'd likely kissed her more out of desperation than true sexual attraction.

Interesting. Perhaps he'd been the heedless sleeper awakened by the kiss.

When he left Ellen, he was in surprisingly good spirits for a man who had found himself more capable of breaking commandments than he'd known. He was also more capable of accepting the truth than either he, his wife, or his congregation had thought. On the whole, the visit with Ellen had been time well spent, and really, she was right: one kiss did not a lecher make, and with some truth between Daniel and his wife maybe he and Olivia could reach a more appropriate accommodation.

Then he read the correspondence that had come in on the day's post, and any hope of such a sanguine outcome fled.

∽

"Mrs. Banks is protecting someone," Douglas Allen concluded, watching Fairly prowl around the library of a town house more elegant than any property Douglas would ever own. "I paid her a call to inform her Guinevere is letting the Newcomb woman go— with a glowing reference and some severance, but good riddance to a lazy baggage."

All of which might have been conveyed to Mrs. Banks in a note, of course. Fairly did not comment to the same effect—didn't offer any reply—so Douglas forged on.

"Your Mrs. Banks is thin, her eyes suggest she's not sleeping enough or very well, and she could not stop herself from inquiring after you. The lady is haunted, my friend. I at first suspected she might be carrying your child."

Douglas had hoped that very thing, in fact.

Fairly wandered the room, looking tired, gaunt, and preoccupied. "But?" He hadn't rung for tea, hadn't inquired if Douglas were hungry or thirsty, though he was neither. Mrs. Banks had insisted he partake of her tea tray, and he hadn't had the heart to refuse her.

"But Mrs. Banks promised me, and I assume she also promised you, that she wouldn't conceal your own child from you. And as to that, her help would tell you were there signs of a blessed event in the offing."

And yet, Douglas had had the strong suspicion the quiet, withdrawn Mrs. Banks was hiding something.

Fairly swiped a small carved elephant from an end table. "Some women have few signs early on."

Fairly was a physician, and yet he was also a man in love. "You are hoping." And wasn't that *interesting*?

His hopeful lordship buffed the little elephant with his palm. "Letty and I parted only a month ago, and without such foolish hopes, I would lose my reason."

He lowered himself to the hearth across from where Douglas was comfortably ensconced on the couch. The morning was warm, the windows open, the scent of honeysuckle wafting through the library.

Honeysuckle, which, according to Guinevere, symbolized the bonds of love.

Fairly was apparently focused not on the fragrant breeze, but on mental machinations he wasn't about to share with even his best friend. "I am nigh certain I know whom she's protecting, but hearing your suspicions is reassuring."

Never had a reassured man looked so tired and dolorous. "At the very least, she's protecting *you*," Douglas said. "She's protecting you from the scandal of having a former madam as your viscountess and the mother of your children."

Fairly rose and half-tossed the elephant onto the mantel beside a small silver angel.

"I was raised the illegitimate son of an impoverished, bigamous lord, and my eyes are different colors. I have been the butt of Society's unkind impulses since birth, which I now regard as the greatest possible blessing. If I say I am willing to take the risk of censure on behalf of our children, Letty should believe me. My sisters both married into a wealthy family whose scandals make Letty's past a mere peccadillo, and I'm convinced that family would receive us."

"Of course we would, which is why I am all the more convinced other interests weigh on Mrs. Banks's decision to part from you."

Fairly scrubbed a hand over a tired countenance. His cuffs were turned back, his cravat limp, and his hair tousled. On the sideboard, a single white rose was beginning to lose its petals.

For the first time in Douglas's experience, David, Viscount Fairly, looked less than exquisite—also entirely human.

"A fellow in Little Weldon assumed liberties with

her," Fairly said, reciting the exact tale Guinevere had conjectured might apply. "The blighter—a damned curate, no less—then confessed their misdeeds to her father, the vicar. As an attempt to coerce Letty into marriage, that ploy failed. Nonetheless, Letty must have been viewed as the sole malefactor, because this despoiler of innocents now holds the living as vicar in Little Weldon, while Letty ended up in your brother's bed."

Tangled webs were tedious in the extreme, and yet Fairly was Douglas's dear friend, of whom he was prodigiously protective, as was Guinevere, as was, for that matter, Rose.

Douglas had not consulted with Sir George or Mr. Bear on the topic, though they were decent fellows and would likely concur.

"Mrs. Banks would have married this curate if she were in love with him."

Fairly picked up the fireplace poker and tried to balance the handle end of it against his palm, the way a callow young swain tried to balance his damsel's parasol.

"Perhaps, had she married him amid scandal, this lusty Christian soldier might have lost his post. Or maybe he was promised to another, or maybe she refused him in a fit of pique then regretted it, too late. I do not have the details from her, but Val Windham went scouting out to Little Weldon. The vicar is esteemed by all, and no hint of scandal attaches to his name."

The poker tilted, nearly drubbing the viscount on his noggin.

"Could the vicar be blackmailing her?"

Fairly set the poker on the mantel, where it did

not belong and might roll off to rap his toes. "In what sense? She ought to be blackmailing him."

"Maybe she has cousins or a grandmother in the country who are ignorant of her former occupation," Douglas suggested. "The vicar could be extorting money from Mrs. Banks to keep her confidences."

"Then the vicar would have to know not only that he himself was indiscreet with Letty several years ago, but also of Letty's situation with your late brother, and at The Pleasure House."

"Clergy gossip," Douglas reminded him. "Where else does one hear the most interesting *on dits* in a small village, if not in the churchyard? The vicar would hear anything anybody in town came across, sooner or later."

Some of the distracted quality left Fairly's eyes. The man was shrewd—even in love and wallowing in heartache, he was possessed of shrewdness. "Where else, indeed? This bears thinking about."

"You do the thinking," Douglas said, rising. "Sir Regis and I must return to Surrey. We've had too much pleasant weather for it to last much longer."

"Spoken like a man of the land. I trust all is well with your family?"

Small talk, *now*? Douglas paused at the door, because before he could return to Guinevere's side, one more salient point remained to be made.

"When I called on Mrs. Banks, she was at first reluctant to admit me to her domicile," Douglas said. "It occurred to her, as it must with every man who even smiles at her, that I might have been interested in getting under her skirts. Guinevere was wounded like that, and it... it breaks something in a man, to see a woman he cares about unable to live fully because other men have stolen her confidence and self-respect."

Plainer than that, he could not be when sober, so Douglas made it his exit line, though Fairly accompanied him through the house.

"Gwen lives fully now," Fairly said, "and even abundantly. My God, she let me deliver her child, and that had to have been terrifying for her."

She had allowed Fairly to *attend* the delivery of her child, but Mrs. Banks had provided the greater assistance.

"The child's arrival was terrifying." And not only for Guinevere. "But you're right. She is recovering from difficult years, and recovering beautifully."

"Because you love her, even when it seemed she turned from you, you loved her."

Finally. "And you love Letty Banks. Love like that should be tenacious as hell. *You* are tenacious as hell. Slay her demons, even if you don't marry her. Hell, slay her demons, and then try to keep her from marrying you."

Fairly might have offered a deft rejoinder—he excelled at the deft rejoinder. Instead, he handed Douglas his hat, gloves, and riding crop.

"I must first discover what those demons are."

Fourteen

Douglas's prediction about the weather turning foul proved accurate. The skies opened up, and three straight days of rain poured down in unrelenting torrents. Several days after David had made a firm decision to travel to Little Weldon, he was still waiting for the roads to dry out enough for travel on horseback.

The delay gave him time to doubt, to lose his resolve, and then regain it.

But nobody in his right mind would travel all day on muddy roads. A horse could too easily pull a shoe in the muck, slip and injure itself, or worse, injure horse and rider both. The day wasn't even fit for navigating the streets of London, so a thumping knock on David's front door late Wednesday afternoon came as a surprise indeed.

David's caller had come on the butler's half day, so rather than rouse a footman, David pushed away from his desk and wondered which of his family members had been sent to check on him—this time.

He didn't recognize the handsome, dark-haired man who stood on his doorstep in the pouring rain, or the small child who shivered beside him, clutching the man's hand.

"I've come to call on Letty Banks." A martial light in the fellow's eye suggested he'd purposely knocked on the front door in broad, if sopping, daylight. The child, by contrast, looked merely sodden and chilled.

"Won't you come in?" David stepped back and opened the door more widely. "And your young friend too?"

"I've no need to set foot in this house. I've business with Mrs. Banks." The man's tone suggested this business would best be transacted over David's dead body.

"Mrs. Banks is not here at the moment, and the lad is about two minutes from catching a lung fever. My guess is he's already started coughing."

The child obligingly coughed.

"Unless you want the boy's ill health on your conscience," David continued, "I suggest you avail yourself of the warmth of the house, Mr...?"

"Banks, late of Little Weldon," Letty's caller replied. At the sight of the boy's discomfort, some of the starch left his spine. "We'll wait for her."

Which saved David the bother of summoning the footmen to ensure Banks—who could be Letty's male relation *or her husband*—availed himself of David's hospitality. "For the sake of the child, might I suggest you wait in the library, where we've a wood fire going and the teapot due to make an appearance."

"My horse—" The fellow gestured to the street, where a large, muddy black gelding was having a fine time spooking himself with the water splashed up by his own undainty feet. An urchin of dubious skill kited around on the end of the horse's reins.

"Take him to the mews," David bellowed through the downpour, "and then take yourself 'round to the kitchen."

The boy saluted, flashing a grin as he led the horse off in the direction of the alley.

Banks took two steps past the threshold, barely far enough for David to close the door behind him. "If Lord Fairly is about, you will please tell him I'd like a word. I insist on it, in fact."

The truculent manner had returned, its effect spoiled by the way the fellow's clothing dripped onto David's polished wood floors.

"I am Fairly," David said, bowing slightly. "And you are sopping wet, Mr. Banks. Whatever needs to be said can be discussed under warmer and dryer circumstances."

Banks closed his eyes, and David had the sense the man was praying—honestly sending sentiment heavenward—for patience. With a hand sporting a wet glove bearing a half-inch-wide hole on the palm, he gestured for David to lead on.

The civilities were endlessly useful as a ploy to allow a man time to readjust his entire concept of the universe. Letty had said she was not married, nor had she ever been, and if Banks was her true name—Windham's visit to the cemetery suggested it was—then this man could be her brother, cousin, or other irate relation.

She *needed* irate male relations, provided they were protective as well, and yet Letty had never mentioned a brother.

David strove for the appearance of calm while he ushered his guests into the library, rang for tea, and stoked the fire. Silence reigned until the tea tray arrived, at which time David murmured some instructions to the footman, and thanked God he'd listened when Letty had suggested he start offering half days to half the staff at a time.

"Tea, gentlemen?" David brought the tray to the low table near the hearth and noted that both the man and child were standing before the blazing fire, and the child—a dark-haired, dark-eyed copy of Banks—was still shivering.

"I'll not break bread with you," Mr. Banks said.

Pride was apparently a familial trait. "Suit yourself, Mr. Banks, but because your fingers are likely too cold to pour yourself a cup of tea, I will do those honors at least. And how about you, young man?"

David knelt before the silent child, whose lips were losing their blue color.

"You will note that my eyes are two different colors. This makes it difficult for you to know where to look, but because *I* can't see that they don't match, I will look at you as if you are a normal, sopping wet, shivering little boy. Would you like some tea?"

The child offered a ghost of a smile, a fey, charming quirking of the lips, and nodded. A glance at Banks the Elder resulted in a terse nod from the adult.

"P-Please, sir."

"Sweet? With a drop of cream, I suspect?"

The child's smile grew more enthusiastic. He was an elfin little fellow, with huge brown eyes and a mop of wet sable hair that needed a trim. His complexion was brown too, as if he spent long hours in the summer sun.

"Mr. Banks?" David asked, rising. "The same for you?"

"If you please. Danny, make your bow to his lordship."

"Danny Banks," the child piped, "at your service." He bowed correctly and ruined the sober effect by beaming hugely at his accomplishment.

"David," his host replied, "Viscount Fairly. Pleased to make your acquaintance, Master Banks." David extended his hand, which the boy shook with appropriate manly vigor, though his little fingers were icy.

Mr. Banks did not comment on this exchange of courtesies. When David passed him his cup of tea, it nearly slipped from Banks's grasp.

David took the little cup back and poured the contents into a heavier mug, which he then topped off. When he handed the tea to Banks, he cupped the man's fingers around the hot mug before he let go.

He served the child in another mug, then poured his own tea into a mug, too.

Banks sipped his tea with desperate restraint. "Where is Let—Mrs. Banks?"

"I've sent for my coach," David said. "I will take you to her, but first I must insist, for the sake of the child, that we get you both warm and dry."

"You insist?" Banks snorted. "*You?*" He didn't give up his tea for all his righteous indignation, and the child was discreetly pinching a biscuit from the tray.

"Mr. Banks, you are no doubt holding your unpleasant sentiments barely in check, and for that, I am appreciative. If we have adult matters to discuss, then we can do so when we have the necessary privacy." David glanced meaningfully at the child, and Banks had the grace to nod once in understanding.

"Does my—does Mrs. Banks reside here?" The tone was marginally more civil.

"She does not," David said as the boy tucked a second biscuit into his coat pocket. "She was a guest here briefly while recovering from a knife wound, because I am a physician and rendered her aid at the time." Aid and a broken heart. "She has since returned to her own dwelling, where I understand she has continued a successful recuperation."

Banks set his mug down with a clatter. "A knife wound? Letty was stabbed?"

"Is Aunt Letty all right?" the boy asked, his eyes filled with concern. "Papa? Is Aunt Letty going to die?"

"She will not," David answered the child. "Though she did need a few stitches, but she was very brave about it. She is well, and you mustn't fret about her."

A discreet tap on the door summoned David, who conferred with a footman and then returned to his guests.

"These"—he held up a stack of boy's clothing—"have been borrowed from the bootboy, though he's a bit bigger than you, Danny."

Danny took the dry clothes from David.

And now for the more stubborn fellow. "You are of a height with me," David informed Banks. "I will offer you a change of clothing. Everything in your saddlebags will take a good while to dry, though I'm sure it's being hung up in the kitchen as we speak."

Banks glanced around the library, his gaze lighting

on the little silver angel David had had cast from
mended porcelain as part of a celestial pair. "My thanks.
The loan of dry clothing would be appreciated."

"The first bedroom upstairs on the right is available
to you both," David said, "and I've had a tray sent
up, for the boy if not for you, Mr. Banks. Though as
to that, if you've ridden any distance in this weather,
your health is jeopardized as badly as the child's. I
humbly ask you to partake of some sustenance—you'll
need it for the coming discussion, if nothing else."

Banks looked like he might take exception.

"It's all right, Banks," David said. "I don't much
want to like you either, but I can hardly fault a man
for being concerned for Letty's welfare, can I?"

Looking even more uncertain, Banks herded his
son out the door and into the keeping of the footman.
The library door closed behind him just as the child
whispered to his papa.

"He's a viscount, Papa! And he shook hands with
me. Is a viscount like a duke?"

A lively child, for all that he'd been subdued in
unfamiliar surroundings. David sat back and poured
himself a second cup of tea, giving his guests time to
get dry, and himself time to collect his reeling thoughts.

Some pieces of the puzzle had fallen into place,
but others weren't arranging themselves as neatly.
Where did Mr. Banks fit, for example? Had the old
vicar tattled on Letty to her brother? Banks was clearly
aware that David had trifled with his sister. Was he also
aware that others had more than trifled with her?

David finished his tea, though his fretting was not
nearly done. What if this man wasn't Letty's brother?

What if she'd had a husband after all? What if Mr. Banks, whoever he was, had come to offer Letty a miserable sanctuary in the judgmental arms of her family— the family about which David knew very little?

He changed into attire appropriate for a morning call, then rapped on the door of the guest room.

"Gentlemen? The horses have been put to. I'll await you below."

Five minutes later, Mister and Master Banks came down the stairs, the one a miniature of the other. The elder polished up quite nicely. He had the same dark, compelling eyes Letty had—a reassuring observation, that—and his features were beautifully designed, strong enough to be masculine, but not a one of them—not nose, eyes, lips, chin, jaw, eyebrows—was in any way disproportionate to the others. If the man had any charm, he'd be a lethal addition to the best ballrooms.

Provided, of course, he learned how to tie a cravat.

"Hold still." David untied his guest's neckcloth.

"Are you *dressing* me?"

"Somebody had better," David muttered as he whipped the linen back into an elegant knot, "or Letty will have to fix it when she sees you. There."

In no time, he and his guests were tucked into the carriage, snug and dry, the floor tiles giving off a pleasant heat.

"Am I to understand," Banks said, staring out the window, "that Letty was at no time a member of your household?"

"She was a guest." And the boy was listening to every word, even as he peered out the window, his nose pressed to the glass. "Further details should be requested directly of her."

"I was told she was your housekeeper."

Told by whom? Did Letty perpetrate that fiction? Told when? And how had Banks discerned Letty was *not* a housekeeper?

"Was she a guest in your household when she was stabbed?" Banks asked in the same toneless voice." The child whipped around to look sharply at Mr. Banks.

"She was not. She was stabbed in defense of me, and I owe her my life." In many ways, David owed her his life.

"She really is well?"

The question planted a seed of liking in David he did not want to feel for Banks, liking and sympathy.

"She lost a lot of blood, but she healed quickly and has been taking good care of herself. The wound may still pain her occasionally, and she will have weakness in her arm for a while yet, but she is substantially recovered."

From the knife wound.

Banks asked no further questions, and because the distance between Letty's house and David's was only a mile, they soon found themselves turning onto her street.

"Before we go inside, Banks," David said, taking his turn staring out the window, "you need to know I have offered for her, and I will offer for her again, but she will not have me."

Banks brushed a hand over the child's hair, which in ten minutes of travel had somehow regained a state of complete disarray. "She will not…?"

"Will not, and yes, I love her." To say that felt good, also a bit pathetic.

Perhaps it was a measure of Banks's preoccupation with David's latest revelation that he allowed David to carry Danny up the steps to Letty's door. David rapped loudly, and the door swung open to reveal Letty herself standing in the front entry.

"Daniel? Danny? *David?* What on earth…?"

"May we come in?" The sight of her, the simple, lovely, soul-gratifying sight of her, set something back to rights in David's chest. She was still in need of more weight, but she looked… so very, very dear.

"Come in." Letty stepped aside and shooed at them. "Please, yes, all of you come in. Danny!" David relinquished the child into Letty's arms, and she held the boy tightly for long moments before she set him on his feet. "Oh, Danny, how you've grown, and how very good it is to see you!"

"We came on Zubbie," Danny informed her. "And it was cold and wet, but Zubbie likes to play in the puddles."

Letty beamed at the child, her smile unlike any she'd ever bestowed on David—or the patrons of The Pleasure House. "He does, doesn't he? He's a very naughty boy sometimes, but he has a good heart, and he brought you all the way here from Little Weldon, didn't he?"

"I never fell off once." Danny beamed back at her, the sight doing queer things to David's insides.

"And Daniel." Letty held out her arms to Mr. Banks, who enfolded her in a quiet, snug embrace.

Daniel? The name registered in David's mind with a

shock, and it wasn't until then that he realized Letty's *brother* was the vicar. *Vicar Daniel*, to distinguish him from his father, likely, who would have been Vicar Banks.

The child looked like both Letty and her brother, which told David nothing. But the sober regard in Banks's eyes, and the light of battle dawning in Letty's, suggested that some truths were about to be aired.

"Letty? Might I suggest that Danny make his way to the kitchen for a cup of chocolate while Mr. Banks and I join you in the family parlor?"

The child commenced dancing in place. "Oooh, chocolate. May I? Papa? Aunt Letty? Mister Viscount? Please?" Despite the situation, all three adults smiled at Danny's misconstruction of the title, and he was sent off to the kitchen.

David didn't trust himself even to put a hand on Letty's arm, but he was standing close enough to catch a whiff of her rose scent. "I'll excuse myself if you prefer, Letty, and wait in the front parlor. You should know the gentlemen are welcome to bide with me if you're not up to guests."

Banks made no reply, while Letty patted David's lapel. A single, presuming, familiar gesture, which Banks also observed—and did not comment on.

"His lordship is my friend," Letty informed her brother. "What we have to discuss affects him too. He will join us."

David felt no sense of victory, for Letty's decision turned Banks's expression unreadable, and "what we have to discuss" might not be what David sought to discuss. And yet, a declaration of friendship was a far cry from a solitary tray in the front parlor.

"Shall we wait for tea?" Letty asked when she'd taken a seat in one of the rocking chairs in her small parlor.

"I've had my fill for the present," Banks replied. "Lord Fairly was most gracious." The vicar made "gracious" sound like a one-way ticket to the ninth circle of hell.

"So you went to his lordship's house, looking for me?"

"Where else was I to look for you? I'm told things that aren't true, and then I receive correspondence that I cannot fathom. I wanted to come sooner, but the rain arrived in a deluge, and then I had to get here, hang the floods—"

"Perhaps," David interrupted, "you could tell us about that correspondence? And, Letty, may we sit?"

"Please." Her tone told him she would not resent his efforts to steer the conversation; her eyes told him—lovely woman—that she'd missed him and worried for him. David took the other rocking chair, leaving Banks the small settee, onto which he dropped with a weary sigh.

"Olivia—my wife—has been called to her mother's sickbed—possibly her deathbed, though I've had little news yet on that score. In Olivia's absence, the church has received two letters addressed to the Ladies' Charitable Guild, which organization my wife founded and directs. The first epistle, Letty, was from you, and included an astonishingly sizable bank draft."

Banks paused, while from the direction of the kitchen, a child's laughter rang through the house.

"Imagine my surprise," Banks said softly, "when I went to the banker over in Great Weldon and found that the Ladies' Charitable Guild is wealthy enough that I could soon retire on its assets. All these years, I have counted among my blessings a wife who is clever with figures, one whom I've allowed to copy my signature on any bank drafts, sparing me—she said—tedious bookkeeping, so I might have more time for the Lord's work." He paused again, looking at his hands as if expecting to see them filled with pieces of silver.

Letty went utterly still in her rocking chair. "That money was for Danny. Olivia was to save that money for Danny. That was our arrangement."

David laid a quieting hand on her arm when Banks blinked at her in confusion.

"The second piece of correspondence?" David prompted.

"That missive," Banks said, "had been penned to my wife by Mrs. Fanny Newcomb. Mrs. Newcomb cheerfully related that because Letty's current protector was every bit as titled as the last one, and much, much wealthier, the Ladies' Guild could expect a great deal in the way of remuneration. Mrs. Newcomb hinted that Letty might bring this gentleman up to scratch, which would cost her the position of madam at his brothel—'A pity, that'—but would ensure the greatest gain for the Guild in the end. Viscounts, Mrs. Newcomb noted with appalling authority, are particularly susceptible to blackmail."

Banks had a beautiful voice, one that likely beguiled his parishioners to services for their weekly dose of scripture and gossip, but he also had beautiful eyes, and those eyes were devastated.

"My dearest sister, what have we done to you?"

❧

"You alluded to an arrangement, Letty," David said into the strained silence. "What was that arrangement?"

Brother and sister shared a look, and some communication beyond David's ken passed between them.

"Tell him," Banks said. "I've never been comfortable with the deception, and I see little point to it now."

A pure white cat came strutting into the parlor. It hopped onto Letty's lap, and David felt a spike of resentment for the beast and its presumptuousness, until the cat gazed at him with one blue eye and one green eye.

"The money I sent to Olivia," Letty said, stroking the cat's back, "was for the support of my son, and to buy Olivia's silence. She implied, Daniel, that you knew the money was coming in, but I wasn't to bring up any particulars in your presence, lest your pride be offended."

Letty's admission was made softly, and she did not so much as glance at David when she spoke. He wanted to take her in his arms, to shout with relief, to toss Banks from the room and kiss the lady senseless, because her secret no longer stood between them.

Instead, David twitched the crease of his breeches and prayed for wisdom.

Banks was apparently not a man made for bitterness, but neither did sorrow look well on him. "My pride is in tatters, Letty, that you could think I would ever ask for money to support my own nephew. I love that boy, and I love you, and I never asked you for money."

"Olivia did." Letty lifted the cat to cradle it against

her shoulder. "She made my own home a hell for me, with her veiled insults, her hints, threats, and false piety, and then, when I resolved to leave, she told me I'd pay a price for that as well."

"I don't understand," David said as the cat began to purr. "You lived with your brother when Danny was born?"

Letty did not reply, her silence an echo of the same silence David had been enduring from her for months.

Banks provided the answer, regarding his sister with such compassion, David suspected the man qualified for sainthood.

"Letty found herself with child when she approached her seventeenth birthday. The child's father, Uriah Smith, had been our father's curate, and while Father was hardly fair to Letty, he was properly incensed with Smith. Smith departed for parts unknown in the dead of night, though we later learned he took a post in the North and perished of influenza. I became my father's curate, and then replaced him when, shortly after the whole situation erupted, Papa died of a heart seizure."

Letty cuddled the damned cat, while David wanted to pitch the beast through the window and draw her into his arms.

"Olivia and I," Banks went on, "had not been blessed with a child in the five years of our marriage, but it still surprised me when she suggested raising Letty's baby as our own. Letty was willing, however, so at the appropriate time, the ladies went on an extended holiday and repaired to the home of Olivia's mother, where Danny was born."

"And the vicar's beaming wife," David supplied, "came home with his son in her arms, just like that."

Letty set the cat down. "This scheme was a chance for my son to be respectable. To have a gentleman for a parent, not a slut—"

"Letty," Banks remonstrated her, but it was David who passed her his handkerchief.

"So what went amiss?" David asked, picking the cat up, despite how easily white hairs would show against excellent tailoring. "You could have remained in the vicarage household, a significant figure in your son's life, and he in yours. The situation would not be ideal, but I suppose something like it happens more frequently than we know."

"Letty decided to leave," Banks said. "She could not bear watching the child refer to Olivia as Mama or see him crawling up to Olivia for comfort and reassurance."

Letty abruptly stopped dabbing at her eyes. "I did no such thing. Olivia told me to go when I'd weaned Danny and it became obvious he still viewed me as his mother. The day Olivia overheard him call me Mama was the day she started campaigning for my departure."

The cat in David's lap purred contentedly, while brother and sister regarded each other with bewilderment.

"Campaigning? Olivia assured me you wanted to go."

"For God's sake, Daniel, I never wanted to leave my son. What kind of mother do you think I am?"

David thought she was a heroic mother, a mother who'd stop at nothing to see her child safe and well cared for.

"Then why did you go?" Banks asked.

"To earn the money," Letty retorted, tears tracking down her cheeks. "To earn the damned money and to keep Olivia quiet."

"Quiet, how?"

The question took courage. David rather wished Banks hadn't been able to ask it.

"Olivia became convinced she needed to confess our situation to the bishop, much as Uriah Smith had been smitten by the need to confess. You were involved in a monumental deception, Daniel, and allowing a woman without virtue to live at the vicarage, among your congregation. Olivia implied, amid much reference to Christian duty and my immortal soul, that if I did not leave and begin producing the money you had admitted would be a welcome contribution, then her conscience would continue to plague her."

The irony of Letty's fate, ending up in a brothel as a result of the selfishness of a curate and a vicar's wife, had David on his feet, the cat vaulting to the floor and scampering for the door.

"I'm sorry, Banks," David said, "but your wife is a scheming, conniving, heartless, unfeeling, unnatural—"

"Bitch," Banks concluded wearily.

"But clever," Letty added as the cat stopped in the doorway, sat, and curled its tail around its haunches. "She made the choice easy: I could leave, allowing my son to grow up as a gentleman, while I contributed to his welfare and provided a blessing Olivia and Daniel had given up hoping for. In the alternative, I could live in constant fear that Olivia would expose my brother and my son to scandal, while every day Olivia hurt me through the people I loved most. The decision was simple."

"It was not easy," David said, but this tale smoothed all those small puzzle pieces into a single image of sacrifice and sorrow. Letty had protected first her son, then her brother, and then—humbling realization—David, too.

Viscounts being particularly susceptible to blackmail—in the opinion of some.

"Living apart from my son was miserably difficult. It still is."

"So you did not decide to leave of your own volition," Banks said. "You were blackmailed into leaving."

Ugly word, though the man's fortitude was impressive.

Letty regarded David's handkerchief—one she'd embroidered with pink roses—rather than meet her brother's eyes. "I can't blame Olivia for the fact that, having surrendered my virtue, I chose to trade on that lapse to make my living on my back."

"Oh, can't you?" David said softly. "Let me speculate here, and suggest Olivia fixed for you a sum you had to regularly remit, lest she bring her fears to the bishop, and such a sum would never have been within the ambit of a woman in service even in London, though you likely didn't know that when you agreed to her scheme. When you left the shires, your sister-in-law's carping was fresh in your ears, insisting you could not expect decent men to take an interest in you, and you would be well-advised to use your venery to support your son. Am I right?"

The cat hopped into Banks's lap, which meant more of David's own fine tailoring would be sporting white hairs. "And," Banks said, stroking a hand over the presuming cat, "Olivia recruited Fanny Newcomb to keep an eye on you, or maybe their collusion was a simple, rotten coincidence."

Letty folded David's handkerchief into quarters on her lap, probably adding cat hair to that too. "I've wondered how Olivia knew where to find me. She sent letters to The Pleasure House when I worked there, but I never indicated to her where I was employed, or in what capacity. She just knew."

"And exploited the knowledge," David added. "Does Olivia at least love the boy?"

Banks found it expedient to scratch the cat's chin. "He does not go hungry or want for clothing and hygiene, but she is not warm toward him—toward him *either*, truth be known. When he was a baby, she delighted in showing him off, but now that he's older, she seems to resent him. I love him," he added quietly. "I love him like he was my own."

David guessed Banks loved the boy like a man who had no children would love the only youngster ever to come into his keeping.

"It grows late," Letty said, tucking David's handkerchief into a pocket. "I am sure you have more questions for me, Daniel, but you've had a long, trying day, and I should see about supper."

When she left the room, Banks cradled the cat against his shoulder, exactly as Letty had. "Does your offer of marriage still stand? Knowing my sister bore a child out of wedlock, would you still have her for your viscountess?"

A brother was entitled to ask. "I knew months ago she'd borne a child."

"She *told* you?"

"She didn't need to. But yes, of course I would still offer for her. The issue is, will she have me?"

～

Letty returned to the parlor to find both men rocking silently in the chairs near the hearth. They were not at each other's throats, but then, on what grounds would one castigate the other? David had slept with Letty— albeit with her enthusiastic consent—while Daniel had failed to protect her from his own wife, in which arrangement, Letty had also been complicit.

What were they thinking of *her*?

"I propose we share a simple meal here," she said. "Daniel, I have an extra room for you and Danny, though Lord Fairly has also offered his hospitality."

And the idea of housing Danny and Daniel in the front bedroom turned her stomach.

Daniel considered *his lordship*, who looked all too dear and hard to read in his rocking chair. "My horse is enjoying the viscount's accommodations as we speak, so perhaps Danny and I had best do likewise."

This was no relief, not when Letty hadn't seen Danny for months. "As you wish."

She wanted to argue, wanted to point out that with her secrets splattered all about like an upended tea tray, she no longer had a reason to tolerate separation from her son.

Except, she had a reason. For Danny's sake, she would not start ranting and weeping—again.

Danny joined them for the meal, volubly excited to be at table with guests, and to have his Aunt Letty as his hostess, which was a small consolation.

"London is muddy, wet, and cold, but I don't want to go home," Danny announced, shooting an anxious glance at Daniel.

"We won't be going home tonight, Danny," Daniel explained. "We will ride in Viscount Fairly's coach and stay at his house, where Zubbie is staying."

"Will we see Aunt Letty again soon?" Danny asked, fiddling with his potatoes.

"We will see her tomorrow. Now eat your potatoes, and there might be some pudding for well-behaved young men from Little Weldon."

The exchange was prosaic, and yet, in Letty's wildest, most irrational moments, she never would have guessed she'd one day have her brother and son sharing a table with her—*and David*. And yet, Letty kept missing parts of the conversation, turning over in her mind how willing she'd been to believe Olivia's venom and mischaracterization. Very likely, Daniel, who was married to the woman, was experiencing the same sort of consternation.

Several times, Letty caught herself staring into space, preoccupied with odd memories, times when Daniel had looked puzzled by a remark she'd made, times when he'd not responded as she'd expected to something she'd said.

Daniel, too, dropped out of the general discussion at odd moments to stare at his plate. David took up the burden of keeping the child entertained, though Danny was tiring.

"Might I suggest," David said when the trifle had been served, "that I take Danny with me to Tatt's tomorrow? They won't be holding a sale, but I'd like to have a look at some of the new stock, and Tatt's is a stop a young man ought to make when he comes up to Town."

Whom was he asking? Letty, as the child's mother, or Daniel, as the man who'd raised the boy since birth?

"I would appreciate some time to visit with my sister," Daniel said. "You'll have to watch Danny, though. He's spent a lot of time with my gelding, Beelzebub, who's a hotheaded young fellow, but Danny's lively, and he's only five—"

All boys should be lively, though Letty did not argue with her brother, not when David was regarding her with amused eyes.

"How many am I up to now, Letty?" he asked. "Three nieces and four nephews, of some sort, all under the age of seven? Danny and I will manage splendidly, won't we?"

Danny's answer was obscured by his yawn, which prompted the departure of the menfolk for David's town house. As they assembled at Letty's front door, Daniel leaned in and kissed her cheek.

"We'll get this sorted out, Letty. I won't go back to Little Weldon until we do."

Some comfort there, though Daniel's position had been all too clear when he'd announced that he loved the boy as if he were his own.

"Good night, Letty." David kissed her cheek as well, causing Letty to start, then blush and fix a stare on the little silver angel, whose wings she'd taken to polishing for luck. "I will see you tomorrow when Danny and I drop the vicar off, say, around eleven of the clock?"

Fourteen hours. She could manage to part with her son for another fourteen hours—and her brother, *and David*.

She tousled Danny's hair, though he dozed so contently against Daniel's shoulder his eyes didn't even open. "That will serve, and perhaps you'll stop by on your way home?"

"Of course." He offered her one of his golden, beaming, special smiles. A smile that warmed the spirit with kindness and understanding, that offered a sense of sincere and personal appreciation.

She had been dying, *dying*, for want of the sight of one of those smiles. She went up on tiptoe to return his kiss—while Daniel nuzzled Danny's crown—and then ushered her guests out to their coach.

In the silence that followed their departure, Letty felt weightless. She had seen her son, and acknowledged him as her son before David, and David had not raised even an eyebrow. And the rest of it, the abandonment of her only child, the terrible deception she'd perpetrated on Daniel regarding her livelihood, and the even worse deception Olivia had perpetrated on them all... David had listened, and calmly assisted her and Daniel to sort out the tangled threads of truth.

More sorting lay ahead, between her and Daniel, and between her and David. Most especially, she had sorting out to do with her son, for no power on earth would compel her to return the child to Olivia's care.

Still, for all that was yet unresolved, Letty felt for the first time in years more hope than despair. She'd seen her son, her brother, and the man she loved sit down at the same table and break bread together.

It was a start. Where it might lead, she could not say, but it was a start.

Fifteen

"TUCK HIM IN," DAVID SUGGESTED, NODDING AT Danny where he drowsed on Banks's shoulder. "Then join me in the library, if you don't mind?"

Banks's hand absently rubbed the boy's back as he carried him up the stairs, the child clearly a familiar and treasured burden. Danny roused enough to lift a hand and offer a sleepy grin to David in parting. David winked at the child and left father and son—uncle and nephew—to their bedtime ritual while he enjoyed a few minutes of solitude in the library.

He built up the fire then took a perch on the sofa, his thoughts running riot in the quiet and shadows.

Douglas had been right: Letty had been protecting a son, a brother, *and David himself*, and the threat Daniel's wife wielded was still real. While David could easily provide for Letty and the child, the scandal of the situation for a man of the cloth was something to be reckoned with.

His musings were interrupted by Banks's arrival to the library.

"Danny is asleep?"

"Out like a candle," Banks said. "He's such a good child, and this—"

"This will mean complications for him. Might I offer you a drink while we consider the situation?"

"You may, though these are hardly your problems to consider."

The vicar did not lack for tenacity or courage, and he was protective of his sister. David filled two glasses with brandy. "This will take any lingering chill off," he said, handing Banks a drink. "And in my household, we don't particularly stand on ceremony, so you'll pardon me if I take my boots off and put my feet up."

Banks shrugged and did likewise, sitting some distance away from David on the couch.

"My lawfully wedded wife," Banks mused, "would scold me vociferously for putting my feet up on the furniture, setting a bad example for Danny, allowing disrespectful informality to sneak into a godly household. To realize I have married a worse incarnation of my own father is a... lowering development."

"What would you like to do about her?" David had a few suggestions, which when implemented, would break at least one signal commandment.

"What I would like to do would require penance until my dying day—and it might even hasten that."

Agreement in principle, then.

"You might be able to send her to jail. In whose name was the bank account kept?"

"Mine. The banker was a member of the congregation, Olivia had handled the church money for years, and to all appearances, I'm sure my signature will be found on any relevant documents."

Well, damn. "What are your other options?"

"Why do you care?" The question was curious rather than rude, or perhaps exhausted rather than rude.

"You are the victim of several serious deceptions," David said, "and out of a simple instinct for justice, this rankles. You are also Letty's brother, she loves you, and you made a good faith attempt to help her when her own father would not have been so kind. But for you, Letty could have died of the pox in the gutters of London before her son was two years old—and he along with her."

"Do you really own a brothel?" Banks asked, apropos of nothing, except perhaps a rural vicar's curiosity.

"I inherited one, and Letty was the manager there for a few months. She had no duties above stairs, if you take my meaning. If you have further questions on this topic, they're for you and her to discuss."

Banks took his first sip of the liquor, closed his eyes, and leaned his head against the back of the couch. "We haven't spirits such as this in Little Weldon."

The observation bore some significance David could not grasp. "My brother-in-law owns a distillery or two in Scotland, and some vineyards in Germany and Portugal—or possibly France. Demon drink is quite profitable."

"How many titles does your family hold?" Banks asked without opening his eyes, though David had purposely not mentioned Heathgate's title.

"I am but a viscount," David said. "One sister married a marquess; the other married his brother, the Earl of Greymoor. Their cousin married a brother of my younger sister's first husband, Viscount Amery. That makes four, including mine."

And Rose's grandfather was the much-respected Duke of Moreland, though no blood relation to David himself.

"Only four." Banks took another small sip of his drink, eyes still closed. "We can go three years in Little Weldon without seeing anything more impressive than the local squires in their hunting pinks. How did you and Letty meet?"

David had not anticipated these questions, though a vicar would be adept at coaxing confessions from those who clutched their sins tightly. The fire sent shadows flickering against the cupids above, while David debated whose story this was to tell.

Perhaps the tale was easier to hear from someone besides Letty.

"Letty was mistress to the present Viscount Amery's older brother, Herbert, who was married to my younger sister. I called upon Letty to ask her about Herbert's finances upon his death."

"Why would she know anything about that?"

Abruptly, David felt not merely tired and bemused, but aged as a function of experiencing too much wickedness.

"Mistresses hear all sorts of things that wives do not. Herbert's estate was left in significant disarray as a result of his bad management. He was, however, generous with Letty, even giving her some of the estate jewelry. She returned it to the man's surviving brother when she realized what had transpired."

"She would. Did you know this man, this late Viscount Amery?"

Not well enough, considering the bastard had made

David's younger sister miserable. "He was my brother-in-law for the last two years of his life."

"He was not kind to your sister, not in the ways that count," Banks concluded with what was probably clerical instinct. "A woman should not have to tell her brother some things, but my wife, and indirectly I myself, forced Letty into these circumstances. I would rather know how much I have to atone for."

The entire discussion had taken place in a room illuminated by little more than the fire in the hearth, and yet there was light enough for David to see that Banks had tears on his damned handsome cheeks.

"I have sisters," David said as he handed Banks his handkerchief.

"And yet you own a brothel. Do you tell yourself those women secretly enjoy what they do?"

"I am ending my association with the brothel and ensuring any of the women employed there have the means to do the same if they so choose." If the notion had been tentative, it was plain fact now. He and Bridget were in negotiations. "And for your information, Vicar, a few of them do enjoy what they do, though not as many as the patrons would like to think."

Or did they learn to *appear* to enjoy what they did, because the alternative was hurling a knife across the kitchen at their employer?

Rather than endure more of Banks's questioning, David went on the offensive. "You've yet to decide what you will do about your wife."

"God help me." Banks lifted his glass in a mock salute. "Didn't see that one coming, Lord Fairly. Well done."

"Letty will want to know, and I don't think she'll allow Olivia anywhere near Danny, even if you might consider it." David had the influence and determination to ensure Letty's wishes were respected, too.

"I would not consider it. In fact, Olivia shouldn't be allowed anywhere near *me*."

Letty's brother was not so very hard to like after all. "Olivia has much to answer for."

"My father was not in favor of the match. He refused to attend the ceremony, and was quite vocal on the matter. I've never known quite why, but I suppose he's vindicated on this count too."

"What do you mean, on this count too?"

"He didn't want me going into the church. Thought I was too stubborn to accept the hierarchy, and now, I can see that was probably something he struggled with."

A log burned through on the hearth, sending a shower of sparks upward, leaving less illumination than before. "Odd, isn't it, how we come to understand our fathers only after they're no longer about to hear our apologies?"

"They know. Somehow, I think they do know. Our mamas too."

"As we will one day."

"You, perhaps." Banks swirled his drink, holding the glass under his perfectly proportioned nose. "I doubt I will ever have children of my own."

"Because you are not in charity with your wife, or because she is barren?"

"Neither," Banks replied, heaving to his feet and fetching the decanter. "I am the one who... I don't even know what the word is for a man who is barren."

"Sterile." A terrifying word to most men. "What makes you think it's you?"

"Measles. A serious case, shortly before I married. The physician told me my wife might have difficulty conceiving. It doesn't make any difference now," Banks said, lowering himself back to the couch. "I wouldn't touch the woman again if she begged me."

And abruptly, the conversation had reached truly difficult ground. "So you will live apart from her, raising Danny on your own?"

"I don't know," Banks said softly. "I love that child, and because I love him, this continued deception *of him* sits ill with me."

As it did with David, for as a child, David had understood much that no adult had ever explained to him—all of it painful.

"You think Danny knows you are not his papa? He seems to love you, and to regard Letty as his aunt." And how hard was it for Letty, to be only an aunt?

"When I explained to him that Olivia had to go away for a long visit, he offered one word in reaction: 'Good.'"

Brilliant child. "So he doesn't like his supposed mother, but Olivia doesn't sound very likable in general."

"Now she isn't, but ten years ago, she was a different woman."

"Was she?" David mused. "Or were you more easily deceived? I married young, and my bride turned out to be a very different person as a wife than she was as a fiancée. Her death spared us both a lifetime of making each other miserable."

"I'm sorry for your loss, and sorry your experience of marriage was so trying."

The saintly bastard offered the most genuine condolences David had received, and maybe the most timely, too. "I assume you will send Olivia packing to her family?" Though even the north country was not as far as the woman deserved to be banished.

"I don't know. Olivia deserves punishment for this—her actions affected Letty, who was still very much an innocent at the time. They affected me and Danny, both of whom she ought to have loved. They affected my standing with my congregation, or so I was informed even before all of this business came to light. My very profession is jeopardized, too."

For all his fatigue, and for all the developments of the day, Banks was still thinking with brutal clarity.

"In what regard? You meant well."

"Those words—I meant well—they pave the road to hell, at least in the eyes of the church. My bishop is a good sort, and he will not personally condemn me for trying to raise my sister's child as my own. He will, however, have no patience with this whole Ladies' Charitable Guild fund, or the fact that I refuse to live with my wife hereafter."

"Don't be too hasty. If the account was only in your name, and the only deposits came from Letty, the church has no involvement in it."

"You're shrewd." A compliment, not an accusation. "Do you engage in trade?"

"I wallow in it." Or tried to lose himself in it. Lately, Jennings's reports had been sadly neglected. "I'm also wallowing in filthy lucre as a result. You should be aware that because Letty saved my life, I was able to impose a substantial financial settlement on her before we parted."

Not substantial enough, though. Not nearly substantial enough for a mother and her child.

"I am confused." Banks uncrossed his feet and crossed them the other way. "I was under the impression that she... that you and she... Oh, bother, just what went on between you two?"

The answer to that would take all night. "You came to London in the midst of a deluge to call me out, Banks. Do I see equivocation here?"

"Fleeting humility. Enjoy it while it lasts, and answer the question. I could still call you out. Will you marry my sister?"

And the good vicar was not bluffing or teasing, despite the fact that the difference in their stations should have meant dueling was not an option. "I am still not confident Letty will have me, though you give me reason to hope."

Banks undid his sleeve buttons and turned the cuffs back. "Hope. Explain yourself."

If Banks had used that tone of voice to ask for a recitation of the Ten Commandments, David would have dredged them up from memory, and in the correct order.

"Letty can leave the boy to you," David said, "in which case he is the son of a defrocked vicar, or she can raise him on her own, the problems there being self-evident. In the alternative, she can raise him with me, giving the child the benefits of wealth, title, and a large and influential family. For Danny's sake alone, Letty will at least consider my suit."

Now, she would consider it—provided the vicar agreed with David's reasoning.

While David debated pressing his guest on the issue, Banks took another parsimonious sip of his drink. "Your reasoning is… ruthless. I like it, because Danny is what matters here. I will give my sister the benefit of my thoughts on the matter."

Hope germinated, a small, glowing warmth in David's heart. While he hurt for the vicar, he rejoiced for Letty and for her son, though the boy faced a significant adjustment.

David rose, a lightness suffusing his fatigue. "The hour isn't so late, but I have an important appointment in the morning, and you rode in this weather from Upper West Bogtrot to hell and back. Will you return there, by the way?"

"I will," Banks said, yawning. "If only to make my good-byes and tidy up for my successor. There's no question I will be leaving the church."

This would be a significant loss to the church, and to the sinners of Upper West Bogtrot and other parts. "You can't be a curate somewhere?"

"I am not suited to leading a flock, and I'm not being humble. Some responsibilities I manage very well, others I loathe. And if one's marriage is in shambles, perhaps that situation should take precedence. I was content in the church, Fairly, but I went into it in part because my father said not to, and in part because I didn't know what else to do with myself."

"So what will you do now?" This would matter to Letty, but it also mattered to David. "Particularly when you've a small boy to consider into the bargain."

"I will sleep on it." Banks rose and took his glass to the sideboard. "I am resolved that I will leave my post and separate from my wife, which is a vast difference from the resolutions I had when I knocked on your door. Let's see what the good Lord provides for me tomorrow."

Such… self-possession was worthy of a duke. "Shall I send my valet to you?"

"I wouldn't know what to do with him." He tucked his boots under his arm, likely his only pair. "If you could untie this?" He lifted his chin, indicating the knot David had put in his neckcloth.

"I know why Letty loves you," Banks said quietly, as if to himself while David worked at the knot. "You are genuinely decent. You are startlingly, quite unexpectedly, astonishingly honorable."

"And you"—David smacked Banks gently across the cheeks with the ends of the neckcloth—"are halfway to being foxed. Force yourself to drink water before retiring tonight, and to sip water throughout the night. Your head will thank you in the morning. I want you to consider a question."

"I'm not that foxed. What's your question?"

"If you could divorce Olivia or have your marriage annulled, would you?"

Banks did not deliberate as a proper saintly bastard ought to when faced with such a question.

"Yes, I would divorce her, though Olivia is the last woman who'd commit adultery and divorce is something I'd not know how to pursue."

And yet, Banks had lit out hotfoot in the direction of divorce, mentally. If Banks were under one-and-twenty at the time of the marriage, and his father had not approved the match, then annulment was indeed a possibility.

"Pursue a good night's sleep for now," David suggested, lighting a branch of candles. "I'll see you to your room."

Banks followed, saying nothing until they reached the door of the guest room.

"I wanted to hate you, you know. Not very vicarly of me." More saintliness, suggesting it was a bad habit that would take some time to break.

"Letty is not your congregation. She's your sister, and your feelings were brotherly." About which, David knew a great deal.

Banks leaned his forehead against the doorjamb. "My feelings were murderous, which is part of why I brought Danny. I would not initiate violence while I was responsible for him."

"The strategy was effective. What's the rest of the reason?" Because there was more. David already knew Letty's brother well enough to know there was more.

"I could not leave him in Little Weldon without knowing when Olivia would return. If she got her hands on him, I have no doubt she'd use him against Letty, and against me."

"You'll meet with my solicitors about an annulment," David said. "You've said your bishop is the sympathetic kind, and he'd hear the case. Either that, or you'll have to leave the country, and Letty and Danny will both need you."

"We could all three go away," Banks said, head

lifting like a hound catching a fresh scent. "In fact, I think that's an excellent suggestion."

"It's an awful suggestion." David opened the door to the guest room. "Get the hell into bed, Vicar, and do not think of taking Letty and Danny out of the country. Don't forget to drink plenty of water."

"Right." The vicar bowed a little carefully. "Plenty of water, do not leave the country, but *do* leave the church and annul my marriage. From your lips to God's ears."

When David closed the bedroom door, his last glimpse was of Daniel Banks staring down into the face of the child he loved like a son, his expression stark with devotion and loss.

❧

"I had a long and interesting discussion last night with your viscount."

He's not my viscount, Letty wanted to retort, but Daniel hadn't been trying to bait her.

"He's an interesting man. What did you discuss?"

"We discussed how you've managed to avoid dying in the gutter these past several years," Daniel said.

"You are angry with me." Because the day was—finally—showing the promise of sunshine, they were in the front parlor. The teapot sat between them, but Letty had yet to pour.

"Angry," Daniel repeated, as if tasting an exotic dish. "Disappointed, then. Profoundly disappointed, *again*."

"Again?"

She could not read him, as if he'd shifted internally from being her brother to being a vicar on his way to a bishop's see, a man mortally good at hearing confessions and handing out exquisite penances. "I disappointed everyone from God on down when I was sixteen." This was why her name upon arriving to London, had shifted from Elizabeth to Letitia, because the creature she'd become did not deserve her mother's name.

"You became such a disappointment by not agreeing to marry Uriah Smith?"

That too, of course. "By allowing him the liberties that resulted in the need for marriage."

Daniel rose to pace the room, while the tea grew cold in the pot. "You were not to blame. You were fifteen when that man got his hands on you, sixteen when you tried to bring a halt to it, only to find he'd raised the stakes. He was nearly twice your age, Letty. Did you think I wanted to see you wed to him?"

They were going to rehash this *now*? "You never said one way or another, and Father certainly made his wishes clear. If you disagreed with him, you kept it to yourself."

Daniel had come home from a comfortable post as curate in the Midlands as tight-lipped and unsmiling as she'd ever seen him.

"Honor thy father and mother," Daniel bit out. "I'm sorry, Letty. Very, very sorry. I did not want you to marry that beast, and I will be forever glad you did not."

"Thank you for telling me." The words should have comforted; their timing left her with a hard ache in her throat. "Tea, Daniel?"

He leaned back against the mantel to study her,

which struck Letty as a not very vicarly posture. "He loves you, you know. Really loves you."

Letty busied herself pouring, though she might have put six lumps of sugar into the same cup. "Lord Fairly?"

"Who else?" Daniel ambled across the room to drop into a rocking chair. "I understand your former… associate is deceased."

The cup and saucer nearly slipped from Letty's grasp, so unexpected was Daniel's angle of inquiry, for his inquisition of her had only started.

"If we're going to fight, Brother, then have at it. His lordship was good enough to give us some privacy to do so, and I have the sense you'd like to tear my head off."

He picked up the teacup but didn't take a sip. "A part of me would like to rip up at you, but it's nothing, Letty, nothing at all, compared to the anger I feel toward Olivia, and toward myself."

"Yourself?" The teacup in Daniel's hand trembled minutely—with temper? With some other emotion? Perhaps Daniel shared Letty's compulsion to pitch the entire service against the wall. "Olivia and I lied to you, and you are angry at yourself?"

"I understand why you did what you did, Letty. You saw no alternatives, and as young and inexperienced as you were, as pretty as you *are*, Olivia didn't want you to see alternatives. Things could have gone much, much worse for you here in London than they did. I can only conclude that the good angels kept you under constant watch. You've suffered at the hands of at least one man who makes me ashamed of my gender, but your suffering seems to be at an end."

There was suffering, and then there was suffering. If Letty could help it, she still didn't go into the bedroom where she'd lain with Herbert Amery. But then there was the pain of having parted from David, and that suffering might not ever end.

"So explain to me," she said, pouring herself a cup of tea she did not want, "why you direct your anger at yourself."

"Because I have been blind," Daniel said. "Absolutely stone, stubborn blind. A few days ago, one of the members of my congregation tried to tell me Olivia was a backstabbing, ungrateful, godless bitch, but I didn't want to believe it. All around me, I had evidence that Olivia was at the very least a hypocrite. Oh, I knew she was unhappy with me, and I made allowances, but this… Whatever Olivia told me, I believed. The evidence of my own heart, the evidence before my eyes, I did not."

And then, there was suffering. That Letty should hear her brother's confession seemed only fair. "Evidence such as?"

"Your dresses." Daniel waved a hand at her. "When you came to visit, you were always so tidily turned out, and in finery even a frugal housekeeper would not be found in. The presents you brought for Danny were beyond what a housekeeper should have been able to afford. Your attachment to Danny never faded to that of an aunt who was merely visiting. You look at him now the same way you looked at him when he was one week old, like he's the answer to all of your prayers. You aren't merely fond of him, Letty, you love that boy as fiercely as any mother loves her son."

"I do." Even those words—a little refrain from the wedding ceremony—were hard to get out around the lump in her throat.

"And that, my dear," he said gently, "is why you're going to take pity on Fairly and accept his suit."

He was still her older brother after all, and battle had finally been joined.

"Daniel, you don't understand. David is a good man, and he has a title, and he was above my touch before I met Uriah Smith. He will love his children to distraction, and when they are not accepted socially, it will be my fault, and there will be nothing I can do to make it right."

Daniel rose and closed the parlor doors. When he turned back to face Letty, his expression was incongruously relaxed and untroubled.

"Letty, it is for Fairly to say whom he loves to distraction, and for me to protect Danny from the disgrace association with me will visit upon him. It is for you, my dearest sister, to recall the simplest tenet of faith: with love, anything is possible."

He was a man facing ruin and the loss of all he held dear, and yet he was smiling. Letty pitched into her brother's arms and started to cry.

Sixteen

"Zubbie's a good sort," Danny said, "but he's only four, and little boys are bound to get into mischief at that age."

How expertly he mimicked his father—his uncle.

"And how old would you be, Danny? Eight at least, I'd guess. Maybe even nine, judging from those muscles in your arms."

Danny giggled from his perch on David's shoulders, a sound that went wonderfully with the bustle and bonhomie of Tatt's at midday. "I am five and a half, and soon I shall be six."

"Why will you be six?" For that matter, why be twenty-eight?

"Six comes after five. You only get to be five for one year, and then you have to go to the next number. How old are you?"

Children were so patient with their elders. "Four thousand seven hundred eighty-two," David replied, eyeing a chestnut mare. "How do you like the looks of this one?"

"Chestnut mare, better beware. She's pretty. Zubbie would like her."

"She isn't for Zubbie. She would be for your Aunt Letty."

Because the child was sitting on David's shoulders, David experienced physically the tension that straightened the small spine and had the boy clutching David's hair more tightly.

"Shall we watch her trot out?" David hefted the child off his shoulders and settled him on his hip, and sure enough, Danny's expression was one of wary tension. "Danny, is something wrong?"

Danny shook his head, then buried his face against David's neck.

"Well, let's have a look at the mare, shall we?" They watched her walk, then trot up the aisle, and David liked what he saw. Her gaits were rhythmic, smooth, and relaxed, and the mare regarded the hubbub of the stables with placid condescension. She put David in mind of a more elegant version of his own mare, so he asked to have her saddled.

He sat Danny down on a pile of straw, while he tried the mare out himself. She was sound, patient, and every inch a lady. She responded to his aids with alacrity, and was as comfortable to sit as she had been to watch.

"Danny, lad," David called to the child, "up you go. You tell me if your aunt would like her."

Danny scrambled aboard and barely let David shorten the stirrups before he was off around the yard, posting the trot as if born knowing how.

A grizzled stable lad shook his head. "Them little ones. The horses just know…"

"Have you any ponies?" Because David had been little once long ago, and because back at Letty's modest house, two adults needed time for a difficult conversation.

"Have we!" The man thwacked his cap against his thigh, which sent a nearby yearling dancing on the end of its lead rope. "The Quality is all leaving Town for summer, and we've ponies coming out our arse, pardon me language."

"The boy is clearly well off the lead line," David said as Danny guided the mare through a change of direction. "Show me what ponies you have that are safe both in harness and under saddle."

Young Danny had fun with the mare, and the mare with him. They trotted every which way, halted, backed, trotted some more, and eventually came to stand right before David.

"She's splendid," the child cried, beaming. "Do I have to get off now?"

"You do," David said, reaching up for him. "You think Aunt Letty will like her?" A cloud passed across the boy's expression, so fleetingly that David would have missed it were he not watching closely.

"She will," Danny said, watching as the mare was led away.

"But?"

"I know some things," Danny said, looking abruptly sullen and mulish.

"Are they important things?" David asked, taking a seat on a saddle rack.

"They are *secret* things. Bad secrets."

"And who," David asked, not a murderous thought to be seen—on his face—"asked you to keep these secrets?"

"She didn't ask me, she *told* me. If I tell, she'll

throw me on the rubbish heap." He glanced around nervously, probably checking for a nearby rubbish heap.

"That does not sound like a very nice or fair thing to do to a fellow who isn't even six yet," David said, settling a hand on Danny's bony little shoulder. "Do you want to tell the secrets, Danny?"

Danny nodded, staring down at the dirt floor, then rubbed his nose on his sleeve. "I mustn't. She said."

"Do you know, Danny"—David began to rub the child's back in the same soothing circles he'd seen Banks use the night before—"a viscount is a very important fellow. We're such important fellows that I've met the regent himself."

"You've met Prinny? Oddsboddykins! Is he quite stout?"

"He's very grand, and because the prince was once himself a little boy, he told me he takes a dim view of anybody who thinks they can toss little boys—English little boys, in particular—onto rubbish heaps, as do I." The stable manager led up a Welsh pony gelding, but the beast was quite small, and David shook his head.

"I won't get thrown on the rubbish heap if I don't tell."

"You won't get thrown on the rubbish heap no matter what. I won't have it, Danny, and I am a viscount." For once, David could say that with relish. "The vicar would not hear of it either, nor would your aunt Letty. Not if you teased Zubbie, not if you said very bad words, not if you punched an old lady in the nose and knocked her into a hog wallow. Nobody is allowed to throw little boys onto the rubbish heap, particularly not little boys whom I happen to like."

"But you're not my papa," Danny said in a miserable whisper.

David spoke very quietly, knowing the exact contour of a boy's torment when his paternity was in doubt. "Who is your papa?"

Danny shook his head and buried his nose against David's thigh. David scooped the child into his lap and *felt* the boy start to cry, felt the heat welling up from the small body, felt the tension, misery, and bewilderment overcoming the child's fragile dignity. He wrapped his arms around Danny and prayed—honestly and sincerely *prayed*—for fortitude.

"Might I ask a favor of you, Master Banks?"

"What favor?" The child's tone suggested important viscounts shouldn't need favors from anybody.

"I know a young lady whose name is Rose, and she loves ponies. I was wondering if you'd try some of these ponies out and let me know if there are any you think she might like."

"I get to ride them?" Danny asked, head coming up.

"You can't ride all of them, or your papa will wonder where we are." The cloud passed across Danny features again, but his attention was on the ponies lined up down the aisle.

"Select three." David put the child down, though Rose had already chosen her steed—a gift from old Moreland, no less—and nobody and nothing would part her from Sir George.

An hour later, David had made his decision—decisions, rather—and he and Danny were on their way back to Letty's house, Danny up before him on his gray mare.

"She's bigger than Zubbie, even," Danny marveled. "What's her name?"

"Honey," David said, patting the mare on the neck. "And she has to be big, because I'm big."

"You're as big as my pa—" Danny's face fell and he went silent.

David spoke close the child's ear. "I don't know what your secrets are, because you haven't said one word to me about them. But I do know Vicar Daniel loves you, and loves you and loves you. He would never toss you on the rubbish heap, and he would be *exceedingly* angry at anyone who did. You should tell him your secrets and let him help with this other person who is threatening such mean things."

"But he's not..." Danny fell silent again, a child struggling to explain the simplest logic to a thickheaded adult.

"Even if he isn't," David said firmly, "he is your vicar, and vicars protect the innocent and weak, like the sick people and the old people, and little boys who are being threatened. He loves you, and you can tell him. If you want me to, I'll come with you."

Danny twisted around in the saddle to peer at David.

"What if he gets mad?" Danny asked in a small voice. "She said he'd get mad, and then..."

"Then he'd throw you on the rubbish heap? My God, the nightmares you must have."

But Danny had nodded and was looking to David for further reassurances.

"I will keep you safe, lad," he said, tightening the arm he had around the child's waist for emphasis. "No matter what, I will keep you safe. It's what viscounts do."

It's what this viscount would do, and devil take the

hindmost. Danny faced forward again and seemed lost in thought. As they turned onto Letty's street, Danny whipped around and speared David with a look.

"You'll come with me?"

"I shall." David swung off, tossed the reins to the groom who had accompanied them to Tatt's, and lifted the child from the saddle to his hip. "Do you want to tell him now?"

"Will Aunt Letty be there?"

"Do you want her to be there?"

"Aunt Letty is nice," Danny said. "She loves me, and she's my... he's her brother." Complicated business, indeed, from a small child's perspective.

"So why don't we ask Aunt Letty to join us?" David suggested as he climbed the steps. He didn't knock on the door, but opened it as if he were family and hallooed in the entryway.

"We're in here," Letty said, emerging from the parlor. "How were the stables?"

She'd been crying, though she looked... not unhappy.

"Fun," Danny murmured, again burying his nose against David's neck.

Letty frowned at the child then at David. "Is somebody tired?"

Several somebodies were likely weary to death.

"Somebody," David said, leaning in to kiss her cheek, "is burdened with secrets, but not for much longer. Is the vicar about?"

"Here," Banks said, coming up behind Letty with a smile. "I smell the most wonderful perfume—like horses, only mixed with little boy. Did you see anything you liked, Danny?"

Danny wasn't to be cajoled, and Banks shot David a perplexed look.

"Into the parlor, shall we?" David suggested. Letty and Banks followed him, both clearly puzzled by Danny's behavior—and David's. David sat in one of the rocking chairs, Danny in his lap, and set the chair in motion.

"Danny has matters to discuss, but first you must both promise him sincerely that you won't be mad at him, and you won't toss him on the rubbish heap, *no matter what*."

"I promise," Letty said instantly. Banks paused a moment though, waiting for the child's eyes to meet his—probably a maneuver taught in vicar school.

"Danny," he said, "I will not be angry with you, no matter what you tell me. And I would not toss you on the rubbish heap, or suffer anyone else to do that, no matter what. I promise. Do you believe me?"

He was good at being a vicar, at being a papa. And Banks was just plain good, as Letty was good.

As David himself could be good, when he tried very hard and didn't own any brothels.

Danny returned Banks's regard, looking very like him. "But you are not my papa."

That was all he got out before bursting into tears and pitching against David's chest. Banks fished out a handkerchief and hunkered beside the rocker, while Letty crouched on the other side, looking dumbstruck.

"Danny, hush," Banks coaxed, taking the child from David's arms. "I love you, Danny, that's what matters. I love you."

"But you're not my papa!" the child wailed, clinging to Banks's neck. "I haven't a papa at all!"

While Banks slowly paced the room with the

child in his arms, Letty rose, her movements burdened and creaky.

"Take it," David said, shoving his handkerchief
at her. He rose and kept an arm around her waist as
Banks continued to try to reason with Danny.

Who was only becoming more and more upset.

❧

A mother, a real mother who hadn't abandoned her son
to the care of a viper, would know what to do. Letty
hadn't the right to interfere between her brother and her
son at that moment, and yet, she could not keep silent.

"Daniel Temperance Banks, hush before you scare
my cat." The heartrending sobs ceased, as both Danny
and Daniel turned surprised expressions on Letty.
"Thank you, that's better. Gentlemen, if you'd have
a seat."

She put as much command into her tone as she
dared, more than she'd ever used on David's employees at The Pleasure House, more than she'd attempted
on David himself. Almost as much as her own mother
might have used when in a taking with her offspring.

And it worked. The Banks menfolk subsided,
Daniel into a rocking chair, Danny to a corner of the
sofa near Letty's chair.

"Danny, listen to me: everybody has a papa. My
own papa died before you were born. Lord Fairly's
papa is gone too. Your papa got sick and died, the
same as my own mama and papa did. That's all. It's
sad that your papa died before he could know you, but
I've loved you since the day I knew God was sending
you to us, and that's what counts. So has Daniel."

"But she said…" Danny sniffled, dragging a finger under his nose.

Letty shifted to the sofa and used David's handkerchief to tidy up her son—another skill mothers laid claim to that Letty could apparently appropriate.

"Tell us," Letty said, slipping an arm around the boy. "Tell us, because she's far away, and the people who love you need to know what she said."

"She said I was nobody's, that I have no mama and no papa, and if I was bad, I'd end up like Malkin Tidebird."

Even Letty had heard this tale of the boy from Little Weldon who'd been lost for weeks in London.

"Malkin's family found him, didn't they?" Daniel prompted. Across the room, David rocked slowly and petted the cat, who'd found its way to his lap.

"Nobody would look for me," Danny protested. "I would have to eat garbage and I'd be cold and the rats would get me and I would die of an ague!"

"If you belonged to nobody," Letty said, gathering the boy onto her lap, exactly where he should be, "then maybe those bad things might happen. But you belong to me, and to Daniel. You belong to the people who love you, and we will not let bad things happen, Danny. Even Zubbie loves you." That merited a small smile from the child, at least.

"He's always a good boy for me."

"See?" Daniel gently poked the boy in the tummy, provoking a giggle. "Even a horse knows you're lovable and special, and tries to get you to be his friend. I don't want to hear any more talk about rubbish heaps, if you please."

"But did you know her?" Danny prompted. "Before she died, did you know my real mother?"

Letty smoothed a hand over her son's unruly dark hair. Perhaps in this one instance, Olivia had been attempting to be kind to the boy, offering a version of the truth, because the girl Letty had been—gullible, inexperienced, self-centered—she surely had died.

Though her maternal instincts were apparently alive and well. "Daniel, if you would please explain this to Danny?"

"That is an entirely different matter," Daniel said, straightening his lapels as Letty had seen him do many times in the churchyard.

"You knew her?" Danny pressed.

"I am looking at her."

Never had Letty loved her brother more, and yet, it was David's steadying gaze, David's slight smile that fortified her. Danny followed Daniel's gaze, and his little eyes went round as comprehension dawned.

"Aunt Letty is my real mother?" he whispered.

"She is," Daniel said. "She always has been, but she couldn't always take care of you. That's why she spent most of her visits with you, Danny, because she missed you so much."

Danny pulled away to study his mother. "Why is Aunt Letty crying?"

"I can answer that," Letty said. "I'm crying because I could not stay with you once you were no longer a baby. I'm crying because I'm sorry I lied to you. I'm crying because I have missed you every d-day since I left Little Weldon, and I'm crying because I'm happy for you to know the truth, even though it might be hard."

The child looked bewildered, but Letty could only wipe at her cheeks and try not to hug the stuffing right out of him.

"She's crying," David said, "because she's worried you will be angry with her. You are not the only one who's been afraid of a trip to the rubbish heap."

Danny was a bright child, and David had put the matter in terms he could understand.

"I'm not mad."

"Good," Daniel said as Letty tried to find a dry spot on the much-used handkerchief. "We'll give your mama a chance to collect herself, then. But, Danny?"

Your mama. Letty nearly dissolved into outright sobs at two simple words.

"Yes, sir?"

"Were there any other secrets?"

"Just one. She said she was going to go away soon, and I wouldn't know where to find her. But that wasn't a bad secret. That was a good secret."

"It was also the truth," Daniel replied with a sardonic smile. "At least the part about her going away. She and I won't be under the same roof anymore, Danny."

"Good," the boy replied firmly. "Is there any more chocolate?"

The question assured Letty that her son would weather these revelations well enough, in time.

"There is," Letty said. "Would you like to come with me to the kitchen so we can see about getting you some?" Because she was *his mama*, and a mama could spoil her son in small ways whenever she pleased.

"Yes!" Danny bounced off her lap, grabbed Letty's

hand, and dragged her toward the door. David rose to meet them and put a staying hand on her arm.

He said nothing, merely kissed Letty's cheek and winked, then shooed her into the front hall and closed the door.

Seventeen

DAVID SURVEYED THE REMAINING VICTIM OF OLIVIA Banks's scheming—for Letty and Danny would find their way, of that he was sure.

"Letty keeps decent liquor on the premises, if you'd like me to scare you up a medicinal tot," he offered. Though when he'd stocked Letty's sideboard, he'd never envisioned the liquor would be used for medicinal purposes.

Banks slumped in his chair. "Last night was rather adventurous for me. That will have to serve as my signal incident of drunken excess."

"You've a lot to learn about drunken excess, Banks, but as a papa, you did splendidly," David said, taking the other rocker. "Broke my heart to see it."

And he'd never admired a man more.

"Broke my heart too, and Letty's heart broke every time she saw the child in my care. God above, to think what Olivia did to that innocent little boy…"

"Tried to do." Because she'd failed. Danny was in no way headed for any rubbish heaps, and never would be. "His trust has been abused, but in the end, he was honest with the people he could rely on and was relieved of his burden. He certainly wasn't going to tell me a thing. Who was Malkin Tidebird?"

Banks sat up a bit. "Malkin is one of eleven Tidebirds, and when he turned six, his parents apprenticed him to a cooper here in London. The arrangements got confused, and Malkin was left at some tavern, while the cooper awaited him at another tavern. The boy wandered the streets for weeks, begging, eating scraps, and sleeping in doorways, before a letter from the cooper reached the family, and they could come searching for him. They eventually found Malkin filthy, emaciated, and barely existing as a mud lark."

"A cautionary tale." Which could have ended even more unhappily.

"Terrifying," Banks said. "We set up a prayer chain, so until the boy was found, somebody was praying for him at every moment. On second thought, I'll have a small tot."

"Of course." David opened a sideboard that stood along one wall. He poured two glasses of brandy and took one to Banks. "Will you be all right?"

Banks tossed back the liquor in a single swallow and held out his glass for more. David considered he'd just watched a man take his first step away from a religious vocation, and added Banks to the list of people he'd pray for each night.

"I will not be all right, not for a long, long time."

David refilled the glass, Banks being a substantial fellow, despite lack of familiarity with strong spirits. "You can't drown your sorrows in truth, you know," David said, putting the bottle away. "And you have done the right thing and the only thing, under the circumstances."

"I love that child," Banks informed his drink. "But I was a fool to believe Olivia when she said Letty chose to leave him to go into service. Letty's his mother, for God's sake. She carried him in her body, nourished him at her breast for the first year of his life... And I was willing to think she left him behind with a relieved sigh to go beat rugs for the Quality in Town. I was deluded."

Good people often were. They viewed the world as full of others like them, until experience proved them wrong. "You can't abandon the boy now."

Daniel tossed him an incredulous look. "You've seen to it—and Olivia has seen to it—that Letty can provide for him better than I can. She's his mother. I am only an uncle who is about to part company with spouse, church, and livelihood."

Progress, not away from sainthood, but perhaps in the direction of being human. The cat hopped into the vicar's lap and went to work shredding another pair of borrowed breeches.

David silently toasted his companion. "I'm relieved to hear you pouting. Nobody could sustain the nobility of character you've displayed here today."

"I'm not pouting."

He was grieving, or he would be soon. "Glad to hear it, but don't sulk, then. Don't slink off and think you've no place in the child's life. You are the person he loves most in the whole world right now, and if you disappear, he will blame himself."

Banks petted the cat, and the beast began to rumble.

"I thought you didn't have children, and yet you seem to understand their funny little minds. That is exactly what Danny would do."

"My aunt collected me from my mother's humble Scottish household when I was about Danny's age, for a 'visit' to England. I took two years to comprehend that I would be visiting England for the rest of my childhood, and I never again shared a household for any length of time with my mother. You can't run out on Danny now, Banks. I won't allow it."

Because left to his overdeveloped theological tendencies, Banks would fashion an emotional hair shirt and depart for parts distant.

"You," Banks said around another sip of his drink, "and your allowing can go hang."

The kind thing to do was goad the saintly bastard, because he'd probably refuse to get drunk. "Such talk from a man of the cloth."

Banks smiled then, a small, genuine smile that reminded David that Letty's brother was a damned good-looking saintly bastard. "I am looking forward to cursing, and to overindulging on occasion, and having a second helping of pie, and owning more horses like Zubbie. Being a vicar—a good example—is a lot of work."

"A damned lot of work."

"A bloody damned lot of work, and I've done enough of it."

Cursing sounded good from the saint—relaxed, casual, fun, the way a man should curse.

"If we leave them alone in the kitchen much longer, there won't be any chocolate left."

"Nothing for it then." Banks tossed back his drink,

set the cat down, and pushed to his feet. "Time to defend the damned chocolate."

※

"How does Daniel seem to you?" Letty asked David as they strolled his back garden two weeks from what she thought of as That Day. That Day she'd become a mother once more, a proper sister, and a woman who took responsibility for her own happiness.

"I don't know your brother well, but he seems lighter, more aware of the potential gain before him, less preoccupied with the losses."

Since Daniel had come to Town, Letty and David had spent many pleasant hours like this. They walked in the garden or in the park. They indulged in a quiet chat over tea. They took time for Danny and Daniel to adjust to the changes in their lives. But at no time had David pressed more than chaste affections on her.

"I agree with your assessment," Letty said, "though I think my brother would find this whole process easier if he knew Danny and I would be provided for."

David paused to snap off a white rose and pass it to her. "You have enough money at your disposal…"

Letty accepted the rose, which was pretty but had thorns and little fragrance. "I meant, if Daniel knew we were *loved*, provided for in that sense."

Because that was the sense that mattered most. Around them, the gardens were approaching their finest summer glory, and yet Letty wanted only for David to look at her the way he used to—with love.

"You *are* loved, Letty Banks," he said quietly. "You know this."

How many men had hidden behind the fig leaf of passive voice because women had driven them there?

Letty kissed his cheek and leaned against him. Slowly, his arms stole around her.

"What I meant, David Worthington, is that my brother's conscience would be more at ease if I were married to you, and Danny was a part of our household." She'd meant to *ask* if David might still be interested in fashioning a life with her.

"You'd marry me to appease your brother's conscience?" He didn't kiss her back, didn't stroke his hands down her spine, didn't brush his fingers over her nape.

She would stand here all day having this discussion if necessary—and all night. "Daniel's welfare is a concern. Then, too, I want to set a better example for *my son*."

How she loved those two words. Probably the only two words more lovely would be "our child."

"Setting an example is important," David murmured. "Very important. May we sit?" He gestured to a bench near the roses, a spot where they'd spent hours before Letty had parted from him weeks ago.

"You have refused proposals of marriage from me in the past," David said when Letty had arranged her skirts. "What has changed your mind?"

This was not a proposal from him, but neither was it an academic inquiry. Letty sorted through the available answers and found the most honest.

"If Daniel ever asks you, you must tell my brother my change of heart was entirely his doing, and know you'll be imparting a falsehood." That falsehood, though, she could live with, easily, provided David accepted the truth from her.

She set the rose aside and took David's hand. "After weeks apart from you, what affected me most was regret that I had left you."

"Your brother must have delivered quite a sermon to you in that parlor while Danny and I were at Tatt's. What did he say?" His arm rested along the back of the bench behind her; his hand brushed her nape, his touch spilling a sensation like sunshine down her spine.

"When you proposed to me before, I was concerned that Olivia's blackmail would only get worse were I to marry you. If I had told you what she was about, then you would have become involved in her web, and Daniel's position would suffer. If I didn't tell you, then it would always be between us, a dirty secret that Olivia could use to undermine Danny's happiness and Daniel's dignity. I did not want you to attempt to wrest Danny from her... But all of that is moot, now, isn't it?"

"It never was of merit. Never."

Disparate impressions came together in Letty's memory: David, smiling at her across the parlor as the truth of Danny's parentage was revealed. David, insisting on the language in his legal documents.

"You weren't surprised to meet Danny, were you?"

"My love, I fear you will be wroth with me."

He hadn't used that endearment for weeks. Letty was anything but wroth, though she was anxious. "Tell me."

"You have stretch marks on your belly and other indicators that, to a physician's eye, shout your status as a mother. I noticed even before... I noticed some months ago, the first time I saw you as God made you."

He'd walked in on her in her bedroom, and Letty had been torn between modesty and the hope that he'd be interested in what he saw. How slowly she'd donned her robe, and how mistaken she'd been about what she'd seen in David's eyes.

The bench was solid beneath her, David's arm came around her shoulders, and that was good, because Letty's world threatened to slip off its axis. "You've known all along that I have a child?"

"I knew you had carried a child," David said, kissing her jaw. "I did not know if the child lived or had been taken from you or was dependent on you but dwelled in some Scottish croft. I knew only that you had carried a child. You could not trust me with your secrets, and I had to respect that. I was not very forthcoming about my own past, was I?"

She leaned into him, needing to breathe in sandalwood and a forbearance that had respected her more than she'd respected herself. "That's why you wrote up a document that required me only to prove I'd conceived, didn't you?"

His arm around her became more snug. "I wanted you to have independence. I wanted to know you were safe, and you would not have to ever again manage a Pleasure House or put up with a Herbert Allen, unless you chose freely to do so. Or a David Worthington."

A David Worthington. A man who had kept her secrets, who valued her independence, who'd offered her marriage when he'd had more questions than answers.

And yet, he was not precisely proposing.

"I am concerned, David, about how our children would be received were we to marry. I worried about it when Danny was going to be raised as the vicar's treasured son, but now… I don't expect he can be raised as my indiscretion, much less in a viscount's household."

David reached past her to retrieve the white rose, and gently touched it to her nose. "We can raise him as the vicar's son, if you like."

We.

We can raise him.

If you like.

"What do you mean?"

"Olivia has two options," David said, very much the man of business sizing up a contretemps. "She can take a settlement and let Banks dictate the terms of their separation, or she can contest those terms. She is shrewd and was planning on leaving him anyway, so let's assume she'll cooperate."

"Cooperate with what?"

"Banks's decision, at this troubling crossroad in his life, to place the child with his wealthy brother-in-law, the viscount, where the child will have love, stability, every material advantage, and a doting aunt."

How long had David been hatching this scheme; how many angles had he considered before broaching it with her?

Every possible angle, no doubt. "It could work… I don't know if Daniel would be comfortable with it."

David enfolded her hand against his heart, a steady, reassuring beat under Letty's palm. "The thought of abandoning this child is killing your brother. He can do it only because he saw you make the same sacrifice at a young age, followed by other sacrifices of similar magnitude. In the eyes of all save Olivia, this is Daniel's son. Your brother does not love by half measures."

Daniel did nothing by half measures, and thank God for that. "The truth is that Danny is illegitimate, and my son. You would have him legitimate, and my nephew."

"The very same outcome you sacrificed greatly to bring about, with two significant differences. First, the relevant parties, including the child, all know the truth. Second, Olivia is no longer an element in the equation, and even if she were, as a married woman, she has no legal right to the child whatsoever. The children of a married woman belong exclusively to her spouse, as if they were his chattel, and his alone."

What a wonderfully cheering thought. "You're still not telling me everything."

He rose, and though that meant they were not touching, it also meant Letty could think more clearly.

"My willingness to suborn this scheme is derived in part from the fact that I was regarded by my peers as a bastard, at least when I was a child. I would spare your son that experience, and if I have to do business with Olivia to ensure it, then I will."

"I forget the twists and turns your life has taken, David, and that you did not spring up out of the ground, whole cloth, Viscount Fairly at your service. You've traveled, held a profession, found your sisters, you were married, lost a child, for heaven's sake... Will you ever tell me about these things? Really talk to me about them?"

She wanted to know—wanted desperately to know—and yet she had firsthand experience with the burden a troubled past could be.

"Will you marry me, Elizabeth Temperance Banks? Will you be my viscountess and the mother of our children?"

His diffident tone belied the intensity of his gaze.

"Gladly. Twice a day, if you like."

All manner of tension drained from his posture, as if against all odds, a royal pardon had been handed down with his name on it, even as a noose of loneliness and misery hung inches from his neck.

"That's all right then." He resumed his place on the bench, taking Letty's hand in his. She limited herself to that connection and waited for him to gather his thoughts.

And his courage.

"You know I went to Philadelphia to start my medical practice," David said, "and that I met a woman there, whom I took to wife before understanding how troubled she was. You know she bore me a child, a daughter." He paused, took another deep breath, and a breeze brought Letty the scent of honeysuckle and fresh-cut grass.

"What you do not know was that I named the child… I named her Hannah Grace. Her eyes were so blue, perfectly blue, Letty, not like mine. And we shared… one sunrise. She smiled at me, Letty. I swear to God… she smiled…"

His voice broke, his grip on Letty's hand became desperately tight, and among the fragrant flowers and the soft evening sunshine, the tears finally, finally came.

❧

"So what necessitated this ingathering of the clan, Fairly? With the Season winding down, shouldn't you be larking off to Kent?"

The Marquess of Heathgate was at his customary perch, sitting on his vast mahogany desk, David's sister Felicity beside him. Greymoor sat with Astrid on the hearth, holding hands in plain sight, for God's sake. Douglas and Gwen were on the couch, indulging in a similar shameless display, and David had never been more aware that he loved each and every one of them, and their children. Hell, he even loved their horses and their dogs.

"I've done it," he said. "Earlier today, Miss Elizabeth Temperance Banks was married by special license to yours truly, her brother Daniel Banks presiding."

They'd not asked Banks if he was willing to officiate, he'd insisted—rather colorfully.

Greymoor shot to his feet, grinning and thwacking David on the back. "Well done, old boy." He pulled him into a hug that ended only when Astrid and Felicity came at David at once, followed by the rest of the assemblage. Last to come was Amery, who was as close to smiling as Amery ever got.

"I'm proud of you," Amery said, his blue eyes beaming. "I'm happy for you, and proud of you. When is the baby due?"

The question detonated a silence, a surprised silence, but not a shocked one. David was among family, after all.

"Well, as to that…" David's demurrer was greeted with whoops and hoots and general ribaldry, all intended in good fun. When the riot subsided, David took up his usual spot by the French doors.

"I was concerned you would not understand the need for haste," David said. Heathgate treated him to an arched eyebrow half the City had reason to dread. "Or even the need for marriage, given the circumstances."

The eyebrow lowered. "I believe," Heathgate said, "every person in this room was married at least once by special license. Only Astrid and perhaps yourself were initially married with full honors. Even so, you might have let us know."

As scolds went, particularly scolds from Heathgate, that was the merest observation of good form.

"Letty is concerned her past will necessitate that we live quietly, for there's more to the story than most of you know."

Heathgate pulled his marchioness closer, and Felicity made not even a token resistance. "Then I suggest you give us the details sooner rather than later."

David launched into an explanation of Danny's upbringing, and the vicar's current marital situation. When he was finished, the room was ominously quiet.

Astrid spoke first. "My heavens, David. When you land in a pickle, it's the pickle to end all pickles. I can see why Letty anticipates a quiet life."

"It might not be so bad as all that," Felicity said soothingly. "In time…"

"And it might not come to an annulment for the vicar," Gwen added philosophically. "Many couples married that long don't dwell together."

Another silence fell, this one more awkward.

Amery crossed his legs at the knee, a gesture that would be fussy on anybody else but looked elegant on him. "What is needed is a betrothal ball."

"What?" Greymoor was off the hearth and pacing in an instant. "Do you want to hold Letty up to contumely from the entire peerage? They'll cut her in the damned receiving line, and not all David's gold or Heathgate's intimidation or my own considerable charm will be enough to prevent that."

Bless Douglas, for he'd anticipated David's plan wonderfully. "We have something better than gold, intimidation, or even your charm," David said.

"I don't know…" Felicity exchanged anxious looks with the other ladies.

"Madam," Douglas interjected, "this family has survived bigamy, illegitimacy, suspicious deaths, adultery, all manner of misbehavior on the part of the Alexander brothers, as well as Guinevere's silly contretemps with Moreland, and we are received *everywhere*. We will still be received everywhere after this."

More murmuring followed, but then a grin spread across Heathgate's face. It was an unholy, dangerous, decidedly not-nice smile, and it had the rest of his family looking at him worriedly.

"My dears," Heathgate said, slipping off the desk and crossing the room to stand before David, comprehension in the marquess's gimlet blue eyes. "Fairly has a plan, and it's a very good plan, brought to us by one of the most diabolical minds of all time. There will be a ball, and Letty and David's children will be received—all of their children. Viscount Fairly, you have the floor."

❧

"Chin up, my lady." The Duke of Moreland smiled down at Letty, age making his courtly gallantry all the more impressive. "The jackals want to see you cringe and duck, so flirt your eyelashes off. I will endeavor to return the favor within the limits of my maturity and station."

He whirled her away to the strains of the waltz, only to be succeeded by his son and heir.

"Is it working?" Westhaven asked. "Has my mother once again cowed the tabbies of titled Society and their camp followers into doing her bidding?"

Letty smiled up at him, a genuine smile that acknowledged him as a friend when a friend had been needed. "I hope so, for my husband's sake, but as for my own, all I know is that the most handsome men in the room seem to be dancing with me."

Westhaven was not above a bit of flattery, which was probably a good thing in a ducal heir. "While your husband glares daggers at our backs."

"Oh, you really mustn't do that."

"Do what?"

"Smile, my lord." She let him turn her under his arm. "When you smile, you look so convincingly human."

"And when you steal a glance at Fairly, you look so convincingly happy."

"I am, you know. I am so happy, and it's generous of your family to make this effort on my behalf."

"To have two weeks at Morelands with her grand-daughter," Westhaven rejoined, "my mother would present Attila himself at Court. In a dress. With a smile."

"Rose seems to be looking forward to the journey, provided she can take Sir George, of course. Will you be joining them?"

"That was part of the bargain," Westhaven said,

holding Letty a trifle too close on a turn. "To keep His Grace in check, of course. But I'll take any excuse to leave Town, as will Valentine."

The dance came to an end, and when the next set started, Letty whirled off on the arm of the marquess. She spent the entire evening partnered by one impressively titled gentleman or another. The Duke and Duchess of Moreland had mustered unbelievable influence to make it so, but Letty was also touched to see that many of the former patrons of The Pleasure House were present, and to a man they treated her with utmost courtesy and sincere good wishes—though their ladies were a much cooler group.

She scanned the Moreland ballroom, looking for her husband. By agreement, David was to partner her in the supper waltz, and happily, that time drew near. When he found Letty, she stood flanked by David's family—Heathgate, Greymoor, Amery and their ladies, Westhaven and Lord Valentine, a brooding Thomas Jennings, and her own brother. Decked out in evening finery, they ranged around her, tall, handsome, and impressive, even at play.

One of Letty's memories of her mother involved an outing to a stone dance favored by the locals as a picnic spot. As a small child, she'd found the place daunting, the silent monoliths intimidating in their height, mystery, age, and sheer mass.

Standing with David's family at a ball held in her honor, Letty felt again as if she were surrounded by a dance, but a dance of men and women, people whose honor, integrity, and sheer force of will rendered them every bit as impressive as the actual stones that had withstood the centuries.

"My love?" David interrupted her musings. "May I have the pleasure?" He made her a formal bow, she curtsied, and placed her hand on his.

"I cannot believe," David said as they waited for the music to start, "this scheme has worked so well. I haven't heard even an innuendo all evening."

"I've heard plenty of innuendo," Letty countered, assuming waltz position. "All about a rake reformed and wonders never ceasing."

David slid one hand around her back, tucked her other hand into his, then curled it against his chest. "I am reformed in so many ways."

The music started, and to Letty's surprise, the orchestra dropped away to leave only a solo piano. The tempo of the waltz changed, slowing into a more romantic, intimate cadence, and Letty recognized the work as one of Valentine Windham's.

"I wanted this night to be perfect for you, Letty-love," David said. "To make it so, we must endure this waltz and stay at least twenty minutes into supper."

"And *then* you'll make it perfect for me?"

"As many times as you like, my love."

When the waltz ended, they lasted all of twelve minutes in the supper room, stole a bottle of Heathgate's finest, and made it perfect twice in the coach as the horses sedately walked them home.

Their first child—a darling girl with lovely green eyes—was born a mere seven months after the wedding.

Acknowledgments

David and Letty's story concludes the Lonely Lords series proper, and what a series it has been! My first historical romance hit the bookstore shelves little more than three years ago, and I know of no other editor, publisher, or publishing house that would have shown an author this much support this early in her writing career.

Getting out a full-length title per month (plus a few novellas!) for a year takes tremendous organization and commitment on the part of the entire publishing village. Though the manuscripts had been completed in draft some time ago, editorial, art, marketing, publicity, production, sales, EVERYBODY had to endure a schedule that was, quite honestly, not always fun.

So my thanks go to that village, and to the readers who make that village a wonderful place to be. The Lonely Lords has concluded as a series, but I plan on writing love stories for many more lonely lords and lonely ladies—and possibly even a few lonely lawyers!

About the Author

New York Times and USA Today bestselling author Grace Burrowes hit the bestseller lists with her debut, The Heir, followed by The Soldier, Lady Maggie's Secret Scandal, and Lady Eve's Indiscretion. The Heir was a Publishers Weekly Best Book of 2010, The Soldier was a Publishers Weekly Best Spring Romance of 2011, Lady Sophie's Christmas Wish won Best Historical Romance of the Year in 2011 from RT Reviewers' Choice Awards, Lady Louisa's Christmas Knight was a Library Journal Best Book of 2012, and The Bridegroom Wore Plaid, the first in her trilogy of Scotland-set Victorian romances, was a Publishers Weekly Best Book of 2012. All of her Regency and Victorian romances have received extensive praise, including starred reviews from Publishers Weekly and Booklist.

Grace is a practicing family law attorney and lives in rural Maryland. She loves to hear from her readers and can be reached through her website at graceburrowes .com.